To Pat
Best Wishes

Larry

7/11/21

Three Days in Tripoli

A Spy Thriller

By Lawrence Scofield

Acknowledgments

This book would not have been possible without the efforts of Judy, my wonderful editor. My thanks and love go to my family for everything they do to enrich my life: Jennifer, Elizabeth, Daniel and John. They're the best.

Neither products nor brand names used in this novel represent or imply any relationship with, or endorsement by, the author or publisher.

Copyright Notice and Disclaimers

Books by Lawrence Scofield

"The Laura Messier Files"

Three Days in Tripoli
Two Days in Moscow
One Day in Lebanon

Three Days in Tripoli

A Spy Thriller

Contents

Prologue

Sunday, April 13th, 1986

Located beneath the White House, the Situation Room's contact with the outside world comes only through video, telephone and telex. The room's only access point is one heavily guarded elevator. On the particular morning in question, the video screens were turned off, the telephone and telex were silent and the insulated quiet of the environment served to amplify the conversation around the conference table.

Senior staff came into the building underground through the White House tunnels to avoid alerting the press. There was a certain tension in the air, the kind that could be expected given the gravity of a situation where military action was imminent. Secretary of State George Shultz, Chief of Staff Don Regan, National Security Advisor John Poindexter, Chairman of the Joint Chiefs Admiral William Crowe, Director of the Central Intelligence Agency William J. Casey, and National Security Agency Head General William Odom, all sat at the conference table talking quietly among themselves awaiting President Ronald Reagan. Secretary of Defense Caspar Weinberger, who would normally have been present, was traveling abroad that day. Vice-President George H. W. Bush would arrive late, having just returned from a trip to Saudi Arabia.

As President Reagan entered the room a few minutes late, he flashed his signature smile. "Good morning," he said, shaking his head. "Sorry I'm late, guys. Nancy and her damn questions." That caused a fair amount of amusement around the table, but the comment served a purpose, for Reagan wanted to put his colleagues at ease. Reagan carried himself with an air of confidence which projected onto his staff. He had sound judgment and made clear and convincing decisions. Reagan was a big picture president and his people liked that about him.

"Okay, fellas, let's run Operation Eldorado Canyon from top to bottom," Reagan said as he lay a briefing book on the table. He sat at the head of the table, opened the folder and studied it while his subordinates waited for the President to speak. He raised his head and looked around the table. "Let's go around the room and ask everyone if we're ready. Mr. Secretary?" Reagan asked the Secretary of State George Shultz.

"Yes, Sir," Shultz responded. "Prime Minister Thatcher gave permission to use the bases in England last week. I would remind you, Mr. President, that we must notify our allies tomorrow morning. It would be wise to avoid informing the Soviets until shortly before the bombing commences."

"I agree," Reagan said. "It would be just like those bastards to inform Gaddafi in advance. What about Congress?"

"We're required to brief Congressional leaders, Mr. President, but if we want a surprise attack, we should brief them late tomorrow afternoon after the planes are in the air. White House meetings attract the press."

The President turned to his Chief of Staff, Don Regan. "What about the press on this, Don?"

"Mr. President, as you know, there's been speculation about an attack for weeks. The networks and wire services already have people in Tripoli. They'll begin reporting as soon as the attack begins. We should be prepared to have you address the nation shortly afterward."

The President nodded his head. "Get Larry Speakes to write something for me. Wait until late tomorrow to reserve time on the networks. We don't want rumors coming out of the Press Office."

"Yes, Sir," Regan answered.

Reagan looked at Joint Chiefs Chairman Admiral William Crowe. "Bill, how are we doing on the military side?"

"Mr. President," Crowe replied, "we're ready to go. NATO has scheduled a joint military exercise called 'Salty Nation' starting tomorrow in Britain. We'll use those maneuvers as cover for our aircraft. We should be able to take off without being noticed. France and Spain will deny overflight permission, but we've planned for that. We'll be flying around the continent and through the Strait."

"That'll be one hell of a long bombing run, won't it?" Reagan asked.

"The longest in history, Sir. We're confident we can execute it. The Air Force has practiced for it and our pilots are ready."

"Fine," Reagan said, nodding his head.

"What about the NSA, Bill?" Reagan asked William Odom.

"Mr. President, we've heard nothing in our phone intercepts that lead us to believe the Libyans know anything about our plans," Odom said. "At the present time, only the British have advance knowledge of the mission. Our concern is Gaddafi could receive a last minute warning of the attack from aircraft flying through the Strait or carriers moving into position near Malta. Gaddafi will want a radar confirmation before he calls a full alert. If we're able to shut down Libyan long range radars, they'll be caught by surprise."

"It's my understanding we have someone from CIA in Libya this weekend working on that. Is that right, Bill?" Reagan asked CIA Director William Casey.

"Yes, Sir," Casey replied. "She's coming out of the country today."

"She?" Reagan asked. Reagan paused for a few seconds as though he didn't hear Casey properly. "You have a woman in there?" That raised eyebrows around the room.

Luckily, Casey had brought Messier's personnel file with him in case the subject came up. "This is Laura Messier, Mr. President, the agent we sent into Libya," Casey said as he slid the file across the table.

Reagan began thumbing through the pages. "She's pretty, Bill," Reagan said, looking at her pictures. "Isn't it dangerous to send a woman?"

"That was the point, Mr. President. Women are one of Gaddafi's weaknesses."

Reagan passed some of the pictures around the table for the others to see. SecState looked at Messier's modeling pictures. "This is her as a model, Bill?" Shultz asked.

"Yes," Casey said, hoping the entire subject would go away. "She was a runway model before she joined CIA."

"Wow," Shultz said. That raised the interest of others and parts of Messier's file were spread across the table.

"The others are more recent?" the President asked.

"Yes, Sir," Casey said. "In the first one, she's walking into the American Embassy in Paris. That was taken just a few months ago. Her cover job is an aide to the French Minister of Foreign Affairs in Paris."

"I remember this girl, Mr. President," Shultz said to Reagan. "Every time we have meetings with the French, she's in the room on the French side. She acts as a kind of personal aide to the Minister. I always thought she was a clerical employee."

Reagan smiled when he spoke to Casey. "You mean we have people on both sides of the table when we talk to the French?"

"Yes, Sir," Casey replied.

Reagan laughed, "Too bad we don't have someone in the Libyan government."

"We do, Mr. President," Casey said. Every person in the room stopped, looked up and stared at Casey.

There was a pause in the room before the President said, "Go on, Bill."

"Well, he's not American. He's a French double agent positioned inside the Libyan government. Messier will bring the radar and missile codes out of Libya today. We'll relay them to the double agent. He'll be the one who shuts down the radars."

"Well, I'll be damned," Reagan said with a smile. He sat back and slapped the table with his hand. "Gentlemen, this is how you win wars. Nice job, Bill."

"Thank you, Mr. President."

The Vice-President entered the room with appropriate apologizes. "Mr. President, I apologize for being late. I just got back. Barbara insisted I change my clothes before I came over," he said. That brought a few chuckles from the group.

"You're lucky, George. Nancy would have asked me to walk the damn dogs," Reagan said with a smile. Bush sat down next to the President.

Reagan directed his next question to Shultz. "How's the world going to react to this?" Shultz hesitated before he answered. "Mr. President," he finally said, "the Canadians, Australians, Israelis and British will support us. The rest of NATO will, too, although they'll appear neutral in the press. The Italians and the French are big trading partners with Libya so they'll issue mild condemnations, but the French, as we heard from Bill Casey, are helping behind the scenes. The Chinese, Soviets and East Germans will offer strong criticism, but it's unlikely to go further than that. We don't believe they'll interfere."

"George?" the President asked the Vice President, "what about the Saudis?"

"Mr. President, I spoke with King Fahd yesterday. He feels Gaddafi's had a destabilizing effect on the Middle East. They'll support us even though they'll publicly condemn the raid."

"That's good news; thanks."

Reagan heard what he needed to hear. He made his decision. "Gentlemen, here's what we're going to do. If our agent gets out of Libya," Reagan hesitated. "What's her name again, Bill?" Reagan asked, looking at Bill Casey.

"Messier. Laura Messier."

"If Ms. Messier gets out with the codes, that's great, but whether she does or not, we're moving ahead with the attack. Tomorrow morning, I'll call the allies to inform them of our plans. I'll brief Congress later in the day. What's the timetable from there, Bill?" Reagan asked Joint Chiefs Chairman William Crowe.

"Our bombers in Britain will leave around 6:00 p.m. tomorrow local time, twelve noon here," Crowe replied. "We'll fly around the continent and through the Strait of Gibraltar. That will put our forces in Libyan airspace about 2:00 a.m. local time, 8:00 p.m. here in Washington. They'll get in and out in fifteen minutes and return to base."

"Caspar should be back this afternoon," Reagan said to Crowe. "I want you fellas over at the Pentagon running the show. Keep me informed. Gentlemen," he said looking around the table, "let's keep this quiet. Everyone continue their normal routine today and tomorrow. Okay?"

"Yes, Sir," everyone answered nearly in unison.

"Bill?" the President asked William Casey.

"Yes Sir, Mr. President."

"Keep me updated about our agent. Call Don with any information, day or night."

"Yes, Sir," Casey replied.

"Gentlemen, we stand adjourned. Good luck and may God Bless the United States of America."

Chapter One

It wasn't unusual that John Brownley answered his own phone calls. Brownley, the Central Intelligence Agency Station Chief at the American Embassy in Paris, could best be described as a hands-on administrator. When the call came in to Brownley's office on Thursday afternoon, August 8th, 1985, at 3:10 p.m., he picked up the line himself. "Brownley," he said simply in the flat tone of voice that businessmen use when their mind is engaged elsewhere.

"John, it's Clair George over at Langley. How are you?"

"Doing well, Clair. How can I help you?"

"I need to find Laura Messier. She's not at the Ministry of Foreign Affairs and I couldn't catch her at her apartment. Do you know where she is?"

"She's on vacation, Clair, not due back until Monday. Hang on a minute, let me confirm that." Brownley took the roster sheet from his middle desk drawer, ran his finger down to the M's, saw Messier's name and said, "Yeah, Clair, she'll be back Monday."

"I need to get in touch with her today," Clair said. "Do you know where she went on vacation?"

It was unusual that Clair George, the CIA Deputy Director of Operations, would contact a field agent directly. Field agents worked the street. Like men hanging off the backside of a garbage truck, they got their hands dirty. Brownley would have been delighted to put Clair in touch with Messier; she was a constant irritant, someone he'd dearly love transferred somewhere else.

"She usually goes back to the States, Clair," Brownley replied.

"Any guesses where?"

"The only contact we have is her parents in Illinois. Have you tried there?"

"They don't know where she is, either," Clair said.

"I'm sorry, Clair, I don't think I can help."

"Okay, John. Thanks."

Clair George decided to try Roger Wilson. As the CIA Chief of Staff, Roger seemed to know everything about everyone. Not that he told everything he knew, far from it, but Wilson knew for instance that Steve Tilton, one of the Assistant Deputy Directors of Intelligence, and Laura Messier had been romantically linked since Messier's first days at CIA. This was a secret which Laura Messier thought had been well hidden. Clair dialed Wilson's extension at Langley.

"Wilson here."

"Roger, it's Clair."

"Morning, Clair."

"I need to find Laura Messier," Clair said.

"She works out of Paris Station."

"I tried over there. They said she's on vacation."

"Geez, she could be anywhere." Wilson thought for a minute. "Hang on, Clair, I've got an idea." He punched his secretary's line, "Nancy, I need to find Steve Tilton's number out at his cabin in Colorado."

"Sure, hang on a minute." After a few seconds, Nancy found the number.

"Clair, my best guess is she's with Steve Tilton. He owns a cabin out in Ouray, Colorado. Here's the number," Wilson said.

"Thanks, Roger,"

"You bet."

Clair George leaned back in his chair to consider Steve Tilton and Laura Messier as a couple. He had no idea they were seeing each other. Steve, already well known to Clair, was a rising star in the agency. Coming from a wealthy, blue blood Boston family, Steve was in his early 40s, well educated, extremely bright and had a confidence about him that played well in the upper echelons of administration. Steve was quickly becoming someone of influence within the agency.

Laura Messier, on the other hand, came from a lower middle class background in Des Plaines, Illinois. At age 32, she was stunningly beautiful and had one of the best minds at the agency. The CIA had embedded her inside the French Foreign Ministry in Paris where she worked directly for the Minister himself. She was brilliant in that role and her information was some of the best material that came out of Western Europe. It's just that she was a bit rebellious at times which gave her boss, John Brownley, something of a challenge. Laura Messier didn't play by the rules and while that often put her in conflict with her boss, it also made her perfect for the mission Clair had in mind.

However, office romances were off limits at the CIA and although Steve Tilton was quickly becoming an indispensable asset, Laura Messier was not. Bill Casey would hand pick the personnel for this mission. At a time when Messier needed to keep a low profile at the agency, apparently she was doing exactly the opposite. If considered for this mission, she wouldn't escape the scrutiny that accompanied the vetting for high profile missions. While Clair thought Messier might be the only agent capable of performing this mission, he knew she'd be a tough sell to Casey because of her track record as a rebel. That would make the next call awkward.

Ouray, Colorado, is one of the best kept secrets in America. Dubbed "The Switzerland of America," Ouray sits on Highway 550, between Montrose and Durango in the San Juan Mountain Range. Steve Tilton's cabin, on the eastern edge of town, sat just a short walk from a waterfall that overlooked the town. Late at night, the sound of water crashing into the rocks below could be heard from the cabin.

The phone rang at 7:20 a.m. Steve had been up for a while. He had risen early to stoke the fire in the fireplace. The heat in the cabin had been turned off for the summer and temperatures had fallen into the high 40's overnight. The scent of brewing coffee permeated the air.

"Hello?"

"Steve, this is Clair George back at Langley. Sorry to bother you on vacation."

"No bother. Always great to hear from you, Clair." Steve laughed. "You're not calling to tell me I'm fired are you?"

"You mean for taking Laura Messier up in the Colorado Mountains?" Clair asked in the manner in which men banter with each other.

"Hey, she's gorgeous."

"That she is. Can't blame you at all. No, I just need to speak with her this morning."

"Sure, hang on a minute."

Laura heard the conversation and pretended to be asleep. Steve touched her shoulder, "Honey, Clair George is on the phone."

"Tell him I went hiking." She burrowed herself farther down in the comforter.

"Honey, I can't do that. Here," he said, pushing the receiver into her hand.

Laura slapped it away. "Tell him to call me Monday when I get back to Paris," she said bluntly. Frankly, she didn't care who the hell was calling from Langley.

"I can't do that and you know it. Take the call." Steve pushed the phone under her nose.

"Oh, all right," she said, disgusted that work had found her on vacation.

"Good morning, Clair. How'd you find me?"

"We're the CIA, Laura. We can find anyone," Clair said, trying to brighten the conversation.

"Hilarious. What's up?" she asked.

"I need you to stop at Langley on your way back to Paris."

"No, Clair, you don't."

With any other agent, Clair might have fired them on the spot, but he considered her essential to the mission's success. "Laura, don't be difficult. I have a meeting arranged Monday morning at 10:00 a.m. I expect to see you there."

"Do I need to prepare anything?" Messier asked with resignation in her voice.

"Nope. We'll be in one of the conference rooms on the Executive floor. See you then." Clair said.

"Fine."

Laura could already feel her anger building. She was frustrated that she'd be meeting men who didn't have a clue what she did to obtain intelligence. Well, not really. Clair was a street agent through and through. In his long and illustrious career, he had served in every hot spot around the world. Laura liked Clair immensely.

"Can I get you a cup of coffee, honey?" Steve said.

"No, I'm going back to sleep."

Laura rolled over and buried herself underneath the comforter. "No, you're not," Steve said. He slid under the comforter and made love to her, ever so much more pleasant than talking on the phone with Langley.

After spending the rest of the morning changing flight arrangements to include a Monday layover in Washington, calling the Foreign Ministry in Paris to tell them she wouldn't be in on Monday and the CIA Station in Paris to update them on her schedule, Laura was back into her work far too soon. By the time they arrived back at Steve's Georgetown row house Saturday night, Laura felt cheated, two days of vacation ruined by Langley.

Laura found Steve at the kitchen table early Sunday morning studying briefing reports. She came downstairs in a bathrobe, put her arms around him and kissed him good morning.

"There's fresh coffee over there, honey, and I bought a coffee cake," he said, without looking up. "Go ahead and grab a piece."

"Reading so early in the morning?"

"Just trying to get ahead of things," he said.

13

Laura poured herself a cup of coffee and sat down across the table, curling her feet up under her. She stared at him. He looked up over the top of his reading glasses.

"Here, read this," he said, tossing the front section of The Washington Post across the table. "You're staring."

"What are you reading?" she asked, expecting Steve to share his work with her. Steve had already returned to reading his briefing reports. She waited a minute, then interrupted him. "I can read upside down, you know," she said.

"Yes, I think I knew that."

"What's so important about Libya?"

"Nothing yet. This is just image analysis of a terrorist training camp Gaddafi runs." Steve stopped, took off his reading glasses and smiled. "You're not going to give up, are you?"

"Nope."

"All right. Just so you know, the meeting tomorrow is about Libya."

"How come you didn't tell me before? You let me hang around the cabin Thursday and Friday and didn't tell me?"

"Yep."

"Why?" she asked. "Honestly, Steve, you're getting so ..." Laura struggled to come up with the word she wanted, "bureaucratic these days."

"I didn't want to ruin the rest of vacation."

"You could have mentioned something about it," Laura said.

"Okay, I'm telling you now. The meeting is about Libya," he said, putting his glasses back on to read.

"Gee, thanks a lot."

"You're still staring, you know," Steve said. "Don't you need to wash your hair or something?"

"Oh, now he's being sexist," Laura said with a smile. Steve laughed and closed the briefing folder.

"I can see you're not going to leave me alone. Let's get dressed, go out to lunch and catch a movie. I don't want to think about this stuff anyway."

Chapter Two

NEITHER OF THEM said much on the drive to Langley the next morning; the first day back from vacation is always tough. As they walked into the building, Laura tried once more to get Steve to talk about the meeting.

"Anything else I need to know about the meeting?"

"Whatever this is, it's coming from outside the agency. It could be something the White House is pushing."

"That doesn't sound like anything I'd be involved in," Laura said.

"You're right. I was surprised when Clair called you. He might be planning an operation in Libya."

"We don't have any assets there, Steve."

"That's true. But the French do."

"I've got an hour and a half before the meeting," she said. "I'm heading over to Research."

"Listen, one thing you should know."

"What's that?"

"If I were you, I'd keep your head down in the meeting."

"Okay," she said.

"I'll be in my office. See you at ten."

"Bye."

Messier went over to the North Africa and Middle East section and asked to see briefing reports on Libya. "Do you have clearance for that?" the clerk asked. Messier had no idea, so she suggested he call up to Clair George's office. After placing the call, he turned to Messier.

"Yes, you have SCI clearance. What would you like to see?"

"Start with the most recent." She sat down at the closest table. He disappeared for a few minutes, then brought out a stack about a foot high. "Is that all you have?" she asked.

"No, Ma'am, I just brought you the stuff since the first of the year."

"I need to see more," she said.

"Yes, Ma'am."

Laura was an incredibly fast reader and she had finished the first stack by the time he brought the second. He couldn't bring documents faster than Laura could read. She'd worked her way back through the 70s when she looked at the clock and realized she'd spent too long reading. "That's all I need to see. Thank you."

"You're welcome, Ms. Messier. Do you mind if I ask you a question?" the clerk asked sheepishly as Laura prepared to leave.

"Sure. What is it?"

"I've never seen anyone read that quickly. How do you do it?" he asked.

"Anyone can do it. Words fall into patterns. Start by reading groups of words at once. After a bit of practice, you'll be able read entire paragraphs at a glance."

"Have you always been able to do that?"

"Listen, I'd love to talk, but I'm in a real hurry. Thanks for your help this morning," she said with a smile.

"You're welcome."

Laura headed over to the Military Affairs research room. She walked up to the counter and spoke with the clerk. "I need to see information on all U. S. military aircraft stationed in Western Europe and on the carriers in the Sixth Fleet. Types of aircraft, numbers, payloads, specs on fighters, bombers, electronic countermeasure and refueling aircraft. Oh, also Soviet radars and surface to air missile systems."

"Are you cleared for that?" the clerk asked.

"Call Clair George's office."

The clerk made the call, hung up the phone and said, "That's a lot of material Ms. Messier. Where do you want me to bring it?" She sat down at a table and tapped the tabletop with her index finger impatiently.

"Right here."

After a quick review of the files, Laura walked to the counter and looked at the clerk.

"I saw a reference to a new plane, the F-117."

"That's a secret program run by the Air Force. We don't have that here."

"Okay, how about Stealth Technology then?"

"Whatever we have would be in Science."

"Thanks," she said as she turned to leave.

One of Clair George's assistants tracked Laura down in the hallway on the way to the Science Department. He gave her a new ID badge with SCI Above Top Secret clearance.

"Excuse me, Ms. Messier; Deputy Director George said you needed this."

"Thanks."

With a new ID, Laura had no trouble getting information at Science. They took one look at the badge and she received everything she asked for, although there wasn't much on Stealth Technology, just a few research articles. After finishing, Laura glanced at her watch; she had just enough time to use the restroom before going upstairs to Clair George's office. She checked her hair and make-up. Like it or not, Laura would be stepping into an "old boys' club" at Langley; the upper level administration was entirely male. In Paris, she would have worn the latest French fashions. The Minister insisted Laura make a fashion statement at meetings, especially those with foreign delegations. The fashion industry is important to the Paris economy and beautiful women were a part of French culture. At Langley, such statements were out of place, so Laura wore a conservative gray pinstriped business suit with the skirt cut at the knee. However, giving a nod to her prior work as a runway model, she couldn't resist a form fitting blouse beneath the jacket and three inch heels. She unbuttoned the blouse a bit and folded it over the lapel of her jacket. *Conservative, but nice,* she thought to herself.

Exiting the elevator on the seventh floor and finding the row of executive offices, Messier walked toward the double doors at the end of the hallway with the name William J. Casey, Director, Central Intelligence Agency, in large letters beside the CIA seal. Everything about it was intimidating. She found Clair George's office along the hallway, walked inside and glanced at a clock. It was 9:55 a.m. The secretary said, "You must be Ms. Messier?"

"Yes."

"Deputy Director George and the others are already in the Director's office." She pointed down the hallway. "At the end of the hall, go through the double doors; you're expected."

Entering the Director's outer office, Laura found the room crowded with people chatting. Clair George spotted her and walked over. "Ah, there you are." He smiled broadly. "Nice to see you again, Laura."

"Hi, Clair."

"Come on in," he said motioning her to follow. "I'll lead you back to the conference room."

Clair led Laura through a labyrinth of hallways into an elegant conference room with a large oval table in the center. It was one of the building's corner rooms with windows that looked out over the forested areas of the complex. The table was of the highest quality mahogany with a number of executive chairs lining the oval. A flower arrangement graced the center of the table with miniature flags on either side, the U.S. flag on the left and the CIA flag on the right. It had the look of a room where serious people made serious decisions regarding the fate of nations.

There were a half a dozen people standing around talking when Clair and Laura entered the room.

"Laura, you know Bill Bates, the Deputy Director of Intelligence." Laura had met Bill during her early days at CIA.

"Hi, Laura." He smiled and stuck out his hand. Laura liked Bill Bates a lot.

"This is Michael Pratt, one of my Assistant Directors of Operations."

"Hi, Michael," she said. He nodded.

"And, of course, you know Roger Wilson, the Chief of Staff."

"Morning, Laura."

"Morning, Roger."

People continued to file into the room and take seats at the table. It was then that Laura noticed Steve standing across the room. Their eyes met briefly. *What a handsome man he is,* she thought. *Tall, with gray hair that falls onto his forehead and those incredibly attractive steely blue eyes; if anyone could be a male model, it's Steve.* Laura took a seat well apart from him, opened the briefing folder and studied the agenda. There were afternoon sessions to follow. Apparently, this would be an all-day affair.

William J. Casey entered the conference room and began tapping his water glass with a pen.

"Ladies and gentlemen, please take your seats. Let's get the briefing underway," he said loudly.

Bill Casey looked like everyone's favorite college professor. He was in his early seventies, paunchy, bald, with glasses that hung awkwardly about his rather wide head. He was quick to smile and had an exceptional ability to read people. He was a longtime political operative, having worked in the Nixon administration and had been Ronald Reagan's campaign manager in 1980. However, he also had intelligence experience going all the way back to the OSS during World War II. He was a pro.

A projection screen dropped from the ceiling behind Casey and a small door opened in the wall at the other end of the room. A projector lit the screen showing a map of North Africa with Libya highlighted in red. He waited until everyone was seated and then began reading from a prepared statement.

"Ladies and gentlemen, good morning. The President of the United States, after consultation with our allies, has determined that a military strike against Libya may be necessary to defend the assets and interests of the United States and our allies around the world. Such action as we may take against Libya is permitted under Article 51 of the United Nations Charter.

"Diplomatic initiatives are continuing. Economic sanctions against Libya have been in place since the Nixon administration and President Reagan is considering another round. If another round of sanctions do not change the behavior of Muammar Gaddafi, we believe a military strike to degrade Libya's ability to wage terror around the world may be our only option to protect American lives and interests, along with those of our allies. The President has asked the Pentagon to begin planning for such an attack.

"The United States has clear and convincing proof that Libya continues to fund and provide logistics to major terrorist organizations around the world including, but not limited to, the Palestine Liberation Organization, the Abu Nidal Organization and the Red Brigades. Their actions have resulted in the deaths of many innocent people. Gaddafi continues to train and arm terrorists at training camps in Libya with the intent of expanding a global campaign of terror.

"We also suspect Gaddafi has aspirations to build a nuclear bomb. His occupation of Chad has given him access to uranium. In addition, he's sent assassination teams to kill American envoys around the world.

"Today's briefing will outline the Pentagon's plan for a proportional military strike and the support this agency will provide to the Armed Forces of the United States should such an attack be necessary. With that, I'll turn the briefing over to Rear Admiral Mike Sullivan, United States Navy, and our liaison at the Pentagon. Mr. Sullivan?" Casey asked, looking toward the Admiral. Sullivan stood and walked to the front of the room beside the screen.

"Thank you, Director Casey, and good morning everyone. This mission is named Operation Eldorado

Canyon and will be a joint effort between the United States Air Force and the United States Navy. We'll be assisted by the Central Intelligence Agency who will provide the actionable intelligence necessary for the success of this mission. Tactical strike aircraft from bases in Britain and off our carriers in the Mediterranean will hit targets in Libya with the support of fighters and electronic warfare aircraft."

The Admiral began changing slides using a remote control.

"As you can see on the next slide, the targets under consideration include military barracks, command and control centers, airfields and terrorist training camps throughout Libya. The strike requires that aircraft remain in Libyan airspace for only a short period of time, perhaps only minutes, making the coordination of Navy carrier aircraft and the land based Air Force jets crucial to our success. Several exercises and practice bombing runs will be conducted this fall to insure the operation goes as planned. As of now, there is no precise date for the mission, but it could go active at any time after our planning and preparations have been completed.

"We anticipate that France and Spain will refuse over flight permission forcing our planes from Britain to fly around the continent and enter the Mediterranean through the Strait of Gibraltar, making this the longest bombing run in history. The entire mission, from take-off to touchdown, will take twelve hours and require several airborne refuelings along the way. To maintain operational secrecy, Air Force tanker aircraft will accompany the group to keep the planes in the air for the duration of the mission.

"Options under consideration by the Pentagon differ significantly in operational detail, starting with the type of aircraft used. In one scenario, the Air Force will use the F-111 aircraft, the Air Force all-weather ground attack fighter. In the other, a new type of plane will be used that incorporates top secret features that fall under the heading of stealth technology. This technology makes them nearly invisible to enemy radar.

"One important consideration is how large the strike should be. The administration wants a larger strike, one that includes multiple targets around Tripoli and Benghazi. That would necessitate bringing a larger strike force from the U.K., along with a number of tanker aircraft to refuel them. We'd also need a larger contingent of strike aircraft off the carriers to suppress Libya's air defenses and to perform Air Combat Patrol duties. The number of aircraft involved in the mission gets out of hand quickly. We're talking in the neighborhood of 100 aircraft for an operation of this size. Can we actually perform a strike of this size and be successful? Furthermore, can we keep it secret?

"There are also political ramifications to consider. What will the reaction be around the world? How will the Soviets react? The Middle East? What about our allies in Europe? In the event of a Libyan retaliation, Europe would be a convenient target. Finally, what's Gaddafi likely to do following an attack? Will it result in a decrease in his support for terrorism?

"Ladies and gentlemen of the Central Intelligence Agency, I'm here today to ask for your support. There is much you can do to help make this mission successful. However, I'm also here to seek your advice and counsel. You know this area of the world. We'd be interested in hearing your reaction to such a proposed mission. At this time, I'd like to open my part of the briefing to questions and general discussion."

An intense discussion followed, much of it centered on the political considerations of a military strike. Laura felt much of that discussion to be conjecture, but necessary. The CIA analyzed the intentions of every country in the world and Bill Casey took those evaluations directly to the White House. The CIA was in the prediction business and the wrong prediction about something like this could start a war.

Nothing more was discussed about the mission itself, which on the face of it, wasn't unusual. Few of the men around the table were able to talk with authority about military hardware or strategy. However, if the Pentagon only wanted image analysis, the agency could easily support that. If the President wanted Casey's advice or a written analysis, all he needed to do was place a call. Something was missing from the presentation and while that might become apparent in the afternoon meetings, it was certainly left unsaid so far.

Messier found herself thinking about Sullivan's description of the attack. *Sullivan left out a lot of material. How would the Air Force and Navy keep their planes safe from Libyan SAMs? How would the Reagan administration appear if Gaddafi paraded blindfolded pilots in front of television cameras? And those American carriers stationed somewhere off the Libyan coast? Aircraft taking off in the middle of the night would be seen. One phone call could give the Libyans time to prepare.*

Chapter Three

THIS WAS LAURA'S first high level briefing. She'd never met Bill Casey and was hesitant to speak up. Still, there were a number of issues she'd discovered during her reading that morning that hadn't been mentioned. Whether that was by omission or design, it was impossible to know.

"Admiral, before the discussion ends, I have a couple of questions if you'd care to respond," Laura said. Fearful she might lose her job, she leaned forward with her body full of tension.

"Yes, ma'am, go ahead," he said.

"Regarding the use of planes with stealth technology, are you referring to the new Air Force F-117?"

Sullivan hesitated, then finally said, "Yes, ma'am, that's correct."

"They're being flown out of Tonopah, aren't they?" Laura asked coyly.

Sullivan looked surprised by the question. "The F-117 is supposed to be a secret program. If you don't mind me asking, how did you come by this information?"

"Sir, Director Casey signs my checks and he pays me to know that stuff," Laura said with a smile. The entire room burst out in laughter, all except Steve, who seemed a bit uncomfortable.

"Fair enough," Sullivan said with a smile on his face.

The laughter broke the tension in the room so Messier decided to ask a follow-up question. "Using the F-117 would alleviate much of the concern with Libyan SAM sites, but if one were shot down, wouldn't it give the Soviets a chance to look at the plane?"

"That's the main issue with using the F-117. We wouldn't have a problem penetrating Libyan radars, but the Soviets aren't aware we've built the plane. If one were shot down, it'd compromise twenty years of research," the Admiral said.

"Does the Pentagon plan a surprise attack? If so, have you solved the problem of Libyan long range SAMs?" Laura asked.

The Admiral gave her the hint of a smile. "Yes, we do plan a surprise attack and to be perfectly honest, their long range SAMs are a problem."

Laura glanced at Bill Casey and suddenly realized she might be in trouble. Bill Casey didn't look pleased. She ignored him. "Sir, whatever plane is used and let's say, for argument, that it's the F-111, if they come through the Strait of Gibraltar, they'll need one last refueling around the Tunisian coast. To accomplish that, they can't stay below the radar deck, so the Libyans will pick them up on their long range SAMs, the S-200s, or what NATO calls the SA-5s. The S-200 system can see, track and fire on targets up to 250 miles away. Libya could fire on those planes as they refuel. How do you plan to deal with that threat?" Laura began scanning the room using her peripheral vision. It didn't appear anyone in the room, other than Admiral Sullivan, had considered the issue, except perhaps Casey.

The Admiral gave her a confident smile. "That's excellent technical analysis, Ma'am; my compliments to you. The entire element of surprise could hinge on neutralizing their long range systems. We think it's best to eliminate that threat before the attack. That's an area where we could use assistance from the CIA," Sullivan said, as he looked right at Casey.

At that point, Casey stood up. "That's a perfect note to stop on. Its 11:45; let's take a break for lunch. We'll reconvene at 1:30 and split into two working groups. The Intelligence Directorate, led by Deputy Director Bates, will meet with the Admiral and his staff in this room to discuss imagery analysis of current targets and what may be needed to further refine their mission. The Operations Directorate, led by Deputy Director George and myself, will move to the conference room down the hall to talk about a proposed CIA mission to help neutralize the long range missile threat we just heard about. It's been a great discussion so far. I appreciate everyone's input. Lunch will be served downstairs in the Executive Dining Room next to the cafeteria. We stand adjourned until 1:30."

As people filed out of the conference room, Sullivan walked over to Laura and introduced himself.

"Hi, I'm Mike Sullivan."

"Nice to meet you, Sir. I'm Laura Messier, ops officer working out of Paris."

"Ms. Messier, I was impressed with your knowledge this morning. If you ever need a job, give me a call. We'd love to have you over at the Pentagon."

"Why, thank you, Admiral. What a nice thing to say."

Bill Casey happened to be in the general vicinity. He walked over and put his hand on Sullivan's shoulder.

"Hey Mike, no fair recruiting my employees here in my own building."

Mike laughed. "Oops, I thought you were out of earshot, Bill. I may have to outbid you for this young lady's services."

Casey turned to Laura with a cold expression. "I don't believe we've met. I'm William J. Casey, Director of the CIA."

"Nice to meet you, Sir. I'm Laura Messier, one of your ops officers."

"Thank you for coming today," he said stiffly, more as a formality than an honest gesture.

Laura waited to leave until the room cleared, hoping to walk to lunch alone. Casey wasn't friendly and she began to regret speaking up in the meeting. By the time she exited the office, only Steve was left in the hallway. "What were you doing in there this morning?" Steve asked.

"What do you mean?" Laura asked, although she knew exactly what Steve meant.

"The meeting was strictly background information for you. You have zero experience analyzing weapons systems and military strategy. You had no business speaking up."

"I think Sullivan liked it," she said, trying to defend herself.

"You don't work for Sullivan," Steve said, raising his voice. "Casey was angry, Laura. He could fire you." He looked down the hallway to make sure no one else had heard. Even though the hallway was deserted, this was no place for an argument.

"Well, if I still have a job after lunch, we'll be in different meetings," she said. Laura eyed a women's restroom down the hall. "Excuse me, I've got to use the restroom."

Steve had gone by the time she came out of the restroom. Lunch in the Executive Dining Room would've been awkward. Laura was upset. She walked down to the employee cafeteria, bought a package of crackers and a soft drink out of vending machines and headed outside. She walked along the sidewalk until she found a bench away from the foot traffic of the building. Listening to the birds chirp, she wondered who it was that said the forest would be a very quiet place if only the best birds sang. She couldn't remember. *I was invited to the meeting; I've got a right to speak my mind, dammit,* she thought. Looking at her watch, Laura still had about an hour. She closed her eyes and listened.

In the Executive Dining Room during lunch, Casey pulled Clair George aside for a private chat. "Clair, would you walk with me for a moment? I have questions about the young woman who attended the meeting this morning. Laura Messier, is that her name?"

"Yes, Bill, that's right," Clair said, somewhat confused. Casey knew who she was. What was the pretense about?

"Step out in the hallway with me, would you?" Casey offered.

"Sure, whatever you like," Clair replied, shrugging his shoulders.

They stepped into the hallway and Casey started walking away from the dining room with his hands in his pockets, as though he were taking a stroll in a park on a Sunday afternoon. "I was told by Roger Wilson she'd be the smartest person in the room. We certainly found that to be true," Casey said.

"She's one of the brightest people we have, Bill."

"Despite her talent, I wonder about her maturity level. How old is she?"

"I believe she's thirty-two," Clair said, after thinking a moment.

"I wonder whether she's ready for this mission or any mission, to be honest. She's impulsive and immature," Casey said with an honesty that surprised Clair. Bill was known to be oblique in his comments about people.

"I agree she shouldn't have spoken up this morning, but, and I'm not trying to disagree with you Bill, she's one of our best people," Clair replied.

"I also wonder if she's tough enough."

"You mean tough enough for the mission?"

"Yes," Casey said nodding, "emotionally ready to handle the pressure."

"Her field reports are excellent. People in Paris have nothing but praise for her."

Casey stopped, turned and faced Clair. "Yes, I know, Clair, but Paris isn't Libya."

Clair didn't want to appear an apologist for Messier, but he figured he ought to defend her. She had a great record with the agency. "That's a good point. Paris isn't Libya. She's the agent who planted a transmitter on Markus Wolf that allowed us to track him. You remember that, don't you?"

"Yes, I remember."

"Markus Wolf! The East German spymaster who operated for thirty years without ever being seen. No one even had a picture of the man, Bill. It was a coup for us."

"Clair, step outside with me for a moment," Casey said patiently. Casey led George out a side door onto the sidewalk. "I question her entire employment here. It was a mistake to hire her in the first place. She's a troublemaker. She doesn't respect authority or the chain of command. We have no idea what she might do in Libya."

It was clear that Casey didn't like Messier. He didn't care for what he'd observed this morning; he was uncomfortable with who she was. The CIA had plenty of talent. He felt they didn't need her. "When you gave me Messier's file last week," Casey continued, "I was shocked to read she's been accused of trading sexual favors in exchange for intelligence. In fact, she's ignored the 'Code of Conduct' her entire career. She's had conflicts with supervisors and I heard today she's personally involved with another agency employee. We need to get rid of her. She works in your division so you do it."

"Yes, Sir. I'll do it right away," Clair said stiffly. He didn't agree with it, but he was obliged to follow orders. "How do we handle the meeting this afternoon? Would you like me to excuse her?"

"No," Casey said, waving his hand dismissively. "Let's go ahead and let her attend. The French Intelligence man we're bringing in expects to meet someone he's supposed to work with. We'll change the person later. For now, let's just get through the meeting. Let her go at the end of the day."

"As you wish, Sir."

"Thank you, Clair," Casey said. Casey could have found no better right hand man than Clair George. When Casey needed to get tough things done, it was Clair George he turned to. Clair was a veteran spymaster with a drawer full of medals; he was as loyal as anyone in the agency.

Chapter Four

AS DEPUTY DIRECTOR of Operations, Clair George had a conference room as part of his office suite. Not as large or elegant as Casey's, it was nevertheless a nice room by corporate standards. As Laura approached Clair's office for the afternoon meeting, she thought about the plans that had been made in this room over the years. *This was the place they planned to shoot people and a lot of shooting had been going on since Reagan took office. Okay, maybe the CIA didn't exactly do the shooting, but with all the secret arms deals I've heard about, somebody, somewhere was shooting people. This room was where it was discussed.*

There was a new face at the meeting she hadn't seen before. Clair made the introductions.

"This is Jean Broussard, from the DST, the intelligence service of the Republic of France. Jean will be working with us on this mission. Mr. Broussard, this is the Director of the Central Intelligence Agency, Mr. William J. Casey."

"A pleasure to meet you, Director Casey," Broussard said.

"This is Michael Pratt, my Assistant Director of Operations," Clair said, "and this is one of our field agents, Laura Messier."

"A pleasure to meet everyone," Broussard said.

Clair directed them toward a furniture grouping at the end of the room and immediately took control of the meeting. "Mike, would you kick the door shut? Please, everyone take a seat and let's get started." Laura chose to sit on the sofa where she could look out the window at the rolling hills that surrounded the complex. Broussard sat next to Laura; Clair and the others took seats in the chairs around the coffee table. Clair spoke first. "I want to thank everyone for attending today. I'm going to ask Director Casey to give an introduction to a proposed mission in conjunction with the Pentagon's plans we heard about this morning. Director Casey?"

With that introduction, Bill Casey leaned forward to tell a tale Laura thought might border on fantasy. She'd done the necessary research. *There's no way to shut down those missile systems without getting someone inside,* she thought. *Clair, I respect. He's been in the field. Casey doesn't have a clue.*

"Thank you, Clair," Casey said, "and welcome back for this afternoon's session. Let's just dive right into this thing, shall we? The goal of this mission is to obtain the launch codes for the Soviet S-200 pods which surround Tripoli. With those codes, we can disarm the system and our planes can approach the Libyan coastline without being seen on radar. This mission will begin shortly before the attack. It will be run from the Operations Center here at Langley. We'll insert one agent into Libya who will be out of contact and operate largely alone. The goal is to obtain the launch codes, then exit the country within twenty-four hours of the attack. Clair will provide the operational details. Clair?"

"Thank you, Director Casey," Clair said. "To be clear in our definitions, the Soviet S-200 SAM system, what we call the SA-5, is the long range Libyan radar and missile system that concerns us. That system must be compromised before the attack to maintain the element of surprise. The system is powerful. It can identify and track targets 250 miles away and up to 60,000 feet in altitude. It can fire automatically. Each pod of the S-200 system consists of six missiles grouped in a circle around a command center. There are six pods scattered around the Tripoli area. The commanders are stationed at the command center in the middle of each pod. Each commander enters a six digit number into the electronic control to activate the radar and arm the missiles. However, the commanders do not possess the codes.

"The codes are kept by Gaddafi himself in a briefcase he carries with him at all times. In an emergency, Gaddafi provides the codes to his commanders who activate their systems. It is possible to activate the pods manually without the codes, but it's difficult. Disabling the system should give our aircraft the time they need to perform their bombing run and leave Libyan airspace before those systems can become operational.

"Our plan will put an agent into direct contact with Gaddafi himself. The agent will access Gaddafi's briefcase, obtain the codes and exit the country. To explain how this will be accomplished, I'd like to call upon Mr. Broussard."

Jean Broussard was an attractive man in his early 60s. He was short, slight of build, with graying hair and a closely cropped beard. He had an internal energy that emanated in every direction. He had a sharp mind, a quick smile and eyes that caught every detail in a room. He also appeared to have a great deal of kindness behind his eyes. His native language was French, but he was proficient in English and also knew a fair bit of Arabic. He wore the casual clothing typical of French men, slacks, a black turtleneck and a tweed jacket. Jean was exceedingly polite in the manner that the French do business. Laura was accustomed to this style and she liked him immediately.

"Yes, Sir. Thank you, Monsieur George. First, allow me to say that I'm delighted to work with you as a representative of the DST. I am a French native of North African descent who has business interests in Libya. I'm in the entertainment business. I operate four nightclubs, two in Paris, one in Beirut and one in Tripoli. I provide the DST with intelligence in regards to Lebanon and Libya. The clubs in Beirut and Tripoli operate as traditional nightclubs that cater to local traditions. You'd be most interested in the Tripoli location, so allow me to explain the special circumstances surrounding that facility.

"The club in Libya is technically illegal. Officially, the club does not exist. It's a secret known only to certain government officials and foreigners who visit the country. Colonel Gaddafi permits its existence to allow foreign businessmen to negotiate with him privately. Late at night, unseen by the public, Gaddafi conducts secret negotiations at the club; arms deals, contracts to buy equipment for the oil industry, airplanes and other goods and services all done in the club's private areas.

"The club operates in the basement of a downtown building. There is no street address, no signage, nothing to identify that it exists. Entry to the club is through an unmarked door in an alley. The Colonel personally approves the guest list and the guards at the entrance are from Gaddafi's personal security detail.

"Gaddafi likes to watch performances by Western entertainers. Such entertainment is illegal in Libya, but

Gaddafi often requests I bring performers from my Paris clubs to entertain him and his business associates."

Laura wondered who had thought up this incredibly stupid plan. *Sending someone to perform for Gaddafi?* she asked herself. *I've heard a lot of stupid ideas come out of Langley, but this one is, by far, the worst.*

Broussard continued...

"On occasions where Gaddafi completes a negotiation, he holds a reception at his compound for invited guests. When this happens, my performers and I are among his guests.

"I have seen the briefcase you speak of. His guards carry the briefcase into his personal quarters which are nearby. The reason I know this to be true is I've personally seen it there. Gaddafi meets privately with businessmen in his personal quarters during the receptions.

"I think it's possible to slip away from the reception for a short time and gain access to the briefcase in his personal quarters. That concludes my analysis, Mr. George."

"May we ask questions, Mr. Broussard?" Clair asked.

"Of course."

"What about Gaddafi's family? Aren't they present in Gaddafi's personal quarters?"

"No, Gaddafi's family lives in another part of the compound. Gaddafi's wife is largely unseen by the public."

"What about Gaddafi's kitchen? His security?" Clair followed.

"The kitchen staff is kept busy serving the reception. His security staff is comprised of his female guards; they guard him at the reception. The quarters are vacant unless Gaddafi has a private meeting," Broussard said.

"One more question, if I may," George said.

"Of course."

"Where are the receptions held?"

"They're held at the Libyan Military Headquarters, called Bab al-Azizia, south of downtown Tripoli. Inside the compound, Gaddafi has a vast underground bunker which contains living quarters, his office and a reception area. Upon entering the Azizia complex, guests are led to a small building and walk down several flights of stairs. Once underground, there's a hallway that leads to the area where the reception is held."

"I have another question for you, Mr. Broussard," Casey said.

"Of course."

"Does the DST use hidden listening devices to eavesdrop on Gaddafi's negotiations at the club?"

"My apologies, Director Casey. My government prevents me from giving you that information."

"Thank you, Mr. Broussard," Clair said. "Our plan is to put an agent into Tripoli through Mr. Broussard's business. To gain access to the briefcase, we must penetrate Gaddafi's personal quarters. That, we believe, is our best chance to obtain the S-200 missile codes. The entire attack on Libya depends, in part, upon our success in obtaining these codes. It will save the lives of American servicemen and women involved in this military action."

Clair turned to Laura, "The best qualified candidate is you, Ms. Messier. You have the unique attributes and skills necessary to perform this mission."

"Sorry to disagree, Clair, but I'm definitely unqualified for this mission." Laura responded.

"You were a music major in college weren't you?"

"Yes. I played the violin."

"That's close enough."

"What do you expect me to perform? A violin concerto?"

"No. You'll have to sing and dance. If you can't do it, we'll teach you," Clair said a little too casually for Laura.

"You think that stuff is easy?"

"We have no other agent who's a trained musician. You have one other attribute that's important. Pardon me for saying this, Laura, but you're a beautiful woman. Gaddafi has a weakness for women. We do not believe he'll suspect you're an agent."

"Surely, you're joking."

"No, I'm not. This is our best chance to get inside Gaddafi's personal quarters."

"Quite right, Clair," Casey said, supporting Clair's comment now that he'd heard the plan in detail. "Gaddafi's weakness for women is well known. And she's sexy as hell," Casey said enthusiastically.

"I'm right here, Bill. You can talk to me directly."

Casey ignored her. "I see what you're doing now, Clair."

Laura became visibly angry. It was bad enough that Clair suggested Laura walk into Gaddafi's personal quarters surrounded by thousands of Libyan military, a place where women were known to be raped and abused. But to reduce her years of experience at the agency to being "sexy as hell" was more than she could tolerate. Clair sensed Laura's anger and tried to move the meeting forward. "At this time, I'd like to open the meeting for additional input," Clair said.

The damage had been done. Watching Messier stand and begin to gather her personal items, Clair tried to forestall her exit. "Mr. Broussard, is there anything you'd like to ask Ms. Messier?"

Laura interjected before Broussard had an opportunity to speak. "Clair, I've heard quite enough, thank you. Excuse me, but I have pressing business elsewhere. It was nice to meet you, Mr. Broussard." She turned to leave.

Broussard gently laid his hand on Laura's arm. She hesitated for a moment and turned as he spoke to her. "Mademoiselle, I understand you speak excellent French. Would you mind speaking with me in French for just a moment before you leave?"

"Aucun," she said, turning back toward the door.

Broussard spoke in French. "Please, one moment, Mademoiselle, then I'll keep you no longer." The conversation became private since none of the others understood the language. "Please, Mademoiselle. I know what was said insulted you. Just talk with me for a moment."

Laura turned and spoke to him in French. "Mr. Broussard, may I call you Jean?" she asked.

"Please, Mademoiselle, address me as you wish."

"Jean, I have no intention of sitting here and allowing myself to be degraded in this fashion. My bosses are nothing but pigs. The one sitting there," she said, nodding at Casey, "is fat, old and ugly. The one at his side is his errand boy. The other one," motioning to Pratt, "does not speak because he doesn't have a brain. They're all idiots."

Broussard stared at Laura for a moment, then began to laugh. He threw his head back and slapped his hands together. "Mademoiselle, you are a true French woman, proud and strong. I like you very much already."

Broussard stood up. "May I greet you in the traditional French manner?" Jean asked.

"Yes. Show these rude Americans a proper form of greeting," Laura replied.

She leaned toward Jean who air kissed her on both cheeks. Jean smiled broadly. "Mademoiselle, I've never had the pleasure of meeting you, but I know of you. The Eastern Bloc calls you the 'Shewolf' and you have become a legend in Europe." Jean said. "Mademoiselle, it's an honor to meet you."

"The pleasure's mine, Jean. I can't wait to leave these fools to their folly and return to Paris."

"You must come visit my club in Paris as my guest."

"Thank you. I'd be delighted," Laura said. "Jean, these idiots have no idea what they're asking me to do."

"You're quite right, they do not. However, I understand. Mademoiselle, I wonder, could I speak with you privately away from your employers?"

"Fine. Get me out of here before I punch the big fat one in the face."

Jean laughed. "I understand completely," he said. "I often have that urge with my employers. Allow me to explain that you and I will take a short walk."

Jean switched to English. "Director Casey and Mr. George, I wish to speak with the Mademoiselle privately. We shall take a walk and be back shortly. Please wait for us here."

Clair looked at Casey, who appeared bewildered by the entire exchange. Clair said, "Please, Mr. Broussard, take all the time you need." Jean and Laura left the room and began chatting like old friends out for a stroll on one of the boulevards of Paris.

41

After they'd left, Clair turned to Casey. "With all due respect, you can fire Messier and I'll respect your decision. Bill, you've just insulted one of the best agents we have in the field. If you want her fired, I really don't think you'll have to go to the trouble."

Casey responded harshly. "Clair, I want that woman fired immediately after ..."

Clair George interrupted his boss. "Excuse me, Director Casey!" Clair shouted. He leaned uncomfortably close. "Whatever you think of her is your business, but in her presence and in mine, for however long she remains at this agency, you will refer to her with respect or you shall have my resignation as well as hers!" Clair was incensed when he finished.

Casey could barely contain his anger. No one talked to William J. Casey in that manner, not even the President of the United States. Casey had too much clout in Washington. On the other hand, he could ill afford mass resignations. He'd lose Messier, which wasn't important. But if this incident blew up, he could possibly lose Clair George, a Deputy Director and probably that boyfriend of hers, Steve Tilton. That isn't the kind of thing that can be buried. It would get out in the press. Questions would be asked; even the President would ask for an explanation.

Clair watched Casey run the political calculation in his mind. After a minute or two, Clair made an attempt to lower the temperature of the conversation. He leaned back in his chair and spoke in a relaxed tone of voice. "Bill, did you see how Messier handled Broussard?"

"What do you mean handled?" Casey shot back.

"Bill, this woman could charm the socks off a rattlesnake. She can, literally, shape her personality at will.

She's a consummate actress, Bill. If we were to send one person into Libya to face Muammar Gaddafi, she might be the only person with enough talent to pull it off and get out alive. Let's wait and see what happens when they return."

"We don't have a choice. We've got to wait for Broussard. We can't afford to offend the French," Casey said, still angry, but tacitly acknowledging that Clair's logic was sound.

"Can I get you a soft drink?" Clair asked Casey.

"Diet, please."

Chapter Five

LAURA AND JEAN continued talking in the hallway. "Jean, would you take me outside the building?" Laura asked.

"With pleasure, Mademoiselle. I noticed benches along the walkways. Would you feel comfortable talking there?"

"Yes, please."

As they exited the building, Jean took Laura's arm and picked the very same bench she had used earlier in the day.

"Mademoiselle, I want to apologize for the manner in which you were treated by your employers. It's not my place to apologize on their behalf, but I regret the manner in which they described you."

"Thank you, Jean, for those kind words."

"I can't change the attitudes of Americans, but in France, we recognize everyone's talent equally, regardless of their gender."

"Thank you, Jean. I'll be fine. Just give me a minute to calm myself."

Jean Broussard was a patient man and watching her, he realized he'd found a partner. Deputy Director George had been right, Messier was perfect for the mission and it had nothing to do with her beauty. After a long while, Jean spoke again. "Mademoiselle, it's not my place to influence your decision to perform this mission. I can only explain it fully, not as those bumbling fools would, but in every detail."

"Go ahead, I'm listening," Laura replied.

"I am here at the request of my government. The French strongly object to Gaddafi's terrorism, but we also have diplomatic relations with Libya and there's much trade between the two nations. France will punish Gaddafi through trade sanctions. My government also understands the desire of the United States to use force. I'll explain the help I'm able to provide and your role in this mission.

"I would ask that you perform at my club in Paris for a few weeks to learn the nature of the kind of performing Gaddafi likes to see. I'll pay you a small sum to create the illusion that you're legitimately employed. Do you have French documents?"

"Yes," Laura said. "I have everything I need."

"Excellent, because those documents will be examined. The Libyans have eyes everywhere. We must wait for your American President to approve the mission, then we must wait until Gaddafi requests a performer. When the time is right, you'll accompany me to Tripoli. Gaddafi and his friends will view your performance. Do not worry; I'll be in the room also. You will not be harmed.

Gaddafi often asks my performers to sit with him for a few minutes after their performance. It's a harmless gesture. He's never hurt any of my performers. Gaddafi will invite us to his reception. There will be others there; government officials, foreign businessmen and personal friends. Gaddafi will be busy entertaining. He'll pay no attention to us. Everyone will drink Arak, including his guards. It has a high alcohol content and their senses will become dull after a time. Security will become lax.

"At an appropriate time, you'll slip away on the pretense of using the restroom and enter the door the kitchen staff uses to serve the reception. You should be able to leave unnoticed, but if the guards do happen to stop you, merely apologize and ask where you may find the restroom. Once you access the personal quarters, you'll be alone. The briefcase should be nearby. Find it and obtain the information you seek. Do not stay away long. You must return to the party in the time it would take you to use the restroom.

"Upon your return, we'll leave the party together and return to the hotel. My performers and I usually leave these receptions early, so if you're unable to obtain the information, we'll leave without it.

"The following morning, we'll leave the country together. The French Embassy will be aware of our plans and will have someone watching to make sure we leave safely.

"This is also important. If you're able to access the information, do not take the code sheet with you or it be discovered the next time Gaddafi opens his briefcase. Copy the codes and return the code sheet to his briefcase."

"May I ask I question at this point?" she asked.

"Of course, Mademoiselle."

"If the code sheet is left in Gaddafi's briefcase, won't he arm the missile pods once he's alerted of an attack?"

"No, and this is a part of the mission that hasn't been told to you," Jean said. "A high ranking official in Gaddafi's military headquarters works for French Intelligence. For reasons of security, he'll remain unknown to you. You'll give the codes to the Americans once you arrive back in Paris. They'll pass them to our agent inside Libyan headquarters. The next day, on the pretext of an inspection, that agent will use the codes to access the system and enter new codes. Libyan missile commanders are accustomed to the codes being changed periodically. Nothing will appear contrary to their normal routine. However, Gaddafi will not be informed of this change. When Gaddafi discovers an American attack is imminent, he'll provide the wrong codes to his commanders and the missile system won't operate."

"Why don't you obtain the codes yourself?" Laura asked.

"Mademoiselle, this is an American operation. While the French may assist behind the scenes, officially, we are at peace with the Libyans. I'm unable to help any further than my government permits. They desire to keep me in place as an active agent and I'd like to continue to operate my business."

"What happens if I'm caught?" she asked.

"In that case, you'll say that you're a thief and you intended to rob Gaddafi. The Libyans have no method to identify you as American. Libyan intelligence does not reach into the CIA. You speak French perfectly and your documents are in order. The Libyans will classify you as a common criminal. They'll release you to the French and you'll be expelled from the country. The Libyans do not take French hostages. They're unwilling to risk offending the French government due to the trade between the two countries. You'll be questioned, of course, and perhaps severely so and afterward, you'll be brought back to France. Do you have any other questions?"

"Yes, Jean, if you'll permit me. What's he like?"

"You mean Gaddafi?"

"Yes."

"He's very intelligent, Mademoiselle, well-educated with an interest in many things, especially history. He's a dynamic leader with great powers of perception. He has a vision of himself as a world leader so he's filled with much pride. However, there are many in his country and around the world who oppose him. To those people, he is ruthless. He's a man of many faces. He'll show you only the part of him he wants you to see. He's not to be trusted."

"Thank you, Jean."

"You may have other questions as this mission draws closer. We'll have other opportunities to speak. Now, let's go deal with your employer," Jean said.

Jean took Messier's arm and they walked together back into the building. They entered Clair George's conference room and found Casey and George waiting. Apparently, Pratt had left the meeting. Jean spoke to them in unusually blunt terms.

"Gentlemen, the French government permits me to work with you on the condition that I endorse the agent I work with. The Mademoiselle is one of the finest agents in your CIA. However, you have not treated her well here today. I must ask you to apologize to the Mademoiselle for the disrespect you've shown her. I expect that apology to be forthcoming immediately or you shall receive no further help from me or my government."

Jean turned to Laura and spoke in French, "This is how you deal with Americans, Mademoiselle. They're a rude and arrogant people."

"Mr. Broussard, I'm afraid I don't understand what you mean," Casey replied.

"Director Casey, this woman should not be judged by her appearance. Your country brags about human rights, but I've seen little here today that assures me you honor them. I wouldn't be surprised to see her resign her position from your employ immediately. She doesn't deserve the disrespect and discrimination she's received. As a representative of the French government, I'm in a position to demand certain things of you. If you would rather hear it from my Ambassador, I shall call him immediately. I'll give you one more opportunity to apologize to the Mademoiselle or you'll receive no further help from either the French government or me."

Clair George and Bill Casey were stunned. There was a brief silence as Casey began to understand the serious nature of the threat being made. Clair spoke first. "Ms. Messier, on behalf of ..."

Casey interrupted, "Excuse me, Clair. This is my responsibility. I speak for the Central Intelligence Agency. On behalf of the agency and the United States government, I sincerely apologize to you, Ms. Messier, for any disrespect and discrimination, either overt or implied, that you may have suffered at any time during your employment here at the CIA. We are a nation of values and we try to reflect that in everything we do. On a personal note, Ms. Messier, I'm an old man who grew up with certain prejudices that have proven, over time, to be false. It wasn't my intent to disrespect you and I hope that you'll accept my apology and continue the fine work you're doing for this agency and the American people."

Without even glancing at Laura, Jean responded on her behalf. "The Mademoiselle accepts your apology. Let us talk no more of such things because there will never be a need. Mademoiselle, do you have anything to say?"

"Yes," she said. "Director Casey and Deputy Director George, Mr. Broussard has briefed me completely on the proposed mission. I understand it fully. If you choose to offer the mission to me, please contact me in Paris and I'll consider it. However, please know that if I accept, I require extra compensation for the risk. I require $100,000 to be placed in a numbered account for me at Credit Suisse Bank in Zurich, Switzerland. Or if you prefer, I'll drop my letter of resignation off at Personnel on my way out of the building. Respectfully, Sir, that's all I have to say."

"Gentlemen, the Mademoiselle has made her statement. We've finished our duties for the day. I'll be escorting the Mademoiselle out of the building. Have a pleasant day."

With that, Jean took Laura by the arm to the lobby where he called a taxi. Her confidence and dignity had been restored by a complete stranger. Life does have its oddities.

After Messier left, Casey asked Clair to walk with him back to his office. Not a word was spoken until after Casey slammed the door behind him, "Dammit, Clair, a lowly field agent with the aid of the French government, just extorted $100,000 from the Director of the Central Intelligence Agency."

"Now you know why the Soviets call her 'Shewolf'," Clair said.

"Surely, we have someone else who can do this job," Casey said more as an aside than a comment.

"Bill, if I thought there was anyone else, I'd use them. Could I ask you one question?"

"What is it?" Casey snarled, seething at the thought of a hundred grand going to Laura Messier.

"Did you mean that apology?"

"Yes, I did," Casey said. "If I didn't say something that satisfied Broussard, I'd have had the French government up my backside and the Pentagon over here asking what happened to the mission. The President may have even gotten wind of it. I can't afford that. This attack is very important to the President."

"What do you want to do?"

Casey looked out his window at the agency grounds and said without looking at Clair, "When Messier gets back to Paris, make the offer. Get rid of her at the end of the op."

"Fine. What about the money?"

"Set up the account and wire the damn money," Casey hissed.

"Where am I supposed to take the money from, Bill?"

Casey turned around and screamed at Clair. "Dammit to hell, Clair, how in hell am I supposed to know that? Take it from one of our slush funds. You figure it out."

"Yes, Sir."

As Clair walked back to his office, he had a smile on his face. Damn, that woman is good.

Chapter Six

ARRIVING BACK IN Paris late Tuesday night following the disastrous meeting at Langley, Laura found nothing in the refrigerator to prepare for dinner. She warmed a can of soup on the stove top, poured a glass of red wine, put on a recording of Tchaikovsky and curled up on the sofa to read. Laura liked reading novels, but she laid the book aside after a while, preferring to sip wine and listen to the lush scoring of Tchaikovsky's 5th Symphony. Her left hand automatically fingered the notes in the violin part. Her vacation had a poor ending with the brutal meeting at Langley yesterday. Why do I judge vacations by how they end rather than how they begin? she asked herself. As she took her soup bowl back to the kitchen, she looked out her kitchen window at the lights of the Eiffel Tower which could be seen over the rooftops. It's nice to be home.

Laura was late to work the next morning, her first day back at the French Ministry of Foreign Affairs. Grabbing a taxi instead of walking, Laura didn't see the chalk mark on the building down the street which indicated John Brownley wanted to meet. She saw it the following morning and left the Ministry for an early lunch to visit the embassy. Chatting with the guards as she usually did on each visit, she found that Rick Williams had been promoted to Head of Security. Laura made a point of spending a couple of minutes with him. Rick's Georgia accent reminded Laura of her own childhood; Laura's mother was a southern girl.

"A fine looking woman just walked into my embassy. How's my girl today?" Rick asked.

"I'm doing great, Rick. Congrats on the promotion; it's well deserved."

"Thanks. It doesn't get any better than this, Miss Messier."

"You gonna be too big to say hello to me from now on?" Laura teased.

"Yep. You're gonna have to make an appointment with me," Rick said, teasing her back.

"Well, Rick, I only have two words for you," she said as she leaned close to his ear. "Chicago Bears."

Rick leaned back and laughed. He followed football closely and judging by his well chiseled frame, he'd probably been a pretty fair player at one time.

"I don't think anyone's gonna beat them Bears this year."

Messier pointed at the ceiling, "Is the boss expecting me."

"Yep, you're in trouble. He expected you yesterday," Rick said with a smile.

"Well, you'll just have to come and rescue me then."

"Anytime, Miss Messier. You know I've got your back."

"Can I go on up?" she asked.

"Yep, go right ahead."

Upon entering Brownley's office, he looked up, "I thought we were supposed to meet yesterday."

"Gee, John, it's nice to see you, too. I had a great vacation, in case you wanted to know."

Brownley leaned back in his chair and smiled, "Okay, how was your vacation, Laura?"

"It was fine."

Laura had confidence she would finally loosen Brownley up one of these days. Inside that administrative attitude, somewhere there was a real person.

"And, that boyfriend of yours? How's Tilton doing?"

"You know about that?" she asked, somewhat shocked at that revelation.

"When Clair George tracks you down at your boyfriend's cabin, Laura, I think you can assume everyone knows about it," Brownley said.

"I give up." Laura laughed. It was good to be home again. "What have you got for me today?"

"Clair George tells me you'll be working a special assignment for a while."

"Yes, but I should be able to continue my duties here."

"I have the upcoming Ministry schedule here. You've got a busy fall."

"I was looking at that myself yesterday. I may have to travel back to Langley once in a while for meetings, but that's it for now," Laura said.

"Fine, we'll be able to work around that. As usual, keep me informed as to your whereabouts and for goodness sake, Laura, remember that we operate safely because of our attention to the tradecraft we use in the field. So please be aware."

"Sorry about missing the mark on the wall. I took a taxi to work yesterday morning."

"Very good. That's all I have for you, Laura. Have a nice day."

"You, too, John." *I've made some progress*, she thought, leaving his office. *John is calling me Laura now.*

There is a sense of comfort that comes from the routine of work. Leaving the apartment each morning and coming home at the same time, seeing the same faces doing the same work day after day, it's like wearing an old pair of shoes; they just feel right. Yes, small things do change, the bookstore down the block has a new display, the diner has a new lunch special or it rains one day and not the next. It's the small things that make life interesting. It was that kind of comfort Laura felt in the fall of 1985. In retrospect, she'd gotten a bit lazy.

When Messier received a letter from Credit Suisse in Zurich requesting her presence to complete the registration for her numbered account, she didn't have a sense that tumultuous times lay ahead. On the contrary, the money gave her an added sense of comfort. When a Top Secret communication arrived at Paris Station from Clair George offering Messier the Operation Eldorado mission, she accepted it largely because it meant she could keep the money. Nothing was urgent at the moment; Laura's life was calm and she welcomed the sense of peace.

Beneath that calm exterior, though, Laura felt a sense of pressure about the mission. She knew the stress of waiting could psychologically defeat her so she channeled that emotion into action. The French Foreign Ministry offered language classes for employees and Laura went about the task of learning Arabic. She was a quick study with everything she learned, but Arabic was a unique challenge. Laura already had fluency in French; she could speak German, Italian and Spanish as well. The written form of Arabic was impossible to grasp in a few short weeks. She decided to concentrate on the spoken language, figuring that would be what she needed most for the mission. After finishing the Ministry course, she turned to the American Embassy, which also offered beginner's courses in various languages. Once that was completed, she hired a private tutor. *Arabic's going to be a longer term study,* she thought. However, her study did serve its intended purpose. She needed to maintain her focus during the intervening months.

The attack on Israeli athletes at the Munich Olympics in 1972 was a prelude to what would become commonplace years later. The 1980s saw terrorism enter the vernacular of ordinary citizens as accounts of terrorist incidents appeared on the front pages of newspapers around the world. Muammar Gaddafi's name was linked to nearly every incident. Libya was a major source of funding for terrorist organizations. When a senior commander of the PLO was captured on a yacht off Cyprus in early September, 1985, Gaddafi denounced it in the press. Following that, when the PLO hijacked an Israeli yacht in retaliation, Gaddafi called a news conference to praise the terrorists. Finally, after the Israelis destroyed the PLO headquarters in Tunis on October 1st, Laura realized an American strike against Libya was inevitable.

Chapter Seven

Winter, 1985-86

OVER THE CHRISTMAS holidays, Laura met Steve's parents in Brookline, Massachusetts, a suburban area southwest of downtown Boston. Jack and Linda Tilton were wonderful people and made Laura feel a part of their family. It seemed to family members that Steve and Laura could be headed toward marriage.

Right after Christmas, the two headed to Key West for afternoons on the beach, followed by evenings of drinks and quiet dinners. It was to be their time away from the worries of the world. The Rome and Vienna airport bombings on December 27th brought them back to a harsh reality. If terrorists could bomb Rome and Vienna, they could bomb New York and Washington.

Both were surprised they weren't called back to work. It was the top story in the media for days and Steve made more than a few phone inquiries back to Langley. Otherwise, Laura and Steve tried to enjoy their well-earned time off, returning to Washington after the first of the year. However, neither could shake a sense of fear about the future. The Abu Nidal Organization claimed responsibility for the bombings and that could mean only one thing: the Libyans were involved.

Clair George requested a meeting with Laura before she left for Paris so she drove out to Langley alone to meet him on a Saturday. They went over the mission, step by step, to make sure things were in place. Laura told him of Jean Broussard's plan to create a legend for her as a performer and mentioned her language training. Clair told her the Reagan administration would introduce further economic sanctions in January. If Gaddafi stopped his involvement with terrorism, then perhaps the mission wouldn't be necessary. He urged Laura to continue her preparations. Study Libya, memorize a map of Tripoli and read everything she could about Gaddafi. When she asked about a timetable for the mission, Clair said if Libyan involvement in any future terrorist attack could be proven, the mission would be activated.

Steve drove Laura to the airport for the flight back to Paris. As they said their goodbyes, Laura casually mentioned she could be back in town for briefings soon. That told Steve what he needed to know; Laura was working on Eldorado Canyon. Laura had failed to tell him. Steve had advised her earlier against getting involved and on the flight home, Laura wondered if he had been right; perhaps the money wasn't worth the risk.

Upon returning to Paris, Laura received word that John Brownley had requested a meeting. That usually indicated trouble, for Brownley and Laura often had difficulty working together. Brownley had no argument with the quality of the information Laura produced, but rather the manner in which she obtained it. Brownley could not accept Laura's penchant for conducting business on the fringes of permissible activities according to the CIA. While Brownley was determined to rein in Laura's approach to intelligence gathering, Laura was equally determined to prevent it.

"Laura, you're literally having sex with every man you meet in Paris," Brownley shouted as soon as she walked in his office.

"Bullshit. Don't be ridiculous, John."

"Miss Messier," Laura hated the administrative tone of voice Brownley was fond of using, "the Central Intelligence Agency expects a certain code of conduct which we are not seeing from you. You attended the opera with the Minister last week and I read it in the damn newspaper," Brownley said, holding up the society page of a Parisian daily newspaper.

"Yes, I did. It was Puccini, so what?"

"Learning about your activities in the newspaper, Miss Messier, is unacceptable," he shouted.

"His wife took ill at the last minute, John. He's an important government official. The press follows him around."

"What about the evenings he spends at your apartment?"

"I fix dinner for him once in a while. So what?"

"This relationship you have with your boss over there at the Ministry is contrary to the Code of Conduct."

"John," she said, "there is a social aspect to my job at the Ministry that I am expected to fulfill. We've been over this before."

Brownley was getting nowhere, so he paused and when he started again, he was gentler. "Laura, American agents have started disappearing around the world. We lost one in Eastern Europe last month and one in Southeast Asia the month before that. We believe there's a leak out of Langley."

"You believe what?" she asked.

"We think there's a leak."

"What are they doing about it?"

"Langley started an investigation, but it's going to take a while to track it down. Until they do, you should consider the possibility that you've been compromised. I want you to assume the Soviets have your file."

"I'm not sure what to do about that, John. I can't just stop working."

"You're not safe enough, Laura. You use no tradecraft, you never tell us where you are and you don't tell us who you're with. If you turn up missing, we need to know where to look."

"John, the Minister sends me to embassies all over Paris each week. I'm visible and that public persona is my protection."

"It won't protect you from an assassin."

"The agency put me under cover and I've got to act the part. It would be dangerous to do otherwise."

"I'm concerned for your welfare, Laura."

"I understand that."

"Then inform us of your schedule in advance."

"To the extent that's possible, I'll try to do better."

"Very good, that's all I have for you today," Brownley said. "Oh, one more thing before you leave."

"What's that?"

"Stay out of the damn newspapers," he said.

Chapter Eight

THE LETTER THAT appeared in early February, 1986, for Laura at the French Ministry of Foreign Affairs did not have a return address. Inside the envelope was only a business card for the Club Marais with an address and phone number, but she knew its meaning. The following day, Laura made her way to the Marais District, an upscale area of nightlife and found the club, which appeared to be closed. After ringing the doorbell, someone who looked like a bouncer unlocked the front door, stuck his head out and inquired as to her business. Laura mentioned the name Jean Broussard; the bouncer nodded and led her inside to a table near the bar. The building must have been recently renovated; it had the smell of freshly cut wood. The large room had an open, airy feel, with high ceilings and windows that looked out upon the street. Laura watched the bartender restock the bar for the evening's business until Jean walked through the club with a big smile.

"Mademoiselle, it is so nice to see you again."

They gave each other a big hug, Jean kissed her on both cheeks, took her by the hand and spun her around. "Mademoiselle, you look absolutely wonderful this afternoon. Come, sit, and tell me all that goes on in your life." They chatted about every day kinds of things; Jean and Laura had an instant rapport that made her feel they had been friends for years.

"I noticed, Mademoiselle, that your picture was in the news from the opening night ball at the Paris Opera. What a beautiful gown you were wearing. You were the essence of elegance. A young, beautiful woman on the arm of an older man. Typically French, I think."

"Thank you, Jean, what a nice thing to say. The Armani gown was absolutely fabulous. It was loaned to me by one of the fashion houses."

"And the jewels?" Jean asked.

Laura laughed, "Also borrowed. I was Cinderella at the ball."

"The man in the picture? He is the Minister, no?"

"Yes," she said, with a smile that was more an admission than a fact. "His wife became ill at the last moment."

Now, it was Jean's turn to laugh. "I think powerful men in France have wives who suddenly become ill quite often, Mademoiselle." They both laughed at the realities of French society.

"Mademoiselle," Jean said turning serious, "I think it's time for us to prepare, no?"

"I've been waiting for your contact."

"Here's what I'd like to do with your permission. Come and watch my shows over the next couple of weeks. Sit far enough away from the stage to go unnoticed. I want you to get a feel for what goes on."

"Of course, Jean. I will come this weekend, if that's convenient."

"Excellent! We have our best performers on weekends."

Jean's show consisted of five performers who performed in what could best be described as a variety show. Singers and comedians took the stage, one by one, to do various types of entertainment. Each performer interacted with the audience and the bawdy, raucous behavior of the crowd was part of the show. The performers were talented and interesting individuals, each with an innate ability to communicate with the audience.

After studying their shows, Messier realized much of her life's experience was completely useless insofar as performing was concerned. An intelligence officer is inconspicuous by design; a runway model is coached to avoid any attention that would divert from the clothing she wears, so attracting attention is contrary to her sense of self. While Jean's performers instructed Laura in singing, movement and showmanship, she wasn't nearly as polished as the others. However, she had one thing they didn't, her beauty. That was a source of interest for men in the audience and a key part of her popularity.

It is the feedback from an audience that a performer enjoys most. After a couple of weeks, Laura began to enjoy herself and once again, put Operation Eldorado Canyon out of her mind. Only briefly, though, because Langley called her back to Washington for a consultation in early February.

It was only for little more than a day, but Laura looked upon the trip more as an opportunity to see Steve than discuss the Libya mission with Langley. With Eldorado Canyon drawing ever closer, an underlying tension had developed between them that was never mentioned, but they made love with a passion neither of them had felt before. Riding out to Langley with Steve the following morning, Laura became determined to transfer back to Washington once Eldorado Canyon was finished.

During Laura's meeting that day, Clair George and his operations staff went over the plan again and again, searching for variables, weaknesses and alternatives if the plan were to fail. It reminded Laura of refinishing a piece of fine furniture where each time one thinks it's finished, another spot is found that needs work until finally one realizes that nothing is ever perfect. The two most basic of questions were unanswerable. Would she obtain the missile codes and would she get out of the country? Jean had tried to ease her worry on those two points, but no one had definitive answers to those questions.

DST provided new information in the form of photos taken of Gaddafi. In the first, Gaddafi was in the act of opening the briefcase. The lock was a three digit combination and the photo showed two of the three numbers. His hand, unfortunately, blocked the last digit. Laura now knew she may have to try as many as ten different last digits to open the case.

In the second photo, the open briefcase appeared in the background sitting on a table. Inside, on top of a stack of documents, rested the laminated code sheet. One column of six numbers, each number consisting of six digits, could clearly be seen on the sheet. Written in Arabic, the headings were in red, the text and numbers in black. The agency provided a translation and if that translation was to be trusted, the picture positively showed the code sheet. Laura knew exactly what she'd be looking for.

She practiced memorizing the codes as a long string of thirty-six numbers divided into three groups of long distance telephone numbers. Over and over, Clair tested Laura. She'd glance at different sets of numbers, slowly decreasing her memorization time to less than a second. It reminded her of card counting in the casino game of blackjack. By the end of the meeting, everyone became convinced her part of the mission was ready. Clair added one caveat at the end, something Laura already knew but which he was required to say.

"Laura, there's one more thing we haven't discussed," Clair said as Laura was preparing to leave.

"Sure, what's that?"

"As you know, you'll be alone in there."

"Broussard will be with me, Clair. What are you talking about?"

Clair hesitated, looked at the floor and said, "I mean you'll have no American help."

"I knew that from the beginning," she replied.

"I'm required to tell you that if you're caught, Laura, we can't acknowledge that you work for us."

"You won't be coming to get me, then?" she asked. Clair became quite grim in his expression and tone of voice. "We can't. I'm sorry, Laura. The CIA will not admit having any knowledge of you or what you're doing. We must deny everything."

"That must mean the CIA can't acknowledge the hundred grand, either," Laura said with a smile. That brought a hearty laugh to both of them.

"Casey's still pissed off about that," Clair said.

"Yeah, well, you tell that bastard he's not getting the money back, no matter what."

"What money?" Clair asked with a sly smile.

Laura described Jean's plan if she were captured. "I'm to say I'm a thief and intended to rob Gaddafi. I'll be classified as a common criminal, handed over to the French and expelled from the country."

Clair nodded. "I like it."

"That should be enough to get me out if things blow up."

"All right then; have a nice flight back to Paris and I'll be in touch when we go active."

"Thanks, Clair."

On the plane ride home to Paris, Laura wondered about the timing of Operation Eldorado Canyon. She suspected the Reagan administration was waiting for one more terrorist incident to activate the mission. It sounded odd to think of it this way, but while the military practiced bombing runs, Laura performed in a nightclub. Both would be needed for Operation Eldorado Canyon to be successful.

Chapter Nine

WAITING CREATES DOUBT, the kind of indecision borne of a lack of knowledge, unpredictable outcomes and unknowable fates. Doubt lingers in the back of one's mind, gnawing at the consciousness, following as a shadow whose manifestation comes in the form of fear. This was the emotion Laura felt during the weeks leading up to her mission; a fear that something could go terribly wrong. She fought it through preparation, ordering every analysis Langley had on Libya. The diplomatic pouches between Langley and Paris Station were heavy with files each week. She read them at the American Embassy which meant Laura changed her schedule, a red flag for those who might be watching. Those eyes were real, the Soviets, the East Germans, and especially the Libyans. They watched Jean; would it be so difficult to imagine they'd watch her, too? Laura disguised her movements, sneaking out the back of the Foreign Ministry building during the day and making her way to the embassy using unpredictable routes. Sometimes, she'd go early in the morning, other times late in the afternoon. She'd leave her apartment out the back door, crossing the alley to pass through the butcher shop onto the next block. As Jean had cautioned her, the Libyans had eyes everywhere.

One disturbing aspect of Laura's research was the activity of a rogue CIA agent named Edwin Wilson, who had lived for a number of years in Libya. Wilson was a gun runner who created a number of front companies that engaged in arms deals. A number of those weapons had been traced to assassinations of Libyan dissidents living abroad. Whether Wilson actually worked for the CIA at the time was debatable; he said yes while the agency said otherwise. Laura's mission would take her into the heart of Libyan military power, the Bab al-Azizia compound. If it were discovered she worked for the CIA, Clair had already warned her; she'd be on her own. Laura decided if she were caught, she wouldn't become a small back page denial by the agency in an American newspaper. She fought her fear through another kind of preparation: combat training.

When Laura asked to join the para-military workouts Rick Williams ran for his embassy guards, Rick was hesitant. Laura was one of the most beautiful women Rick had ever seen and he'd grown up believing women were to be protected. Rick's workouts were tough; they emulated the training he'd received at the Marine Officer Candidate School at Quantico. When Rick suggested Laura join the jazz dance class run by one of the embassy secretaries, Laura laughed and asked Rick to meet her in the gym one evening. They met the following night.

"Okay, Laura, what are we doing here?" Rick asked. "You want me to show you a few self-defense moves?"

"I want you to gear up," Laura said.

"Nah, that's not necessary. Here, let me show you a couple of moves you can use on the street."

When Rick walked up to Laura, she planted her hip into his pelvis and used one of the many Aikido moves she had learned from Master Kwon in Chicago, flipping him over her shoulder and tossing him to the other side of the mat. Rick rose with a smile on his face; the kind smile that indicated he'd just been issued a challenge. "I guess we'll gear up then," he said.

Laura laughed. "No, I don't need to wear anything, Rick; I just don't want you to get hurt," she said.

This thin, wisp of a woman just threw me six feet across the mat. How is that possible? Rick asked himself. He unlocked a closet and broke out the pads and headgear he used when training his staff in hand to hand combat. "I really think you ought to wear something, Laura," he said.

Rick had five inches and a hundred pounds on Laura, but she just smiled. "Rick, with all due respect, you won't be able to lay a hand on me. If it makes you feel better, though, go ahead and throw the stuff over here. I'll put it on," she said.

After they donned padding and headgear, Rick said, "I'm not going to fight you, Laura. I don't fight women. Forget about it."

"Then prepare to defend yourself," she said and in the blink of an eye, she reverse roundhouse kicked Rick with a full extension of her right leg, turning her right heel slightly outward to hit Rick flush in his headgear.

Rick wasn't prepared for the move. He smiled as she backed off. "Oh, this is going to be fun," he said.

Laura motioned him forward with her index finger. "Come, let's dance," she said with a smile.

In an instant, Rick and Laura were attacking each other. Rick's size and strength versus Laura's speed and agility. Rick found Laura's admonition to be true; she was difficult to lay a hand on. His offensive moves were either blocked, deflected or he missed entirely, which left him open to Laura's counter moves. *She's fast,* Rick thought, *too fast.* The velocity of her kicks and punches was jarring. Laura's combinations, sidekicks, reverse side kicks, snap kicks, spin kicks and jump kicks, left Rick with no choice except to defend himself because he was unable to get close enough to generate any offense. Whenever she moved in to punch, it was because Rick found himself unbalanced and each time he tried to use his size and strength advantage, Laura deftly moved away where she could use her superior speed.

When it was over, both of them were exhausted. They sat down on the mat together, breathing heavily. "Damn girl, you can fight," Rick said. "Where did you learn that stuff?"

Laura smiled, "Oh, I just picked up a few things along the way."

Picked up a few things along the way? That's a bunch of horseshit. You're a pro."

"Can I join your class?"

"Hell, yes," Rick said with a smile. "You can teach it if you want."

Rick had no way of knowing it was the CIA's training school near Williamsburg, Virginia, called The Farm where Laura became recognized for her hand to hand combat skill. Within the agency, that garnered her a fair amount of respect.

Jack Helms, a retired Army Ranger, ran the hand to hand combat training at The Farm. His training was some of the toughest there. He taught a form of mixed martial arts, which was familiar to Laura coming from a Taekwondo background, but she never showed any skill in class, preferring to learn Helms' techniques instead. Helms, a talented combat expert, would teach a technique to the class, pair students against each other to practice while he roamed the room, stepping in to issue brutal corrections. Helms was never pleasant; he was never encouraging. Every recruit suffered under his harsh teaching methods.

Laura had taken up Taekwondo a few years earlier after being beaten outside an elevated train stop in Chicago. Determined to walk the Chicago streets unafraid, she spent years in the black belt class at Master Kwon's studio in River Forest, Illinois. Eventually, she learned to hold her own during tough sparring sessions each week against Kwon's satellite school instructors and his tournament team. Over time, she learned to fight as well as they did. However, in keeping with the original purpose of Taekwondo, Laura refused to take promotions and wore just a beginner's white belt. Laura fought for survival, not status. She didn't list Taekwondo among her skills on her CIA employment application because it never occurred to her that it was one.

The day in question was marked by Captain Helms' vicious attitude toward his students. Helms went beyond teaching that day; his lesson plan was humiliation. He had hurt a couple of classmates that morning and as he stalked the class looking for his next victim, Laura began to view Helms more as an adversary than an instructor. When Helms saw Laura staring at him, he issued a challenge.

"What the fuck you looking at, baby doll?" Helms asked. Helms was fond of calling Laura "baby doll" as a measure of disrespect. Laura refused to answer him. Instead, she began removing her boots and socks. That should have given Helms a warning.

"Why are you taking off your fucking boots, baby doll?" Helms shouted in anger. "You'll never be in combat without your shoes."

Laura smiled. "Oh yes I will," she said calmly.

"Really? And when will that be? In bed with your fucking boyfriend?"

Laura walked to the edge of the mat and bowed. "Now."

He was amused. "Well, look'ee here, the little baby doll wants to fight today."

"No, Sir, I don't fight."

"What are you gonna do then? Kiss me?"

"I win," Laura simply said.

Helms laughed at her. "You think you're going to beat me, little girl?"

"You've already lost. You just don't realize it yet," she said.

That statement enraged Helms, who had never seen a woman fight as well as a man. Helms couldn't wait to humiliate her for her insolence. As Laura stood at the edge of the mat, she bowed to Helms with her eyes up. She thought Helms was too confident to notice the important signals that tell one the strength and skill of an opponent.

"Okay girlfriend, make your move and be prepared because I will make you suffer," Helms said with a wicked smile as Laura moved to the center of the mat just inches away. Helms was accustomed to observing fear in the eyes of his recruits, but this is not what he saw. Laura gave him the stare of a focused, confident opponent.

The first blow came so quickly, Helms never had time to defend himself. Starting with a reverse roundhouse kick that seemingly came from nowhere, Laura put her heel into

Helms' cheekbone and the force of the blow stunned him. She followed with an attack that kept Helms struggling to stay on his feet. She moved inside with her hands; the punches had tremendous speed behind them. Once Helms' reactions had slowed, Laura used her hands and feet interchangeably, pummeling every part of his body.

Finally, to show her superiority, Laura swept Helms' legs out from under him. When he tried to rise, she allowed him to climb to his feet only to use an Aikido move to throw him clear across the mat. Helms finally gave up. Laura backed away and allowed Helms to pull himself up to his knees. He looked at her with an utter hatred. "You'll be dismissed from The Farm by morning, bitch. Pack your bags."

"Captain Helms," Laura said with a calmness that came from victory, "with respect, Sir, thank you for sparring with me today." She bowed again, moved off the mat and sat down with her classmates. Helms ended the class early.

Laura had seen that kind of hatred many times sparring in Master Kwon's studio. It was a hatred of losing, a different quality than hatred of an individual. To Helms' credit, Laura was not dismissed from The Farm; quite the opposite. She received the top ranking in hand to hand combat and was excused from any further training.

So when Laura joined Rick Williams' training class, he saw her do things he'd never seen anyone do before. She could stand straight with her back against a wall, lift either leg above her head and touch the wall with her foot. She could do it facing the wall, too. She could do the splits, then put her hands underneath her and rise to a handstand and simply walk off the mat on her hands. Back flips,

73

forward flips; it seemed that whatever Laura wanted to do, she managed to accomplish.

When she asked Rick if he could find 6" by 6" wood beams to bring into the gym, Rick found old railroad ties thrown behind the motor pool. He propped them against the wall and Laura broke every one of them with her kicks. When she requested he bring concrete blocks into the gym, the embassy guards watched as she broke them with her hands and feet. The day she asked Rick to stack four of them on top of each other, the room grew quiet as she approached the stack, focused herself, then yelled loudly and broke all of them with a single stroke. *This is the stuff of legends,* Rick thought.

During sparring sessions, Rick had to put four guards against her to equal the odds, but she used ancient Taekwondo forms, developed over centuries in Korea, to put each man on the floor. Her speed was blinding, her tactics impeccable and yet, she was as humble a person as Rick had ever met. She didn't fight for pride or the pleasure of victory. She simply thought of fighting like she thought of breathing; she took her skill for granted.

Laura needed help with weapons, but Rick was kind enough to teach her. She would never be a great marksman, but she found herself equal with the rest of his detachment. Rick found it odd she insisted on learning Soviet made weapons and instead of learning one, she learned them all.

Rick finally decided to ask John Brownley if Laura had been assigned a mission. He stuck his head inside Brownley's office.

"Chief, mind if I come in for a minute?"

"Not at all, Rick. What can I do for you?" Brownley asked.

"I want to talk about Laura Messier."

"Ah, well, okay. What do you want to know?"

"Is she training for a mission somewhere?"

"Yes, she is, but it's classified," Brownley said.

"Have you seen that woman fight, Sir?"

"No, I haven't, but I've heard she's been putting on quite a show down in the gym."

"In all my years in the military, Sir, I've never seen anyone like her," Rick said.

Brownley laughed out loud. "You haven't seen her file have you?"

"No, Sir."

"Well, I have and I can tell you she has a reputation for that sort of thing."

"You wouldn't know it from looking at her," Rick said.

"When I first got here, Rick, I didn't understand her. It's taken me awhile. I read her file from Langley. I watched her, studied her. Rick, she's the best field agent I've ever seen."

"I can tell you she's the best fighter I've ever seen," Rick said. "My embassy guards are kind of frightened of her, to tell you the truth."

"Did you hear about the incident last year in the alley behind her apartment?"

"No, Sir."

"The Soviets hired a couple of thugs to kill her. They caught her alone at night walking down the alley behind her apartment. Both of them were armed, but when they went to shoot her, so the story goes, she saw their shoulders stiffen before they fired. She hit the ground and they missed. She disarmed them and killed both of them with her bare hands."

"Jesus," Rick said.

"After that, she tracked down Volkov, the KGB man at the Soviet Embassy. Cornered him one night in a bar and told him she'd kill him if he ever sent anyone else after her. He didn't. The Soviets left her alone after that."

"Wow," Rick said.

"She's produced a gold mine of information for us during her time here. Embedded in the Ministry over there, she's privy to information we can't get any other way. She's in the French delegation for every meeting. She accompanies the Minister on his trips abroad. She's made all kinds of contacts around the world that she uses for information. Hell, I don't even know where she is most of the time."

"I had no idea," Rick said.

"That's why the Soviets wanted to kill her. She's the real deal. She'll do whatever it takes to get the job done. Underneath that facade, she's one of the nicest people you'll ever meet. I've never seen anyone like her."

"Me either, Boss."

"I've heard the mission she's doing comes straight from the White House. They're sending in the A team on this one, and believe me, Laura Messier is the A team."

"Thanks for telling me, Boss," Rick said.

"I've heard she likes you, for what it's worth. Anything else today?"

"No, Sir."

Chapter Ten

ONE OF LAURA'S stops each week was the bar at the Paris Marriott where many bureau and network journalists congregated during the evening hours. Laura came to know many of them during her tenure in Paris and she felt comfortable in their midst. Journalists had a unique perspective, being so close to the events of the world, yet apart from them. They were natural storytellers and their stories were often told with such flourish, they seemed to be writing them as they talked. None were covert operatives that she knew of, except one, Jane Nelson. Jane was Laura's contact at British Intelligence, MI-6, and Jane's cover as a journalist for the Daily Telegraph in London gave her the opportunity to engage a wide group of people. Jane was the closest thing to a friend Laura had in Paris.

Although a bar stool at the Paris Marriott wasn't the place to share intelligence, it was a place to compare notes on the upcoming week. It would be a busy week of diplomacy with the quarterly winter meeting of the G7 finance ministers in Paris. While delegations wouldn't arrive until the day before the meetings, security teams had already begun arriving. The lobby of the Marriott had the look of a convention with media types milling around looking for interviews.

It was early evening when Jane and Laura were sitting at the bar, squeezed by people standing three deep behind them, all shouting for the bartender's attention. It made for excellent cover as Jane and Laura were able to talk freely.

"Check out who's sitting at a table in the corner," Jane said.

"Yuri Volkov? When did he get back in town?" Laura asked.

"Don't know. I thought they'd have sent him to a gulag," Jane said. Both of them laughed because Volkov had been caught by the Paris police breaking into Le Monde's offices in the middle of the night a few weeks ago. Moscow claimed diplomatic immunity and shipped him back to the Soviet Union for consultations. Volkov's idea of intelligence was snooping through file cabinets.

"Do the Soviets know he's a drunk?" Jane asked.

"He's a piece of shit, Jane."

"You have to give him credit, though. No one can drink like Volkov."

"They must give him one hell of an expense account," Laura said. "Who's he sitting with?"

"Marie Colvin. American. UPI's new bureau chief," Jane said.

"Obviously she's new if she's talking to that clown." Laura watched Colvin leave the table and walk toward the restroom. Laura leaned over and whispered in Jane's ear. "Jane, I'll be back in a minute. I'm going to warn her."

Laura followed Colvin into the restroom and ran a brush through her hair waiting for Colvin to exit a bathroom stall. Colvin emerged a minute later and stood next to Laura in front of the mirror.

"He's KGB, you know," Laura said in perfect English.

"Who are you talking about?" Colvin asked.

"Volkov. He's a piece of shit with a capital S."

"You sound American. Are you with the U.S. delegation?" Colvin asked.

"Volkov is giving you a false flag, Ms. Colvin. He's planting a story. If I were you, I'd take your phones apart. He's bugged them."

"How do you know Volkov?"

"He's not a diplomat. He's KGB's man at the Soviet Embassy," Laura said with a shrug as though it were common knowledge.

"Well, if you must know, I'm lining up an interview next week," Colvin said indignantly. "Why is it any of your business?"

"It isn't. I'm just trying to help. Volkov knows nothing."

"So, who are you?" Colvin asked. Laura wasn't sure Colvin believed her.

"No one special," Laura said with a smile. "Have a nice evening."

Laura left the restroom and pushed her way through the crowd to the bar. Laura shook her head in disgust. "Well, I tried to warn her," she said to Jane.

"Don't look now, but she's on her way over," Jane said. Colvin squeezed through and made her way to the bar.

"Hi Jane," Colvin said.

"Hey, Marie. You covering the G7?"

"Who isn't? I was wondering who your friend is?" Colvin asked

"Laura Messier, personal aide to the French Foreign Minister. Laura, Marie Colvin, UPI," Jane said.

"I think I saw your picture in the paper the other day," Marie said to Laura.

"I'm sure you did," Laura said.

"You mean the one of you coming out of a restaurant with Cheysson?" Jane said, stifling a laugh.

"Ha, ha, not really all that funny, Jane," Laura said. Laura was a bit sensitive about her relationship with the Minister. Laura dug into her purse and pulled out a business card. "Here's my card, Marie. Do yourself a favor. When you get back to your office, take the phone apart; the one in your apartment, too. Volkov's clumsy. The bugs will be easy to find. If I'm right, give me a call and we'll talk."

"All right, you've got a deal." Colvin looked confused, as though she wasn't sure how Laura would know such things.

"Volkov promised you an interview with Andropov next week, didn't he?" Laura asked, nodding at Volkov, who was watching them. Laura smiled and waved at Volkov. "Hi, Yuri," she said, although Volkov couldn't possibly have heard her. Volkov smiled and waved back. Laura turned to Marie. "Listen, Volkov couldn't get you an interview with the Kremlin gardener."

Colvin looked very much like she was getting angry. Jane noticed it and pulled Laura off the bar stool by the arm. "Marie, Laura and I were just leaving." Jane started pushing Laura toward the exit. "I'll see you next week at the G7," Jane said to Marie, over her shoulder. She pushed Laura into the lobby of the hotel.

"You can really be a bitch sometimes," Jane said.

"I know. I'm sorry. That didn't turn out the way I wanted."

"One thing you should know about Marie, she wants to cover the Middle East," Jane said. "She could be a good person to know."

"Oh, how's that?" Laura asked, sarcastically.

"She'll do whatever it takes to get a story."

Laura considered that for a moment. "All right, if she calls, I'll talk to her. Are you staying here at the hotel?"

"Yeah, the Telegraph got me a room."

"I'll see you next week at the meetings, Jane," Laura said, before walking out of the hotel and grabbing a taxi.

The next morning, when Laura answered her phone at the Ministry, she found Marie Colvin on the line.

"Laura, its Marie Colvin."

"Good morning," Laura said stiffly, still feeling awkward about the conversation last night.

You were right about the phones. They were bugged," Colvin said.

"Well, I'm sorry I was such a bitch. Let's start over."

"I've been told you're an important person to know."

"That depends. Information flows two ways, Marie," Laura suggested.

"Are you offering a deal?" she asked.

"I'm suggesting we form a relationship."

"When do you want to meet?" Colvin asked.

"I'm going to leave you a message at the front desk of the Marriott. Follow the instructions on the message and we'll go from there."

At lunch time, Laura took a taxi to the Marriott where the lobby was packed with check-ins for the G7 meeting. Standing in line at the front desk, it was impossible to avoid people she knew and Laura spent more time than she desired chatting with acquaintances in the lobby. She managed to write a short note giving Marie the phone number to what Laura purported to be her apartment phone. It wasn't. It was an answering service for Operations at Paris Station, a number Laura gave to diplomats and their aides. Laura put a cute message on the line saying she

81

wasn't in at the moment and asked the caller to leave a message. Operations monitored the line, ran a trace on the calls and did a voice analysis of every caller. Laura picked up the messages when she stopped by the American Embassy.

For clandestine contacts like Jane Nelson, messages were left at the coffee shop a few doors down from Laura's apartment. Where Jane Nelson was discreet and knew how to spot a tail, Marie Colvin was a journalist who attracted attention. Brownley also used the coffee shop, although his men put a white chalk mark at the base of the building.

That fortuitous meeting with Marie Colvin began a fruitful relationship. Marie had her eyes set on the world's hot spots where she was fearless in pursuit of stories. She was loyal only to the victims of war and her stories were brilliant exposes of the horrors of conflict. To get those stories, Marie went where no other reporter would go, right into the midst of the shooting. Marie Colvin was someone who got her hands dirty and she turned out to be an incredibly important person to know. As different as their jobs were, Marie Colvin and Laura Messier were similar. Both pushed the boundaries of their profession, going further than their colleagues would dare, to gain the information they wanted. That's what made them successful.

Chapter Eleven

Early spring, 1986

The talks between France and the German Democratic Republic (the GDR) in late March were unusual since East Germany was closely allied with the Soviet Union. However, economic and political pressure was building toward reunification with West Germany and the East Germans brought a large delegation to Paris for talks on a range of mutual interests. Laura was included on the French side but, as usual, her role was limited to being a low level functionary. She had studied the files on the major players, but many of the low level East Germans were unknown to the CIA.

Laura began chatting with the GDR staff during breaks, many of whom had never traveled abroad. They were eager to talk and she found them to be quite pleasant. A reception scheduled the first evening at the hotel provided a greater opportunity for intelligence gathering. East German security was extremely tight, but Laura knew all the secret passageways in every hotel in Paris. She had been slipping in and out of hotels unseen since she started working in Paris. She even had master keys to a few of them.

Many of the East German men were interested in the famed Parisian club scene. Apparently, the reputation of French women had managed to pierce the Berlin Wall because when Laura explained how to slip out of the hotel unnoticed, a couple of young East Germans became excited at the prospect. After the reception, Laura led them out of the hotel right under the noses of their East German handlers, along with an attractive female colleague from the Ministry.

They hopped in a taxi and ended up in a trendy bar in the Marais District, where the disco music was overly loud and the women were under dressed. After several rounds of drinks, despite the language difficulties, things were going rather well. Apparently, drinking is a universal language. Laura smiled at Arno, her dance partner, as she drew herself close to him, pressing her body into his. She kept rubbing her leg into his very hard penis, moving her hands underneath his jacket while kissing him. He was so overcome with sexual energy that he did not feel Laura slip her hand into his breast pocket and pilfer his billfold. She spun around and as he pressed himself into her hips, Laura wedged the billfold into her bra.

Laura suddenly feigned fatigue, exited the dance floor and excused herself for a restroom break. Down a little used stairway, she found an empty employee's lavatory, filthy, but serviceable. Once inside, she checked a frosted glass window on the far side to use as an emergency exit. She ran her fingers over top of the frame, unlocked it and pulled up slightly to loosen it. She looked underneath the stalls, saw no one, locked herself into one and inspected the billfold. Exiting the stall, she stood before the mirror; damn, she looked horrible. She put her purse on the counter, dug out a tube of lipstick and applied color to her lips. She thought, *Why can't I ever find lipstick that will stay on for more than an hour?*

She heard a click, a door latch. She immediately turned and found an elderly man had entered the restroom. He locked the door behind him. Laura instinctively grabbed her purse and stuck her hand inside. She had no idea what she was looking for since she carried no weapon.

"Hello, Shewolf, it's nice to finally meet you," he said. *He knows my Soviet code name,* she thought. Laura looked toward the window, her escape route. Observing this, the man sought to calm her. "Do not worry, Shewolf, I am not here to hurt you. I am an old man ..." he spread his hands wide, "... see, I have no weapon." He spoke slowly and deliberately in French.

"No one's ever called me Shewolf before," Laura said, looking him straight in the eye.

"You are familiar with the name, aren't you?" he said.

"Yes, I've heard it."

"It's the code name the KGB has given you in Moscow," he said.

"Who are you?" she asked.

"Don't you know, Miss Messier?"

Laura thought for a minute. *Well, he's about the right age, but I've heard he never leaves East Germany. No one in the West has ever met him. He's a ghost; very little is known about him. I'll take a chance.* "You're Markus Wolf."

"Very good, Shewolf. I've been told you're very bright." He began walking toward her. Laura put up her hand. "That's far enough."

He stopped. "I have no intent to harm you."

"You're far from home, Mr. Wolf."

He shrugged. "A short vacation, I think." He paused; his eyes were judgmental. "You speak excellent French for an American."

"You speak excellent French for a German," she countered.

"It's important to know the ways of our enemies, don't you think?"

"It is a wise thing to learn," Laura said in German. "You're a legend in the West. At CIA, they call you the man without a face."

Wolf replied in English. "As you can see, I have one, not unlike the picture you have seen?"

"You were much younger then," she said switching to English.

"You are quickly making a reputation for yourself in the East, Shewolf," he said. "I want to tell you how much we admire your work. Your methods are very much like our own."

"Allow me to pay a compliment in return," Laura said. "Wasn't it you who said that sex and money were the two most powerful tools in espionage?"

"Yes, and you pay me a great compliment by quoting me."

There was silence for a minute. Laura leaned back against the counter and felt the vibration of the music from upstairs.

"You like music, Shewolf?"

Damn, he just read me. He's better than me, she thought. She studied him, but could read nothing in his face, his body posture, in his demeanor. She listened to the sounds about the room, hoping to receive advance warming of an attack by Wolf's men. The drone of music upstairs, the faucet drip slowly beside her, an occasional voice in the hallway; every sound gave her information. Slowly, a smile crept upon Wolf's face.

"You remind me of when I was young," he said.

"How is that?"

"You are a hunter, Shewolf. You isolated that young boy, Arno, I believe is his name, and you know all about him by now. How is your family at 1742 Linden Street, Des Plaines, Illinois?"

Wolf was doing Laura a favor. He was telling her the rumored leak at CIA was true.

"You've seen my file, haven't you?"

"I see many things, Shewolf," he said.

"Would you care to tell me how you obtained it?"

"It came into my possession from the KGB. Their sources are unknown to me."

After a moment to consider that, Laura said, "We're watching, you know."

"I imagine you are. Will the Minister be in your bed when you return home this evening?" Wolf asked.

"I rather think he'll be home with his wife this evening."

"You are pretty, Shewolf. I can see why he likes you."

This was a war of wits and Laura had to respond with something. She remembered the background reports she'd read on Wolf. "You don't need to worry about your granddaughter, Anna, at Chateau Du Rosey, 1180 Rolle, Switzerland, or is she still in Gstaad this time of year?" His eyes turned cold and hard. "Don't worry, we don't touch families," she said.

"Neither do we," Wolf replied.

There was another pause; Wolf appeared to be waiting for something. Laura realized what he wanted and she reached into her purse, pulled out Arno's billfold and tossed it to him. He opened the billfold as Laura recited the information on the ID. Wolf looked up and just for a brief moment, she saw something in his eyes. Her memory surprised him. *He's good, but he's not perfect,* she thought.

"Shewolf, how do you think I found you this evening?" Wolf asked and then answered his own question. "I know all those secret passageways, too. I have been to that hotel many times. You take too many risks, Shewolf. You ignore tradecraft. That's how an old man was able to isolate you tonight."

"I made a mistake," she admitted.

"Watch yourself, Shewolf. Make sure you remain the hunter and not become the prey." He paused, thinking about his next comment. "I am old and I will retire soon to a villa and write my memoirs. You, Shewolf? You are young and have an entire life to live. Make sure you are never caught, Shewolf. I'd like to see what you can accomplish in life. Good night." And then, he was gone.

Laura waited before she approached the door. She listened; she heard nothing, except the steady drone of music upstairs. Should she leave using the window? Laura suddenly felt frightened. Wolf would never come alone. Where were the others?

She thought for a moment, *What did I learn from the encounter? Face to face with the head of the East German Stasi Foreign Division. They're getting information from a leak somewhere in the CIA. The risk was worth it, though. I just planted a bug on the top spymaster in the Eastern Bloc.*

Laura quickly found a phone after she left the lavatory. She made the call. "Do you have him?"

"Three men just left the bar. Which one has the bug?"

"The older man. Get every picture you can. Nobody's got pictures of this guy."

"Thank you." The line went dead. A panel truck started its engine and pulled away from the curb. As it happened, Laura had done a bit of tradecraft that evening and asked Operations to follow her. She carried two small electronic transmitters and planted one inside Arno's billfold. She was sure Wolf would find it and it wouldn't take him long to recognize a tail, but they'd get pictures.

Laura rose early the next morning. She had to be at work by 9:00, but her encounter last night was something she had to report. She left the apartment at 8:00 and looked up and down the sidewalk. *I'm paranoid*, she thought. *If he wanted me dead, he had the opportunity.* She grabbed a taxi and arrived at the embassy at 8:20.

"Hi Rick, have you seen Brownley this morning?"

"Hi, Laura. Yes, he just went upstairs." Laura walked around the corner; Brownley was still waiting for the elevator. She grabbed him by the arm.

"John, we've got to talk."

"Ride the elevator with me," Brownley said. When the elevator closed, she told him the story.

"You had our men with you last night?"

"Yes," Laura said.

"That means we have pictures."

They got off the elevator and walked down the hallway to Brownley's office. "Alice, find me one of those cable forms, would you? I've got to send a message to Langley. Get a diplomatic pouch ready, too. We'll have photos this morning to send back. Oh, and please find a car for Laura. Unmarked, no diplomatic plates. She's got to run over to the Foreign Ministry before people notice she's late."

Chapter Twelve

IN LATE MARCH, a brief military conflict erupted between Libya and the United States. Gaddafi had claimed the entire Gulf of Sidra as sovereign Libyan territory which was contrary to the United Nations Convention on the Law of the Sea. The United States, citing the right to open navigation in international waters, continually sailed aircraft carriers into the Gulf of Sidra to conduct military exercises. While several confrontations occurred, none resulted in violence until March 24th, 1986, when Libyans fired SAM missiles at American jets. The battle that ensued took the lives of a number of Libyans while the Americans suffered no losses.

Following that incident, Jean left Laura a note at the club asking her to stop by his office before the performance that evening. The note wasn't unusual; Jean often asked to speak with performers, but Laura knew this was different. Upstairs in his office, Jean said, "Mademoiselle, would you please shut the door so we may have a private conversation?"

"Yes, of course," she replied.

Once the door was closed, Jean motioned her to a couple of stuffed chairs. "There is the possibility of an opening soon for a performer at one of my foreign clubs and I wondered if you would be interested?"

"I'm delighted that you'd consider me," Laura replied. "Yes, I'd be interested."

"Then, I need you to perform every show for the next couple of weeks to make sure you are fully prepared. I only take my best performers overseas and I want you to be ready."

"Yes, Sir, I'll be here every night from now on."

"Thank you, Mademoiselle," Jean said. "I think I'll stick around and watch your performance this evening. You are always a delight to watch."

"I'd be flattered, Sir," Laura said.

"Excellent! That's all I have for you."

That conversation left Messier with the impression Jean thought his office might be bugged. She remembered Jean's comment that the Libyans had eyes everywhere. Would it be unusual for Libyan agents to monitor someone with business interests in Tripoli? Laura noticed whenever Jean talked of important matters it was downstairs in the club, each time at a different table with music playing in the background.

Then, on Saturday, April 5th, the gates of hell opened in West Berlin. La Belle, a discotheque popular with American servicemen, was bombed by terrorists. The bomb exploded late on a Saturday evening when the club was crowded. It was a brutal scene, two dead, one being an American serviceman, 230 injured, 79 of them Americans. Another American serviceman died later from his injuries. The National Security Agency intercepted messages from Libyan Intelligence in Tripoli to the Libyan embassy in East Berlin congratulating them on the bombing.

The following Monday morning when Laura left the apartment, she spotted the chalk mark on the wall of the coffee shop. Laura went to the embassy immediately where Brownley looked up from his desk as she entered his office.

"Good morning, Laura."

"Hi, John. What have you got for me?"

"A message for you came in from Langley marked Urgent. I suggest you read it in my office, then shred it."

She opened it. "Ms. Messier, your mission has been activated. Jean Broussard will contact you with instructions. Good luck, Clair."

Laura looked at Brownley, "John, I must go out of town."

"I figured as much. I wish you the best of luck, Laura."

"Can you do something for me?"

"How can I help?" he asked.

"I need to meet with a reporter named Marie Colvin ASAP. Can you provide security for the meeting?"

"Sure, just tell me when and where."

"I'd like to meet at the Paris Marriott and I'd like to do it in the next day or so."

"When you know the details, let me know. I'll set it up," Brownley said.

"Thank you, John."

"You're welcome. The shredder is right outside in Nancy's office. Once again, best of luck."

Laura destroyed the communication and called the Ministry to inform them of her absence. She headed back to her apartment to wait for Jean's call. Jean had a plan for emergency contact; he would call Laura's apartment phone, but he wouldn't speak. She was to listen for a church carillon in the background. If she heard it, Jean wanted to meet immediately.

The message was already on her machine when Laura arrived back at the apartment. She took a deep breath, paused a minute to collect herself, then left for Jean's club. Leaving through her back door, she walked across the alley and entered the back door of the meat market. She waved hello to Louis, her butcher, as she went out his front door onto the next block. She hailed a taxi after making a mental note to enter the apartment the same way when she returned.

Stopping along the way at an instant messenger service, Messier wrote a short note to Marie Colvin and had it delivered to United Press International's Paris bureau office. Jean's club was closed when she arrived, however Jean appeared soon after Laura rang the bell. He unlocked the door with a big smile. "Mademoiselle, how nice to see you. Please step inside for a moment." Jean locked the door behind her and put a finger to his lips requesting her silence. "Mademoiselle, shall we take an early morning walk to sample the fresh air? It's chilly this morning. I have a wrap for you." As he draped the coat about her shoulders, he frisked Laura. "Do you mind," he asked with a smile. She immediately recognized the technique of searching for listening devices, under the collar, along the seams, around the belt. Finding none, he said, "Shall we go?"

Once outside, Jean locked the club and Laura took his arm. They began strolling as lovers might, out for a walk on a normal morning. "Were you followed, Mademoiselle?" Jean asked.

"No, of course not."

"Is the Mademoiselle sure?" Jean asked.

She laughed. It was wonderful to be with Jean. She squeezed his arm. "Yes, Jean, I'm sure," she said. Laura Messier felt safe in Jean's company.

"Good. The Mademoiselle is very thorough. I presently have a team of DST officers shadowing us. Foreign surveillance will be impossible. Let us walk."

They walked for a long while saying nothing, falling into the rhythm of walking as any couple would. As they passed a cafe, Jean asked, "Would the Mademoiselle enjoy a cup of coffee this morning? This shop serves coffee in paper cups with plastic tops for those who wish to walk. This, I think, is not civilized. It is the American fast food service that has invaded France. Today, I think it serves our purpose." When they approached the counter, Jean ordered on her behalf without asking her preference. "The lady will have her coffee with heavy cream and two sugars, please." *How did he know that?* she wondered.

As they left the shop, Laura tugged at his arm, "Jean, you are an amazing intelligence agent."

He laughed, "I am experienced in the ways of women. I observe their habits closely."

"Are you married?" Laura asked.

"No, Mademoiselle, and I am too old for you," he said with a wry smile. Jean had such a quick and clever wit, it was impossible not to like him. "However, we are much the same in our tastes, Mademoiselle. You have your Minister and I have a wealthy woman who is well beyond my own age. She has a cottage in the south of France along the ocean. We have wonderful times together."

"That sounds so romantic, Jean," Laura said. "My lover does not live in France and I miss him terribly."

"This I also know, Mademoiselle. He is a very lucky man, this Steven Tilton," Jean said.

"You've been doing your research, Jean."

"Yes, Mademoiselle. I know all about you now." They both laughed. Jean had a way of making Laura feel comfortable and relaxed.

They walked for another long period, sipping coffee as they walked. He finally spoke. "Mademoiselle, fortune has worked in our favor. The Americans have planned your mission for this weekend and, as luck would have it, Colonel Gaddafi has requested I bring a performer for this coming Saturday evening. Both our conditions have been met. Can you be ready to leave Friday morning?"

"Yes. The agency sent me a note activating the mission. I was prepared for your call."

"There is a plane ticket in the right pocket of your coat, along with information regarding the hotel reservation. Do not view it now. Just check to make sure it is there."

She felt inside the pocket.

"Yes, it's there."

"I will meet you at de Gaulle for the flight Friday morning."

Jean had led Messier around a circular path that led back to the club. As they approached the entrance, Laura confided in him, "Jean, I'm frightened."

"I know, Mademoiselle. It is the anticipation before a mission. Have confidence in our preparations. Have faith in God. They will carry us forward to success."

"Thank you, Jean."

"Have a wonderful day today, Mademoiselle and I shall see you Friday morning."

"Bye, Jean."

He kissed Laura on both cheeks and disappeared into the club.

Chapter Thirteen

LAURA MANAGED TO arrange a meeting with Marie Colvin late Wednesday afternoon at the Paris Marriott. As United Press International's Paris bureau chief, Marie had an interest in Middle Eastern affairs and it had been rumored she had actually met Muammar Gaddafi, which is what Laura wanted to confirm. The Foreign Ministry provided a car and driver for Laura while Brownley booked a conference room and assigned four men to secure the meeting. One of Brownley's men met Marie in the hotel lobby and escorted her to the room. A second man secured the conference room. A third followed Marie from her UPI office and the fourth followed Laura from the Ministry. They arranged to arrive at slightly different times, Marie first. Laura came a few minutes later, entering through the employee entrance and went up the service elevator.

When Laura entered the room, she found Marie sitting at the table, sipping a soft drink. Brownley had ordered coffee, tea and soft drinks on a cart.

"Hi, Marie," Laura said cheerily.

"Hi Laura. What's with all the security?" One of Brownley's men entered the room.

"Hang on a minute, Marie," Laura said, before speaking with Brownley's man. "Was she followed?"

"No, Ma'am," the guard said.

"What about me?"

"From the Ministry, yes, but you lost them at the cafe," Brownley's agent said. As a precaution, Laura had requested the Ministry car stop in front of a corner cafe that had entrances on both intersecting streets. She entered the shop, went in the restroom, changed into a spare blouse she carried in her purse and reversed her coat. She pinned up her hair, put on a floppy hat and sunglasses. She bought a cup of coffee to go, went out the other entrance, walked up the street in the opposite direction and hailed a taxi. The tail continued the surveillance on the Ministry car, continuing to watch it a full twenty minutes before it returned to the Ministry.

"Do you have any idea who they were?" Laura asked.

"We're not sure, but we suspect the KGB, Ma'am," he said.

Why are the Soviets watching? she wondered.

"Did you fellas sweep the room?" she asked

"Yes, Ma'am. It's clean, except ..." Laura waved her hand and interrupted him.

"That's fine. Thank you so much. Would you mind stepping outside?"

"Yes, Ma'am. We'll be in the hallway if you need us," he said. Laura poured herself coffee and sat down next to Marie.

"So, what's all the security about?" Marie asked.

Laura thought it better to ignore the question. "Muammar Gaddafi. The Minister wants to know about him," Messier said, getting right to the point.

"Planning a vacation to Tripoli, are we?" Marie asked with a mischievous smile.

"No, the Minister just asked me to gather background. You've met him, right?"

"If the Ministry just wanted background information on Gaddafi, why all the security?" Marie asked. "For God's sake, Laura, give me something. What's going on?"

As much as Marie and Laura might have desired to be friends in other circumstances, their relationship operated strictly on the barter system. Each of them gave up something.

"Okay, here's a scoop for you," Laura said. "I hear Western Europe is planning to slap economic sanctions on Libya next week. It's a huge shift in policy."

"Can I use you as a source?" Marie asked.

Laura shook her head no. "You can't even use me as an unnamed source. You'll have to confirm it some other way, but the information is accurate."

"Thanks, I'll run it down. What do you want to know?"

"What's Gaddafi like, personally?" Laura asked, getting back to the subject.

"This meeting is interesting timing. I just interviewed him two weeks ago."

"Really? Where?"

"At his underground headquarters in Tripoli."

"In the Azizia complex?" Laura asked.

"Yes."

"What were your impressions of him?"

Marie thought for a minute before answering. "Well, he's under tremendous pressure, of course," she said. "He thinks the Americans are going to bomb him. I think he's right about that. It's only a question of when. He spends a lot of time in that underground bunker of his."

"Anything else?" Laura asked.

"He launches into these diatribes about Reagan; calls him a madman. He thinks Reagan is out to get him."

Laura laughed. "Well he might be right about that," she said, more as a joke than a serious comment. "How were you able to get in to see him?"

"I walked up to the front gate at Azizia, showed them my press credentials and asked to see him."

Laura was astonished. "You didn't go through channels to request the interview?" Laura asked, puzzled at Marie's description.

Marie smiled at Laura's confusion. "I just walked up to the front gate unannounced."

"You're kidding. They just let you in?" Laura asked.

Marie laughed. "You have to know Gaddafi to understand why," she said.

"Do you think it had anything to do with you being an attractive woman?" Laura asked.

"For Christ's sake, I'm not attractive, Laura. What the hell are you talking about?"

"Yes you are, Marie. Just stop the bullshit. Let me rephrase it. Does it have to do with you being a woman?"

Marie thought for a moment, "He's a very weird character when it comes to women, especially Western women."

"When I see him on television," Laura said, "he's guarded by women. That seems odd to me."

"I never felt safe around him," Marie admitted. "I had the feeling he would have raped me if I hadn't had press credentials. After I met him, the next evening his security team woke me in the middle of the night at the hotel, told me he wanted to see me right then."

"Did you go?"

"Fuck, no. I wasn't going to go meet Gaddafi in the middle of the night. Are you crazy? When I saw him again the next day, he laughed about it. Get this; he had a pair of shoes he wanted me to wear. Really fucking weird."

"Did you put them on?" Laura asked.

"I had to. He wouldn't talk to me otherwise."

"Did he ever try to touch you?"

"Well, yeah, he tried," Marie said.

"Did you let him?"

"Hell, no. I think the only thing that protected me was my press credentials."

"I've heard rumors about his mistreatment of women. You know anything about that?" Laura asked.

Marie stared at Laura for a minute before responding. When she did, she grew serious and looked Laura straight in the eyes. "I think if you went to Libya as part of a delegation, you'd be safe, but if you were alone, he'd probably rape the shit out of you. Does that answer your question?"

Laura fell silent for a minute, thinking about the possibility of being trapped inside Gaddafi's personal quarters. The thought of being raped sent chills up her spine. She walked to the catering cart to refresh her coffee. "Would you like another soft drink, Marie?" she asked, hesitating for a moment to think about the dangers of the mission.

"No, thanks." Marie looked at her watch. "Laura, is that all you wanted to know? I've got to get back to the office. Anything else?"

"I just have a couple more questions, if you don't mind. There's a lot of speculation in the press about the Americans bombing Libya. What do you know?"

"Nothing officially," Marie replied. "But after that nightclub bombing in Berlin last weekend, everyone thinks it's coming soon."

"What do you know about the Berlin bombing?" Laura asked.

"There's some talk going around among the wire service people that Libya was behind it."

"Where are they getting their information?"

"Leaks from the White House."

"It wouldn't surprise me if the Libyans were involved, given Gaddafi's support of terrorism."

"Alleged support," Marie reminded her. "Gaddafi says the CIA is telling lies about him to give Reagan an excuse to attack him."

"You believe that?" Laura asked, not understanding how Marie could be so impartial.

"I'm just telling you what he says, Laura. The CIA has their version, he has his."

"Come on, Marie, you're an American. Surely you have some loyalty?" she asked.

"I'm in the press, Laura. My job is to be impartial. Any loyalties I have are with the victims of terror. The innocent civilians that are killed and injured by governments and terrorists who don't give a shit who they hurt," Marie said pointedly. "That's why I'm going back down there this weekend. I want to cover the civilian casualties if the U.S. stages an attack."

"Wait a minute; you're going back to Libya this weekend?" Laura's eyes widened.

"Yes, and I won't be the only one. The networks already have people there."

"You're just going there to wait for an attack?"

Marie nodded her head. "You wouldn't believe all the journalists down there in the hotels. They're filing daily reports on location."

"If the Americans bomb Tripoli, won't that be dangerous?"

"They're not going to bomb the fucking hotel we're staying in, Laura. Don't be ridiculous," Marie said.

"Okay, good point. Let me ask you this, are you planning another interview with Gaddafi?"

"Sure," Marie said with a shrug. "He wants to talk to me. I think he trusts me. We're going to do another interview this weekend and he's invited me to a social function on Saturday night."

"Did I hear you correctly?" Laura asked. "Gaddafi's invited you to a social function Saturday night?"

"Yes, he wants me to report on it. He wants to give the world a different image of himself."

Damn, if Marie sees me on Saturday night, it could compromise the op, she thought. Laura had no choice, except to address the situation immediately. "Marie, hang on a second, I've got to talk with security outside the room," Laura said abruptly. Marie glanced again at her watch as Laura walked to the door and stuck her head out to talk with Brownley's men. "Hey guys, I need you to get hold of Dan Jenkins at the embassy," Laura said. "I need him over here right now."

"Ms. Messier, he's already here. He's sitting in the truck listening to the conversation."

"Get on your radio and tell him to get up here! Now!"

"Yes, Ma'am."

Brownley's men had put a bug in the room and Dan Jenkins, the FBI's representative at the embassy, was

103

listening from a panel truck outside the hotel. Laura walked back to the table and talked again to Marie, stalling to allow Dan Jenkins time to arrive.

"Marie, would you mind clarifying something for me? You said you're going back to Libya this weekend, you're going to meet with Gaddafi and attend some kind of party he's hosting on Saturday night?"

Marie was confused. "What's the problem?" she asked.

"I've got someone on the way to the room I'd like you to meet," Laura said, trying to keep Marie in the room until Dan arrived.

Marie stood up, gathering her purse and jacket. "I'm sorry, Laura. I've run out of time. We'll have to do this later." Fortunately, Dan knocked on the door before Marie could leave. He stuck his head inside. "We have a problem here, Laura?" Dan asked.

"Yes. I need you in the room."

Chapter Fourteen

Laura made the necessary introduction. "Marie, this is Dan Jenkins, the United States Federal Bureau of Investigation representative at the American Embassy. Dan, this is Marie Colvin. She's an American citizen and UPI's bureau chief in Paris."

"The FBI? What's going on?" Marie said, raising her voice.

Laura turned to Dan. "Dan, I need to detain Ms. Colvin briefly while I consult with Langley."

"Of course." Jenkins flashed his badge at Marie. "Ms. Colvin, I'm sorry to inconvenience you, but I must ask you to stay here for a short time."

"Fuck you assholes. I know my goddamn rights!" Marie said angrily. She rose from her chair and moved toward the door. Jenkins blocked her path. Laura asked one of Brownley's men to step into the room. "What's the problem," he asked.

"We need a little help," Laura said.

Three people now surrounded Marie. "Once again, I apologize, Ms. Colvin," Jenkins said, "but due to a possible threat to the national security of the United States, I must ask you to wait here while we straighten this matter out. Please sit down and relax. I'm sure it will only take a few minutes."

Marie sat down again and looked at Laura. "What the hell are you doing?" she asked.

Laura turned to one of Brownley's men. "Do you have equipment in the truck I can use to place a secure call to Langley?"

"Yes, Ma'am. I'll get it right away."

Laura tried to reassure Marie. "Just hang on, Marie," she said. "As Dan mentioned, we'll have this all straightened out in a few minutes."

"Are you with the FBI?" Marie asked.

"No," Laura said.

"You're CIA, aren't you?"

"Yes," Laura said flatly.

"Fuck you, Laura! You've been playing me from day one!" Marie gave Laura a disgusted look as she slammed her purse on the table. "I want to call the embassy!"

"We'll give you that opportunity in a few minutes, Ma'am," Jenkins said. "Right now, we just need your cooperation. Please sit down and be patient."

Marie angrily threw her coat onto the table and sat down. With Marie upset, the tension in the room was palpable and Laura was uncomfortable waiting until Brownley's man came back with the equipment and installed it on the phone. Before Laura placed the call, she said to Brownley's man, "I'm sorry, I've seen you around the embassy, but I can't remember your name."

"It's Phil, Ma'am. Phil Gregory."

"Thanks. What's going on in the rooms on either side of us, Phil?"

"Nothing. We're secure. Chief Brownley rented all three rooms so there wouldn't be anything on either side of you."

"You've got four men, right?" Messier asked.

"Well, six if you count Mr. Jenkins and the van driver."

"Great. Dan will stay here with me. I need you to put a man in each of the rooms on either side of us. You stand outside the door and I need one more man in the hallway at the elevators. Pull your van driver inside to watch the lobby. Let's see, that makes ..." she counted to herself, "that's six. Can you do that for me, please?" she asked.

"Yes, Ma'am. Do you need help placing the call?"

"I think I can figure it out," Laura said with a chuckle. "I used it at The Farm a couple of times."

"Okay. I'll get the entire area secure for you."

"Thanks, Phil," she said.

Laura placed the call and put it on speaker. "Good morning, Clair George's office. Can I help you?"

"Karen, this is Laura Messier calling from Paris."

"Hi, Laura, what can I do for you?"

"I need to speak to Clair."

"I'm sorry, Laura, he's in a meeting. Can I take a message?"

"Karen, this is an emergency. Would you put me on hold and get him please?" Messier asked.

"Of course. Please hold." It took a couple of minutes to pull Clair out of a meeting. Laura reminded herself to talk to those clowns over there about the music they play while people are on hold. The stuff was horrible.

"Hi Laura. Is your line secure?" Clair asked after coming on the line.

"Yes."

"Go ahead. What's the problem?"

"Clair, I've put you on speaker. I'm here at the Paris Marriott in a conference room. I've got Dan Jenkins, the FBI rep from the embassy here and I'm sitting with Marie Colvin, a UPI reporter here in Paris. Apparently, she's going to be in Libya this weekend and by coincidence, she and I will be in the same room together at the same time on Saturday night. What can we do about this?"

Clair George directed his comment to Marie. "Ms. Colvin, can you hear me?"

"Yes, Sir."

"I'm Clair George, Deputy Director of the Central Intelligence Agency, talking with you from Langley, Virginia. I'm sorry for your inconvenience today, but having you and Ms. Messier in the same room in Tripoli this weekend compromises a classified operation we're doing," Clair said.

"I'm sorry, Mr. George. I had no idea," Marie responded.

"I'm sure you were unaware. Dan?"

"Yes, Sir," Dan Jenkins said.

"We're going to have to detain Ms. Colvin briefly while we figure this out. Ms. Colvin, I want to emphasize that you're not being taken into custody. Due to national security implications, I want you to voluntarily stay in the room while we figure out how to handle this. Are you willing to cooperate?" Clair asked.

"Do I have a choice?" Marie asked with bitterness in her voice.

"I'm afraid not," Clair said. "If you aren't willing to cooperate, then Mr. Jenkins will have to take you into custody for the duration of the operation. If you can wait a few minutes, I'm sure we can have you on your way in an hour or so."

"I'm sorry, Mr. George, but I need to check in with my office," Marie said. "I'd like to use the telephone."

"I'm sorry, but we can't allow any breach of security, Ms. Colvin. I'm sure you can understand that lives are at risk, possibly your own. Please be patient and give us some time to sort this out, okay?"

"Fine," Marie said. She sounded resigned to the detention.

"Laura, I'm going to talk to Casey and see what he wants to do. I'll call you back in a few minutes."

"Thanks, Clair."

Once the call ended, Dan Jenkins spoke again to Marie. "Once again, I apologize, Ms. Colvin. Do you need anything right now?"

"I need to use the restroom," Marie said indignantly.

"Dan, take her phone from her," Laura said.

"Laura, just fuck off," Marie said in anger. "Don't even speak to me."

Dan Jenkins walked Marie into the hallway. "Wait here just a minute, please," he said as he waited for Phil to clear the restroom. Once Phil gave him a signal, Dan looked at Marie. "Okay, let's go, but I'm going to need to take that phone. I'm sorry." Marie handed him the rather large cell phone UPI provided her. "If you'd allow me to give you a piece of advice?" Dan asked while walking Marie down the corridor.

"What would that be?" Marie shot back, still angry over the detention.

"I wouldn't piss Laura Messier off, if I were you. She's the best hand to hand combat expert in the agency. I've seen her work out with the guards over at the embassy. She commands a lot of respect over there."

"I'll keep that in mind," Marie said.

Clair George called Bill Casey's office and explained the situation. "Clair," Casey said, "only the publisher can make the decision to hold a story. The request must come from the President and it can only be for a national security issue. Does this qualify?"

"I think it does, Bill," Clair said.

"All right, give me a couple of minutes, I've got to call the White House," Casey said.

Bill Casey called the President's Chief of Staff, Don Regan, and explained the situation. Regan briefed the President who agreed to call Maxwell McCrohon, the head of UPI in Washington, to enlist his cooperation in withholding information connected to Eldorado Canyon. A non-disclosure agreement was quickly drawn up by agency attorneys, sent over to McCrohon's office and faxed to the American Embassy in Paris. John Brownley had his copy delivered to the conference room at the Marriott, where there was a knock on the door. Dan Jenkins answered. "Mr. Jenkins, this just arrived from Washington for Ms. Messier," Phil Gregory said.

"Thanks, Phil," Dan said. He handed the file folder to Messier. When the phone rang, Laura picked up the line and heard Clair say, "You need to push the switch to red on the scrambler." Once she changed the setting, Clair said, "Laura, we're ready for a conference call between Bill Casey, Maxwell McCrohon, the President of United Press International, Marie Colvin and you. It should come through in a couple of minutes. Do you have the document we sent over?"

"Yes, Sir."

"Please give it to Ms. Colvin to review. The call will come through any time now. Good luck."

"Thanks, Clair." Laura handed the non-disclosure agreement to Marie.

Laura picked up the phone when it rang. "Laura Messier," she said.

"Ms. Messier, this is Bill Casey. I have Maxwell McCrohon on the line with me. Can you put us on speakerphone?"

"Yes, Sir, you already are."

"Let me start this conference by telling everyone that this call is being recorded. Would everyone please identify themselves for the record and who they represent? We'll start on our end. I'm William J. Casey, Director of the Central Intelligence Agency. Go ahead Mr. McCrohon."

"I am Maxwell McCrohon, President of United Press International.

"On your end, Ms. Messier?" Casey asked.

"Laura Messier, Central Intelligence Agency."

"Marie Colvin, Paris Bureau Chief for UPI."

"Dan Jenkins, Federal Bureau of Investigation."

"Thank you," Casey said. "Would you like to start Mr. McCrohon?"

"Marie, I just got off the phone with the President of the United States. He asked me to hold any and all information you've heard today indefinitely for reasons of national security. I've agreed to do so. I order you to keep what you've heard confidential and I need you to sign the non-disclosure agreement."

"Yes, Sir."

"Thank you, Marie," McCrohon said.

"Ms. Colvin," Casey said, "You have accidentally stumbled into a classified CIA mission in Libya this weekend. None of this is your fault, of course, but by signing this agreement, you are pledging under the threat of prosecution for treason that you will not divulge the identity of Ms. Messier to any living person, nor will you reveal the existence of this classified mission to anyone. If you agree, please sign the agreement and you're free to go."

"She's signing the document now, Director Casey," Laura said.

"I've signed it as well," McCrohon said.

"Thank you both. Ms. Colvin, would you please pass your executed copy to Ms. Messier and Mr. McCrohon, would you please give your copy to the messenger at your office?"

"Yes, Sir," they both said simultaneously.

"Thank you, ladies and gentlemen, for your cooperation. We have concluded the call and Ms. Colvin is free to go. Good day."

As they packed up to leave, Marie turned to Messier, "Laura, are you able to give me any information at all? Is your mission to kill Gaddafi?" she asked.

"Marie, I'm sorry, but I can't talk about it."

"When is the bombing?"

"Marie, once again, I'm sorry. Remember, if you even hint to Gaddafi that I'm CIA, he'll kill both of us. Our lives depend on your ability to keep this confidential."

"I will, Laura. You have my promise. I guess I'll see you down there," Marie said.

"No, Marie, you won't because I was never there."

"I understand" Marie said.

Chapter Fifteen

Mission Day One, Friday, April 11, 1986

FRESH FROM A near catastrophe with Marie Colvin two days earlier, Laura arrived at the airport well in advance of her 9:00 flight to Tripoli on Friday morning. Jean Broussard was a very cool customer at the gate, showing none of the stress Laura felt. Looking very much like he was leaving for holiday, Jean gave her a big smile. "Good morning, good morning, Mademoiselle! You look radiant this morning. Are you ready for our little adventure?" Jean asked.

"I think I am, Jean," she said weakly.

Jean hugged her. "You have nothing to worry about, Mademoiselle. It is a lovely morning, we're leaving on an exciting journey and we shall enjoy our time together."

"I wish I could share your enthusiasm, Jean," Laura said.

Jean gave her a confident smile. "Look around you this morning," he said, motioning at the gate area. "The people around us are defenseless against acts of terror. We have a responsibility to protect them, Mademoiselle. We should feel happy that our burdens are great. We're making a difference in the world."

Laura was comforted by his words. "Jean, somehow you always make me feel better." Laura hugged him. "You're a wonderful man."

Jean had a twinkle in his eye. "Yes, I agree with you." Once again, Jean had her laughing.

Laura relaxed and thought no more about the trip. It was just past 1:00 p.m. when they stepped off the plane into the warm Mediterranean climate of Tripoli. The difference in weather was remarkable, but the culture even more so. Arabic had proven difficult for Laura and even though she had studied it the last few months, the written language was impossible to understand. She struggled with everyday language, such as talking to an impatient customs official who, expecting fluency, treated her rudely. While Arabic is a language for poets, with a beauty of expression unmatched in the world, it is not a language of science and technology. Gaddafi had purged Western influences from Libya and where Messier expected international norms to be in place, she found relatively few.

The second language of Libya, if one existed, was English, not that Messier found anyone who spoke it. Gaddafi was reported to be fairly fluent in English, but most Libyans lived in the old ways, speaking the same language their ancestors did. It was a society steeped in tribal and family traditions that offered continuity from one generation to the next, but whose language and lifestyles were ill suited to the technological advancements of the West.

Every woman wore a head covering of some kind. The hijab was worn by many, a head covering that left the face open, but wrapped around the head and neck. Many older women wore a niqab, too, a veil that covered the lower half of the face. Some younger women forswore traditional head coverings in favor of a colored headscarf which was what Jean suggested Laura wear.

In public, women covered themselves completely with heavy clothing, even on the hottest days. Women needed men to accompany them in public to avoid being subjected to harassment. On the occasions Laura did see women without men, they were in large groups.

Jean booked rooms at the downtown Radisson which overlooked the Mediterranean Sea. Traveling by taxi north from the airport toward the downtown area, the Abu Salim prison and the Bab al-Azizia military compound were within view. The city was pretty, with many modern buildings similar to those found in the west. Construction cranes could be seen all over the downtown area. Tripoli was experiencing a building boom.

Jean handled the hotel check-in, something Laura would have found difficult, despite being proficient in several languages. The room was clean, with freshly laundered linens and towels and a wonderful ocean view. However, Laura couldn't be seen alone in public areas of the hotel without being accompanied by a man, so she was forced to wait for Jean to accompany her to dinner. Standing on the balcony looking out over the ocean, she used the time to think about Libya, trying to put what she had studied into the perspective with what she had just experienced.

Muammar Gaddafi had come to power in 1969 as an agent of change. Son of a poor Bedouin sheepherder, Gaddafi grew up in the eastern part of the country listening to the radio broadcasts of Egyptian strongman Gamal Abdel Nasser, who rose to power by staging a coup against the monarchy in Egypt in 1952. Gaddafi, at the age of 27, engineered a remarkable bloodless coup with the help of only 30 young officers from the Benghazi military academy. He overthrew the pro-western monarchy of King Idris while the King was out of the country. Drawing from Nasser's style of governance, Gaddafi sought to change the entire social and economic fabric in Libya.

Gaddafi had developed an egalitarianism that stemmed from his tribal childhood in the deserts of eastern Libya. Free education, medical care and a pension system for the elderly were among Gaddafi's new programs. The government guaranteed jobs, farmland, homes, and expanded rights for women. Libya became a country in which per capita income equaled many Western democracies.

To finance programs, Gaddafi nationalized the oil industry, taking up to a 60% stake in the operations of Western oil companies in Libya. It created boom and bust cycles in the economy. Gaddafi's economy operated almost solely on oil revenue and when oil prices were high, times were good. When oil prices dropped, the economy struggled and the Gaddafi regime struggled to maintain basic services.

Seeking to exert absolute control, Gaddafi abolished private business ownership. He confiscated the assets of the wealthy who fled the country. An exodus of the country's highly paid business class and skilled labor followed and left Libya without much of the expertise needed to run the economy.

Gaddafi tried to break the tribal loyalties that the Libyan people had lived under for hundreds of years. He formed committees to manage the daily affairs of the population. Neighborhood committees, municipal committees and regional committees all came to be dominated by people with a strong revolutionary fervor.

Gaddafi called each change a revolution and ordinary Libyans endured one revolution after another.

Gaddafi controlled the country through a huge military created to enforce his changes and keep him in power. He was ruthless in his persecution of the perceived enemies of the regime. Executions were common as ordinary citizens became caught in Gaddafi's paranoia; people simply disappeared with no explanation.

Gaddafi's foreign policy aims were expansive. He proposed creating one vast Pan-Arab state with the power to confront the West. Rebuffed by Arab leaders, Gaddafi turned to conflict. He turned natural allies into enemies. He developed a hatred not only for Israel, but for any country that made peace with the Israelis.

Gaddafi believed revolution was the proper mechanism for change. He turned his embassies into terrorist havens. When Gaddafi's terrorist groups were not blowing up commercial airliners or taking hostages, Gaddafi sent assassination squads after the sizable expat community of Libyans living in foreign lands. He supported assassination attempts on world leaders. After every attack, Gaddafi offered public support for terrorism. By 1986, Muammar Gaddafi was one of the most hated men on earth.

Laura was thankful when Jean finally stopped by the room and offered to take her downstairs for dinner. While the decor was pretty, reading the menu proved to be impossible. It didn't matter; only traditional Middle Eastern dishes were available. Jean ordered for both of them and they were served a seafood dish of some unspecified fish mixed with rice, overcooked vegetables and covered with a brown sauce that had the pronounced flavor of cumin. "Not exactly the menu choices we'd find in Paris," Jean said.

"Apparently, they don't go to great lengths to make Westerners comfortable," she said.

"Things will be better inside the club. Gaddafi allows a certain amount of Western influence there to promote business dealings with the West," Jean replied.

Although Laura wasn't scheduled to perform until Saturday, Jean persuaded her to come to the club Friday night to become accustomed to the environment. Gaddafi wouldn't be there, but Jean could show her the stage she'd perform on, she could sit at the bar, talk with foreign businessmen and become familiar with the surroundings.

Chapter Sixteen

IT WAS WELL past 9:00 by the time Jean and Laura arrived at the club. She was ready for a stiff drink, outlawed in Libya, but which Jean's club managed to serve due to bribing the local authorities and enjoying the protection of the Colonel. Apparently, Gaddafi's version of Islam included serving alcohol to foreigners who might be able to sell him the next generation missile system or fighter jet.

Jean's club was nicely decorated and looked much like his clubs in Paris, surprising considering what Laura had seen in Tripoli so far. Getting inside the club was a bit uncomfortable. When Jean said it was an unmarked door in an alley, he wasn't kidding. The entrance reminded her of prohibition speakeasies she'd seen in old movies. The two military men with AK-47s standing outside the door were intimidating, although she had seen armed men everywhere. The airport was filled with guards, military trucks moved through the city and military personnel were prominent on the city's streets.

Even though the club was located in a basement, the ceiling was high enough to create an open feel. There was plenty of space and the recessed lighting gave it a relaxed atmosphere. Jean had built semi-circle cushioned sofas around permanent tables along the walls that gave people a bit of privacy and there were plenty of doors into private rooms along the sides. Jean showed Laura the private viewing area she'd perform in the following evening and it was quite nice as well. All in all, Laura was feeling a bit more confident about the plan.

She dressed in Jean's dressing room backstage, opting for Western style dress inside the club and while she might have been arrested for such clothing on the streets of Tripoli, inside the club Laura was quite popular with foreign businessmen. Sitting at the bar, men continually pushed drinks and conversation in her direction. Several of them were French which made conversation easy. Her popularity may not have been solely due to her attractive looks, though. Laura was the only woman in the room.

Jean did a perfect job of hosting. In Paris, he would rarely be seen in the club among guests. In Tripoli, however, he greeted every customer with a smile and handshake. He worked the room like an experienced politician. Sitting on a high bar stool, Laura observed that Jean's communication skills far exceeded her own. When a group of oriental businessmen entered the club, Jean began conversing in Chinese. Looking very much like they wanted to have a good time, the Chinese delegation spotted Laura instantly. Jean was kind enough to walk them over and introduce her. They were full of laughter and although Laura had no idea what they were saying, she enjoyed their company. Laura thought things were going exceedingly well and she should have known something would go awry. It did, and in the worst possible way.

She looked toward the foyer and saw the unexpected entrance of the Leader of the Revolution, the Leader of the Libyan people, the Commander in Chief of Armed Forces of the Great Socialist People's Libyan Arab Jamahiriya, Colonel Muammar Gaddafi. Apparently, he arrived without any prior warning. All activity in the club stopped and all eyes focused on Gaddafi.

He was about six feet tall and his military hat made him seem taller. Black, frizzy hair stuck out from underneath the hat in all directions. Gaddafi's face was pockmarked, as though he'd been left with small scars from a serious acne infection. The eyes were what Laura noticed most, intense and dark; they darted quickly in every direction, back and forth, giving him the look of someone of an insecure nature. An air of superiority enveloped his every movement. *It's an attitude kings and royalty might adopt,* Laura thought. Given what she'd heard about him, seeing Gaddafi for the first time gave Laura an opportunity to analyze him. Her instinct told her this man was dangerous and unpredictable. Despite Jean's assurances, Laura knew she wouldn't be safe around him; she wondered whether any woman could feel safe in his presence.

Gaddafi's entrance looked well rehearsed. The foyer was two steps above the floor of the club and Gaddafi, wearing his full military regalia, stopped under an overhead light. His hat shadowed his face so Laura could not get a close look at him, but she had little trouble seeing his eight female guards. They fanned out, walking down into the club wearing military fatigues with red berets. They wore belts with full ammo clips and held AK-47s in front of them, barrels up. Although they wore full make-up, nice hairstyles, high heels and manicured fingernails, they looked quite capable of violence. Gaddafi raised both hands and stood there smiling while everyone in the room gave him a standing ovation. Gaddafi expected a tribute and he got one.

Jean appeared surprised by Gaddafi's unexpected visit, but he recovered quickly. Jean stood there smiling with his arms open wide, paying respects like everyone else to the Libyan strongman. Laura looked for some kind of signal whether to stay in place or go backstage, but Jean didn't glance over. The patrons in the club lined up to greet the Leader like a wedding reception receiving line. Many were known to Gaddafi and needed no introduction, but Jean provided introductions for others, such as the Chinese for whom language was a barrier. Laura could hear bits and pieces of Gaddafi's conversation. He English well, which provided a language in common for those who did not speak Arabic.

Laura's chief concern was her visibility; she did not want Gaddafi to see her. Her position on a high bar stool gave her more prominence than she would have preferred. Looking down into the club from the foyer, the bar ran along the right side of the room while the semi-circular cushioned sofas were placed on the left. In between, in the center of the room, were widely dispersed cocktail tables. Opposite the foyer at the far end of the room, a small performing area existed where a local guitarist quietly strummed, but had temporarily stopped his performance.

Gaddafi's receiving line formed on his left, so Gaddafi turned slightly in that direction, taking Laura out of his view. Her hope was that Gaddafi would enter a private side room for a negotiation which would allow her to walk backstage unseen. Her instinct, though, was to move while Gaddafi's attention was elsewhere, so she casually left her spot at the bar and began walking the length of the room toward the stage door along the right hand wall. Once she reached the backstage area, she found herself sweating profusely from the stress she felt seeing Gaddafi for the first time. While she sat in the dressing room, she dabbed herself with tissue and did a make-up correction in front of the dressing room mirror. She was out of view and safe.

Once the club patrons had paid their respects, Gaddafi requested Jean escort him to one of the tables with semi-circular seating. As Jean led him to a table, Gaddafi's guards moved along with him, two staying at his side while others adjusted their positions to protect him. Jean snapped his fingers and a waiter brought a small set of glasses containing ice and two pitchers of clear liquid. When Jean mixed both liquids together, the contents turned a milky white color. This was Arak, a traditional Arab liquor. Gaddafi strictly disavowed alcohol of any kind, however when one is about to negotiate the purchase of a couple of dozen army tanks, apparently rules can be bent. One by one, Gaddafi requested Jean bring patrons to his table where he engaged in conversation and the drinking of Arak, something that looked very much like an audience with a king.

As luck would have it, Gaddafi had been advised of Messier's presence when guards saw her walking through the club. When Jean explained her presence by telling Gaddafi that Messier was his performer on Saturday evening, Gaddafi asked Jean to bring her to his table. Jean appeared in the dressing room doorway moments later. "Mademoiselle?"

"Hi, Jean. Gaddafi was not expected this evening, was he?"

"No, Mademoiselle, it was a surprise to everyone. He would like to meet you," Jean said.

"He knows I'm here?"

"Yes."

"I slipped backstage when he was engaged in conversation. I'm sure he didn't see me," Laura said.

"His guards alerted him to your presence. I'm afraid you'll have to accompany me to his table."

"Do I need to be worried?"

"No. He knows you are here to perform tomorrow. But you'll have to come with me now."

Chapter Seventeen

AS JEAN LED her through the club, Messier noticed the club had reverted to normal, the guitar player had resumed playing and patrons had taken their seats and were talking among themselves. The only ominous sign of trouble was Gaddafi's guards. Several of them stared at Laura as she walked.

"Colonel Gaddafi, I present Ms. Laura Messier, your performer tomorrow evening," Jean said. Laura had insisted Jean use her real name. The best legend for an intelligence agent should contain as much truth as possible.

Laura held out her hand. "It's an honor to meet you, Colonel," she said, looking straight at the floor. Gaddafi took her hand and kissed it. He responded to Jean in English.

"You have brought me one of the most beautiful women in the world," Gaddafi said to Jean.

"Thank you, Colonel. I try to find the very best entertainment for you."

Gaddafi stared at her and this time he spoke to Jean without taking his eyes off her. "I have seen this woman before."

"With all respect, Sir, I doubt it. I've never brought her to Tripoli before."

This time he spoke to Jean in a commanding tone of voice. "I'm sure of it, perhaps photos of her. I will investigate this woman, Broussard. Leave us to talk."

When Jean hesitated for a moment, Gaddafi shouted, "Now, Broussard! Leave us!"

"Yes, Sir, as you wish," Jean said. He bowed and stepped away.

Gaddafi motioned for Laura to sit on the opposite side of the table. The table was large and a great deal of space existed between them, but to Laura's left a guard appeared with a fully loaded AK-47. To Gaddafi's right, another of his equally armed female guards stood at attention. Laura felt trapped and wondered briefly whether she could make a run for the door. She felt she could subdue the guard closest to her and perhaps disarm the guard next to Gaddafi, but there were two guards on the top step of the foyer and others behind her. She would never make it to the street. There were too many guards, too widely dispersed to fight all of them. Gaddafi noticed her assessing the guards.

Gaddafi was silent and his stare made her uncomfortable, but once Laura raised her eyes, she realized she had a greater problem. Laura Messier had seen this man's expression in others, the look of a man sexually attracted to her. However, once in a while, she saw the look of a predator; someone who would take a woman forcibly if given the opportunity. This is what she saw in Gaddafi's eyes. Marie Colvin had been right and despite Jean's assurances that Gaddafi's sexual appetites extended only to his female guards, Laura was sure of what she saw. She looked down again only because she did not want Gaddafi reading fear in her eyes. Control and fear were sources of enjoyment for a rapist. If Laura's hunch was true, Jean could get help from the French Embassy in the morning, but there would be none this evening.

When plans collide with reality, unpredictable events occur. Even the best plan requires some kind of change in the face of random accidents. Variations and alternatives may be allowed for, but some situations simply cannot be predicted. Laura had never thought of the possibility that Gaddafi may have seen her modeling pictures. No one had. In all the planning stages of the mission, that possibility was never mentioned. Laura wondered if this mission was about to disintegrate.

Gaddafi took his time; he was accustomed to holding an advantage. He gave Laura a look of kindness as though it was a civilized convention to be honored. It wasn't sincere; underneath she saw violence in his eyes. As Gaddafi and Laura took the measure of each other, she tried to keep her mind quiet. *This man's very, very smart,* she thought. *Don't give him nonverbal information.* When Gaddafi started talking, it was in the manner of an interrogation.

"What is your name, again?" Gaddafi asked.

"Laura Messier, Colonel," she replied without emotion in her voice. She intended to show no signs of stress that might encourage him to rape her.

"Pronounce it slowly for me, please."

"MESS – ee – ay."

"You live in France?" he asked.

"Yes, Sir."

"Where have I seen you before?"

"Perhaps from pictures. I was a fashion model before I began singing," she answered.

"You are from Paris?"

"Yes, Sir."

The idea behind passive resistance in an interrogation is that answering questions with the fewest words gives your interrogator little information. You've answered the question, but he's left to fill in the gaps because you've given him no help.

"Why are you a singer if you work as a model?"

"I quit modeling."

"Why?"

"I became too old."

"I see. You support yourself by singing?" Gaddafi asked.

"It is a part time job, Sir."

"You have two jobs?"

"Yes."

"Who do you work for?" he asked.

"I am a clerk."

"No, I mean the company you work for."

"I work for the French government," Laura said.

He'll find out sooner or later, she thought. She reasoned that the truth lent the perception of credibility. Gaddafi was surprised. He raised one eyebrow.

"Ah, and in which part of the government do you work?" he asked.

"The Ministry of Foreign Affairs, Sir."

He smiled, "Yes, I know these people. I have negotiated with them many times." France and Libya were trading partners and although Laura had participated in meetings with the Libyans, Gaddafi had never been present. He went on.

"And where is this place you work and who is your supervisor?"

"I work at the Ministry building, Quai d' Orsay, on the left bank in the 7th Arrondissement. I am one of the Minister's clerks."

"I see. You work for the Minister himself?"

"Yes, Sir."

"What is your specific job there?" Gaddafi asked.

"I make coffee; I distribute the mail; I am a typist."

Hearing that, Gaddafi smiled. That was the truth of Messier's cover job and she guessed Gaddafi would soon discover it. As Jean told me, the Libyans have eyes everywhere. Gaddafi gave her an inquisitive look.

"Perhaps I have seen your picture in a fashion magazine," Gaddafi said. "I know your face. It is also possible that the French sent you to spy on me. Are you a spy?" Gaddafi asked.

Laura smiled. "I'm a clerk and part time singer."

Laura saw the intelligence in his eyes. He was judging her appearance, her movement and tone of voice. Suddenly, she watched anger creep into Gaddafi's face. "We shall see. Guard," he said, looking at the guard standing next to her, "Teach this woman how to talk to the Leader of the Libyan people." The guard slapped her across the face. "No person enters my country and lies to me," Gaddafi said. "Answer the question truthfully, please." He repeated the question, this time with more tension in his voice, as though he wanted a different answer.

"I am not a spy," she said putting a hint of confusion in her voice as though she didn't understand why he'd ask.

Gaddafi thought for a moment. He relaxed and changed subjects. Laura was familiar with the technique of tension and release that was meant to confuse an interrogation subject.

"You work for Broussard, too?" Gaddafi asked.

"Yes, Sir."

"If you work for the Foreign Ministry, why would you need a second job?"

"The government does not pay their clerks well, Sir. I need the money," she said.

This time, Gaddafi's response was immediate. "A woman should not be forced to work two jobs. A woman should be permitted to work if she desires, but your husband does not support you well enough," he said.

"I'm not married." Laura said.

His response was quick, as though it was common knowledge. "A beautiful woman should be married. Otherwise, she's wasting her talent."

"In France, customs are different."

"No, in your country and in mine, women are still women. They need protection."

The server approached and Gaddafi motioned him forward. He mixed fresh glasses of Arak in front of them. Gaddafi pushed one toward Laura and motioned for her to drink. The taste was reminiscent of licorice, but with a bitter aftertaste. The liquor was accompanied by a platter of finger food of a kind Laura could not identify. Gaddafi had drunk two glasses while they had been talking while Laura could only manage a few sips. Arak had 50-60% alcohol content and she felt the effect of it immediately. Gaddafi took another long drink before he spoke again.

"Why did you want to perform in Libya?" Gaddafi asked.

"Mr. Broussard offered me extra money."

"You didn't work today at the Ministry?"

"I used one of my vacation days."

Gaddafi took one last drink of Arak, looked at Laura and said, "I have decided I have no interest in seeing you perform."

From that decision flowed all the unpredictable events Laura hoped to avoid. "I am sorry, Sir, that I have disappointed you. Please accept my apologies for wasting your time," Laura said.

"No, you haven't wasted my time. I am pleased with your appearance. However, I suspect that Broussard brought a spy into my country."

"Colonel, if I were a spy, would I dress in this manner and make myself conspicuous to you?"

Gaddafi laughed, "We shall see. Beautiful women often lie."

"Colonel Gaddafi," Laura said, "I assure you, performing is my only interest."

When Gaddafi spoke again, he lifted his eyes and spoke to Jean, who was standing close by. "Broussard," he said sharply. Jean approached the table into Laura's line of sight. Laura glanced up and saw the concern in Jean's eyes as Gaddafi spoke. "Broussard, I wish to talk with this woman further. She will be a guest this evening at my personal quarters."

"Colonel, I must ..." Jean tried to say.

Gaddafi cut him off with a wave of his hand. "It has been decided. Do not worry, Broussard. I will return her to you safely. Guards!" he shouted. Guards immediately moved to his side. "Take this woman to my automobile and wait for me there." With that command, four heavily armed guards wrestled Laura from her seat and led her out of the club. As she reached for her purse, one guard hissed at her in English, "We will bring it."

Jean protested Gaddafi's decision. "Colonel Gaddafi, I must politely ask you to reconsider. Ms. Messier is my employee and is in my custody."

Laura heard the next exchange as the guards took her toward the door. "Broussard," Gaddafi shouted, "you have no rights in my country. I will question this woman at my compound. The decision is final. I shall return her to your hotel tomorrow." With no further explanation, Colonel Gaddafi walked out of the club.

Chapter Eighteen

LAURA WAS THROWN into Gaddafi's limousine. Marie Colvin's comment regarding rape caused Laura to consider giving up the mission. *What are my escape options?* she wondered. The limo looked impossible to escape from; heavy doors, bulletproof glass, partition between the driver and passenger compartment, plus the driver controlled the door locks. Even if she could escape the vehicle, there were armed guards standing on either side.

Could I take Gaddafi hostage when he enters the vehicle? She quickly looked around the passenger compartment for anything that could be used as a weapon. She found nothing. Laura knew she could easily defeat Gaddafi hand to hand once he entered the automobile, but without a viable escape, it would be useless to try.

Overhearing Gaddafi say she'd be taken to his personal quarters, it appeared Laura would be going to her ultimate destination anyway, she reasoned. Unfortunately, it would be without Jean. *I could possibly obtain the codes some other way and meet Jean later, if I make it through this evening,* she thought. *How will I protect myself tonight?*

When Gaddafi entered the limo, he sat on the opposite seat and reeked of perfume and liquor. As the car pulled away from the curb, Laura looked out the window at the Western style skyscrapers scattered amid one and two story flat roof buildings. They were headed south.

She wouldn't look at Gaddafi, but could feel his stare. Using peripheral vision, she saw a triumphant look on his face as though he had won a victory. He spoke in the tone of someone giving a command. "Look at me," he said. He waited a few seconds, then said again, "Look at me." Laura wouldn't make eye contact and oddly, he didn't force her. She continued to consider escape scenarios in her mind. Could she manage to elude the guards when the car stopped? Would it be possible to wrestle a weapon away from a guard when she exited the vehicle?

"You cannot escape," he said with a slight smile. "Thousands of women would love to be sitting in my limousine, yet you do not appreciate it. You are sitting alone with a world leader, but you do not show me the proper humility."

Gaddafi had experience taking women against their will and Laura guessed he was entertained by reading defeat in their faces. She would not give him the pleasure even as Gaddafi continued his propaganda. "Do not worry, my beautiful flower," Gaddafi said. "You will be treated well. It is a great privilege to be a guest of the Leader of the Libyan People at his dwelling."

Laura wondered about the time. *Surely, it must be past midnight.* She saw little traffic on the roadways. She had studied maps of Tripoli and knew they were on the same expressway she had traveled earlier in the day. Jean and Laura had passed the Bab al-Azizia military compound on their way to the hotel and she guessed that was Gaddafi's destination now.

"I'm amused at your thoughts," Gaddafi said as though her thoughts were a matter of fact. "You do not realize yet what has happened to you." He reached over the small table and grabbed Laura by the throat and forced her to look at him. "You have used your beauty to manipulate men your entire life. Now you will learn what it means to submit to one. In the West, women do not serve their husbands." He released her with a shove that sent her sprawling back onto the seat. "You will soon realize why women were put on this earth."

"You can go fuck yourself," she said bluntly, looking him briefly straight in the eye. *I don't give a shit who you are. World leader or not, if I get the chance, I'll take you down.* Then, she looked away again.

However, Gaddafi just smiled at her comment and continued talking as though he hadn't heard her. He motioned out the window with his hand. "You are wondering about the time. It is past midnight. In Paris, the streets would be busy with people wasting their time in revelry. Here in my country, we are a hardworking and devout people. The evenings are used for prayer and devotion to family. This is something you never learned."

Laura was determined to avoid reacting to his words. Using words to break down the resistance of a subject can be a powerful technique. "As I said before, Colonel, you can go fuck yourself," she said flatly.

"You are thinking of your life in France. That is a natural thing to do, but Allah planned for you to come to me. You do not realize it yet, but He wishes me to teach you to become the faithful and devout woman you have always secretly desired to be," he said.

A key statement, Laura thought. *Gaddafi is announcing his intent.* He'd told Jean she'd be returned to the hotel tomorrow, but Laura was hearing something else. She suspected Gaddafi would treat her like other women he'd captured. She doubted Gaddafi could keep her long. She was a French citizen, an employee of the French government and the French Embassy would demand her return.

The street signs were in Arabic, but Laura knew they were getting close to Gaddafi's compound. The limo took a cloverleaf exit; they were headed toward the Bab al-Azizia compound, probably the biggest site on the American target list. *The Air Force is going to bomb the hell out of the place. I can't be there when they do.* Obviously, she needed to find a way out before then and meet Jean somewhere, but how?

The limo slowed briefly at the front gate where the guards recognized Gaddafi and they waved him through. "You are wondering where I have taken you," Gaddafi said. "Welcome to my humble home, my flower. In a Muslim household, the guest is considered part of the family. So, this is your home as well. Welcome to your new home, my flower."

The limo stopped at a small building, much like the one Jean described in his briefing. The guards pulled Laura from the car and they weren't gentle, perhaps sending a message that she shouldn't resist. She tried to remember every detail, the front gate, the military vehicles and the buildings.

The small building housed a stairwell that led underground. Laura was taken down four flights of stairs, through double doors guarded by military personnel, then down a long hallway past a large room. *This could be the reception room Jean described in his briefing.* It was large enough that support pillars were needed every few feet in the middle of the room. Led past that room through another set of double doors, also guarded, she was taken into what appeared to be living quarters. *How many guards have I seen?* She counted two above ground at the entrance, two near the bottom of the stairs at the first set of doors and two more at the second set of double doors. Gaddafi followed and she heard him direct the female guards who brought her from the club, "Take her away and prepare her!" he said.

Laura was led further down the hallway, past what appeared to be a kitchen, a dining area, a living room and an office. Concrete pillars every few feet supported the ceiling, but the walls were drywall as one might find in the States. The baseboards, door frames and doors were made of an expensive wood. The facility looked similar to a stylish office building in the States, except there were no windows. Not one.

The ceilings were high with recessed lights every few feet. Laura did not feel a sense of closeness that one usually feels when underground nor a sense of dampness. The floor of the hallway was white ceramic tile with inlaid colored tiles that created elaborate patterns. She looked for air handling vents large enough to use as an escape. The air smelled fresh and lightly scented, although Laura could not discern the fragrance. She heard no sound, except that of the female guard's high heels hitting the floor.

Laura was led to what looked to be a bedroom. Four guards pushed her inside and onto a bed. "Do not try to escape," one of them said. "Any attempt will be punished severely. Sit on the bed and wait. Someone will be with you shortly." Laura's purse was thrown on the bed beside her and the guards stepped into the hallway just outside the room.

She grabbed her purse, looking for anything she could use as a weapon. Much of the contents were missing; her identification was gone, the plane ticket back to Paris as well. Only make-up items remained. This, too, was a common interrogation technique, stripping a subject of their identity to isolate them and remove all connection to their previous life. Laura felt glad to have had interrogation training at The Farm.

The bedroom was huge, larger than the living room in her apartment. The height of the ceiling was the same as the hallway; Laura guessed ten feet. It had a dropped ceiling of foam tiles and recessed lighting. The walls were drywall with the same expensive looking woodwork. This room had thick, plush brown carpeting, slightly darker than the wall color. It was, in many respects, a modern Western style bedroom. The bedroom set looked expensive; a king size four poster bed with expensive linens, two end tables with lamps on either side of the bed, a dresser and three piece vanity set with a large mirror rested against a wall. Two stuffed chairs were pushed against another. Laura walked around the room inspecting every inch for a means of escape. The bathroom was large and quite pretty; a glass enclosed shower, a separate tub, a marble vanity and white ceramic toilet. The room was eerily quiet; she couldn't even hear the air handling system.

When the servant came into the room, she closed the door behind her. She carried two black, vinyl bags which she set on the dresser. "Hello, my name is Yani." She spoke English with an eastern European accent. She smiled politely. She was pretty, about Laura's age, slight of build and wore fashionable Western style clothing and black four inch heels. She wore pearl earrings and a matching necklace. Her nails were long, manicured and painted bright red. Her light brown hair was full of highlights and she wore full make-up, something Laura found odd for the middle of the night.

"I am here to help prepare you for Daddy," Yani said. "Come, we must hurry. He will be expecting you shortly. Take off your clothes and shower, please," she said.

"Who is Daddy?" Laura asked.

"It's what the Colonel insists the women on his personal staff call him," she said. "We will talk as I get you ready to meet him. Please undress yourself in front of me so I may inspect your body, then please use the shower."

Laura made no move to comply. Yani spoke with more urgency. "You will be killed if you disobey. Please, do as I ask," she said, pleading. Laura took off her clothing and Yani inspected her like one might judge livestock. "Daddy will be pleased. Go shower while I prepare your clothing."

All the amenities Laura needed were in the bath. A brand of body wash, shampoo and conditioner with labels written in Arabic, expensive oversize towels, one of which Laura wrapped around her body and her hair in another as she exited the bath after showering. "Come, I will dry your hair," Yani said, as she took a blow dryer from a bag. Laura sat on the vanity chair while Yani dried her hair.

Afterward, Yani said, "Please remove the towel from around you and lie on the bed. I must oil your body." She rubbed a scented oil into Laura's skin, then powdered her body with what appeared to be talc. Once that was completed, she pulled a tube of personal lubricant from her bag. "Moisten yourself where Daddy will show you his love this evening." Seeing that, Laura couldn't help but speak up.

"You're kidding, right?"

"No, my lady," Yani said. "You must push the lubrication inside yourself and make sure you are moist."

"You can go tell the Colonel to kiss my ass," Laura said firmly. She tossed the tube back to Yani.

"Guards!" she said loudly. Four of Gaddafi's female guards quickly entered the room. "Please instruct the lady on the behavior that's expected of her."

They leveled their automatic weapons and pointed them at Laura's head. One guard put the barrel against her skull and said with a vicious hatred in her voice, "You will comply with every command given you or I will take you outside and execute you. Do you understand?"

Laura said nothing. Another guard hit her hard on the head with her open hand. "Do you understand?" she shouted.

"Yes, I understand," Laura replied.

"Good." The guards left the room.

"I apologize for that, my lady," Yani said politely. "You need to know what will happen if you resist. Young women are brought here and many disappear the very first evening. If you fight this, my lady, you will not survive the night," Yani said. "I am trying to save your life. Please obey me."

Yani's admonition seemed sincere enough that Laura believed her. Laura briefly entertained the thought of twisting a weapon away from one of the guards and side kicking the others to gain a temporary advantage, but it would have been suicide. With so many guards between Laura and the surface, escape was not possible. Laura applied lubrication to herself. Yani handed her a towel, "Now, please wipe the excess off so your clothing will not become stained." Laura complied with that request also. "Now, please apply your make-up while I watch. I will instruct you as to what Daddy expects."

Apparently, Laura's make-up technique passed Yani's inspection. She used the make-up from her purse. As Laura sat at the vanity, she continued to think about the guards outside the door. Observing how they entered the room, she knew they could be subdued, although she might have to shoot them. Laura had practiced with an AK-47. Once she killed the guards in the room, she'd have to take extra clips with her as spares; they'd be needed to fight her way up the stairs and exit the building. There could be as many as eight guards before she escaped the personal quarters and perhaps more. With hundreds of military personnel on the surface and no ready transportation, the probability of a successful escape was low. She decided to keep thinking about it and refine the idea as she was able to observe more of her surroundings.

"It is time to put on your undergarments," Yani said. As Laura stood, Yani dug into one of the bags and produced a cream foundation. "Take this and cover every blemish on your body. You must be absolutely perfect for Daddy or he will reject you." After that had been accomplished, Yani removed a white push-up bra and bikini panties from one of the bags. "You will wear these," she said, handing them to her.

The bra was far too small and Laura felt herself falling out of it, but Yani smiled, "Daddy will be pleased. Here, put on these," she said, holding out a pair of dark colored pantyhose. "Then, this skirt and blouse." It was an extremely short, black leather mini-skirt, accompanied by a tight, form fitting sleeveless silk blouse which Yani unbuttoned nearly to Laura's navel to expose her breasts. Yani took several pairs of four inch heels from her bag, which Laura tried on until one was found that fit reasonably well. "Don't worry, my lady. You won't have to walk far this evening. In the morning, we will find shoes to fit you, gather appropriate clothing and take you to the salon where we will improve your looks. Here," Yani said, handing Laura a fragrance. "It's Daddy's favorite. Apply it to yourself, please."

Yani said, "Now, stand up and let me look at you." Once Laura stood before her, Yani said, "We're almost finished." She glanced at her watch and frowned. "We must hurry. Daddy will be waiting for us. Sit down at the vanity." Yani gave her pearl earrings and put a wide, pearl choker around her neck. "This choker will identify you to the staff as Daddy's possession. You will wear it at all times unless Daddy orders something else. Do you understand?"

Laura did not answer. In a lengthy interrogation, inquisitors force a subject to focus their mind on obeying instructions. Yani, whether it was her intention or not, was doing an excellent job of it.

"Stay seated while I work on your hair," Yani said, as she looked through her bags. She removed a teasing comb and hairspray. She proceeded to build up Laura's hair, then fix it in place with a horrible, cheap holding spray. "Now, stand before me." Upon standing, Yani said, "I have made you as presentable as possible this evening. We will do more work on you tomorrow. Guards!" she shouted as she turned toward the door. The guards entered the room and took Laura by the arms. "No!" Yani shouted at the guards. "Do not touch her. She will cooperate. Let's take her to

Daddy." As they turned to leave, Yani said, "My lady, I must impress upon you the importance of cooperation this evening. It's the only way to survive."

In any long interrogation, the subject learns to anticipate torture and Marie's words about rape were ever present in Laura's mind. Everything Yani said supported the notion. Laura was being emotionally defeated by the thought of rape torture.

"My lady," Yani said quietly as they left the room, "you must accept what has happened. I know this may be different from anything you've ever done, but you must learn quickly or you will be killed. I've seen it time and time again. Please, I want you to survive." Once again, Laura felt Yani's words were genuine.

Chapter Nineteen

TWO GUARDS TOOK Laura to a large common area with a sofa, a television, a coffee table and various other smaller pieces of furniture. Yani followed behind them. Gaddafi was sitting on the sofa and rose to greet them. "Ah, there she is, my beautiful flower," Gaddafi said as his eyes moved up and down the length of Laura's body. "Thank you, Yani. You may leave now."

Gaddafi and Laura were somewhat alone. Two guards from the bedroom stood outside in the hallway. Gaddafi studied Laura far longer than was comfortable. "You will learn the household rules over time, but tonight, I will teach you how to please me," Gaddafi said with the look of a predator. His voice had a pretense of kindness, but there was violence beneath it. "You must never look a man in his eyes unless you are commanded to do so. Cast your eyes downward, please." Laura complied. "Only I will enjoy your gaze. Never any other man. Do you understand?"

"Yes, Sir," she said.

"Yes, what? Did they not teach you how to address me?" He slapped Laura hard about her head.

"Yes, Daddy."

"Very good," he said. "Now, you will come sit with me. You will sit straight, legs together with your hands folded across your lap." He slapped her hard again about her face. "No! I have not told you to raise your eyes. You are a slow learner, my flower."

Gaddafi was using another established interrogation technique. Demand so much that it forces the subject to think of nothing else, except following instructions. Laura recognized the technique was working. She was having trouble thinking of anything else. Gaddafi read her instantly. He slapped her hard about her head again. Laura could feel the ring on his finger come into contact with her skull. It briefly stunned her.

"No!" he shouted. "You will keep your mind pure at all times. It will take a while to train your mind, but you feel yourself changing already, don't you?"

"Yes," Laura admitted. No matter how much one trains to resist an interrogation, over time one is forced to submit in order to survive.

Gaddafi turned suddenly and punched Laura hard in her gut. She did not see the blow coming and her lungs collapsed. She leaned over, gasping for air. "Yes, what?" Gaddafi shouted.

"Yes, Daddy," she croaked softly, trying desperately to draw breath.

"You're learning," Gaddafi said with an air of triumph. "I see you are wearing your choker." He said it with a lift to his voice at the end of the sentence as though he expected a response.

"Yes, Daddy," she said with much effort as she was still recovering from the blow to the stomach.

"It's a sign of my ownership of you. You will wear it in the household so the staff recognizes your status."

"Yes, Daddy. May I be permitted to ask a question, please?" Laura asked.

Gaddafi smiled. "Of course, my flower. You are permitted to ask questions."

"Where is my identification? It was taken from me."

"What is this identification you speak of? I know of none," he said.

"My French identification. My driver's license, my health ID, my credit cards."

"You have none of these things. You have no identification and you need none," Gaddafi said.

"My government will come looking for me," Laura said.

Gaddafi laughed. "What government do you speak of?"

"I am a French citizen. They know I'm here."

Gaddafi gave her a slight smile in a patronizing way as though he did not feel the need to elaborate.

"You are a member of my personal staff. You have no other affiliation. When governments ask us to look for people, we try to find them, but often we cannot. Libya is a big country. So, we tell these governments that, sadly, their people cannot be found and that is the end of the matter."

"Jean Broussard will look for me. He will speak to the French government for me. He knows I am here," she said.

"Broussard? There is no such man in my country. I do not know him," Gaddafi responded with a shrug. "Foreigners have no power in my country. I often remove those who cause problems." Apparently, Gaddafi wanted a response. He slapped Laura hard on the cheek. "Do you understand, my flower?"

"Yes, Daddy."

"On this point, you must be clear. Your value comes from pleasing me. There will be no talk of anything else. You will not think of anything else. Do you understand this?" Gaddafi asked.

146

"Yes, Daddy," she said. Gaddafi had given her important information. Broussard would be sent out of the country in the morning, at least, that's what he wanted her to think.

"Now, enough of this talk. Kneel between my legs," Gaddafi said as though he were commanding his guards.

As she knelt in front of him, he unzipped his pants and withdrew his penis. "You have a rare privilege, my flower, to see the manhood of a world leader. Thank me for the opportunity, my flower," Gaddafi said harshly.

"Thank you, Daddy," Laura said.

Gaddafi suddenly grabbed her hair and jerked her head back. With his other hand, he withdrew a revolver from a drawer in the coffee table. He laid the barrel against her temple. "You will now please me, my flower, but if I feel your teeth against my skin, I will pull the trigger. Open your mouth and accept one of the world's greatest leaders into yourself." He pushed Laura's head forward; she opened her mouth and accepted him. He pushed himself deep into her throat. She gagged, coughed and Gaddafi pulled the trigger. The chamber was empty.

"You are trembling, my flower," Gaddafi said with a smile. "I have two rounds and four empty chambers. You were lucky this time. Now, we will try again and this time, you will perform well enough to please me."

He plunged himself into deep into her throat. This time, she held her breath. He came to orgasm soon after and she felt his warm semen go down her throat. She had no choice, except to swallow it. "Now, rise and sit beside me," he said.

As Laura sat down, Gaddafi slapped her hard about her head. "Wipe your face. Straighten your make-up." He reached for a box of tissue on the coffee table. She scrambled to find her purse which had been laid on the coffee table. She wiped her face, found a tube of lipstick and used the mirror inside her compact to re-apply lip color. When she had finished, Gaddafi said, "Continue to look down, my flower and feel the honor of having pleased your master. You hold the manhood of the Leader of the Libyan People inside your body. Do you feel the pride of the Libyan people inside you? Gaddafi asked.

"Yes, Daddy."

"Yani!" Gaddafi yelled, as he zipped up his pants. Yani appeared from around the corner. "Take her to my bedroom and prepare her."

"Yes, Daddy," Yani said. She came around the coffee table and lifted Laura by the arm. She and four guards led Laura down the hallway. As they walked, she whispered, "My lady, you did well, but he will take you again this evening. Prepare yourself for it. He will not be gentle."

The guards took her to a different bedroom. Yani asked the guards to leave and she helped Laura undress. As Laura began to remove the jewelry, Yani cautioned, "No, my lady. Do not remove the choker. Only Daddy may remove it. You will wear it constantly, except when you shower." Once Laura's clothing had been removed, Yani said, "Please lie on his bed." Yani took silk ropes from her bag. "Do not panic at what I am doing, my lady," she explained as though it were common for women to be tied. "It is for your protection. Many women try to hurt themselves. Your body belongs to Daddy and you must be protected from yourself." She tied Laura's hands behind her back, tied her feet together with a second rope, after which she connected both together and pulled them tight in the manner a calf might be tied at a rodeo. Laura was left lying on her side with her back arched, barely able to move. "Daddy will be here shortly," Yani said, as she left the room. Laura was alone, except for the guards posted outside the door.

The tears began to come and Laura could not hold them back. At the Farm, recruits were taught that everyone eventually breaks down during a sustained interrogation. There was no shame to be found in it. However, it was not the blows to Laura's body, or the isolation, or the threats, or fear for her safety, or even the propaganda that defeated her. It was simply the act of rape.

During interrogation training at the Farm, women in Laura's class had special training on rape torture. However, it was far different in person than the agency training. Before meeting Gaddafi in the living room, Yani's preparations served as psychological torture to convince Laura that she would be raped. Once Gaddafi forced oral sex on her, it was a coup de 'tat of sorts. Gaddafi was adept at breaking women for the purpose of using them as sex slaves and though Laura recognized the technique, she could not help but respond emotionally to it. Laura sought a way to survive and, instinctively, that meant pleasing Gaddafi sexually.

When Gaddafi entered the room, he saw the tears in Laura's eyes. He smiled as he sat on the bed beside her. As he released her from her bonds, he talked gently and began to stroke her body. "I see acceptance in your eyes, my flower." Laura's body could not have been tenser. Gaddafi's touch only created more fear. "Ah, I see you already enjoy my attention," he observed with a smile of contentment. "Your name will be Asila, which means pure in Arabic. Say your name for me."

"Asila," Laura repeated. Gaddafi was pleased at her instant response.

At that point, Laura's mind closed off all thoughts and feelings, except those of survival. She was determined to live even if that meant being a willing participant in her own rape. Laura would do a brilliant acting job because her life depended on it. Gaddafi took her by the hand and raised her from the bed. He began to undress and when he was naked, he kissed her and Laura became mentally detached from her body.

As he lay Laura down on the bed and mounted her, she felt his hands push her legs apart. She fought no longer and discovered her body involuntarily react as he plunged himself into her. She groaned as she felt him enter and he looked into her eyes. "Submit to me, Asila, and become the woman Allah desires you to be." He used his physical strength to control her as her body unconsciously became an unwitting accomplice to the act. It was frightening that she could turn off her feelings when necessary. She learned an ugly truth about herself: she would do anything to survive. It wasn't heroic or courageous. It was nothing more than an instinct for self-preservation. Gaddafi, however, sensed her acquiescence and it gave him a renewed sexual energy. He made one final, violent thrust and emptied himself into her body.

Gaddafi lay on top of her for a time, stroking her, caressing her and Laura was unable to think. "I see purity in your eyes, Asila. I feel it in your body. You have accepted who you are. You are my woman now," he said gently.   "Sleep, Asila, for tomorrow will be a day of discovery for you." She tried to sleep, but could not.

Chapter Twenty

LAURA WOKE SUDDENLY, startled. She sat up, her movements quick. *Where am I?* She remembered; she was in Gaddafi's bedroom. She was alone. Looking about the room, one lamp had been turned on and clothing was strewn about the chair along the wall. She judged time to have passed, but how much? There was no clock in the room. She guessed it was the next morning, but she could not be sure. There was no sound. In Paris, even in the middle of the night, something could always be heard, the sound of brakes squealing or an occasional siren in the distance. Here, she heard nothing. Or did she?

She heard water splashing. The shower was being used and as Laura glanced at the bathroom door, it was closed; the bedroom door as well. She rose to rummage through Gaddafi's pockets and as she lifted his clothing, she saw it. The black briefcase. It was sitting on the chair seat underneath his clothing.

Instantly, Laura's mind snapped into focus. She reasoned she must have been the victim of a temporary psychosis brought on by hours of interrogation and torture the previous evening. How could she have missed the briefcase? Gaddafi must have carried it into the room. He would come out of the shower soon and the torture would begin anew, but not yet; the shower was still running. She had a moment of clarity; *I have a mission to perform.*

152

She wondered about the women who had been made to suffer and then killed by Gaddafi. Apparently, all of them were eventually killed. Laura knew she was now one of those women. Laura looked down at the briefcase. By opening it, she could fight back. It felt good to fight. She scanned the room; the shower was still running. Both doors, the shower and the door to the hall, were shut. *Video cameras?* She saw none.

The briefcase was the one she had seen in photos at Langley; she was sure of it because of a slight scratch in the handle that could be seen in the photos. There were two combination locks, one on each side of the handle. One photo showed the briefcase in the process of being opened, a three digit combination of which only the first two numbers could be seen, the numbers 6-2. She suspected the third number could be a five because 625 represented the birthday of Gaddafi's favorite son and handpicked heir, Saif. She tried 625 on each of the locks, pushed the latches and the briefcase unlocked.

She raised the lid and the code sheet lay on top of a stack of documents, just as she had seen earlier in the photos. She stared at it briefly. Yes, halfway down the page, she saw one column of numbers, a list of six numbers each composed of six digits. Laura memorized them, six numbers, thirty-six digits, then closed the briefcase and locked it. Laura used Gaddafi's clothing to wipe her fingerprints from the case. The shower stopped and Laura heard the shower door open. She threw the clothing back over the briefcase and crawled back into bed.

Gaddafi had read Laura's mind the evening before by watching her eyes. She wondered whether he would suspect her now. Laura spoke to herself. *Play his game.*

153

Be patient. Laura knew she had not been defeated. Opening the briefcase proved her fight was just beginning.

"I see that you are awake, Asila," Gaddafi said as he walked out of the bathroom. He removed the coverings and began stroking her naked body. He climbed on top of her and kissed her hard as she spread her legs around him. She cooperated as a means to survive. She could not think, nor did she want to. He entered her and she arched her back, instinctively moving with him as she felt Gaddafi tense. Afterward, he lay on top of her, kissing her and she looked in his eyes. "You are my woman now," he said.

"I know," she said softly in return.

"Tell me your name."

"Asila," she said.

"No, tell me your last name."

"I do not know it," she said.

"Your name is Asila Gaddafi and you are mine forever."

Gaddafi had taken Laura because a Western woman was special in her significance. She was symbolic of a victory over the West. She was weak just like the West was weak. She was easily trained and Gaddafi would show this woman to the West and they would wonder why this woman was so loyal to him?

Gaddafi rose, donned a thick, white robe from his closet and picked up the phone on the nightstand. "Send Yani in to me. Yani knocked and entered a minute later. "Good morning, Yani," Gaddafi said. "From now on, her name is Asila. Prepare her. She will dine with me over the noon meal."

"Yes, of course, Daddy," Yani said.

Yani carried a black bag. She helped Laura rise and drew a white robe from the bag, similar to the one worn by Gaddafi. She wrapped it around Laura's shoulders.

"Come, Asila. We have work to do," she said. Yani handed her the pumps she had worn the previous evening. "Don't forget, you must wear these at all times," she said with a smile.

Laura walked with Yani toward the bedroom she used the prior evening. She noticed there were no guards accompanying them. After they entered the bedroom, Yani shut the door and took Laura's hand. "Daddy really likes you, Asila. You will be successful here."

"Thank you," Laura said, sitting down on the bed.

Yani sat beside her. "Surrender yourself to him and love him. Now, I must leave for a moment. Please shower and be ready to dress when I return." She left and Laura rose from the bed and showered. It was easier to come to a conscious mental state this time. She thought she may have found the best technique to endure rape torture; separate your identity from the act, then bring yourself back to conscious thought later. She wrapped herself in a towel afterward and sat at the vanity and dried her hair.

When Yani entered the room again, she smiled. "I see you've dried your hair. Put on your choker and pumps. We must travel down the hall. Wear only the robe. I will dress you later." Yani led Laura down the hallway in the opposite direction of the doors leading to the surface. Yani unlocked a set of doors at the far end and two guards were waiting on the other side with a golf cart. "It's too far to walk, Asila. We will take a cart."

"Where are we going?" Laura asked.

"We are going outside the complex, but we will stay underground. We have many underground tunnels that lead everywhere in the city. They are used by Daddy and the soldiers. Today, I am taking you to the salon."

"Don't I need to dress?"

"No, we will dress you at the salon. Keep the robe closed around you and don't worry. The soldiers are not permitted to look at you," Yani said.

They traveled what Laura estimated to be approximately three miles underground. The tunnel system was, indeed, large. The guards turned at various intersections, but she could not see that the tunnels ended. They seemed to be miles long and were probably one of the security measures that kept Gaddafi in power; it was a method of moving unseen around the city.

Yani and Laura were silent during the trip, but once they arrived at their destination, the basement of another military building of some kind, Yani began to talk again. "Daddy likes you because you are Western."

"Yes, I think so," Laura said.

"He's had many Libyan girls, but he tires of them. Daddy told me this morning he wishes you to look more Western, so we are to change your hair color to blond."

"Do I have a choice in the matter?" Laura asked, as they stood in the lobby of the salon.

Yani laughed, "Do I really need to answer that question?" she asked.

Laura smiled, "I think we're going to become close friends, Yani."

Yani was pleased by the response. She had not become friends with any Libyan women, but Laura was like her, fair skin and green eyes.

The salon had Western influences with pictures of models on the wall, books of Western hairstyles on the lobby tables and all the amenities one would find in a modern salon in New York. Yani told Laura it was a perk for the wives of highly placed military officers. Many of them were present that morning, but a request from the Colonel carried weight so Yani and Laura were given preferential treatment.

Laura was given the obligatory massage which helped soothe the soreness inflicted by Gaddafi. Oil was rubbed into her skin, then her body was powdered with talc. Afterward, Yani brought in a seamstress who measured Laura for clothing, after which she was taken to the nail station where very long nail tips were applied to her hands. Apparently, the length of nails in Gaddafi's household was a sign of status. Now, both Yani and Laura both had extremely long nails. After that, the hair stylist cut Laura's split ends, then gave her a color job which lightened her hair to a rich blond color. Laura had become accustomed to changes in hair color as a model so the look was not unfamiliar to her, but amid the dark haired women of Libya, it gave Laura a distinctive look which she assumed was the purpose of it.

The make-up person did a reasonably good job of painting her face, although she used a cream foundation that Yani supplied which created the effect of a mask. Evidently, Gaddafi eschewed a natural look on his women, preferring a look that might appear on the cover of a fashion magazine. *Perhaps Gaddafi's idea of femininity came from magazines.* Laura was taken back to the massage room where Yani pulled a black leather mini-skirt from her bag, black stockings and a black leather bustier,

157

which suggested the look of a fetish model. Yani gave Laura a set of black open toed heels, the hair stylist teased her hair up and Laura became something of a spectacle to look at. The look was not yet complete until Yani handed Laura emerald earrings and a large emerald necklace to wear. The stone in the necklace setting was the largest emerald Laura had ever seen. The underside was cut flat, set in gold and threaded through a tightly linked gold chain. Yani had the hair technician pin the chain around her head and through her hair so the emerald lay flat on Laura's forehead.

"I've never seen Daddy allow anyone to wear this stone, Asila, not even his wife. It is a sign of high status. You will be held in high regard among the staff."

"How about the guards?" Laura asked with a smile. Yani understood that Laura desired some protection from them.

"I do not believe they are permitted to touch you now," she said with a smile. "The stone indicates that you are special to Daddy, although I'm not sure what his plans are. Here," she said, handing Laura the robe, "It's better to wear this over top of your clothing on the way back to the compound." Laura gathered the robe about herself. "There is no need to wear a head covering in the tunnels, since we're not in public, but when Daddy allows you to go outside, we will wear traditional Muslim dress."

Yani and Laura continued to chat on the way back to the compound, this time ignoring the guards driving the cart. Yani told Laura she had come to Libya from Yugoslavia, where she had served on the kitchen staff of a freighter. Gaddafi's men identified her while the freighter was in port and Gaddafi convinced her to work for him.

158

She had been in the personal quarters for nearly three years. If Laura were to survive in the personal compound, Yani's friendship was needed so Laura intended to talk with her whenever possible.

Laura had a clear understanding of the floor plan of the living quarters now. It was a large rectangular space with a long hallway running along one side of the rectangle. One end of the hallway led up the stairs to the outside, the other led to the tunnel system. In between were the living areas, Gaddafi's office and the bedrooms. Bathroom facilities were distributed along the hall and in the bedrooms. Some of the staff slept in the far bedrooms near the tunnel exit, including a few of the guards, but Laura had no idea how many.

Once back in the personal quarters, Yani returned Laura to her bedroom where she applied Gaddafi's favorite fragrance. It was time to meet Gaddafi in his dining room for the noon meal. As Laura looked at herself in the mirror, she said, "Scheherazade."

Yani gave her an inquisitive look. "What did you say?"

"I look like Scheherazade, Yani."

"Who is that?" Yani asked.

"There is a very famous Arabian book called "A Thousand and One Nights," written centuries ago. Scheherazade was a great Persian Queen and she is the narrator in the book. I look very much like her today."

"That means you are becoming happy, Asila."

"I am determined to survive, Yani," Laura said. "That's what it means."

"I felt like you once, but you will eventually find happiness here, Asila, just as I did. Come, it's time to meet Daddy for the noon meal."

As they walked the length of the hallway toward the dining area, Laura analyzed what advantage could be useful in an escape. Laura observed she was lightly guarded on the way to the salon and there were no guards in the salon itself. That represented the best escape opportunity she'd seen so far.

Chapter Twenty-One

YANI LED LAURA into the dining room where Gaddafi was already seated at the table. He was dressed in military fatigues. He looked up and smiled. "Salam, Asila."

"Salam, Daddy."

"Sit and enjoy the meal with me. You may raise your eyes and look at me," Gaddafi said. "Here, please eat," he said. Gaddafi passed Laura dishes heaped with food. The noon meal was the main meal of the day in Libya and the table was piled high with food; sweet breads, salad, two main dishes and plates of vegetables and fruits. They ate in silence, but Gaddafi looked at her frequently. He had a predatory look in his eyes so Laura prepared her mind for another sex session after lunch.

"Were you happy in your duties this morning, Asila?" he asked.

"Yes, Daddy, I was."

"What was your happiest moment?"

"Changing my hair color to blond," she said.

"Yes, I knew that you would like that. You enjoy looking beautiful for me, don't you?" he asked.

"Yes, Daddy."

Gaddafi asked the kitchen staff to serve more tea. "I wish to continue your education, Asila."

"I'm honored to receive it from you, Daddy."

He smiled, "Yes, I see the humility in your eyes, Asila. You are truly beautiful and humble before me. Do you like the stone I have given you to wear?" he asked.

"Yes, Daddy. It is very beautiful."

"You will wear the stone at all times, Asila, because you are now equal to my wife. She gives me children and you give me pleasure."

"I am honored to serve you, Daddy."

"Look at me, Asila." When Laura looked, Gaddafi stared at her for a long time. "I see nothing in your eyes, except humility, Asila. That comes from knowing a woman's proper role in a household. Now, I wish to teach you another kind of humility."

Just for the briefest second, Laura saw the malevolence in Gaddafi's eyes. He grabbed her, lifted her and threw her on the table amid the food. Dishes crashed to the floor; food splattered in all directions. He flipped her over, lifted her dress, ripped her stockings open and began to rape her. Laura screamed in pain. "Loosen yourself, Asila. Accept your pain," Gaddafi shouted. She tried to loosen herself, but the pain was too intense. She fought him, but he kept thrusting until he entered her anally, ripping her open. It sent waves of pain through her body. She kept screaming and Gaddafi punched her. "Quiet, woman!" But she could not. The act seemed to last forever, pain upon pain, humiliation upon humiliation until he pulled himself out of her. He turned her over and hit her again. She held herself in a fetal position waiting for the next blow. As Laura lay there, Gaddafi spoke to her, "As it storms on some days, and other days are sunny, Asila, so will I take you. You must prepare yourself to accept me with much humility, no matter what kind of love I may show you. Pain is a great teacher, Asila and I have taught you a great lesson today. Be proud that you have served me. Now, leave my presence. Yani!" Gaddafi yelled. Yani appeared around the corner. "Take her away." Yani helped Laura stumble back to her bedroom.

Yani gently laid her on the bed and when Laura looked down at herself, she saw blood dripping down her leg onto the bed. "Here, let me help you," Yani said. "Let's take off your skirt and have a look at your injury." She retrieved a damp washcloth from the bathroom and pressed it between Laura's legs. She handed her a cream. "Rub this on yourself when the bleeding stops. It will numb the pain."

She dug into her purse and gave Laura two white tablets. "Here, take these. They are strong pain relievers." She brought Laura a glass of water. "Lie back on the bed, Asila. Do not move for a while. I will be around the quarters if you need me." Yani paused for a minute. "Asila, I'm sorry this happened to you." She laid her hand on Laura's shoulder. "Now you know how difficult your job is."

Laura could hardly bear the pain. Although she had overcome the shame of being raped, Laura had not prepared herself for Gaddafi's brutality. As the pain relievers began to work, Laura felt her body relax and then eventually she slept.

Yani woke her later with a dinner tray. "I thought you might like to have dinner," she said with a sympathetic smile. Laura grimaced as she rose. "Are you still bleeding? Yani asked. Laura inspected herself.

"No, I don't think so. Thank you for your help, Yani. What time is it?"

"I must remember to get you a watch." She glanced at the time piece on her wrist. "It's just past seven this evening. You have some time yet to rest."

"Will he ..." Laura could not finish the sentence.

Yani laid a hand on her arm. "No, he won't. He knows you're injured. He will allow you some time to heal. Besides, he will become intoxicated this evening. He usually falls asleep after drinking." She smiled, "You did well today, Alisa. The entire staff knows what happened. You have their sympathy. They like you very much, even the guards, well, all except one."

"You mean the one who put a gun to my head?" Laura asked.

Yani smiled. "Yes, Salima is angry at everyone. She wants to be Daddy's favorite, but she's too fat and ugly so she takes her revenge on those Daddy favors. Don't worry, though, she can't harm you. Go ahead and eat. I'll be back later to dress you for the party this evening."

"Party?" Laura asked.

"Didn't I tell you? Daddy is hosting a party this evening. You will attend with him. I will come back after dinner to prepare you."

Laura barely touched the food; instead, she lay back on the bed. She must have fallen asleep again, for Yani woke her, "Asila! Wake up; it's time to prepare you for the party this evening."

"Yani, I overslept. I'm sorry."

"Please go ahead and shower. I'm bringing in people to help you get ready. Hurry, we must get started."

After Laura showered, Yani oiled and powdered her body and the hair dresser came into the room and fashioned a sweeping up-do, pinning it together with expensive clips that had diamond inlays. Once that was completed, Laura sat in front of the mirror and applied her make-up.

"If I might make a suggestion, Asila?" Yani asked. "With your blond hair and emerald jewelry, I think green has become your color. It's also one of the colors on our flag. Why don't you use green on your eyes this evening. Daddy will notice. I think it will please him."

Laura considered it. "Good idea," she said in response. "I'll do it."

"I think you should make your make-up quite heavy this evening," Yani said. "I know you like a softer look, but Daddy prefers you fully made up."

The nail technician came to the room and painted Laura's nails again. Once they were dry, the seamstress carried a gorgeous white satin full length gown into the room. Laura was stunned. It was as beautiful as anything she had worn modeling. Built to be form fitting, with a wide sheer strip that ran from underneath each arm to the floor, it was a fabulous piece. As Laura reached for undergarments, Yani shook her head. "No, Alisa, this gown was made for you to wear nothing underneath. Undergarments would be seen through the sheer sides."

Laura thought about that for a moment. "You're right, Yani," she said.

"Here, let me help you into it." Yani unzipped the back and Laura stepped into a gown that fit her perfectly. The seamstress in the compound was excellent. "Asila, you look beautiful. Let's get your jewelry on." Yani pinned the necklace into her hair so the large emerald lay on Laura's forehead just above her eyes. Yani had brought new emerald earrings so long they nearly brushed her shoulders. "I have white heels for you this evening," Yani said. The shoes fit well also and looking at herself in the mirror, it looked similar to a wedding gown, except for the sheer sides. "Let's apply your fragrance for the evening and, oh, I forgot the gloves," Yani said. Since the gown was sleeveless, long white gloves completed the ensemble. "Every woman in Libya would love to be wearing this gown right now," Yani said with a smile. "Being Gaddafi's woman does have its advantages."

"I could do without the sex," Laura replied with a wry smile.

Yani laughed. "Every woman in Libya has the same thought every day of her life."

Yani led Laura to the living area where she sat waiting for Gaddafi. She noticed a clock that she hadn't seen before. Laura had been trained at The Farm to observe detail, but the shock of Gaddafi's treatment, apparently, had confused her. It was well after 10:00 p.m. when Yani brought tea and Laura laid her head back on the sofa and closed her eyes. She cleared her mind of the day's events. *I must show him no ill will,* she thought. *Otherwise, who knows what he might do.*

Gaddafi entered the room just after eleven. He was wearing the same military uniform he had worn when he entered the club. Gaddafi's hair stuck out from under his hat in comical fashion. She was learning to read his moods and this evening he gave her a kind, warm look. He stood before her and spread his hands apart. "Alisa, you look beautiful this evening. You please me greatly. Stand up and let me have a look at you."

Laura stood up, walked around the coffee table and Gaddafi spun her around slowly to inspect his property. "Yani!" Gaddafi shouted. Yani appeared from around the corner. "You have done a wonderful job with her this evening. She looks like a queen."

"Thank you, Daddy," she said.

"You will leave us now, Yani. Please go to the kitchen and help with the reception."

"Yes, Daddy." Yani bowed slightly and left them alone.

Gaddafi motioned for Laura to sit beside him on the sofa. He reached into his pocket and pulled out a small box. "I see you have recovered from this afternoon," Gaddafi observed.

"Yes, Daddy."

"I see in your eyes that you are in peace."

"Yes, Daddy, I am."

"You have accepted your role in my household with grace and humility. I see it in your eyes."

"Yes, Daddy," she said.

"Asila, I am the Supreme Ruler of all things in Libya. My decisions represent the final authority in my country. The Leader of the Libyan people asks the permission of no one before making decisions. In my country, a man does not need the permission of a woman in order to marry her. The Qur'an permits me to take four wives. I have decided to take you as my second wife," Gaddafi said with a warm, kind smile.

Laura immediately looked down so Gaddafi would not see her shock. She began to get dizzy and feel flush. "I can see you have cast your eyes downward, Asila," Gaddafi said. "You are humble and gracious, a shining star among the women of Libya. Give me your left hand." Laura lifted her hand; Gaddafi removed the glove and took a wedding ring with a large diamond from the box. "I had Yani take your measurements while you were sleeping. It will fit perfectly."

When he slipped it onto her finger, it did fit well. "Look at me, Asila." She looked up at him.

"I now proclaim you to be Asila Gaddafi, my second wife. My first wife raises my children while my second wife raises my spirits. You will be at my side always until the end of your days. And, I think," Gaddafi said, "I will always keep your hair blond."

Laura didn't know what to say so she cast her eyes downward again. "You are wise to stay silent, my lovely wife. Decisions are made by husbands and by looking downward, you have told me that you accept my authority over you. Are you ready to be introduced to the reception as my wife?"

Laura summoned the will to answer him, "Yes, Daddy."

"No, from now on, you refer to me as your husband."

"Yes, my husband."

"Tell me your name."

"My name is Asila Gaddafi."

"Excellent! Let's go to the reception."

Gaddafi was greatly pleased. As Laura walked toward the reception with him, she felt as though she were an adornment; a symbol of Gaddafi's power. He extended his arm to her, which she grabbed only because she had become faint. Gaddafi interpreted her weakness as a sign of humility and he seemed eager to help Laura walk.

Chapter Twenty-Two

AS THEY ENTERED the reception of about a hundred people, there was a standing ovation for Gaddafi. He smiled broadly and waited a minute before he quieted the crowd. "Ladies and gentlemen, I have an announcement to make. Tonight I introduce my new wife, Asila Gaddafi." The second ovation was louder than the first. Apparently, the reception had a dual purpose. This was the reception that Jean Broussard referred to back in Paris, but Gaddafi also used the event to celebrate his new marriage.

A receiving line formed and as people were introduced to Laura, she was not permitted to look upon their faces. When Gaddafi introduced her to a French citizen in Libya on business, she simply held out her hand and looked at his shoes. Neither did she look up at the introduction of an American news person.

During the reception, Laura accompanied Gaddafi around the room as he talked to business partners, military figures and personal friends. Arak was served and Gaddafi drank heavily. Many of his guests offered toasts. When Gaddafi offered Laura a glass, she politely declined which seemed to please him. As the guests became intoxicated, people relaxed, the laughter became louder and Laura noticed the guards drinking as well.

Laura became weary of looking at the floor and requested permission to separate herself from Gaddafi to talk with the guards. Since the guards were female, Laura could look at them and talk freely. Gaddafi nodded his permission and Laura made her way to the open doorway where they stood guard. On her walk across the room, a woman blocked her path. She looked up and Marie Colvin gave Laura a look of concern. "Are you okay?" she asked.

"Marie, you'll get both of us killed," Laura hissed.

"If you need my help, I'm at the Radisson," she whispered before walking away. Laura looked around; Gaddafi had not seen the exchange. Laura approached the guards who bowed to her as she had seen them do with Gaddafi. Laura also observed they had abandoned their weapons.

After a few words with the guards, Laura felt she had been away too long and she turned to find Gaddafi. "Where is my husband?" she asked the guards

"He is in a private conference, Asila. You will become used to this. He will be back shortly."

Without Gaddafi, Laura was unaware of the protocol so she sat down in a large padded chair to await his return. She studied the tile pattern on the floor when a man walked past and dropped a note in Laura's lap. It read, "Meet me at the food table." She got up and slowly made her way to the serving table where Jean Broussard was waiting. She walked to the other end to allow Jean to discretely draw himself closer. Jean came close enough to talk and filled a food plate as he spoke, "Gaddafi has gone to his private quarters with a client, Mademoiselle. Now is our chance. Go out of the building first and I will follow after you leave," Jean said.

"No, Jean, they will not allow me to leave."

"Mademoiselle, you must. This is your only chance," Jean hissed under his breath.

"I'm watched too closely, Jean. Gaddafi would kill you just for talking with me."

"Mademoiselle, there is no time to argue. I will not leave Libya without you."

"Give me a pen and I'll write the codes on the note you gave me. Take them to the American Embassy when you get back to Paris."

Mademoiselle, you are Gaddafi's wife. You have the authority to command the guards. Tell them you're going outside."

Laura thought for a minute, *They would find Gaddafi and seek his permission before they allowed me outside.*

"Do you trust me, Mademoiselle?"

"Yes, of course," Laura said.

"Then reach inside yourself and find the courage. You are a proud and strong French woman, Mademoiselle. It will work."

"If we're caught," she said nervously, "they'll execute both of us tonight. You know that, don't you?" Laura stole a peek at Jean. He stood there smiling at her.

"Do you realize how beautiful you are?" Jean asked. Jean was one of the most composed men under pressure Laura had ever seen.

"Stop it, Jean."

"The Mademoiselle has a regal quality about her. She is a queen and I suggest she act like one," Jean said emphatically. "If you command the guards like a queen, Mademoiselle, they will obey you. I'm putting my life in your hands. Get us out of here. Leave now and I will follow in a couple of minutes so we're not seen leaving together."

Once again, Jean had performed his magic and Laura decided to hold her head high and simply walk out of the reception. She was gripped with fear as she walked across the room. As she passed the guards at the reception door, she said, "I'm going to use the restroom in the personal quarters." They nodded, but when she exited into the hallway, she turned right toward the double doors that led outside.

The guards at the doors moved to block her exit so she took off her glove and spoke with as much authority as she could muster. "I am going outside into the fresh air for a few minutes."

"I'm sorry, Asila, that is not allowed. You'll have to return to the reception," one of the guards replied.

Laura held up her hand to show the ring. "How dare you call me Asila!" she said with an anger she did not feel. "My name is Mrs. Gaddafi and my husband is your Commander in Chief. My power in this country is second only to his. Stand aside, I wish to go outdoors. If you do not, I will have my husband kill you." The guards looked shocked. "Now!" she yelled.

"Of course, Mrs. Gaddafi. Can we help you up the stairs?" they replied.

"I'm quite able to manage on my own, thank you. Stay here at your post!"

Laura raised the hem on her gown as she hurried up the stairs. With each step toward the surface, she became more energized. When she reached the top and swung the doors open into the fresh breeze, she felt alive for the first time since she had been taken underground. The two guards outside turned around and approached her. Laura held up her hand and showed them her wedding ring. "I am Asila

Gaddafi, wife of Colonel Gaddafi, your Commander in Chief. I order you to bring me a car!"

The guards looked confused. "I'm sorry, Mrs. Gaddafi, but we have no such orders."

"I'm giving you the order," Laura said. "Don't test my authority or I will have you killed immediately."

"Of course, Mrs. Gaddafi. Which car would you like?" the guard on her left asked.

"The big one right over there," she said, pointing toward a line of cars parked in the drive.

"I'm sorry, Mrs. Gaddafi, but that's impossible. That one is the Commander's personal vehicle."

"Don't you think I know that?" she snarled. "Would you like to clean toilets for the remainder of your military career?" Laura had no idea which car was Gaddafi's; she just guessed.

"I'll get it right away, Ma'am," he said.

Laura could not believe they obeyed her. They sprinted to the line of parked limos, pulled the big one out of line and began to pull it around in front of her. Jean emerged from underground. "I'll be damned, Jean, you were right," she said.

Both guards got out of the car and Laura, full of confidence now, pointed to one and said, "You are my driver. You will drive this man to the French Embassy. I will accompany him to make sure of his safe passage. You will drop him off, then return me to my husband." She pointed to the other guard, "You will open this car door for me immediately." Incredibly, the guards did just that. The car still had to pass the front gate, but the gate attendants recognized it, the driver waved and they passed through easily.

When Gaddafi returned from his private conference, he immediately looked for Asila. Not finding her, he approached one of the guards inside the reception. "Where is Asila," he asked.

"She's using the restroom, Sir," the guard responded.

"When she returns, bring her to me," Gaddafi said. However, when Laura didn't return after a few minutes, Gaddafi walked into the hall and questioned the guards at the doorway. Discovering that Asila had been allowed outdoors, Gaddafi went up the stairs and out of the building. "Where has my wife gone?"

"She demanded a car for a man at the reception. They left together, Sir," the guard said.

"Did she say where they were going?" Gaddafi asked.

"Yes, Sir. The French Embassy."

Gaddafi became agitated. "Call the police! Have the streets around the embassy blocked. They cannot be allowed to approach the embassy. Take a detachment from my security detail and bring them back here," Gaddafi said. Gaddafi returned to the reception.

As the limo made its way to the French Embassy, Jean took Laura's hand and squeezed it. She needed the emotional support for she knew Gaddafi would quickly realize her absence and spare no effort to retrieve her. The French Embassy was just a few short blocks away, but it seemed to take forever to make the trip. Looking out the window at the darkened neighborhood, Laura wondered how she could have missed the guards bowing to her at the reception. It was a sign they acknowledged her status, but she had failed to recognize it. It took Jean's shrewd observation for her to realize it.

The car slowed at the entrance to the embassy and Jean whispered. "Stay in the car. I will explain the situation to the embassy guards. When you see them open the gate, get out and run as fast as you can. We will be safe inside the gate. They cannot touch us on French territory."

After Jean left the automobile, the driver lowered the glass partition. "Mrs. Gaddafi, how long do you want to wait?" he asked.

"Let's make sure he gets inside the Embassy safely before we leave."

"Yes, Ma'am."

Jean talked to the French Embassy guard for what seemed like an eternity. The guard showed no inclination to allow them to enter. He kept shaking his head no while Jean kept shouting at him. The embassy guard finally picked up his phone and handed it through the fence. Jean talked emphatically into the phone as the first police cars arrived. The street was quickly blocked off surrounding the embassy entrance and spotlights on the patrol cars were aimed at the gate. The police exited their vehicles with guns drawn and began to slowly approach.

Laura opened the car door, preventing the driver from locking it. She heard the click as he tried to lock her inside. The driver panicked. "Mrs. Gaddafi, we need to leave," he said. "The man you brought must be a criminal. The police are trying to catch him. It's not safe for you."

He shifted the car into drive and Laura knew she had to move regardless of whether the gate was open. The driver would pull away any second. Laura jumped out and sprinted toward the gate. Jean turned to her and shouted, "Come on, Mademoiselle," as the gate swung open. The police were shouting in Arabic. The first shot rang out from behind Laura's left. It cracked off the metal rungs of the gate, showering the sidewalk with sparks. *They're shooting at Jean,* she thought, until the second shot passed through the fabric of her gown between her legs. She reached the gate when the third shot bounced off the iron bars sending sparks flying in front of her. Glancing behind her, she saw a hoard of police in pursuit. They were ready to grab her when Jean took her arm and pushed her through. One policeman was able to grab Jean by the arm, but the French guard pulled him inside and slammed the gate closed. The latch engaged with a bang.

At the sound of the shots, French Embassy guards came running from an adjacent guard shack and formed a wall in front of them. "Go, Mademoiselle. Run for the door!" Jean shouted. Laura picked herself up off the pavement, grabbed the hem of her dress and ran to the front door of the Embassy. Someone inside opened the door and they dived inside. The door was quickly slammed shut by a guard stationed in the lobby.

A tense situation developed on the sidewalk as the French Embassy guards stood their ground inside the gate while the Tripoli police stood outside the gate with weapons pointed at the French. They were soon joined by Gaddafi's men and the Libyan numbers swelled to several times the number of French guards stationed inside the gate. A police captain walked forward and demanded the fugitives be returned, but the French guards stood their ground and refused. Several tense minutes elapsed as both sides pointed weapons at the other, but the captain finally relented and motioned for his men to withdraw.

Chapter Twenty-Three

AFTER LAURA AND Jean tumbled inside the front door, the Embassy night duty officer helped them to their feet. "Mr. Broussard," he said in French, "I am Maurice Garnier, the duty officer this evening. I'm sorry for your troubles. I understand you are seeking refuge in the embassy?"

"Sorry for our troubles?" Laura replied in French. "Are you shitting me? They're shooting at us out there. Hell, yes, I'd say we were in trouble."

"You've been through a lot today, Mademoiselle," Jean said. "Let me handle this." Jean put his hand on Laura's arm and addressed the duty officer.

"Yes, Sir. I'm a French citizen in Libya on business. This is Laura Messier, also a French citizen, who was illegally held against her will in the Bab al-Azizia compound by Libyan State Security. She escaped this evening with my assistance. As a result, both of us are fleeing from Colonel Gaddafi's personal security. I assure you, Mr. Garnier, neither of us has broken any laws."

"I see," Garnier said. "I need to see identity papers for both of you, please."

"My passport is at the Radisson Hotel downtown, but here is my remaining identification," Jean said as handed his billfold to Garnier.

"You, Ms. Messier?" Garnier asked.

"All of her identification was confiscated by Gaddafi's security," Jean said.

"You have nothing?" Garnier asked her.

"No."

"I see. I'm afraid I must step away and consult the Ambassador by phone. I would ask you to wait in the lobby for a few minutes, if you please. Can we offer you something to drink?" Garnier asked.

"Yes," Jean said. "Both of us would like water and, if it's not too much trouble, a cup of strong coffee would be helpful."

"I'll see to it immediately."

While they waited, Jean tried to calm Laura. "Mademoiselle, you have had a rough time the past thirty-six hours or so. We're safe here. The Libyans will not enter the embassy grounds."

"In a civilized country, I'd agree with you, Jean. Those guys out there are fucking cowboys."

Jean laughed. "The Mademoiselle certainly has a way with words," he said with a smile.

Laura began to laugh. She hugged Jean. "You saved me, Jean. I don't know how I can ever repay you," she said.

"Oh, I'll think of something," Jean said with a wry smile. An aide came by with a tray of water and coffee. Laura took a long drink of water.

"Have you not been under fire as an operative?" Jean asked as he handed a cup of coffee to Laura.

"Well sure, I've been around live fire before, but never in a fucking wedding dress."

"Perhaps you married the wrong man, Mademoiselle," Jean said with a laugh.

Both of them burst out laughing. It was so nice to be around Jean. Laura had the feeling nothing could shake his confidence.

Duty officer Garnier returned. "Mr. Broussard, the Ambassador is on his way to the embassy as we speak. Our Chief of DST Station is coming as well. They will be here shortly. I'm sorry, but I must ask both of you to remain in the lobby until they arrive," Garnier said.

"Thank you, Mr. Garnier," Jean replied.

It didn't take long. Pierre Doucet, the French Ambassador to Libya and his head of the DST Station, Jacques Martin, arrived and walked through the lobby. Jacques greeted Jean warmly. "Jean, it's good to see you in one piece, my friend. I understand you're in a bit of trouble."

"Hello, Jacques. I'm pleased to see you and you as well, Ambassador," Jean said. "Yes, we are having our difficulties this evening."

Pierre Doucet spoke next and offered his apology. "I'm sorry for the delay, Mr. Broussard. We had trouble getting here due to road blocks around the embassy. What's going on?"

"We need to speak somewhere secure, Pierre," Jean said.

"Of course, let's use my office."

They went upstairs to the Ambassador's office where he offered them something to drink. Laura decided a double bourbon on the rocks was appropriate. "First of all, we must confirm the identity of your colleague, Jean," Doucet said.

"Mademoiselle, do you have any suggestion in that regard?" Jean asked her.

179

"Mr. Ambassador, if you would call DST headquarters in Paris and patch the call through to Operations at the CIA Station in Paris, I can confirm for you," Laura said.

After the connection was made, the voice on the other end said, "Operations."

"Yes, this is Pierre Doucet, the French Ambassador in Libya calling from Tripoli. I have a person with me who is without identification. She says you can confirm her identity. Would you be able to do that for me?"

"Sure, put her on the phone."

Doucet handed Laura the phone. "This is Laura Messier. With whom am I speaking?"

"Laura, its Keith Beal. How can I help you this evening?"

"Hi, Keith. I see you've got the night shift this week."

"Yep, my turn, once a month."

"I need your help. I'm down in Tripoli, Libya and I've lost my identification. I'm at the French Embassy this evening and they need a confirmation before they're willing to help me."

"Sure, Laura. Let me get the code book. Sorry, but I've got to take you through the steps to authenticate," Beal said.

"That's fine. Whenever you're ready, Keith."

"Okay, give me the number," Beal said.

"47992-9-0-0."

"Password?"

Laura thought for a minute. "Songbird?" she asked.

"Yep, that's it. Allow me one minute to voice authenticate you, Laura." Keith was only off the line for a few seconds. "Okay, Laura, I can confirm. I'm putting the threat level at high, the coercion level at zero and your current injury level at zero. Is that correct?"

"Yes."

"Put the Ambassador back on the line," Beal said.

"Great. Thanks, Keith. I need to talk to you again when you've finished."

"Sure," Beal said. Laura handed the phone to Ambassador Doucet. "Sir," Beal said, "I can confirm the identity of the person with you. She is Laura Messier. She has dual citizenship, French and American. She is a resident of Paris and works at the Ministry of Foreign Affairs. She's also a covert operative of the Central Intelligence Agency working out of the United States Embassy here in Paris."

"Thank you."

"Would you mind turning the phone back to Ms. Messier for a minute?" Beal asked.

The Ambassador handed the phone back to Laura. "Anything else I can do for you right now, Laura?" Beal asked.

"Can you report this call to Brownley and send a transcript by telex to Clair George at Langley? I need you to do it right now, if you don't mind."

"Will do, Laura. Anything else?"

"Nope. Take care Keith, and thanks," Laura said.

At Gaddafi's headquarters, the reception had finished when the Colonel found out Asila had managed to enter the French Embassy. Gaddafi gathered the members of his personal guard.

"The man who took Asila is Jean Broussard. He is not important. Concentrate your efforts on Asila. She must not be allowed to leave the country. Release roadblocks to the embassy, but maintain surveillance. I want to know who goes in and comes out. Follow all automobiles coming out. She may leave in a car with diplomatic plates and head to the airport. Do not stop a diplomatic car, but seize her before she boards a flight. Question every Western woman starting now until she is found. If she doesn't try to get out of the country tomorrow, maintain the surveillance indefinitely until she does. Any questions? Good, now get to work."

At the French Embassy, Jacques spoke to the Ambassador. "Pierre, we were aware that Ms. Messier was in the country. This is a joint American and French operation. Headquarters assigned Jean to work with her. Our orders are to assist her in whatever way she requests."

"Ms. Messier, what is it you're asking us to do?" Doucet asked Laura.

"Jean and I need to stay in the embassy overnight, then we need to get out of the country tomorrow. We need a full set of documents and they must be covers because Libyan State Security will be looking for us. They'll probably stake out the airport and watch the embassy."

"Jacques, can you make the necessary arrangements?" Doucet asked Martin.

"We can handle everything from my office, Pierre."

The Ambassador turned to Jean and Laura. "You're in good hands with Mr. Martin. He's experience at making these kinds of arrangements. I'll be back in the morning if you need anything. It was nice to meet you, Ms. Messier. Good night."

Jean and Laura accompanied Martin to his office where their escape planning began. "Jean, we have no government aircraft at Tripoli International right now,"

Jacques said. "Even if we did, they'd have the right to check documents. We might as well try to get both of you out commercial in the morning."

"I agree," Jean responded.

"What about by freighter or over land?" Laura asked.

"They'll follow every car out of the embassy," Jacques said. "They would snatch you as soon as your vehicle stopped for fuel. If we had time to prepare, we could take you out by water. Bribe a ship's captain or something of that nature. If you need to be out of the country by tomorrow, the best way is to arrive at the airport during the morning rush hour. The departure areas will be congested; they'll have difficulty following you. I'll send Henri Thomas, our security chief, with you, Laura. You'll pose as his wife. He has full diplomatic immunity and that would extend to you, too. Jean, do you have any ideas about yourself?"

"I suggest I go out alone under an Arabic name. I'm of North African descent and if I disguise my appearance, I'll probably go unnoticed. My suspicion is they'll focus their attention on Mademoiselle Messier," Jean said.

"Either of you see any problems?" Jacques said.

"What about these?" Laura said.

She had taken off the jewels and wedding band she'd worn at the reception. She handed them to Jacques. "I was wearing these at the time of the escape," she said. "They belong to Colonel Gaddafi. I didn't have time to leave them."

Jacques thought a minute. "Well, Gaddafi's going to want them back." Jacques held up the emerald to inspect it. "This is the largest emerald I've ever seen. If they accuse you of theft, Ms. Messier, they can detain you. If you were willing to wait a couple of days, the Ambassador could negotiate your safe passage in exchange for the return of the jewel."

Laura hesitated before her next comment. "Jacques, I have to be out tomorrow. I'm carrying time sensitive information crucial to the success of an American military operation." Jacques stared at Laura intently.

"Were we notified of this?" he asked.

"President Reagan should be calling President Mitterand Monday morning to inform him."

Jacques turned to Jean. "We were informed that some kind of clandestine op was running here, but we weren't given the details. Is this what you're doing?" Jacques asked Jean.

"Yes, Jacques and I apologize we couldn't tell you. This operation was run strictly out of Paris and Washington."

"Is our source inside Libyan military involved?" Jacques asked.

"Yes, Jacques, he is."

"Do we run the risk of disclosing him?"

"I don't think so," Jean said. "The Mademoiselle knows nothing and I doubt they'll be looking for me."

Jacques considered that for a minute. "Well, if military action is imminent, then of course, we need to get both of you out tomorrow. "

"Thank you, Mr. Martin," Laura said.

Jacques smiled. "Please, call me Jacques. If anything happens at the airport in the morning, we'll deal with it then. For now, let's get the two of you settled for the evening. I'll get operations to work on your documents and we'll meet again in my office tomorrow morning at 07:00 hours."

"Thank you so much, Jacques, for your help," Jean said.

"You're welcome. Get a good night's rest."

Sleeping quarters for the night were provided along with hot showers and Laura was given an assortment of western clothing. Jean and Laura were forced to use the same queen sized bed, but it didn't take much effort to sleep. It had been a very long day.

Chapter Twenty-Four

Mission Day Three, Sunday, April 13, 1986

SAFELY ENSCONCED INSIDE the French Embassy, protected from Gaddafi's security apparatus, Laura and Jean slept soundly for the first time in several days. After a Western style breakfast in the small cafeteria, they met Jacques in his office early the next morning to plan their escape. Jean had shaved his beard and donned a western style suit accompanied by a kaffiyeh, a red and white checkered cloth worn over the head with a cord. His appearance mimicked the traditional dress of Arab businessmen. Laura wore the clothes given to her last night, a discreet neutral colored pantsuit and a headscarf. Both would blend in nicely at the airport.

"Good morning. I trust everyone is well rested?" Jacques inquired.

"We're doing well, Jacques," Jean said.

"Here's what we've arranged for your exit this morning," Jacques explained. "Miss Messier, you are leaving on a flight to Rome at 09:00 hours. From there, you'll connect to Paris. I'd like to introduce you to Henri Thomas. He'll accompany you all the way to Paris."

"Miss Messier," Henri said, nodding his head in acknowledgment.

Henri Thomas was a big, barrel chested man in his early 40s who looked like he could take care of himself in a fight. He had a strong masculine presence, short black hair graying at the temples and brown eyes. He was friendly, with a nice smile and kind eyes. Laura felt comfortable with him immediately.

"Mr. Thomas, thank you for helping me," she said.

"You're welcome, Mademoiselle."

Jacques continued, "Henri will brief you on the way to the airport. He has your documents and plane ticket. Now, for you Jean, following Miss Messier's departure, we have you on a noon flight to Madrid. From there, you'll connect to Paris. We're dropping each of you off at the airport separately in embassy vehicles. We'll have personnel at the airport shadowing you. Should either you be detained, they'll call me and we'll lodge an official protest. In the past, that's been enough and I think it will work this time. If it doesn't, I'll get the Ambassador involved. Any questions?"

"That sounds great, Jacques; I can't thank you enough," Laura said.

"Well, don't thank me yet, you're not out yet, but I think we're in decent shape. Henri?"

"Yes, Sir?"

"Get Miss Messier ready to leave." Jacques glanced at his watch. "Your flight is in less than two hours. Good luck everyone."

Before Laura and Jean parted company, they hugged. "Mademoiselle, I wish you the very best of luck this morning. Let's meet in Paris next week for a drink," Jean said with a confident smile.

"In case I don't make it out, Jean, I need you to take this to the American Embassy and give it to John Brownley, the station chief." Laura handed Jean a small piece of paper on which she had written a series of numbers. "He'll know what to do with it."

"I will, Mademoiselle, but don't worry. We'll both get out. I've known Henri for years. He's a good man."

"Mademoiselle, I'm sorry, but we must hurry," Henri Thomas said. "We haven't much time."

Traffic was heavy on the way to the airport. Sunday morning is the beginning of the work week in Libya and it seemed as though every car in the city was on the roadway. Laura wondered how drivers managed to ignore lane markings without crashing into each other. Henri briefed Laura on her legend during the drive. She would pose as Irene Thomas, Henri's wife, who had been visiting her husband since last Wednesday. French Intelligence provided a passport with various entries and exits around Europe, a French driver's license, credit cards and a health ID. They even included a library card. Her purse contained various personal items; make-up, a small amount of cash and keys to their car and home. She carried a travel bag of clothing the embassy staff gathered together.

As the heavy, black car with French diplomatic plates pulled to the curb in front of the terminal, Henri noticed Laura's apprehension. "Irene, relax. We're fine, no problem at all. We're a married couple traveling to Rome this morning."

"Sorry, Henri. It's just I was trapped in Gaddafi's personal quarters and I'm a little nervous about the possibility of going back," Laura said.

"You're not going back," Henri replied with a confident smile. "Now, relax."

The driver took their bags from the trunk and when the two exited the vehicle, they looked like normal passengers being dropped off at Tripoli International Airport. The terminal was full of travelers and the congested ticket counters concealed their presence. Henri chatted with Laura in line at the counter where they showed their identification and received boarding passes. As they passed through customs, Henri glanced at the clock; it was 8:15 a.m. They checked in at the gate and sat down in the small seating area to await the flight. Henri smiled, laughed at his own jokes and did his best to make her feel comfortable.

Colonel Gaddafi answered the private line in his office. "Yes, what's the problem?"

The voice said, "Commander, we followed an embassy vehicle to the airport this morning where a man and woman left the vehicle and entered the terminal."

"Thank you," Gaddafi said.

Gaddafi summoned Salima, the head of his personal security, to his office. "Salam, Salima."

"Salam to you, Commander."

"Asila may be at the airport right now. Take anyone with you who can identify her. Find her and bring her to me."

"Yes, Sir."

Henri noticed an unusual amount of security looking at passengers up and down the concourse. About 8:45, as the flight began boarding, security personnel stood next to the attendant accepting boarding passes where they began pulling Western looking women out of line and leading them out of the gate area. Laura stiffened. "Relax," Henri whispered in her ear. "It appears they're checking Western women. Just stick to your legend, answer their questions and you'll be fine." As they handed their boarding passes to the attendant, a security officer stepped forward, "I'm sorry, Ma'am, I need you to step out of line and follow me, please." That's when Laura felt the gut wrenching panic that had gripped her escaping Gaddafi's compound the previous evening.

Security led her away from the terminal into an administrative area where she saw makeshift interrogation rooms in use. It appeared to be airport security doing the interviews, although Laura could not be sure. If so, they weren't professional interrogators. Most of the rooms appeared to be vacant office space being used temporarily by the security staff. Some had windows where Laura could see women being strip searched, much to their dismay. *Male guards doing strip searches?* she thought. *Let's hope it doesn't get that far.*

Led to a room that looked to be recently arranged for an interrogation, she was told to wait for an investigator. She sat in one of the two chairs that accompanied a metal table with a loop welded into the tabletop. The hallway was visible through a large picture window next to the door and Laura entertained the idea of pitching her chair through the window as a means of escape. This was not a secure area, nothing like an interrogation room one might see in a police station. The security officer who stood in front of the door, hands folded in front of him, did not wear a weapon. Laura considered an escape; the guard was inattentive and bored; he could easily be subdued. *How far would I get? Back to the gate area? Out of the terminal?* She remembered Henri's advice; *stay calm, stick to her legend and respond to questions in short, simple answers.* It was a long wait before the investigator arrived and Laura assumed she had missed her flight.

Three Days in Tripoli

When the interrogator entered the room, she caught a glimpse at his watch; it was 9:30. He was an older man, unimpressive in demeanor and appearance, who looked somewhat disheveled and unprepared for interviews. He spoke to her in English and to maintain her cover, she responded in English with a thick French accent. He was polite, asked the usual questions about her documents and seemed satisfied with her answers. It appeared Henri was right, she was about to be released until the interrogator mentioned he needed the approval of a supervisor. He said one would arrive in the room shortly. Laura wondered if Gaddafi had his personal security at the airport searching for her.

Gaddafi's personal security were the female guards who accompanied the Colonel at all times, whether in the personal quarters or outside the compound. Laura had counted twelve. She saw them frequently in the personal quarters. Gaddafi's State Security were male and far more numerous, numbering in the thousands. If they were searching for her, it was likely she go unrecognized. However, if Gaddafi had his female guards at the airport, she knew she'd be caught.

The interrogator left the room and when he didn't return immediately, Laura wondered how long Henri would wait. When the interrogator returned again, she was able to glance at his watch. It was 10:40 and she was thirsty. The room was hot, the air circulation poor. He was accompanied by one of Gaddafi's female guards. Laura didn't recognize her. She spoke to Laura in Arabic and the interrogator interpreted her question. "She wants you to look her in the eyes."

She studied Laura momentarily, then turned to the interrogator and said something in Arabic before leaving. He stood up and motioned through the window. Four male security personnel entered the room. "I'm sorry, Ma'am, but we are required to search you further."

"I have full diplomatic immunity. You're required to allow me to leave," Laura said.

"Please do not take offense at what we do. We're looking for something that has been stolen and the woman who stole it."

The guards motioned for her to stand and Laura expected a pat down. She spread her arms and legs out while one guard felt her body, making sure he lingered over her breasts. He smiled when he did it. Afterward, they insisted she take off all her clothing and when she refused, they ripped her blouse open. She finally stripped to her panties and bra and stood before them. They whispered among themselves until the interrogator cut them off with a wave of his hand. Handcuffs were put on her wrists and strung through the loop in the table. Another set were put around her ankles and attached to the chair legs.

"We will search your luggage. During this time, please relax and be patient."

"May I put my clothing back on?" she asked.

"Not just yet," the interrogator said, "but we'll find a blanket to cover you. We will re-book you on another flight if you're released and your husband will be informed of our plans. For now, just sit quietly please." He said to the guards, "I will be back shortly. Find a blanket of some kind to cover her body."

The interrogator walked into the gate area and found Henri Thomas still sitting at the gate long after the flight had left. "Mr. Thomas?" he asked.

"Yes?"

"Jalil Tuma, Libyan State Security. I regret to inform you that your wife has been detained and will remain here at the airport until certain matters are resolved. I suggest you go back to your embassy and wait until we call you with information."

"My wife and I have full diplomatic immunity. I protest her detention. I will not leave, Sir."

"You're certainly welcome to wait, but I must ask you to leave the gate area and wait in the terminal."

"What is the problem? She has done nothing wrong," Henri said.

"As I said, there are certain questions to be answered before we can release her. I have two guards who will escort you back to the terminal. Someone will keep you informed as we proceed with our investigation."

Two armed guards walked Henri back to the terminal where he ran his right hand through his hair which prompted a bystander to call the French Embassy. "She's been detained for questioning."

"Thank you," Jacques Martin said. Jacques dialed the Ambassador, then left for the airport to help secure Irene Thomas' release.

Ambassador Pierre Doucet pulled the jewel out of his desk drawer and studied it. It was a remarkable gemstone, surely one of the largest cut emeralds in the world. *It's the only leverage I have,* he thought. *Before I use it, though, let's see what Jacques can do at the airport.*

Jalil Tuma started his day well before dawn. As security manager for one of the concourses at the airport, Tuma and his staff had been kept busy all morning vetting Western women on flights leaving his concourse. It was well past 11:00 a.m. after Tuma spoke with Thomas, so instead of returning to the interrogation, Tuma stopped at one of the airport restaurants.

After lunch, Tuma decided to perform his due diligence with regards to Mrs. Thomas. The interrogation was his responsibility until someone else took over so he stopped by customs and pulled what records they had for her entry to the country. By the time he returned to the interrogation, it was afternoon. The woman had been in the room for over four hours and Tuma thought it was time to move the interrogation along. Tuma didn't like the woman and wanted a dispensation of the matter quickly.

Tuma entered the room and asked the guards to leave. "It's nice to see you again, Mrs. Thomas," Tuma said. "One of Colonel Gaddafi's personal security identified you earlier this morning as a person of interest. Why would she do that?"

"I don't know. May I get dressed now?"

"A rare jewel was stolen from a reception last night at the Bab al-Azizia military headquarters. Later, a young woman matching your description was seen entering the French Embassy. You may be the person they're looking for. What is your response, please?"

"I know nothing of a jewel and I've never been to a military base. I have no idea what you're talking about," Laura said.

"If you had arrived on Wednesday as you claim, we would have a record of you clearing customs on Wednesday. No such record exists."

"How can you say that? My passport has an entry stamp."

"Those stamps can be easily forged."

"Does my name appear on the flight manifest for last Wednesday?" she asked.

"Yes, of course."

"Then I don't know what your problem is."

"We will search your luggage when it arrives. Perhaps that will give us some answers."

Laura glanced at the interrogator's watch. It was past 1:30 and Jean's flight would have left. Security retrieved Laura's bag from the gate area and she watched as they tore it apart, ripping the clothing, even tearing the lining of the bag. They found nothing.

"I apologize about your bag, Mrs. Thomas," Tuma said. "It was in your best interest that we did this. Guards," Tuma shouted and two guards standing outside entered the room. "Allow her to get dressed." The guards unlocked her long enough to allow her to dress, then they applied the restraints again.

Tuma picked up the passport and looked at it closely. "The problem is one of Colonel Gaddafi's personal guards identified you as a person to be questioned." He thumbed through the passport looking at each page. "Some people have the ability to forge passports, Mrs. Thomas. This one looks real, but it could be a forgery. What hotel did you stay at during your time in Tripoli?" Tuma asked.

"I didn't use a hotel. I stayed with my husband at the embassy."

"Did you come into the country using a different name?"

"Of course not."

"You have nothing else except this passport?"

"I have plenty of identification."

"Easily forged." Tuma laid the passport on the table in front of him. He leaned forward and folded his hands in front of him. "One of the great gemstones of Libya disappeared last night. You fit the description of the woman who stole it. That woman was later seen entering the French Embassy. You come to the airport this morning from the French Embassy. One of the Colonel's guards identified you as a possible suspect. These things are not a coincidence. Why don't you tell me who you really are?"

"I told you, Irene Thomas," Laura said.

Tuma was more insist this time. "Tell me who you are and what you did with the stone!"

"My name is Irene Thomas and I don't have your gemstone."

Tuma slammed his hand down on the table and shouted this time, "Tell me your name!"

"Sir, with all due respect, you can easily see the customs stamp from last Wednesday when I entered the country. It isn't my fault that your customs people can't keep their records straight."

Tuma was livid. "Our customs officials are professionals. They don't make mistakes! You are going to tell me your real name or I will force you to do so," he shouted.

"My name is Irene Thomas, but if it takes another name to get me released, I'll give you another name. What if I told you my name was …" Laura thought for a minute. "… Mrs. Gaddafi, for instance."

Tuma glared at her. "You mean Colonel Gaddafi's wife?" he asked.

"Yes."

"That's ridiculous. The Commander's wife is well known in the country."

"Fine, would you like another name?" she asked.

"Please, at this point, I would appreciate the truth."

"I am a French singer who came to Libya to perform in a nightclub."

"There are no nightclubs in Libya," Tuma said. "That is impossible. Lies will not help you obtain your release."

"Apparently, you're having a problem hearing the truth," Laura said.

"The truth? Let's see, you told me you were Irene Thomas, a woman married to a diplomat at the French Embassy. Then, you said you were Colonel Gaddafi's wife. Now, you say you're someone who performs in a nightclub that doesn't exist?"

"Yes, that's it exactly," Laura said.

"You are insane, Mrs. Thomas."

"Well, I did forget to mention that. Yes, I'm also insane."

"I've grown tired of your lies, Mrs. Thomas. Would you agree that I've been patient and reasonable with you?"

"No, I don't agree. My name is Irene Thomas. I have full diplomatic immunity and my documents are in order. You have no reason to detain me," Laura said.

Tuma resented the attitudes of superiority that people from the West often showed coming to his country. "Mrs. Thomas, you clearly need to be persuaded to cooperate."

"I've been totally cooperative. I've been very accommodating with you."

"I've heard nothing but lies from you all day. My guard is prepared to persuade you to tell the truth."

Chapter Twenty-Five

TUMA OPENED THE door, called one of the guards into the room and spoke to him in Arabic. The guard smiled, unlocked the handcuffs on Laura's wrists and ankles and pulled her up by the hair. He started to punch her, but before he could land it, she managed to stick her fingers in his eyes. He screamed as she pushed hard. With her left wrist locked so as to use her knuckles for impact, she quickly uppercut her fist just underneath his chin. That raised his head far enough that she was able to punch her right fist into his trachea, pushing it into his throat.

He grabbed his neck and began gasping for air while she took her left heel and hit his kneecap flush, fracturing it. As he fell, she took his head and slammed it hard on the tabletop. His face exploded in blood. She released him and he fell to the floor, unconscious. The entire fight took less than ten seconds. Tuma stood there shocked by what he had just witnessed.

"Fuck you, asshole," Laura growled in French as she made a move toward Tuma. He retreated to the door, opened it and yelled loudly for help. Three guards entered the room and attacked Laura. She managed to put the first one on the floor with a crushing side kick to the sternum and threw the second one over her shoulder into the table with an Aikido move, but the third guard backed away and drew his sidearm. He fired at the ceiling causing Laura to pause. Additional guards burst into the room and there were too many to fight. They beat her severely to avenge their injured colleagues and when they were done, Laura was lying on the floor, barely conscious.

The injured co-workers were carried out, the room cleaned of blood and Laura handcuffed to the table again. "Insane people can fight like demons, Mrs. Thomas," Tuma said after Laura was restrained again. "That's why they are locked in solitary confinement and fed drugs every day. You have a severe mental illness. I'm going to recommend that you be put on a flight back to France. We will let the French authorities deal with you. However, I must wait for Colonel Gaddafi's security head to approve your release."

Before leaving the room, Tuma asked three guards to stay and watch her closely. Laura could see they were eager to inflict more punishment. While she waited for Tuma's return, she took an inventory of her injuries. A few contusions were bleeding, but only a couple of spots needed stitches. However, she'd hit her head falling to the floor and suspected a mild concussion. She'd not been allowed to use the restroom, nor given water to drink. She was terribly thirsty and would soon have to urinate.

Laura had seen Jacques walk by the window; he was on the scene and would be working to secure her release. *If that fails, perhaps the Ambassador could use the jewel to negotiate on my behalf.* However, hearing that Gaddafi's head of security would soon arrive in the room was a depressing development. *It's going to be a long afternoon,* she thought.

Laura could not hold herself any longer and was forced to urinate in the chair. She guessed it was around 2:00 p.m., which would be 8:00 a.m. at Langley. *If Clair George reads the telex traffic Sunday morning, he'll read the transcript of the phone call I made last night to Paris station from the French Embassy,* she thought. *Perhaps he can be of assistance.* Laura needed to rest so she laid her head on the table and closed her eyes.

When Salima entered the interrogation room, it was 2:45 p.m. Laura had been in the room nearly six hours without food, water or the ability to use a restroom. Severely beaten, when Laura saw Salima, she knew the real interrogation would begin now. This was an endurance test; Laura's intelligence and determination against a foe with every advantage. Salima smiled when she saw Laura; the malevolent, wicked smile that Laura saw Gaddafi use.

"Hello, Asila," she said.

"My name is Irene Thomas, Salima."

"No, it isn't. You are the Colonel's property. He named you Asila. Are you ready to return to the Colonel's household?"

"I'd be happy to talk with you, Salima, but right now I need water."

"Of course, let me arrange it," Salima said with a feigned concern.

Salima rose, opened the door and shouted something in Arabic. In a couple of minutes, a glass of water was provided. Salima threw the water in Laura's face.

"I see you pissed on yourself," Salima said.

"Where else would I go? You have to smell it too, Salima."

"You're no longer the pretty Asila, are you?"

Salima knocked on the window and a guard opened the door. "Clean up this mess," she said, pointing around the room. Guards brought supplies to do a quick cleaning. Laura decided to direct the effort. "You missed a spot over there," she said. "Do you mind wiping my leg? Could you wipe my mouth for me, please?" Obviously, she was stalling, but even an extra minute would help.

When they had finished, Salima resumed. "Now that I've removed your disgusting smell, Asila, you will answer my question. Is the Commander's whore ready to return to her duties?"

"I am his wife, Salima."

"Yes, you are and as soon as I arrange transportation, you will be returned to his personal quarters. Discussion is pointless."

"Every discussion has a point, Salima, even this one."

Salima laughed. "You are trying to delay in hopes the French will help you. It doesn't matter how much the French protest. Under Islamic law, you are the Colonel's wife and you will be returned to him. You will live your life making yourself pretty so the Commander can rape you whenever he wishes. Then, when you are too old, you'll clean floors."

"Has the Colonel made you his whore, too?" Laura asked.

"I'm a military professional, Asila. Your profession, however, is the world's oldest."

"A military professional would not have allowed me to escape, Salima. What will the Colonel do to you once this is over?"

"That's not your concern."

"But you are concerned, aren't you?" Laura asked.

"No."

"Do you see how easily I've turned this interrogation around?" Laura asked. "Now, it is me asking the questions. You're not very bright, are you?"

"You won't be talking once I've finished punishing you for escaping the compound."

"Why don't you release me from the restraints so we can talk freely?"

"You're talking to avoid punishment, Asila," Salima said. "It won't work."

"You won't release me because you're afraid of me. You know what I did to the other guards."

"Afraid of you?" Salima laughed, "No. Don't worry, pretty Asila. The Commander doesn't want your face touched. Once your injuries heal, you'll become the pretty Asila again and ..."

Laura interrupted her. "You said that before, Salima. You haven't asked about the jewel yet. Are you so eager to hit someone that you've forgotten to ask?"

"Ah, yes, the jewel. Where is it, Asila?"

"It's hidden where neither you nor anyone else can retrieve it."

"That jewel belongs to the nation of Libya. You'll not be allowed to use it as a bargaining chip for your life. The jewel has more value than you."

"The jewel belongs to me," Laura said with conviction, "and I intend to keep it unless the Colonel agrees to allow me to leave."

"I will beat you until ..."

Laura interrupted her again. "I know, I know. You'll beat me until I tell you where it is. I've heard that before. There is a way to serve everyone's interest if you're smart enough to listen to me."

"I'll hit you in places that will cause you intense pain." Salima smiled. "You'll tell me. Why don't you make it easy on yourself and tell me now?"

"I'm offering the Colonel a deal. Listen to my offer. Go call him and see what he says."

"Asila, there will be no bargain," Salima said. "You'll return to the compound and wear the jewel on your head to show everyone you're his whore. Those are the Commander's orders."

"I know a secret about you, Salima. Would you like to hear it? You make love with women. When I get back to the compound, I'll tell the Colonel and he'll kill you for it," Laura said.

That enraged Salima; Laura knew from Salima's reaction that the assertion was true. "I will not touch you with my hands, Asila, because you disgust me," Salima said. She opened the door and spoke to the guards outside the room. "Bring my weapon."

Two guards returned with Salima's AK-47 and they stayed in the room to assist her. They unlocked the restraints and stood Laura against the wall. She was too weak to put up much of a fight, but she kneed one in the groin and used her elbow to strike the other in the face before Salima leveled her weapon at her. "Move again, Asila, and I'll kill you," she said.

"After you've finished beating me, you'll realize how foolish you were by not listening to my offer."

"Enough talk. You're a sin against Islam. Feel Allah's punishment," Salima said.

The guards held Laura as the first blow was aimed at her head. She moved slightly to avoid the impact, but the glancing blow stunned her briefly. She began to lose consciousness. Unfortunately, she didn't quite get there. Salima knew exactly where to hit her. Laura felt the crack when her ribs broke. The pain was crippling. After the next blow, Laura felt her shoulder dislocate. She tried to move into the blows to lessen their impact, but they were too numerous. Salima kept pounding her until Laura was too weak to resist. She hung lifelessly as the guards held her suspended by the arms. She was unable to even hold her head up. And then, the shouting started.

"Enough! Stop!" the Libyan officer shouted, bursting into the room. Salima raised her rifle butt for one last blow and the Libyan officer grabbed her weapon and pushed Salima to the wall. "Enough!" he shouted. Libyan Intelligence had arrived on the scene.

Chapter Twenty-Six

THE CALL FROM the airport came into Ambassador Doucet's office at 1:30 p.m.

"Ambassador?" Jacques asked.

"Yes, Jacques. Are we making progress at the airport?"

"No, Sir. The Libyans are adamant. They will not release her, immunity or not. I've tried everything I can think of. I think we need to put the jewel in play.

"I'll call Colonel Gaddafi immediately," Doucet said.

"I had another thought, Sir," Jacques said. "The East Germans are in town advising Libya on intelligence matters. They've got influence with the Libyans. Perhaps a deal can be made to release her."

"Good idea, Jacques. You and Henri stay at the airport. If she's released, you must be there to take custody. Oh, and get a nurse. I would imagine she's in bad shape by now."

"One suggestion if you call the East Germans," Jacques said.

"Yes?"

"Use the code word Wranglestrasse. That's the safe house in Berlin where we meet," Jacques said.

"Thank you, Jacques."

Pierre Doucet dialed the number to Gaddafi's headquarters. Gaddafi came on the line after a short delay. "Mr. Ambassador, how can I help you today?" Gaddafi asked.

"Colonel, I have a jewel in my possession that was dropped off at the embassy last night by a young woman. That woman is at the airport as we speak, trying to leave the country. She wishes to return the stone in exchange for her safe passage," Doucet said.

"That's quite impossible, Ambassador. That woman is my wife and she must be returned to my household. The stone is the property of the Libyan people. We demand it be returned immediately."

"Colonel, I am an intermediary. As far as the French government is concerned, we are neutral in the matter. I cannot release the jewel without the woman's permission."

"Then she'll contact you after she returns to my compound."

"Thank you, Colonel," Doucet said.

Doucet's next move was to call the East Germans. The Eastern Bloc nations had influence with the Libyan government. *Perhaps a deal can be struck for her return. It's worth a try.* Pierre dialed the number to the Tripoli Radisson Hotel and asked for the East German delegation. He was connected to the hotel answering service. He left the message, "Wranglestrasse" with his phone number. The return call came into Doucet's office within five minutes.

"Wranglestrasse," the voice said.

"There's a person of interest being held at the airport you should take a look at," Doucet said.

"Who is it?" the voice asked.

"You'll know her when you see her."

"Thank you. Goodbye."

Chapter Twenty-Seven

THE HEAD OF Libyan Intelligence picked up an elderly man outside the Radisson Hotel just after 2:30 p.m. Their destination was the airport where they intended to view the interrogation of a person of interest captured trying to leave the country.

Major Fareed Hassan was Libya's third highest ranking military officer after Gaddafi and the Minister of Defense. He was a major only because Gaddafi refused to promote any officer to a higher rank than himself. Responsible for Libya's vast network of spies, Hassan was one of the most feared men in Libya. Today, he wore his full military dress uniform. He wanted to take control of the interrogation if his suspicion proved correct.

The elderly man, on the other hand, was not impressive to look at. He wore a simple gray suit. He had graying hair and a kind, scholarly face. He was, in fact, one of the most brilliant intelligence agents in the world. Markus Wolf ran the foreign intelligence division of the East German Stasi. He was something of a legend in the West in that he was a ghost. In over thirty years of service, only one Western intelligence agent had ever met him, a young CIA agent named Laura Messier. It was a coincidence that Wolf was in the country when he heard that a woman had been detained at the airport. He was in Libya advising Major Hassan on matters of mutual interest.

On the way to the airport, Wolf asked Hassan what he knew of the woman. "Not much, Markus," Hassan replied in near perfect German. "Apparently, on Friday night, she was in a secret nightclub that Gaddafi runs downtown. Gaddafi took a liking to her, kidnapped her and kept her in his personal quarters. It's been said she escaped and took refuge in the French Embassy. She was caught at the airport this morning trying to leave the country."

"I would have thought it impossible to escape the Azizia compound," the elderly man said.

"It's impossible to get in and impossible to get out. I'd certainly like to meet the woman who managed to accomplish both." Hassan laughed. "There's a rumor going around that Gaddafi was so infatuated with the woman that he married her last night in some sort of trumped up wedding. She used the wedding ring to command his guards to release her."

"She's French, is that right?" Wolf asked.

"We're not sure. She entered the country on a French passport at some point last week. That's all we know."

"Suppose it were her intent to penetrate Gaddafi's personal quarters. His office is there, correct?"

"Yes, in his personal quarters."

"I will be most interested in seeing this woman," Wolf said.

When they arrived at the airport and found the woman being severely beaten, Wolf said to Hassan, "You should stop this. We need her alive, conscious and talking." Hassan stepped in to control the interrogation.

Hassan's men, two dozen of them, arrived at the airport within minutes. They quickly established a perimeter and locked down the area. These were experienced intelligence professionals, not Gaddafi's undisciplined street thugs. Once Hassan observed the physical condition of the woman, he was seething with anger regarding the inexperience of those who ran the interrogation.

He asked Salima to step out of the room to question her in the hallway. "What is your name?"

"Salima, Sir."

"What were you trying to accomplish?"

"The Commander ordered me to bring her back to the compound."

Hassan slapped her hard across her face. "Answer the question. What were you trying to do?"

Salima showed a flash of anger in her eyes. Hassan snapped his finger and two of his men immediately came to his side. "Restrain her," he ordered. The men grabbed Salima by the arms and Hassan hit her flush in the face. Salima's nose dripped blood. One of the men offered Hassan a handkerchief and Hassan wiped the blood from his hand. "I will give you one last opportunity. What were you trying to do inside that room?" He offered the handkerchief to Salima, who wiped the blood from her face.

"I was punishing the woman for leaving the Commander's personal quarters," Salima said.

"Did it ever cross your mind that she may have been in the compound to spy on the Libyan government?"

"Her?" Salima asked, disregarding Hassan's suggestion. "She's a whore."

Hassan changed his tone of voice to something like a college professor would use. "Salima, do you have any military training?"

"I'm the head of Colonel Gaddafi's personal security."

Hassan punched Salima in the stomach. She doubled over in pain, but Hassan grabbed her hair, lifted her head and struck her in the face again. Salima's knees buckled, but Hassan's men jerked her upright and held her.

"Answer the question! Do you have military training?" he shouted.

"No, Sir," she said, struggling to breathe.

"Do you have a university degree?"

"No, Sir," Salima admitted.

"Have you had any training in intelligence?"

"No, Sir."

"So, how would you know a whore from an intelligence agent?"

She couldn't answer the question. Major Hassan continued, "Tell me Salima, was this whore," he said, emphasizing the word, "allowed access to the personal quarters?"

"I'm not sure I know what you mean, Sir," Salima said.

Hassan punched Salima in the face again. She collapsed. "Stand her up again," he said to his men standing on either side of her.

"You're not real bright, are you? Was she allowed to walk around the personal quarters near the Commander's office?"

"After the first night, yes," she answered.

"Why?"

"The Commander had broken her will."

"Broken her will?" the Major asked rhetorically. His voice dripped with sarcasm, "It doesn't seem odd to you that she began obeying commands all of a sudden?"

"The Commander trains all his whores in this manner. By the second day, they realize escape is not possible. They know they will die unless they obey him."

Hassan took Salima by the arm and dragged her to the window. "Look at that woman, Salima. Look!" he shouted, pointing his finger at the window. Salima stared inside the room. "Do you see anything in that woman's eyes that tell you her will is broken?"

"I cannot tell, Sir," Salima admitted.

"What information did she give you during your interrogation?"

"Nothing! She offered me a deal," Salima said.

"She tried to talk and you wouldn't listen? So, I ask again, what were you trying to do inside that room?"

Salima had run out of excuses. She said nothing and stared at the floor.

"What's your name again?" Hassan asked.

"It's Salima, Sir."

"Salima, here's your first lesson in intelligence work," Hassan said. "When you beat someone in an interrogation, you don't get accurate information."

"Yes, Sir."

"Here's your second lesson. We're going to lock you in one of the rooms across the hall until this interrogation is finished. You will sit quietly and think about what you want to do for a living because you will never be allowed near the Colonel again." Hassan turned to one of his men nearby, "Lock this idiot in a room across the hall. If she gives you any problem, kill her."

Major Hassan was now in control of the scene. He addressed another of his men, "I understand the French are here. Find them and bring them to me." Then he asked no one in particular, "Where's the officer who did the original interrogation of this woman?"

One of his men spoke up, "I'll find him, Sir."

"Very good," Hassan said. "Bring him here also."

Hassan's men brought Jacques Martin, Henri Thomas and a nurse to him outside the interrogation room. "Good afternoon, Jacques." Hassan nodded in Henri's direction. "Henri."

"Hello, Fareed," Jacques said in acknowledgment.

"I apologize on behalf of the Libyan government for the manner in which this woman was treated. Is this your nurse?" Hassan asked, nodding toward the nurse that Jacques had requested.

"Yes," Jacques said.

Hassan spoke directly to her. "Clean her up, tend to her injuries and make her comfortable. If she's able to eat, let's get a meal from one of the airport restaurants. Find clean clothes for her and move her out of that room."

Hassan turned to another of his men nearby, "Go in the terminal and secure one of the airport lounges. We're moving this interrogation there. And find a wheelchair." As the man began to walk away, Hassan spoke again, "One more thing."

"Yes, Sir?" the man responded.

"Do a quick sweep of the lounge. No bugs. Do you understand what I'm saying?" The man was accustomed to reading the hidden meaning behind the Major's words.

"Yes, Sir. No bugs," he said, *except ours,* he thought.

Hassan addressed his next comment to Jacques and Henri, "Gentlemen, my men will secure an airport lounge where we can move your girl. Have your nurse tend to her injuries and once she's been cared for and moved, Jacques, you and I will sit down and have a discussion about her future."

"Thank you, Fareed".

"You're welcome, Jacques. I'm sorry this happened."

"Major, excuse me," one of his men said.

Hassan turned his head, "Yes, what is it?"

"We have the man who did the woman's interrogation."

"Bring him here," Hassan said.

When the man was brought forward, Hassan saw a disorganized, inefficient bureaucrat, one of the thousands of inept workers living on the Libyan government payroll. Hassan had an explosive temper, one held in check by military discipline, but at times it was useful to display it.

"Who are you?" Hassan asked with a vicious anger in his eyes.

"My name is Jalil Tuma, Sir."

"What's your job here?"

"I manage security for the A concourse here at the airport."

"Did you have a nice lunch today, Tuma?" Hassan asked. He softened his tone and Tuma looked confused. Hassan repeated the question. "You heard me. Did you have a nice lunch?"

"Yes, Sir."

"What did you have for lunch?" Hassan asked.

"I ate at one of the restaurants off the concourse, a lamb and rice dish with a salad."

"Did you enjoy it?" Hassan smiled, but Tuma wasn't astute enough to notice it was not a smile of goodwill.

"It was an excellent meal, Sir," Tuma replied.

"How many times did you use the restroom today, Tuma, if you don't mind me asking?"

Tuma didn't know how to answer the question. "I'm afraid I don't understand, Sir."

"It's a simple question, Tuma. Did you use the restroom today? Answer!" he shouted.

"Yes, Sir, I had access to restroom facilities all day long."

"Running interviews all day is hard work, Tuma. Were you provided with refreshments during the day, like water to drink during the interviews?"

Tuma thought he knew where the Major's questions were headed. Tuma relaxed. "Oh, yes, Sir. We were provided with everything we needed all day long. The staff here is excellent. They take very good care of us."

"Did you interview this woman?" Hassan asked, pointing inside the window.

"Yes, Sir."

"When did her interview start?"

"She was brought here before 9:00 this morning, Sir," Tuma said.

Hassan glanced at his watch, it was past 3:30. "So, she's been here almost seven hours. Is that correct?"

"Yes, Sir."

"Did you offer her any food?"

"No, Sir," Tuma replied.

"How about water?"

Tuma began to squirm at the sudden shift in the Major's tone of voice. "She didn't ask for any."

"Was she allowed to use the restroom?"

"No, Sir."

Major Hassan was a strong and fit individual. He commanded the respect of his men by working out alongside them several times a week. So, when he suddenly landed his massive fist in Tuma's face, it was not wholly unexpected by his men. Tuma, however, was caught completely off guard; he collapsed on the floor.

"Get him up," the General told his men. Two men lifted Tuma back to his feet. Tuma wiped blood off his face with his tie. "Did you take notes during your interview?" Hassan asked.

Tuma tried to retrieve his notebook from the floor. Hassan grabbed Tuma by the throat and pulled him up. Hassan had four inches and seventy-five pounds on the man.

"Did I ask you to pick that up?" Hassan screamed at him nose to nose.

"No, Sir." Hassan released him with a shove.

"Then answer the question. Did you take notes during your interview?"

"They're right there, Sir," Tuma said, pointing to the floor.

"Pick them up and hand them to me," Hassan said.

Tuma picked up his notebook, tore a page from it and handed it to Hassan.

"That's it? After seven hours of questions, this is all you have?" Hassan punched Tuma in the stomach with a powerful blow. Tuma doubled over in pain. "Answer me! Is this the extent of your notes?"

"Major, the woman is insane," Tuma said, struggling to breathe. "She talked nonsense the entire time. There was nothing of value to write down. She's a crazy woman, Sir. She put three of my guards in the hospital. One of them might not live."

"She did what?" Hassan asked as though he couldn't believe what he was hearing.

"We let her loose to give her a small amount of punishment and she attacked the guards. Three of them were injured, one very badly."

Hassan looked in the window at the woman with a new found respect. He stared at her for a very long time.

"Sir, do you have any other questions for me?" Tuma asked.

Hassan flashed his anger and punched Tuma again in the gut. Tuma began to fall and Hassan's men pulled him up quickly.

"I'll ask the next question when I'm ready," Hassan hissed. He continued to study the woman in the room. He asked the next question while still staring at her. "Who is this woman, Tuma?"

Tuma struggled to remember. "Uh, she said she was the wife of a French diplomat and then she changed her story and said she was a nightclub singer."

"Did I hear you correctly? A nightclub singer?" Hassan asked.

"Yes. She said she was performing in a nightclub in Libya, which is impossible. There are no nightclubs in the country. She also said she was the wife of Colonel Gaddafi. She's mentally ill, Sir."

"Anything else, Tuma?"

"That was all we managed to get out of her, Sir."

Hassan turned to one of his men. "Could I borrow your service revolver?" The man smiled, "Sure, Sir." He handed his weapon to Hassan. Knowing what Hassan was likely to do, his men retreated out of the line of fire.

"Is it loaded?" Hassan asked.

"Yes, Sir," the man replied. Tuma saw the gun and began to tremble. Hassan laid the barrel on Tuma's forehead.

"Tuma, you make me sick. If I ever see you again, I will shoot you on sight. Get out of here before I change my mind and shoot you right now. Go!" he shouted. Tuma fled down the hallway.

During this time, the elderly man in the gray suit stood close enough to get a clear view inside the window, yet far enough away that he could not be seen. He stared at the girl in the room. *What have they done to you, my lovely and talented girl?* he thought. *Why would the Americans waste you on something like this? The American military could blow up the entire country without anyone's help. No agent in the world could have accessed the personal quarters of Gaddafi and lived to tell about it, yet here you are. Your body is broken, but I see in your eyes that your mind isn't. After seven hours of torture, you haven't told them anything, have you?*

Chapter Twenty-Eight

LAURA'S EYES WERE blurred and her mind moved slowly, but she raised her head slightly to look through the window at the man who stopped the beating. He was a professional, a high ranking military officer of some kind; maybe Libyan intelligence, but she couldn't keep her focus.

The field medic course Laura had taken at The Farm would have proved its value, except the only thing she felt was pain. She was sure of broken ribs. She had all the symptoms of a concussion; mental confusion, blurred vision and nausea. The headache was tolerable compared with the pain of breathing. Her shoulder was at an odd angle and she was unable to move her arm. Other bones could be broken, but she couldn't tell.

Laura looked down; she was bleeding over her entire body. One of the men who inflicted the earlier beating wore a ring that had dug into her skin. The end of Salima's rifle butt was corrugated and that tore her skin, too. Many of the contusions needed stitches. Yes, she would live given time to heal. Laura didn't know whether she would be given that time.

Her mind began to clear a little, mostly because she kept her head still. Each time she heard a sound, though, she turned her head to watch for another blow. A miracle was needed to save her and just as if God answered a prayer, Jacques, Henri and a nurse entered the room.

Jacques and Henri were put to work carrying medical supplies in and out of the room while the nurse began by laying her on the table and covering her with a blanket. There was plenty to do. Relief from the pain was her first treatment, the most important aspect of addressing broken ribs. Whatever she was given was strong enough to dull the pain. In about twenty minutes, she was able to breathe while the nurse worked on a myriad of other injuries.

Laura tried to question Jacques, but he asked that she put everything out of her mind for a while. When she asked similar questions of Henri, he stroked her head and told her things were going to be fine. Laura put her faith in the hands of her allies and stopped thinking for a while.

When the wheelchair arrived, the nurse took her into the restroom where Laura had a chance to use a toilet. The nurse gave her a sponge bath and dressed her wounds. Several needed stitches, but none so large they couldn't be addressed in the restroom. After the nurse applied bandages, the bleeding slowed. Laura's arm was put into a sling to immobilize the shoulder. Laura asked the nurse to wash her hair. She had difficulty standing over a sink, but her hair was washed and someone found a blow dryer. Clean clothes were found and after everything had been completed, they used the wheelchair to take Laura into the terminal where she was gently lifted onto a soft cushioned chair inside one of the lounges. She couldn't eat much of the food that was brought, but she drank a great deal of water. Laura was beginning to feel human again. Finally, they allowed her to sleep while Henri stood guard over her.

Major Hassan conferred with Markus Wolf over dinner while the woman slept. "This is the woman from the club, Markus," Hassan said.

"What do you mean?"

"In Gaddafi's secret club on Friday night, she was waiting for Gaddafi to show up. Gaddafi was there to negotiate an energy deal with the Chinese. When he saw this woman, he forgot all about the Chinese. Women have always been Gaddafi's weakness," Hassan said with disgust.

"What did she reveal during her interrogation?" Wolf asked.

"Nothing," Hassan said. "They pounded her for seven hours and she didn't give up a thing."

"I didn't expect she would," Markus said with a smile.

"Here's something surprising. She's got combat skills. That woman nearly killed three guards when she had the opportunity."

Wolf shook his head in amazement. "She's not a normal person, Fareed."

"What do you mean? You know her?" Hassan was surprised.

"Yes. She's one of the best intelligence operatives I've seen in my thirty years of work, Fareed. If I had a hundred like her, I could rule the world. She's Laura Messier, a French woman who works out of the Foreign Ministry in Paris."

Hassan was intrigued by that statement. Hassan worked closely with the DST and had never heard of a French operative named Messier.

"How do you know of her?" Hassan asked.

"The Soviets have a file on her several centimeters thick. They have a code name for her. They call her 'Shewolf.' Don't let her soft appearance fool you, Fareed."

"You've met her?" Hassan asked.

"Yes, once."

"Why is she here?"

"I wish I knew," Wolf said.

"Well, I'm going to find out," Hassan said.

Wolf opened a briefcase, dug to the bottom and pulled out four pictures. "This is as much as I'm prepared to give you, Fareed. It's funny, but I never expected to see her here. Europe is her area," Markus said.

"Who's the man in the picture?"

"The Minister of Foreign Affairs."

"She's beautiful, isn't she," Hassan said.

"Yes," Markus said. Wolf hesitated before his next comment. "Fareed, I've been thinking for quite a while that it's time you and I retired. We've had our time. The world belongs to her generation now. We'll be in capable hands with people like her running things. She's better than both of us. Let her go home, Fareed. The world will be a safer place if you do."

Hassan thought about the comment for a minute. "I want to talk to her first before I agree to release her," Fareed said.

When the nurse gently touched Laura's shoulder, she opened her eyes and looked for a wall clock. It was 6:45. The nurse smiled and Laura nearly cried thanking her for the help. The nurse asked if Laura felt well enough to talk and after Laura nodded, she said a man would come to speak with her shortly.

Hassan walked into the airport lounge to interview Laura Messier at precisely 7:00 p.m. He was impressive at first glance. *He has to be Libyan Intelligence,* Laura thought. There was a presence about him; he carried himself as though he were accustomed to giving orders. He had an air of toughness, but also an intelligent look in his eyes. He was tall and well built, black hair and a nicely groomed mustache. Laura studied his eyes; they didn't communicate much, but they saw everything. Her instinct was that he might be someone she could negotiate with.

"How are you feeling?" Hassan asked, speaking excellent French. He seems genuine, Laura thought.

"I'm feeling better, thank you."

"I am Major Fareed Hassan, Head of Libyan Intelligence."

"Laura Messier, Ministry of Foreign Affairs, Paris."

He got right to the point. "There is a rumor that Gaddafi met a French performer at his club on Friday night," Hassan suggested.

"I'm a terrible performer, Major."

"On the contrary, I believe you are excellent at your job, but perhaps your job is something other than performing," Hassan said.

"Some people judge a book by its cover, don't you think?"

"I think Gaddafi wanted to read the book," Hassan said with a smile. Laura laughed at that, although it hurt her greatly to do so. She grimaced and Hassan saw it. "My apologies for your treatment today," Hassan said with honest compassion.

"Thank you, Major. To answer your question directly, yes, a man named Jean Broussard brought me from Paris to perform at Gaddafi's club," she said.

"But you work for the Foreign Ministry?"

"I do, but I don't make much money, so I work part time for Jean," she said.

"I have some photos I'd like to show you," Hassan said.

Hassan opened a folder and handed them to her. Laura had seen them before; what was it Markus Wolf told her when they met, *I see many things?*

"Where did you get these?" Laura asked.

"Friends," Hassan said. "They appear to be photos of you."

Hassan could only have gotten them from two sources, Laura reasoned, the Soviets and the East Germans. The Soviets had shut the Libyans off so it had to be the East Germans. Laura looked at Hassan for a very long time. He looked back and Laura thought she saw what she needed. She instinctively looked around the room.

"It's clean," Hassan said.

"You catch everything, don't you? You're very good, if you don't mind me saying so."

"I've heard the same about you," Hassan said.

Still, she hesitated for just a minute. In the field of intelligence, sometimes it's necessary to judge a situation by your gut instinct. If agents can't trust their own feel, they'll never survive in the field. "I do not believe you obtained these from the Soviets, so that leaves but one source," she said.

Laura wondered if she'd misread the man. "Yes," Hassan said after hesitating. "We have a close relationship with them on intelligence matters."

"So, they are here?" she asked.

"Yes."

"They are here by coincidence?"

"I would say that is true. Sometimes in intelligence, as in life, it is better to be lucky."

"Lucky for whom?"

"In this case, lucky for you," Hassan said. "If you were Gaddafi's whore, you would simply be sent back to him. No, I'm here because my friend and I suspect there is more here than you are saying. What can you tell me of the photos?"

"Well, the first one is common enough. It was printed in the society pages of Paris newspapers, but this is an original. This is so like the Soviets to sneak around in the middle of the night breaking into locked file cabinets."

"Who's the man in the picture?" Hassan asked.

"He's the French Minister of Foreign Affairs."

"The other photos?"

"This is Soviet work also. I'd recognize it anywhere," Laura answered.

"That's the American Embassy in Paris, isn't it?" Hassan said, pointing to the background in one of the other pictures.

"Yes, I go in the American Embassy through the front door, just like the tourists."

"What were you doing at the Embassy?"

This is where Laura had to give Hassan the stock answer. It didn't matter whether he was a friendly or not. "I'm applying for a visa. I want to move to America where everyone is rich and lives on the beach."

"Ms. Messier, I've decided to release you in a couple of minutes, but I need to ask you something first. Were you sent to kill Gaddafi?"

"No."

"Then what were you looking for in the personal quarters?"

"I found nothing," she said in return. Laura remembered Jean had mentioned a source within the

Libyan military and Jacques mentioned it again last night. *This could be him,* she thought.

Hassan chuckled as though he knew it was a lie. "Yes, I'm sure nothing was found." He looked at his watch. "We should be able to get you on a flight this evening. Before you leave, I'd like to give you an opportunity to speak with a friend."

As Hassan rose to leave, he hesitated. "Once I release you, it isn't finished. You won't be free of him for a while. He has his own apparatus that I don't control. Be careful, Miss Messier, you have a powerful enemy."

"One more thing, if you don't mind, Major?" Laura asked. Hassan turned to face her.

"Yes?"

"Spring is a beautiful time to visit Europe. Perhaps it's time for a vacation."

Hassan gave Laura a wry smile. "Interesting you should say that. My family and I were planning an extended vacation starting tomorrow, as a matter of fact."

"Glad to hear it. Enjoy your trip," she said.

With that, Hassan walked out and spoke with Markus, "I'm sure she'd like to see you."

Hassan approached Jacques and Henri, sitting outside the room. He spoke in hushed tones, "Jacques, I'm releasing her, but we need to get her on a flight tonight. She has an enemy. I have this area locked down so he can't get to her, but he has people in other places. My men will shadow you to the gate. Send Henri on the flight with her." He turned to one of his men, "Can I borrow your service revolver?"

"Yes, Sir," the man said.

"Henri, here, take this on the flight, just in case."

"Thank you, Fareed," Henri said.

Hassan turned to his men, "Book the woman on the next flight out tonight. Send our people to the control tower. No one gets in or out of that tower until her flight leaves. Do you understand? No one!" His men nodded, "Yes, Sir."

Chapter Twenty-Nine

MARKUS WALKED INTO the room with a smile. He spoke in German, "Hello, my friend."

"You know, I'm beginning to think of you as a father, Markus."

"I would have been proud to have you as a daughter," he said.

"Hassan told me the room was clean, but I can't be sure. You came up during World War II, didn't you?"

"Yes, I did," Markus said with a smile as though he knew what Laura was suggesting.

"Then you still remember the old ways?"

Markus smiled, "I'll be right back."

He walked out and asked for pen and paper. He returned and handed them to her. Laura began to write in Morse Code.

"Much safer, I think," she wrote in Morse.

"I'm sorry I couldn't be here sooner. I had no idea it was you," Markus wrote back.

"You saved my life, Markus. They were ready to send me back to Gaddafi," she wrote, showing Markus a fair amount of relief in her face.

"Doucet called me and told me you were here," Markus replied.

"Thank you, Markus."

"You don't need to say it."

"I know, but it needs to be said. The Soviets have shut these people off. How close are you?"

"Publicly, we'll continue to support them, of course, but I'm here to wrap things up. Privately, we're shutting off intelligence," Markus said.

"It seems odd to say this, but Gaddafi is making allies of us."

"Quite right, Shewolf. No one condones the murder of innocent people. Terrorism will become the battleground of the future," Markus said.

Hassan stepped away and used a pay phone in the lobby. "Are you getting this?" Hassan asked.

"They're not talking, Sir."

"What did you say?"

"Neither of them is talking."

"Thank you."

Markus continued. "They should have never sent you. This was an impossible mission. You are the first woman to ever come out of that compound alive."

"I almost didn't make it."

"Gaddafi will send people after you, you know," Markus said with the concern of a father on his face.

"Hassan said the same thing," she said flatly.

"We will watch him for you. You're familiar with the spot where your CIA leaves messages?" Markus asked.

"You know about the chalk marks?" she asked with a smile.

"Yes. I'll write mine in blue chalk. If you see my mark on your way home, don't enter the apartment. You see it on the way to work, take a taxi. Don't leave yourself vulnerable by walking. It would be advisable, I think, to take a vacation in the States once this is over," Markus said.

"Then I have a message for you," she said. "After 6:00 p.m. tomorrow evening, do not go anywhere near a Libyan military installation. You will not be safe."

Markus smiled. "Thank you, Shewolf. Perhaps you have saved my life." Markus looked at his watch. "They're getting ready to put you on a flight."

"Thank you for not giving them my entire file, Markus," she said.

Wolf leaned over and kissed her on the cheek. "I would never do that to you. Take care, Shewolf." As quickly as he'd come, he vanished.

Laura spent a few minutes converting the dots and dashes into math symbols and letters. She left the pages on the table. Laura laughed. *It'll take them quite a while to decipher it,* she thought.

The call came from the airport to Gaddafi's private office line at 8:30 p.m. "You have information on the woman?" Gaddafi asked.

"Yes, Sir. Major Hassan released her to fly out of the country tonight on a flight at 9:00 p.m.," the voice said.

"Stop the flight. Pull her off and bring her to me."

"I don't know if we can, Sir," Gaddafi's man said. "Major Hassan has established a perimeter around the gate. We can't get to her," Gaddafi's man said.

"Access the control tower and tell them the flight cannot be allowed to leave."

"Sir, Hassan has secured the tower."

"Do not provoke a confrontation with Hassan's men," Gaddafi said. "He will release the tower after the flight takes off. Get in there and have them turn the flight around. Just in case we can't stop it, get two men on the plane. Their orders are to kill the woman in Paris. Do you understand?"

"Yes, Sir, we'll get it done."

"Have Hassan call me immediately." Gaddafi said.

Chapter Thirty

JACQUES, HENRI AND the nurse accompanied Laura to the gate for Air France Flight 642 to Paris, exactly twelve hours after she tried to board a flight earlier that morning. Six of Hassan's men walked with them to the gate, one far ahead, four around them and one trailing. Laura watched them, eyes searching for threats. Their manner showed competence and discipline; she felt safe.

The Paris route was lightly traveled late in the evening and with few passengers sitting in the gate area, the two men seated along the opposite wall were conspicuous. Henri spotted them, too. Laura whispered, "Henri, what do you think of the two men sitting over there?"

"Libyan State Security," Henri said with a shrug. "Gaddafi's men. I'll tell Jacques and he'll have them picked up at de Gaulle."

Jacques walked over and handed Henri boarding passes and ticket receipts. He handed Laura the Irene Thomas ID and passport as well. "Here, you'll need these," he said. Henri motioned for Jacques to come close. "Have those two picked up in Paris," he said, looking across the gate area. "They're Libyan State Security." Jacques nodded and patted Laura on the shoulder. "You'll be fine, Ms. Messier. Don't worry."

"Thank you so very much, Jacques, for everything."

Jacques squeezed her hand, "Good luck, Laura." She had grown fond of these two men. Jacques was smart and polished; he handled himself well in difficult situations.

Henri was rough on the outside, but underneath he was a gentle and kind soul.

Hassan's men moved alongside them as the flight attendant announced boarding would start with special needs passengers of which Laura was the only one. As they boarded the plane, Henri flashed his National Gendarmerie badge and opened his jacket to expose his sidearm. The flight attendant gave him permission to carry it on board. The nurse administered two additional pain pills, Laura's wheelchair was rolled down the ramp and Henri helped her into a first class window seat in the second row. Henri slid into the aisle seat next to her. This was a Boeing 737-200; the first class seats were partitioned off from coach. Laura felt safer knowing coach passengers could not access first class during the flight. Laura stiffened when Gaddafi's men walked down the aisle. Henri withdrew his service weapon and placed it between himself and the arm rest, but no trouble occurred as the Libyans moved through first class into the coach section. The entry door was sealed, the flight attendants gave the usual speech about safety and the pilot swung the aircraft away from the gate.

As the plane taxied on the tarmac, Laura saw the flight ahead take off as they turned onto the runway. In the cockpit, the radio was active. "Air France Flight 642, this is Tripoli Air Traffic Control, you are now cleared for takeoff."

"Roger, Tripoli Control," the pilot said.

Laura felt the rush of acceleration. After lift-off, she heard the landing gear secure itself inside the fuselage.

"Flight 642, increase speed to 300 knots, climb to 5,000 feet and maintain course 180," flight control said.

"Roger, Tripoli Control."

In the control tower, the manager opened the control room door and spoke to Hassan's men who stood outside the room.

"Flight 642 has taken off, Sir."

"Thank you. Have a nice evening." Hassan's men pushed the down button on the elevator. Two men took the elevator down, while two others took the stairs to make sure the stairwell was clear.

"Air France Flight 642, this is Tripoli Control. Turn right to a heading of 320."

"Roger that, Tripoli Control," the pilot said.

"Increase speed to 400 knots and climb to 15,000 feet."

"Roger, Tripoli Control. Turn right to a heading of 320, increase speed to 400 knots and climb to 15,000 feet." the pilot said.

Two of Hassan's men got off the tower elevator at the ground floor. Gaddafi's men began to move, but their leader held them back. "Stop! Four men went up. Wait for the other two to come down."

Laura looked out the window and noticed the darkness ahead of the plane, the Mediterranean Sea.

"Air France Flight 642, you are cleared to climb to your cruising altitude of 32,000 feet. Increase speed to 475 knots. Maintain heading at 320. We will be turning control over to Blue Med FAB in five minutes."

"Roger, Tripoli Control. Have a nice evening," the pilot responded.

"You, too. Tripoli Control over and out."

Flight attendants unbuckled themselves and began preparing drink service. Pilot Claude Levron, a Frenchman with twenty years of commercial experience, loosened his tie and turned control of the craft over to his English co-pilot, Alex Harrison. Levron spoke through his headset to his head attendant, "Pam, we are in serious need of some coffee up here." Pam laughed, "Right away, Sir."

After Hassan's men exited the Control Tower stairway and walked away, four of Gaddafi's men disguised in flight controller shirts took the elevator to the control room.

"Air France Flight 642, good evening. This is Blue Med FAB Control. We'll be with you until we turn you over to FABEC later this evening. Maintain present heading, course and speed."

"Thank you, Blue Med. It's a beautiful night for flying, Blue Med," Alex Harrison said.

"Yes, Sir, it certainly is. Have a safe trip, 642."

"Roger that, Blue Med," Harrison responded.

"Hey, Pam?" Harrison said into the intercom. "Could you bring up a couple of sandwiches along with the coffee?"

"Certainly, Sir," she said. "Coming right up."

Gaddafi's men pounded on the locked door to the control room. The manager answered the door. "Libyan State Security," their leader said as all four pushed their way into the control room with guns drawn. "Has Flight 642 taken off yet?"

"Yes, Sir." The surprised manager looked at his watch, "Ten minutes ago." The leader pointed his gun at the head of the manager.

"Get on the radio and order them back to the airport. Now!" he shouted.

The manager turned to his staff, "Everyone, stay calm." He walked over to the controller who had handled Flight 642, "Do as he says."

The bewildered air traffic controller turned on his intercom. "Air France Flight 642, this is Tripoli Air Traffic Control. We request you immediately turn around and land back at Tripoli International."

Alex Harrison, who had already turned on autopilot, looked at Levron. "What the hell is going on, Captain?"

"I'm not sure, Alex. Any malfunction with the plane?" Harrison and Levron looked across the instrument panel.

"Nothing, Captain. All systems are nominal."

"What's our position?" Levron asked."

"We're exactly on course. Heading 320, 475 knots at 32,000 feet. We're inside Blue Med's territory."

"Don't do anything yet; let me find out what's going on."

Levron spoke to Tripoli Control. "Tripoli Control, this is Air France Flight 642. Would you say again?"

"Air France Flight 642, this is Tripoli Control. We request you turn around and land back at Tripoli International."

"Tripoli Control, give us a moment."

"What should we do, Captain?" Harrison asked.

"Contact Blue Med and ask them what's going on."

Harrison picked up his microphone, "Blue Med FAB, this is Air France Flight 642. Tripoli Control has requested we turn around and land back at Tripoli International Airport."

"Flight 642, this is Blue Med. That is a negative. I repeat, that is a negative. You are not cleared to turn around and land. You have traffic on both sides of you. Continue your present course and speed. I repeat, continue your present course and speed."

"Roger, Blue Med and out," Harrison said. "What do you want to do, Captain?"

Levron spoke to his co-pilot, "We're going to continue the flight plan. Let me handle Tripoli Control."

"Tripoli Control," Levron said. "This is Air France Flight 642. We do not have Blue Med's permission to turn around due to traffic in the area. We will continue our present course and speed. Have a good evening. Over and out." The radio fell silent.

"That was weird," Harrison said, after waiting for a response.

Levron shrugged and pressed his intercom. "Pam, how we doing on the sandwiches and coffee?"

"Coming in right now, Captain."

"I guess we ought to do the opening announcement," Levron said. He turned on the cabin intercom.

"Ladies and gentlemen," Levron said over the intercom, "This is Captain Claude Levron speaking. Welcome to Air France Flight 642 with non-stop service to Charles de Gaulle Airport in Paris, France. We're currently cruising at 32,000 feet, 475 knots and you're free to unbuckle your seat belts and move about the cabin. The weather is calm and we expect no delays into Paris this evening. We're looking at an approximate flight time of two hours and fifty minutes. Our flight attendants will be coming through the cabin with drink service shortly. Thank you for flying with us at Air France."

"Henri, would you order a double bourbon on the rocks for me?" Laura put her hand on Henri's arm.

"Are you sure, Ms. Messier? You're on some very strong pain medication."

"Yes, I'm very sure, Henri, and call me Laura."

As the attendant handed Laura the drink, Laura asked, "Do you have any sandwiches for my husband?"

"Of course, ma'am," she said as she looked at Henri. "We have ham and turkey with Swiss on rye."

"I'll take two of them," Henri said. As the flight attendant walked up the aisle, Henri said, "That was very thoughtful of you, Laura. I completely forgot to eat dinner."

"Don't worry, I'll pay for it," she said.

Henri laughed, "It's free in first class."

"Why do you think I offered?"

Laura sipped her drink and leaned her head on Henri's broad shoulder. The pain reliever had begun to take effect and when she closed her eyes, she felt safe for the first time in days.

As Hassan walked out of the terminal, Gaddafi's man approached. Hassan's men moved in front of Hassan to protect him. "Sir, I have a message from the Commander," the man said. Hassan turned to his men, "Let him approach."

"What do you want?" Hassan asked with a snarl.

"The Commander would like to speak with you immediately."

Hassan pushed them aside, said nothing and continued out the door. Once in his car, he called Gaddafi's private number.

"Sir, Hassan here. You wish to speak with me?"

"Yes, Major, why did you allow the woman to leave? I ordered her to be brought to the compound," Gaddafi said.

Hassan adopted the matter of fact tone he often used with Gaddafi. "Sir, that woman was a danger to you. Earlier today, she nearly killed three airport security guards with her bare hands. We didn't have the opportunity to investigate her in advance. I sent her out of the country to protect you. She isn't worth the risk."

Gaddafi thought for a minute. *There's no use getting into a fight with Hassan over a woman.*

"I see. I'm sure you are quite right. Thank you, Hassan."

Gaddafi leaned back in his chair. *Hassan is probably right,* he reasoned. *I was a fool to give her the stone. I'll have Assaf force her to call Doucet before he kills her.*

Nearly three hours later, Laura awoke at the sound of the warning bell from the airplane intercom. The cabin lights came up and Captain Levron came on the intercom, "Flight attendants, please prepare the cabin."

Pam, the head flight attendant, followed with instructions shortly after. "Ladies and gentlemen, the Captain has turned on the 'Fasten Seatbelts' sign and we have started our descent into Paris, France. Please make sure your seat backs and tray tables are in their full and upright position. Make sure your seat belt is securely fastened and all carry-on luggage is stowed underneath the seat in front of you or in the overhead bins. Flight attendants will be coming through the cabin to pick up any remaining cups and glasses."

"Wow, I slept the entire flight," Laura said.

Henri chuckled, "You needed the sleep. How are you feeling?"

"Tired and I've started hurting again."

"You had a rough day," Henri said.

"It was a rough one for you as well."

"Unfortunately, I missed watching you put a bunch of security guards in the hospital. I would have loved to have seen that," Henri said with a smile.

"They beat me up pretty badly after that."

"They were going to beat you up anyway. Maybe I can mete out a little French justice on the Libyans back in coach for you," Henri suggested.

Captain Levron came on the intercom. "Ladies and gentlemen, we're on final approach to Charles de Gaulle airport. We should have you at the gate in a couple of minutes. Thank you for flying with Air France."

After touchdown, Laura felt the engines reverse. The plane slowed, turned onto the tarmac at the end of the runway and began taxiing to the gate. "Ladies and gentlemen, welcome to Paris, France, where the temperature is 9° Celsius and the local time is 12:20 a.m.," the captain said.

As the plane pulled into the gate area, the captain was once again on the intercom. "Ladies and gentlemen, we are experiencing some minor difficulty. We're going to have to stop about 100 meters short of the gate. We need to ask you to deplane using the front exit down the stairs to the tarmac where you'll have to walk a short distance to the terminal building. Air France personnel will be at the bottom of the stairs to assist you. We apologize for the inconvenience."

Laura looked out the window and saw two American Embassy cars sitting on the tarmac with four United States Marines standing by. She pointed out the window, "Look, Henri."

Henri looked out the window, "You're going to be well cared for, Laura."

"Why don't you come to the embassy with me," she suggested. "They have a nice room where you can rest for your flight back in the morning."

"Thanks, Laura, but I've got to follow the Libyans through customs. I want to make sure they're apprehended."

The plane stopped, the warning bell sounded and attendants opened the front exit door. Laura felt the cool outside air in the cabin. Henri helped her out of her seat and blocked the aisle to prevent other passengers from pushing by. Laura gingerly made her way to the front exit where the attendant smiled and said, "Thank you for flying with us this evening."

She glanced down the stairs. She hesitated; it was impossible to manage them alone. Henri helped her from behind and a Marine came running up the stairs to support her. At the bottom, all four Marines surrounded Laura and escorted her to one of the waiting cars. Henri walked alongside and watched as she was helped into the car. He leaned in the door, "Laura, I've got to track down the Libyans, so I'll catch up to you later. Good luck."

"Thank you so very much, Henri, for everything." Laura reached out, touched his hand and he ran back to the plane.

Once in the embassy car, Laura looked up at one of the Marines and discovered it was Rick Williams, her friend who led the security detail at the embassy. "Rick, what are you doing here?"

"I thought you might need to see a friendly face, Laura." Rick put his arm around her. "We were informed of your condition," Rick said. "You're safe now. No one can harm you. We're here to protect you with our lives if it comes to that."

Laura leaned against him and tears welled up in her eyes. "There, there, Miss Laura," Rick said gently. "We've got to get you healed up so you can fix my biscuits and gravy." She looked up at him, kissed his cheek, and whispered, "Thank you, Rick."

Chapter Thirty-One

HENRI THOMAS RAN back to the plane and bounded up the stairs two at a time. The cockpit door was open, the pilots were preparing to leave and the attendants were in the rear of the plane. Henri looked in the front galley and the two restrooms. Captain Claude Levron walked out of the cockpit.

"Can I help you?" he said.

"Henri Thomas, National Gendarmerie." Henri flashed his badge.

"Can I assist you, officer?" Levron asked.

"Are there any passengers left on board?"

Levron walked a few steps down the aisle and called to the head attendant.

"Pam, would you check the back galley and restrooms to make sure everyone's off the plane?" he asked.

"Yes, Sir. Just a moment."

Pam checked the rear of the plane and then walked up the aisle.

"Captain, no one is left back here," she said.

"Thank you very much, Captain," Henri said.

Henri bolted down the stairs, looked underneath the fuselage, and then ran toward the terminal. Before entering the doors, he looked up and down the tarmac for anyone walking away. Henri displayed his badge to the door attendant, "Have all passengers gone up the stairs?"

"Yes, Sir. No one's left down here," the attendant said.

"Thank you." Henri ran up the stairs.

The gate area was empty, except for one man standing near the check-in counter. As Henri approached him, the man flashed a badge, "Mr. Thomas?"

"Yes, and you are?"

"Paul Perrin, DST. The men you're looking for are walking up the concourse toward customs."

"Is there any way they can avoid customs?" Henri asked, pointing up the concourse.

"No, Sir. We have our agents waiting for them at the end of the concourse. They'll follow the suspects through baggage claim, then through customs and apprehend them once they're in the terminal."

"Did anyone walk the other direction?" Henri asked.

"No, everyone went up the concourse."

"Okay, walk it with me. You take one side, I'll take the other. Let's check every door. Do you have an adequate description of the men?"

"Yes, Sir; I saw them. The one with the beard is wearing a blue jacket, the one with the mustache is wearing a tan jacket," Perrin said.

"Good, let's do our search."

Finding no one, save for a few stragglers in the restrooms, Henri and Perrin moved up the concourse near the baggage carousels.

"They carried no bags, Perrin. Let's check baggage claim, anyway," Henri said.

"Yes, Sir."

They worked their way through baggage claim and not finding the men, they moved on to customs.

"There! See him?" Perrin asked. "Tan jacket. He's in line at customs."

"Yes," Henri said, "I've got him."

"The man behind him is DST. We've got that one."

"Where's the other one?" Henri asked.

Perrin glanced around the area. "He may have cleared customs."

"Let's walk through."

"Yes, Sir," Perrin said.

Both men walked through customs flashing their badges. Once beyond customs, Henri approached DST personnel. "Did you see a man with a beard and blue coat?" Henri asked.

"No, Sir. No one fitting that description has left customs. He's probably still in line," the man said.

"Anyone with a beard walk though?"

"One man, but he didn't fit the description," the officer said.

"Thank you." *Shit,* Henri whispered to himself. "Come on, Perrin, let's search the terminal."

They raced through the terminal and saw no one fitting the description. Henri looked out the windows over the street. He saw a man with a beard getting into a taxi. *No blue coat, though.*

"He took off his coat, Perrin. There he is!" Henri ran to the nearest exit, then back up the sidewalk to the taxi stand as the taxi pulled away from the curb. He caught the taxi number on the license plate. Perrin followed him outside.

"Call your supervisor. Tell him taxi number 446 must be stopped before it leaves the airport," Henri shouted. Perrin pulled the radio from his jacket and made the request.

"Let's go back inside and see if they've got the other fellow," Henri said. As they walked into the terminal,

Perrin heard back on the radio that the taxi had been stopped. The taxi was empty.

"Damn!" Henri said. "Secure the other suspect for questioning. I'll be with you in a minute."

"Yes, Sir," Perrin replied.

Henri walked back up the sidewalk where he had seen the taxi pull away. *Slow things down in your mind,* Henri thought. *What did you actually see?* He searched his memory as though studying a photo. *The man walking across the street with his back toward me. No coat. Can't see whether he has a beard. Why would anyone walk across the street? There's nothing on the other side.*

Henri stood there, analyzing his memory for the man's height, weight and gait. *Why isn't the man wearing a coat? It's nine degrees. Everyone's wearing a jacket. That's got to be him. He took off his coat walking up the concourse, stuffed it in a waste bin. He hurried to get in front of the other passengers, skipped baggage and was the first person through customs. He walked out of the terminal, got in a taxi, immediately got out the opposite door and walked across the street.*

Henri walked into the terminal toward customs and stopped the first security officer he saw.

"Excuse me, I'm Henri Thomas, National Gendarmerie." He flashed his badge. "Was a man in a tan coat apprehended outside customs?"

"Yes, Sir. He's been taken to the detention area for questioning." He pointed down the terminal.

"Thanks," Henri said. Henri walked through the terminal and found the detention area.

"Captain Marcel Lamont, Police Nationale. May I help you?"

"I'm Henri Thomas, National Gendarmerie." Henri showed his badge. "I'm looking for a suspect with a mustache wearing a tan coat, Middle Eastern descent. He just got off a flight from Libya."

"Yes, Sir. DST has him in one of the detention rooms down the hall," Lamont said.

Walking down the hall, he found Perrin. "You got the bastard, Perrin?" Henri asked.

"Yes, Sir." He pointed in the window of the nearest room. Henri walked to the window and saw the man sitting quietly at a table. "He traveled in on this," Perrin said as he handed Henri a Swiss passport. Henri studied it.

"This is likely forged," Henri said.

"Yes, that's what we're thinking, too."

"What's your plan?" Henri asked.

"We probably won't get much out of him," Perrin said. "We'll take him to the lock-up, print him and send the prints to Interpol to see what they've got on him. We'll contact the Swiss tomorrow and check the validity of the passport. We're going to hold him temporarily on illegal entry. What happened to the other man?"

"We lost him. Can you put out an alert based on his description?" Henri asked.

"We already have, Sir. We'll watch the hotels in case he shows up."

"Thanks. Can you have someone search the trash bins along the concourse. They're looking for a blue jacket."

"Of course, Sir. We'll do it right away," Perrin said.

"Thanks. I'm going to check into the Marriott downtown for the night. Call me with updates. Otherwise, I'll be at headquarters in the morning."

"Thank you, Sir. Good night," Perrin said.

On the way out of the terminal, Henri stopped at a pay phone as an afterthought. He dialed DST headquarters and asked to be patched through to the CIA station inside the American Embassy.

"Operations, may I help you?" the voice asked.

"Henri Thomas, National Gendarmerie calling regarding Ms. Messier. Is your station chief available?"

"Yes, Sir, just a moment please."

John Brownley picked up the line. "Brownley."

"Sir, this is Henri Thomas, National Gendarmerie calling. I accompanied Ms. Messier on her flight this evening. Is she back to the embassy yet?"

"No, not yet," Brownley said.

"I suspect a Libyan assassination squad is looking for her. One of the suspects is presently at large. Please take the necessary precautions."

"Thank you, Mr. Thomas. We'll be careful."

"I'll be in town for a few days while we try to apprehend the suspect. I'll be in touch."

"Okay," Brownley said, then he hung up.

Brownley immediately dialed the embassy car phone. "This is Brownley, can I speak with Rick Williams?"

"Yes, Sir," the driver stretched the phone over the seat. "Captain Williams, Chief Brownley calling," he said.

"Hello, this is Rick Williams."

"Rick, this is John. There could be trouble on your way in. Be careful."

"Thank you, Sir. We're about ten minutes out. We'll see you shortly," Rick said.

It was past midnight when Gaddafi's phone rang in his bedroom. "Yes, what's the problem?" Gaddafi asked sleepily.

"We had no chance to get the woman, Colonel. They stopped the plane on the tarmac and U.S. military pulled her off.

"She's CIA?" Gaddafi asked.

"That's what I'm thinking, Sir," Ghalib Assaf said. "She's going to be heavily guarded. I don't think I can get to her."

"I'm calling in a specialist. I'll have Rashid Nazari contact you in the morning."

"Have him call the embassy. I'll stop there once I find where they take her."

"I want her dead, Assaf, as soon as possible," Gaddafi said emphatically.

"I'll wait for Nazari's call, Sir."

"Thank you, Assaf."

Asila's CIA, Gaddafi thought. "The American President sent her to assassinate me," he said out loud. Gaddafi laughed. "She was too weak to even make an attempt; too frightened, just like her president. Reagan is a coward and a fool."

Chapter Thirty-Two

AS THE EMBASSY vehicles pulled onto the grounds, Laura glanced at Rick's watch. It was late, after 1:00 a.m. Only a few security lights were on outside the buildings; the grounds were quiet and empty. Under normal circumstances, she'd never come to the embassy at night. The driver pulled around behind the main structure underneath a portico that sheltered visitors. The lighting was low, just two lights underneath the portico and one in the entryway. Rick and his colleague got out first. Laura noticed Rick had the flap unbuttoned on his sidearm. This was a serious side of Rick she'd never seen; head up, eyes moving, hand resting on the hilt of his service weapon, alert for danger. The two Marines in the car that followed got out, service weapons drawn, and established a position at each end of the portico.

The entrance was not visible from the street. Laura saw no danger, but the Marines were taking no chances. Rick left the car door open and Laura started to move. Rick reached in the car and pressed his hand into her shoulder,

"Not yet." She sensed the seriousness in his voice.

Rick spoke to the guard at the doorway, "We good here?"

"You're good, bring her on in," he said.

"Okay, Laura, we're clear. Let's get you out." Rick gently helped her out of the car. He seemed to understand she was in pain. "You doing okay so far?"

"I'm fine, Rick" she said. Laura wasn't, but there was nothing else to say. Rick decided to pick her up. "Do you mind?" he asked.

"Not at all. Thank you."

Rick carried her in the entrance and down the hall to the back elevator. There was a guard there, too. He held the elevator door open and said, "Take her on up, Captain." Rick punched the button, the door closed and Laura felt the elevator move. It was quiet, only the hum of the elevator motor could be heard. The two lights overhead in the elevator cast a shadow on Rick's face. He looked down at her.

"You still okay, Laura?"

"Not really, Rick."

"I know," he said gently. Laura had developed a fondness for Rick over the years she'd known him.

When Laura looked at Rick, she saw a man who knew something about pain. She wondered where life had taken him that he had developed such empathy. She heard the elevator bell, the doors parted and another uniformed officer stood in the hallway. He held the elevator door, while Rick carried her down the hallway to Brownley's office.

Brownley moved from behind his desk as Rick entered the room. Rick motioned for him to stand out of the way. "I've got her, Sir."

"Here." Brownley motioned to the sofa, "Let's put her here."

Rick gently set her down on the sofa where she'd sat many times over the last few years.

"Laura, can I get you anything?" Rick asked.

"Water please." Someone she didn't recognize handed her a glass of water.

"Will there be anything else, Sir," Rick asked Brownley.

"No, thank you." Rick started to leave.

"Wait," Laura said. Rick stopped. "Please don't leave." Rick made her feel safe; she wanted him there. Rick looked up and Brownley nodded.

Brownley sat down opposite Laura. She saw a certain tenderness in his eyes she'd never seen before. *Wow,* she thought, *I must really look like shit.*

"Laura, this is Dr. Humboldt, our physician here at the embassy," Brownley said.

"Hi Doctor." Laura turned to look at him.

"Be still. Please don't move." Humboldt said. He looked at Brownley.

"I need to do a brief exam. Help me get the coffee table out of the way."

They slid the coffee table away and the doctor came around in front of her, kneeled and spoke to Rick standing behind her.

"We need to clear the room."

Brownley spoke to everyone in the room. "Heads up, people. You need to exit the room."

"You too, Mr. Brownley," Humboldt said.

"Not you, Rick," Laura said.

"Not to worry, Ms. Messier. I'm not going anywhere."

A nurse accompanied Humboldt. She began taking vital signs while the doctor gently began his work without moving her around. He asked about the bandages, her ribs and shoulder; he looked at her head wound. He asked the nurse, "What do her vitals look like?"

"140 over 90, pulse 110, and she's hot, 102°."

"Thank you."

He started to move her legs apart. "Do you mind me taking a look?"

"No, Sir."

He pushed up Laura's skirt and saw blood stains.

"I need to ask you a sensitive question if I may. Were you raped?"

Laura looked away and said nothing. Her expression betrayed her.

"Ms. Messier, rapes are not the fault of the victim. This is confidential information. No one will know," Humboldt said.

Laura tried to speak the words, but nothing would come. Tears appeared in her eyes. Her reaction told Humboldt what he needed to know. "It's okay. We can talk about it later," Humboldt said. The doctor turned to his nurse, "We need to get an IV going. And call an ambulance. We've got to get her to the hospital."

"Yes, Sir. Right away."

Humboldt continued to question her.

"Have you noticed blood in your urine?" he asked.

"Yes," Laura replied.

"Do you feel light-headed?"

"Yes. It hurts to breath."

Humboldt gently laid his hand on her ribcage. "Does it hurt here?"

"Oh God, yes. Please don't touch it. Doctor, the nurse in Tripoli gave me pain medication. It's in my purse. Could someone retrieve it for me?"

The medication was found, the doctor inspected it and handed them to the nurse. "Go ahead and give her two."

The nurse washed her arm in alcohol. "This will feel like a small pin prick," she said as she inserted the IV into her arm. She stood up and adjusted the drip. Humboldt closed her clothing and walked to the office door.

"Mr. Brownley, we're taking her to American Hospital."

"Is she able to talk?" Brownley asked. "We need to talk with her briefly."

Laura did not turn around, but said loudly, "Doctor, please let them in. I need to tell them something."

Chapter Thirty-Three

IT WAS JUST past 8:00 p.m. on Sunday night at Langley and Bill Casey was sitting at his desk, reading. CIA kept a skeleton staff on weekends and most had gone home for the evening. Casey had driven into the office to receive reports about Messier. Only he and his secretary were left on the executive floor. When the direct line into Casey's office rang, Casey picked it up himself.

"Yes?"

"She's at the embassy," the voice said.

"How is she?" Casey asked.

"She's hurt."

"How badly?"

"We don't know yet, but she's conscious and speaking," the voice said.

"Thank you." Casey hung up. Casey dialed the White House and spoke with Don Regan who informed the President. Regan called Casey back. "The President wants to know if she brought the information out."

"We don't know yet, Don. I should be able to answer that when the next update comes in," Casey said.

"I'll inform the President."

Chapter Thirty-Four

JOHN BROWNLEY CAME back into the room with two military men Laura had never met. She felt Rick begin to move away.

"Rick, please stay."

"Okay, Miss Messier."

"Thank you," she said.

"Laura, this is General James Mattern, United States European Command, from NATO headquarters in Brussels," Brownley said. He turned to the second man. "This is Vice Admiral Sam Johnson, United States Navy, Sixth Fleet," he said, motioning with his hand.

"Would you gentlemen mind sitting down?" Laura asked. "It's a little hard for me to look up at you."

General Mattern smiled, "Yes, of course." Everyone took seats where she could see them without difficulty.

"John," she said, looking at Brownley. "Would you please hand me a piece of paper and a pen?"

He retrieved a yellow legal pad and pen from his desk. Laura spoke to Mattern. "General, you're looking for a series of numbers. Is that correct?"

"Yes, Ma'am."

"I found them in Gaddafi's personal briefcase on a laminated code sheet which looked identical to the one I saw in photos at Langley," she said as she began to write.

"I'm surprised you were able to get that close to him," the General said.

"It wasn't pleasant, believe me."

"I apologize for interrupting you, Ma'am. Please go on," General Mattern said.

"You're expecting to see six numbers, each number containing six digits."

"Yes, that's right."

"That's fortunate because I would hate to have gone to all this trouble to bring back the wrong fucking numbers." Laura smiled.

That released some of the stress in the room. Everyone smiled at her. She handed them to General Mattern. "What level of confidence do you have that these are correct, Ma'am?"

"Those are the correct numbers, General. I've written them here exactly as I saw them on the code sheet. The title of the document was written in Arabic, but the designation S-200 was written on it in English. If you want that radar and missile system shut down, Sir, that's the information you need."

"Thank you, Ms. Messier. Do you mind if I ask you a few other questions?" Mattern asked.

"Go ahead," she said.

"Were you interrogated?"

"Yes."

"Did you reveal your identity?"

"No."

"Did they know what you were after?" the General asked.

"No."

"Can you remember the floor plan of the Gaddafi residence?" Mattern asked.

"Yes," Laura said. "Here, hand me the pad back and I'll draw it for you."

As she drew the diagram, Laura said, "I wasn't in every room, but most of them. He keeps a separate residence for his family above ground in another building, but his office and personal quarters are where he spends most of his time." She handed the drawing to Mattern.

"This is inside the Azizia complex?" Mattern asked.

"Yes, the entrance I used was about 150 meters from the front gate." Laura pointed to the drawing. "It's this entrance here. The other end is connected to a large tunnel system. Gaddafi can leave his quarters that way, too."

"Can you talk more about the tunnel system?" the General asked.

"I was in the tunnels briefly. They extend for miles in every direction. Gaddafi uses golf carts to travel in the tunnels."

The General asked about each room on the diagram. "This room," he said, pointing to the floor plan, "is Gaddafi's office?"

"Yes."

"Is that where you found the codes?" Mattern asked.

"No, Sir, I found them in his bedroom." She pointed to Gaddafi's bedroom on the floor plan.

The General hesitated. "Were you were recorded by any video surveillance when you accessed the briefcase?" Mattern asked.

"No. Gaddafi doesn't keep recording equipment in his bedroom," Laura said.

Mattern looked embarrassed. "I'm sorry, Ma'am. I was only trying to find out whether you might have been seen."

"There was no one in the damn bedroom when I opened the briefcase, General," Laura said, raising her voice. "No, I was not seen."

"Once again, I apologize, Ms. Messier. I only have one other question if you'd care to answer. Do you have any personal impressions of Gaddafi you'd like to share?"

Laura looked General Mattern straight in the eye. "General, the man's a monster. Kill him."

The General hesitated for a moment. "We're not intentionally targeting Gaddafi, Ma'am. We would not be unhappy, though, if he were accidentally killed."

"Well, if you don't accidentally kill him, I'm going back to intentionally kill him," Laura said harshly. The General didn't know quite how to respond. Laura continued, "The bombing is tomorrow night?"

The General looked at his watch, "Yes, Ma'am. We're about fifteen hours away from wheels up," he said. "You got here just in time. Ms. Messier, we have the information we need." The officers stood up to leave. "You'll have to excuse us. This information is time sensitive. I want to thank you on behalf of the Armed Forces of the United States." He reached out and held her hand. "At great sacrifice to yourself, you are saving the lives of hundreds of American military personnel. Thank you, again, and I wish you the best of luck."

Laura glanced at the clock, it was 2:45 a.m. Doctor Humboldt entered the room and said, "Ms. Messier, the ambulance is here. We're moving you to the hospital."

Rick lifted Laura into a wheelchair and moved her downstairs where emergency personnel transferred her to a stretcher. Rick helped load her into the ambulance, then sat with her and held her hand. She noticed he still had his service weapon unbuttoned.

Chapter Thirty-Five

THE CALL CAME in to Langley about 9:00 that evening. Bill Casey picked up and the voice on the other end said, "She brought the intel out with her, Bill."

"And?" Casey asked."

"It's rock solid. She did a great job."

"How is she?" Casey asked.

"They've taken her to the hospital. They beat her up pretty good, Bill. The Libyans didn't get a damn thing out of her. That woman is tough as nails."

"Thank you."

Casey leaned back in his chair for a moment and thought about Messier before picking up the phone. *Clair was right about her.*

He lifted the receiver and dialed the White House where he informed Don Regan of the mission's success.

"Thanks, Bill, that's great news. Any further update on the girl?"

"She's in bad shape, but we think she'll be fine," Casey said.

"The President will be pleased."

Chapter Thirty-Six

RICK WILLIAMS JUMPED out at the emergency room entrance and two uniformed United States Marines stepped out of the car that followed. Rick asked the EMTs to keep Laura in the ambulance momentarily. Rick conferred briefly with the Marines. They drew their weapons, secured the hospital entrance, then Rick motioned for the EMTs to bring Laura inside the building.

After what seemed to be a long examination, the doctor admitted her. The pain had been increasing in intensity. After Laura received an injection, Rick smiled, leaned over and said, "Morphine, Laura. I know the ambulance ride hurt. Hang in there, you'll feel better in a few minutes." It was well past 4:00 a.m. by the time they were ready to move Laura upstairs. As they wheeled the bed into the hallway, Williams asked the nurse, "Where are we going?" The nurse replied, "Room 410."

"Stay behind me. I'll escort you to the room," Rick said with a natural authority in his voice.

United States Marine Captain Rick Williams was accustomed to giving orders. As he walked in front, Laura could see his sidearm was drawn. She recognized the head movement back and forth; it was as though he had taken point on a patrol.

Whenever they'd come to a turn, Rick asked them to stop, he'd peer around the corner, then say, "Clear, follow me." At the elevator, he made sure it was safe. They'd seen absolutely no one on their way upstairs, but Rick took nothing for granted. *He's a pro,* Laura thought; *classic urban warfare tactics.*

After Laura settled in the room, Rick stood over her bed and asked gently. "Laura, whatever you need, I'll make it happen."

"I'll be okay, Rick," she answered trying to hide the pain. "Thank you so much for all you've done."

Rick held her hand, "I'll be back in the morning. Would you like me to stop by your apartment and pick up anything?"

"That would be great. Thank you." Laura listed off a few items.

"How do I get in?"

"The back entrance off the alley; there should be a key lying on top of the door frame."

Rick hesitated a moment. "Laura, I have something to give you." He opened a small black bag strapped to his belt. Laura hadn't noticed it. It wasn't regulation and not the kind of thing she'd have missed under normal circumstances.

"Laura, here's a Sig Sauer P226; it's what we use at the embassy. You've used it at the range a couple of times."

"Yes, I remember."

Rick took a metal cylinder from the bag and screwed it on the weapon. "Here's the suppressor. You'll be able to squeeze off a round or two without waking up the entire hospital."

"Do I actually need a weapon?"

"Probably not, but I'd feel better if you had it," Rick said.

Laura felt the pistol's heavy weight due to the added suppressor. "Remember, there's no safety on the P226."

Rick took it back to show her. "Here's the mag release." He released it, the magazine came loose and he pushed it back in. "It's a double action weapon. It's ready to fire. The mag is fully loaded. Squeezing the trigger mechanism unlocks the weapon and fires it. You'll have to put a bit more pressure on it for the first shot, then after that, it's easier."

"It won't go off if I drop it, will it?"

"No, it's safe enough," Rick said. "Just remember you'll have to squeeze hard the first round. Are you right-handed or left?"

"Left," she replied.

"Then I'm going to slide this under your blanket with the handle facing to the left. If you need it, remember to grab with your left. During the daytime, I doubt you'll have any trouble. You can stow it in the drawer beside your bed, but at night I'd put it right on your belly. Trust me, you'll sleep better."

"Thank you, Rick."

"I'll be back in the morning with your personal items and the paperwork for the Sig. We've stationed a Marine guard outside. Get some rest, Laura."

"You're so kind to me, Rick."

"See you in the morning." He leaned over and kissed her cheek.

Outside the door, Rick spoke to the Marine. "Someone will relieve you at noon, Corporal. Go ahead and order food from the nurses. The restroom is down the hall to the right. Make sure you notify the nurse and check that the area's clear before you leave your post."

"Yes, Sir."

"I'll be back tomorrow morning," Williams said as he looked the Marine directly in the eye. "Stay frosty now."

"Will do, Sir."

As Rick walked down the hall, he smiled to himself. *She's my kind of girl, pretty and deadly. That girl can handle herself.*

Chapter Thirty-Seven

RICK WILLIAMS HAD just a few hours of sleep before heading to Messier's Rue Cler apartment Monday morning. He parked in the alley, found Laura's back door and felt on top of the door frame. The key was missing. He looked on the ground and, not finding it, tried the door. It was unlocked. He quietly stepped inside and instinctively pulled out his weapon. He listened, but heard no sound.

He crept up the stairs and found the apartment door ajar. He put his weapon in firing position and quietly pushed the door open with his foot. He heard nothing. His movements were quick and precise. Years of training and experience in the Marines had given Rick the survival instincts he needed; he was calm, alert and confident.

Quietly, Rick entered the apartment through the kitchen. He stopped momentarily to listen, but the only sounds were from the street, the squeal of automobile brakes, and the horn of a taxi. There were two doorways from the kitchen into the rest of the apartment, one to the right that led to a dining room and one in front of him that led into a hallway. Rick chose to go right. At the dining room doorway, he quickly leaned in and scanned the room.

Through the dining area, Rick turned left through the wide doorway into the living room. Upon entering, he quickly looked to his left and could see down the hallway to a half open door, probably a bedroom. Moving to open a closet door in the living room adjacent to the front entrance, Rick heard footsteps in the hallway. He moved back in view of the hall and caught a glimpse of a person running through the doorway into the kitchen. Rick crept down the hallway to the kitchen doorway, looked left into the kitchen and heard the culprit running down the stairs toward the back door. Moving to the top of the stairs, Rick pointed his weapon and squeezed off a round as the lower door slammed shut. *Fuck,* he said to himself as the round shattered a window pane. *Had I gone through the other door, I would've had him.*

Rick turned his attention to searching the remainder of the apartment. He checked the first bedroom, then moved on to the bathroom and second bedroom. The apartment was clean. He looked for signs that a bomb had been planted, finding none. The closet and dresser in the bedroom had been searched and the contents of the lavatory cabinet had been spilled onto the floor.

Gathering what clothes and toiletries he thought Laura needed, Rick phoned CIA Operations from the apartment phone.

"97944 scramble," he said.

"Go ahead, Sir."

"Rick Williams here. I'm at the Messier apartment, 51 Rue Cler. There's been an intrusion. I need a team here to dust the place for prints. Find out if there's a tap on this line, too. Bring a locksmith with you; the back door's unsecured."

"Right away, Sir," the voice said.

"Thanks."

Rick proceeded down the stairs with his gun drawn. He peered out the doorway, glancing in both directions. Seeing no one, he exited the building and walked up the alley. He saw nothing suspicious where the alley emptied into the street. The pedestrians, shops and second floor windows offered nothing out of the ordinary. *I don't see anything, but that doesn't mean he's not watching,* he thought. *We'll put surveillance on the place before she leaves the hospital.*

Rick Williams walked back to the apartment and waited until the CIA team arrived. He picked up Laura's personal items and traveled to the hospital, arriving just ahead of the hospital administrator who insisted on viewing Laura's gun permit. Since Laura wasn't afforded diplomatic immunity, she was required to obey the guns laws of Paris. Rick showed the paperwork to the administrator who left unhappy that she kept the pistol, but satisfied he'd done his due diligence.

"How's my girl this morning?" Rick asked as soon as they were alone.

"A bit better, I think. The doctors changed out the antibiotics in the IV and they've given me more pain medication. I'm still hurting, but it looks like I'll live."

"The morphine doesn't get rid of it all, does it?" Rick asked.

"It hurts no matter what," she admitted.

"Don't move around much. That's all you can do."

He debated whether to tell her about the break-in, deciding to withhold the information. "I brought your personal items from the apartment." He laid the bag on the nightstand. "Sorry about the bag, I couldn't find anything else."

"I'm sure it will be fine, Rick. Thank you," she said.

Rick continued to talk while Laura looked inside the bag. "What are the doctors telling you this morning?" Rick asked.

"They've scheduled a bunch of tests, that's pretty much all I know. I guess I was bleeding internally when you brought me in last night."

"They hurt you pretty badly if you don't mind me saying," Rick said. "Any word on when you might be released?"

"They won't say. I think they're planning on keeping me a while."

"You could use a few days in the hospital. Can I bring you anything else?"

"I've got enough for now. Thanks."

"I'll let you rest for a bit. I'm sticking around for the shift change at noon. I'll be here if you need me."

Rick walked down the hallway to the nurse's station. He waited for a moment until the nurse looked up from her paperwork. "May I help you?" she said in the cryptic tone she used to convey annoyance at the interruption.

"I'm from the American Embassy. I'd like to see the list of doctors who are treating the Jane Doe in 410."

She looked at her chart. "Check the room number. We have no one by that name in room 410."

"That's impossible. I just came from her room," Rick said, confused. "Who do you have listed in 410?"

The nurse shook her head no. "I can't release any information on the patient in 410 unless you are immediate family," she said. She looked back at her paperwork.

Rick got visibly upset. "Did you put her under her own name? I specifically asked that she be put under an assumed name when she was admitted last night. Her life may be in danger," Rick said harshly.

"I don't admit people, Sir," the nurse said flatly. "You'll have to go downstairs to admissions," She was completely unmoved by Williams' protest. She heard people exaggerate special needs every day.

"I want her moved to a new room and placed under an assumed name," Rick demanded, slamming his hand on the counter. When the nurse looked back to her paperwork, Rick leaned over the counter and yelled, "Now!"

The nurse looked up with a cold stare. "Assumed names cannot be used without instructions from the police."

A voice from over Rick's shoulder said sternly, "Then consider yourself so instructed." Henri Thomas showed the nurse his National Gendarmerie badge. Henri leaned over the counter and hissed under his breath, "Give this gentleman what he wants or I'll have you fired in the next five minutes." He gave the nurse a look of impending violence. "Do you understand me?"

"Yes, Sir. Right away." She nervously started shuffling papers around her desk.

"Get me that doctor's list while you're at it," Rick added abruptly.

"Yes, Sir." She hurried off down the hall with a fist full of paperwork.

Henri smiled and held out his hand. "I'm Henri Thomas. I guarded Ms. Messier on the flight last night."

"I remember you from the airport, Sir. I'm Rick Williams, Security Chief for the American Embassy. Nice to meet you." They gave each other a strong handshake.

"Ah, we have the same job then. I handle security for the French Embassy in Tripoli."

"Are you going down to the room?"

Henri nodded. "If you don't mind, I thought I'd check in on our girl today."

"Not at all. I'll walk with you," Rick said, nodding down the hallway.

"Good, we have matters to discuss," Henri said glancing at Rick as they walked. "Two men followed us back to Paris last night. Here's a description of one." He handed Rick the bulletin. "We caught one, but this one's still at large. He may show up here at the hospital."

Rick studied the page Henri had given him. "This might be a coincidence, but Ms. Messier's apartment was broken into this morning. It could be the same man. We dusted the place for prints. If we find anything, we'll run it through the Interpol database."

"Will you share that information with us?" Henri asked.

"Of course. I do have a favor to ask in return."

"How can I be of assistance?"

They reached room number 410. The Marine guard stood up. "Relax, Marine. He's a friendly," Rick said. The Marine stood aside, but Rick decided to finish the conversation outside the room. "Let's talk about this in the hall where she can't hear. If you think this suspect," he said holding up the notice, "might come to the hospital, I don't have enough men to guard all the entrances. I need more coverage."

"Consider it done," Henri said.

As Henri Thomas spoke, Rick studied him as he would an opponent. Henri was big, strong and had a calm, confident demeanor. *This guy's a pro,* Rick thought, *not someone I'd like to meet in a dark alley late at night.* "I'll put plainclothes at each entrance, including the employee entrance and the loading dock," Henri continued. "It'll be done within the hour. Hopefully, we can apprehend this man before he gets inside the hospital."

"If he gets as far as the room, he may be in for a nasty surprise," Rick said. "I gave her a Sig Sauer P226 last night. I have a feeling she can handle herself."

"I can assure you of that," Henri said. "At the Tripoli airport yesterday, she nearly killed three Libyan State Security guards with her bare hands."

Rick smiled. "Why am I not surprised to hear that?"

"She's tougher than she looks, for sure," Henri said.

"Well, it is nice to officially meet you, Mr. Thomas. I'm afraid I can't stay. I've got a lot to do today. Go ahead in and visit with her if you like," Rick said.

"Thank you, Mr. Williams." He handed Rick a business card. "Here's my phone number. Call me with your progress."

"Will do," Rick said, "and thanks for the help with the nurse back there. I appreciate it."

"You're welcome. We'll talk soon," Henri said.

When Henri entered the room, Laura's mood immediately brightened. "Hi, Henri. I didn't know you were still in town," she said.

"Laura, you're looking better today."

"I'm feeling a little better, thanks."

"I stopped by to see how you were doing," Henri said with a kind smile and gentle manner.

"I'm glad you did. What's going on with the Libyans who followed us?"

Henri looked around as if he were doing an inspection. Laura understood the technique. "I have no idea whether the room is clean," she said, watching his eyes move about the room. "I wouldn't think it's dirty. I mean, no one knew I'd be in this particular room."

"We caught one of the Libyans at the airport last night," Henri said. "We're checking his prints with Interpol this morning. The other man escaped, however."

"Is he a problem?"

Henri grimaced. "I'm not sure. We're taking precautions just in case. DST will cover the hospital entrances and exits. Captain Williams has put an embassy guard at your door and they're going to move you to another room this afternoon."

"You look concerned it's not enough," she said, watching Henri's eyes betray his professional manner.

Henri wondered whether any preventive measure could deter a professional assassin. He decided she deserved to hear the truth. "The man who got away could be a spotter. They might have someone else out there."

"If it's someone else, that would be difficult to stop," she said.

Henri wondered if he'd been too blunt. "Perhaps, I shouldn't have mentioned it."

"No, I'm glad you did," Laura said.

"Look, we have an experienced team," Henri said. "If it's the man from the plane last night, we'll get him. Here's a snapshot airport security got of him going through customs."

Laura recognized him immediately. "The man with the beard. He was wearing a blue coat on the plane," she said.

"Yes," Henri replied. "He took the coat off before going through customs. Here's a sketch we made this morning of what he might look like clean shaven," He handed her a sketch made by a forensic artist. "If they use someone else, it becomes more difficult. It could be anyone. He might not even be Middle Eastern."

"Do you think they'll try here at the hospital?" she asked, fully knowing the answer.

"They might. Mr. Williams mentioned he gave you a weapon. May I see it?" Henri asked.

"Yes, it's in the nightstand drawer." Laura motioned to the right.

Henri walked around the bed and pulled out the P226. He immediately popped the magazine out, put it back in, and then lined up the sights using a spot on the wall. "I like it," Henri said. "Double action, isn't it?"

"Yes," she said.

Henri handed it to her grip first. "Keep it within reach. If an attacker enters your room, you'll have to assume the guard outside is down. Once he sees you, he'll line up his shot, so he'll hesitate for a second. That's all the time you'll have."

"He'll come at night, won't he," she said more as a statement than a question.

"That's when I would do it."

"Is there anything I can do?"

Henri nodded his head in the affirmative. "Sleep during the day and try to be awake at night. Keep your door shut. If you hear it open without a knock, that's a warning. Doctors and nurses always knock. Keep all the lights off to force him to make a vision adjustment. You'll see his shadow before you see him because the light will be at his back."

There was a knock at the door. The nurse entered, "Ma'am, we're ready to move you to a different room. Can I ask your visitor to leave for a few minutes?" she asked.

Henri looked at Laura. "Remember, the nurses will always knock, Laura."

"Thank you, Henri, "Laura said. "I'm in your debt. Will you be back?"

"Jacques has given me permission to stay," Henri said. "I'll be in regular contact." Henri gave her that strong, confident smile of his. "Don't worry. My men are guarding the building. If he comes, we have an excellent chance of stopping him. Get some rest and I'll see you soon."

The nurses gathered Laura's personal effects and moved her one floor below to room 346. She looked around the room wondering if Operations had done a sweep beforehand. She studied the configuration; the room was exactly the same as the floor above. The bathroom blocked her view of the door. Anyone entering the room would walk past the bathroom before they became visible. An attacker would be several steps into the room before Laura caught a glimpse of him. *Would he even be a man? It could be a woman disguised as a nurse.*

Field agents are trained to sense danger, so Laura decided to trust her instincts. She took the gun in her hand and practiced lining up a shot using the clock on the far wall as a target. She needed a few sessions at the range in the basement of the embassy to feel confident using it, but much of the preparation for a fight is mental, so she calmed herself and let the events of the day unfold.

Chapter Thirty-Eight

STEVE TILTON DROVE to work Monday morning wondering why Laura hadn't called. She should have returned yesterday. Upon entering his Langley office at 8:40, his secretary handed him a note, "Bill Bates just called. He needs to talk with you as soon as you come in." Bates was the Associate Director of Intelligence and Steve's direct supervisor. Damn, he thought, walking into his inner office. He slammed the door behind him and before he even took off his coat, Steve picked up the phone and dialed Bates.

"Yes?"

"Bill, it's Steve, returning your call," Steve said, trying to keep the apprehension out of his voice.

"We have news about Laura, Steve. Don't worry, she's okay," Bates said. "She had trouble getting out yesterday. Details are sketchy at this point, but apparently she tried to get out on a French diplomatic passport and was caught at the airport."

"What did they do to her?" Steve asked, holding his breath.

Bates began to explain, "Libyan State Security ..."

Steve interrupted. "How badly is she hurt, Bill?"

"Hang on and let me finish." Tilton took a deep breath and waited. "Libyan State Security put her through a tough interrogation at the airport," Bates said flatly. "They roughed her up a bit. Here's the strange part. According to the early reports, Libyan Intelligence stepped in late in the day, stopped the interrogation and allowed her to leave late last night. At this point, we don't know why, but it may have saved her life."

"Where is she now?" Steve asked, trying to wrap his mind around the idea that Laura was injured.

"She's at the American Hospital."

"Oh my God," Steve said involuntarily.

"Don't worry, she's in good hands. Our embassy doctor is on staff at the hospital and she's resting comfortably." Bates glanced at his watch. "It will be just before 3:00 p.m. in Paris. Why don't you give her a call? I'm sure she'd like to hear from you."

"What's her condition," Steve asked, trying to prepare himself for the worst.

"They've listed her as stable," Bates said in an attempt to reassure Tilton. "That's all we know right now. If you're going to call, go through Operations and have them patch it through Paris Station. Her line won't be secure, but yours will be."

"Thanks, Bill. I appreciate the call."

"One more thing, Steve," Bates said.

"Yes?"

"If you catch a flight today, you'll be there by morning," Bates said with a compassion that contradicted his business like reputation. "Tell her we're proud of her."

"Thank you, Bill. I really appreciate it."

Bates hung up the phone, leaned back in his chair and thought for a minute. *Office romances complicate the hell out of things.*

With nurses wheeling Laura around the hospital for various tests, she was lucky to be in the room when Steve called. She heard the click on the line, so she knew he was routing the call in from somewhere else. It would be early Monday morning at Langley.

"Hi, baby," he said. *Smart,* she thought, *he's not using names. He knows the line wouldn't be secure.*

"Hi sweetie," Laura said. "I love you."

"I hear you're pretty banged up."

"Not too bad, I'll be fine. It's great to hear your voice," she said.

"I'm taking the rest of the week off, dear," Steve said. "I'll be there in the morning."

"Really, honey, you don't need to do that. I'll be fine."

"Get some rest and I'll see you in the morning. I love you, baby," Steve said. Laura glanced at the clock after the call; it had taken just a few seconds. Untraceable.

John Brownley stopped by after dinner to see how she was feeling. He handed her flowers. "Thank you, John. They're gorgeous," Laura said, reaching for them. The arrangement smelled wonderful. "Can you put them on the window sill for me?" John set them in a perfect spot, right where they could be seen as she looked out over the city. He handed her the card.

"Read the card," he said with a sly smile.

It read, "Operational phase of Eldorado Canyon commenced at 17:30 this evening. Action in theater due at approximately 02:00 tomorrow"

"Thought you'd like to know," John said. She handed the card back and he slipped it into his breast pocket.

"Very romantic, John," she said. John gave her a hint of a smile.

"You're looking a lot better than when I saw you last."

"You're a smooth liar, John," Laura said jokingly.

"Get some rest and I'll be back tomorrow." He leaned over and put his hand on hers. "We're awfully fond of you, Laura. Take care," he said.

Chapter Thirty-Nine

MAJOR FAREED HASSAN arrived at his headquarters promptly at 9:00 on Monday morning. His employees were accustomed to the Captain's punctuality. Hassan demanded military discipline from himself as well as those who worked for him. Hassan had just settled in behind his desk when one of his aides approached with a telex received earlier that morning.

"Pardon the interruption, Sir," the aide said.

"Yes, Corporal?"

"We received a telex this morning from an unnamed source in Jordan. I think you ought to see it."

"Hand it to me," Hassan said as he reached across his desk.

Hassan studied the telex which consisted entirely of numbers, thirty-six in all, separated by commas after each grouping of six digits. Nothing else, no names or words of any kind. *The aide was right,* Hassan thought, *there was little way to ascertain who sent it.*

"I need to make an immediate appointment with Commander Gaddafi," Hassan told the aide. "Also contact Defense Minister Daghar. Let me know when you've got him on the line."

"Yes, Sir," the aide said.

Hassan laid the telex aside and began the day's work. The aide came back to Hassan's office a few minutes later. "Sir, your appointment with the Commander is at 10:15 this morning at Azizia. I have Defense Minister Daghar on the line."

Hassan picked up, "Good morning, Mihran," Hassan said.

"Salam, Fareed."

"I'm meeting the Commander at 10:15. I'd like you to come along."

"Of course," Daghar said. Hassan's office was tucked away in a nearby residential area while Daghar's office was inside the Azizia compound.

"I'll meet you in the front lot at 10:00," Hassan said.

Hassan had known Daghar for years. Both were approximately the same age; they came up through the ranks together. They had chosen military service because that was the most attractive option for poor, talented young men in the days of the monarchy. They went to the military academy in Benghazi together and although they were older than Gaddafi, they understood the politics of the 1969 revolt correctly and immediately embraced the new regime. It was as much political acumen as it was technical expertise that had raised both men to their present positions.

Major Mirhan Daghar was a man of slight build, graying hair and an intense manner. He managed the largest budget in the government and did so with an efficiency that earned him much praise. Although he was deficient in his knowledge of military tactics and hardware, his strength was organizational, putting in place a top down Soviet style military command structure that pleased Gaddafi. Although he lacked the creative, outside the box kind of thinking that was the trademark of Hassan, he was a loyal Gaddafi man.

There was one difference between the men, however, that influenced each man's thinking. Hassan traveled widely in his job and had observed the powerful economic might of the West. He had come to believe that freedom was an essential part of the West's economic success. Daghar, on the other hand, had rarely gone abroad and was heavily influenced by the Soviet advisers who helped train the Libyan military. He had studied the Soviet system and believed in it.

As Hassan and Daghar walked together to Gaddafi's office on that particular Monday morning, they walked with their jackets thrown over their shoulders and engaged in the usual pleasantries, talking of family, hobbies and vacations. Their faces were known to Gaddafi's guards so they passed through the doors and down to the underground quarters without being stopped. As the men walked down the hallway toward Gaddafi's office, past the room where the reception had been held the previous Saturday evening, Gaddafi walked out to greet them. He was genuinely glad to see them both. They were two of his most trusted men.

"Daghar, Hassan, so lovely to see you. May Allah bless each of you and your families." Gaddafi embraced both men.

"Allah's blessings upon you as well," Daghar said.

"Come, sit in my office," Gaddafi said as he led them down the hallway and into his office. As the men settled into chairs, Gaddafi sat down behind his desk, spread his hands across the desktop, leaned forward and said, "What have you got for me today, Fareed?"

"Sir, we received a mysterious telex from Jordan this morning. I think you need to see it." Hassan handed copies to both men. Gaddafi studied his copy for a minute, then looked up at Hassan. "This is just a string of numbers. What does it mean?"

"I wonder if it's a code of some kind," Hassan answered.

"What do you make of it, Mirhan?" Gaddafi asked.

Daghar recognized the numbers immediately. "Commander, would you mind taking the code sheet for the S-200s from your briefcase and compare the numbers with those in the telex?" Dagher asked. Gaddafi looked puzzled, but opened his briefcase, pulled out the laminated code sheet and compared the numbers side by side.

"Aha! This telex contains the S-200 codes, Daghar," Gaddafi said with a fair amount of surprise.

"I believe someone is politely telling us we have a leak," Hassan suggested.

"Gentlemen, copies of that code sheet exist in only two places, my briefcase and your office, Daghar. How did they end up in Jordan this morning?" Gaddafi asked, looking at Daghar.

"I'm at a loss to explain it," Daghar said. "It's impossible this would happen."

"Mirhan, I keep my copy in my briefcase at all times," Gaddafi explained with an annoyed look. "This briefcase," he said, pointing at the black case on his desk, "stays in my possession twenty-four hours a day. I even take it into the restroom with me. No one has access to it, but me. Where do you keep your copy?"

"Locked in the safe in my office."

"Is it possible someone has access to the safe other than you?" Gaddafi asked.

"No, Sir," Daghar said.

"Do you keep a printed copy of the combination somewhere?"

"No, Sir," Daghar said.

Gaddafi thought for a moment. "Then how would someone obtain the codes?"

"It would be impossible unless someone watched me open the safe," Daghar said. "That's the only possibility I can think of, Sir."

"Are your aides trustworthy?"

"Completely, Sir."

"Is your security a problem?" Gaddafi asked with a certain kind of menacing tone. Gaddafi had a reputation for executing military officers who displeased him. This reputation and Gaddafi's tone of voice sent a clear message to Dahgar.

"No Sir. I've received no reports of an illegal entry of any kind." Beads of sweat began to appear on Daghar's forehead.

"Do any of the commanders of the S-200 pods know the codes?" Gaddafi persisted.

"No Sir," Daghar replied. "I'm the only person authorized to change the codes. The commanders are never present when I do it."

Gaddafi turned to Hassan. "Fareed, what do you think?"

"Obviously, we have to change the codes immediately. Perhaps we ought to have someone from outside the Defense Ministry change them until we find the leak."

"Quite right," Gaddafi said, leaning back in his chair. *This is just a minor problem,* Gaddafi thought. "Fareed, I want you to change the codes this morning and bring the only copy back to me. For the time being, until we straighten this out, I'll hold the only copy. Do you understand, Mirhan?"

"Yes, Sir," Daghar said with a sigh as he looked at the floor. Actually, in the back of his mind, Dagher was worried. Gaddafi had executed men for less.

"I want you to clearly understand me, Mirhan," Gaddafi explained. "You're going to have to figure out better security. A leak like this could be serious."

"Yes, Sir. I apologize for the actions of my office in this matter. I'll find the traitor and he'll be severely punished," Daghar said.

"Very good," Gaddafi said. "Hassan, do you know the procedure for changing the codes?"

"No, Sir," Hassan replied. He looked over at Daghar. "Can you explain it to me?"

"It's better if I just go with you," Daghar said.

Gaddafi rose from his chair. "It's settled then," he said, pleased a solution had been put in place. "Mirhan will go with you and show you how to do it,"

"Thank you, Sir. Sorry to waste your time on this," Hassan said.

"Glad we could straighten it out. I'll see you when you get back with the new codes. Good day, gentlemen."

Hassan and Daghar drove all over the city that morning visiting the six missile installations that housed the S-200 long range SAM systems protecting Tripoli. Dagher introduced Hassan to the pod commanders and Hassan entered the control rooms alone. Using the existing code sheet, he entered the correct code into each system, then asked the system to generate a new code. When Hassan copied each new code onto a sheet of paper, he changed the numbers slightly rendering them useless. Once Hassan had changed all six, he and Dagher drove back to Azizia where Hassan personally handed the worthless codes to Gaddafi.

"We're done, Sir," Hassan reported. "The missiles are secure."

"Hassan, thank you and have a pleasant day, "Gaddafi saluted him. Gaddafi slipped the numbers in his briefcase and thought no more about the matter.

Hassan returned to his office where he immediately summoned his aide. "I want to return a message to the sender of the mysterious telex that came in this morning," Hassan said. "Can you return a message based on the number where it originated?"

"Of course, Sir," the aide responded, thinking nothing of the request.

"The message is to read, 'Who are you?' and nothing else," Hassan ordered.

"Yes, Sir. I'll send it immediately."

Hassan looked at his watch. It was 2:15 p.m. Hassan wondered whether his wife would be packed and ready for this evening's flight to Italy.

Chapter Forty

USING AN ELABORATE plot that worked perfectly, EUCOM (United States European Command) had received the original codes from a CIA agent in Paris during the early morning hours on Monday. The codes were relayed to an intermediary in Jordan who sent them to Hassan. When the return telex from Hassan was received in Jordan, the message was sent back to EUCOM in Germany. It was confirmation that the codes had been changed. The Libyan S-200 long range radar and missile system had been compromised and would be no threat to American war planes during the attack.

President Reagan spent Monday morning giving leaders of Canada, Australia, Israel and the European allies advance notice of the attack which would take place later that evening. Although most were supportive, some European allies with close economic ties to Libya expressed frustration. They considered an attack on Libya to be premature in light of their decision the week before to place economic sanctions on Libya. It was the first time Europe had taken decisive action against Gaddafi and many leaders felt economic sanctions would be sufficient. In addition, some leaders expressed concern that an American attack might provoke Gaddafi to retaliate and Europe would be a convenient target.

Reagan asked Congressional leaders to convene at the While House late Monday, once planes were in the air, to brief them on the attack. During the meeting, Reagan told the leaders he could turn the planes back and call off the attack if they wished, but he received their approval and none of them spoke to the press after the meeting.

Reagan would wait until the bombing commenced before Soviet officials were called to the State Department, where the Secretary of State would provide the Soviets with justification for the airstrike and assure them the bombing was not intended to harm Soviet assets. Secretary of Defense Caspar Weinberger and Joint Chiefs Chairman William Crowe would be at the Pentagon Command Center all evening passing updates to the White House.

Chapter Forty-One

THE ORDER TO execute Operation Eldorado Canyon was personally handed to General Bernard Rogers, the EUCOM Commander by Joint Chiefs Chairman Admiral William Crowe the previous Wednesday, April 9, 1986. The operation would be a joint mission between the Navy and the Air Force. Navy aircraft off the carriers America and Coral Sea, currently stationed in the Mediterranean, would attack targets around Benghazi, while Air Force aircraft, coming from bases in the United Kingdom, would attack targets around Tripoli. The attack would take place early Tuesday morning, April 15, 1986, precisely at 02:00 local time. The entire mission would be under the command of Navy Vice-Admiral David Kelso and the flight commander would be Air Force General David Forgan.

With over one hundred aircraft participating in the bombing, the operation was complex and required perfect timing between the Navy and the Air Force. The Navy's all-weather ground attack plane, the A-6E, would attack Benghazi targets, with Libyan air defenses suppressed by F-18A Hornets. Simultaneously, the Air Force would use its ground attack fighter, the F-111F to attack Tripoli targets, while its electronic countermeasure variant, the F-111A, would jam Libyan radars. Protection from Libyan air defenses around Tripoli would be provided by the Navy A-7E aircraft.

Three Days in Tripoli

As orders began to be disseminated through the ranks, Colonel Sam Westbrook, commander of the F-111s to be used in the attack on Tripoli, received his orders on Thursday, April 10th. Earlier in the year, Westbrook's 48th Tactical Fighter Wing, based at RAF Lakenheath in the U.K., and had flown mock missions across the Atlantic to Canada and across Europe to simulate a bombing at Incirlik, Turkey. Just three weeks ago, they practiced joint exercises with the Navy in the Mediterranean Sea. However, Westbrook's crews had trained for a limited strike and when amended orders expanded the mission, Westbrook saw his mission go far beyond what his wing had prepared for.

France and Spain denied the United States permission to fly over their territory which meant Westbrook's fighters, along with the tanker aircraft needed for multiple refuelings, would take a circuitous route around the continent, through the Strait of Gibraltar to Libya and back. The entire mission would take twelve to fourteen hours flight time, far longer than the F-111 had ever been flown continuously. Westbrook was not even sure the F-111 airframe would hold up under that amount of stress. Maintenance records at the base showed that 40% of the F-111Fs suffered a systems failure when flown over two and a half hours. The solution arrived at by the Air Force was to simply take extra jets to the first refueling point, run a systems check and take the best jets on to Libya. How many fighters would suffer a systems failure after twelve hours flight time? The answer was unknown.

Further, additional targets had been added to the mission which forced Westbrook to recruit extra flight crews at the last minute. Twenty-nine jets would travel to the first refueling point, at which time the best twenty-two (eighteen attack jets and four electronic countermeasure aircraft) would continue on while the others turned back to base. Most of the crews had no combat experience, few had done a nighttime refueling and none had ever done a nighttime refueling in radio silence.

The orders left no discretion to Westbrook as to the number of jets sent to the three targets around Tripoli: the Bab al Azizia Military Compound (nine jets), the Tripoli Military Airfield (six jets) and the Murat Sidi Bilal terrorist training camp south of Tripoli (three jets). When Westbrook showed the final orders to his most experienced pilots, his Vietnam veterans, they voiced objections. They saw no need to attack Azizia, a tight target in the middle of the city, with so many jets. Smoke and dust would accumulate in the air as each jet dropped its ordinance. Laser guided weapons depend on a direct line of sight to target properly and each following jet would have greater difficulty finding its target.

A specific kind of attack on Azizia was ordered; a single file of jets, thirty seconds apart, attacking the target one after another. The Libyans had excellent air defenses, strongest around Tripoli. Giving the Libyans multiple opportunities to shoot at each passing jet, eventually they would be successful. The last few attacking planes would be especially vulnerable.

However, when Westbrook took those concerns to his superior, General David Forgan, Westbrook was denied any input into the mission. Forgan insisted the mission be completed as ordered. This caused pilots to suspect that sending so many jets to Azizia (dubbed the Libyan White

House) meant one goal of the mission was to kill Gaddafi, whose residence was inside the Azizia compound.

Heavy concentrations of surface to air missiles around Tripoli and Benghazi made Libya's air defenses difficult to attack. Gaddafi's SAM systems included many types of Soviet made systems layered one upon another to provide maximum protection. Those systems had fire control radar that searched for targets, pinpointed a target's position, plotted a firing solution for the missile, fired automatically and directed the missile to its target. Libya also had anti-aircraft emplacements around Tripoli to counter aircraft that sought to fly under Libyan SAM radars. Air defenses around Tripoli presented a number of challenges to be overcome.

The plan to neutralize Tripoli's air defenses was threefold. The first challenge was to neutralize their long range surface to air missiles, the Soviet S-200 system which NATO called the SA-5s. Those radars could target and fire upon American aircraft as far as 250 miles away. Westbrook knew the Air Force had a plan to neutralize that system, but it was never explained.

Second, the F-111As, with electronic countermeasure capability, would provide radar jamming during the bombing run itself. The F-111As put radio interference into the air to disrupt SAM radars, but the F-111As had no offensive capability, so joining Westbrook's jets would be A-7Es from the carriers. They could attack missile installations directly. However, the Libyans had developed methods for avoiding such attacks, such as turning radars on and off again once missiles had been fired. The photos of SAM installations were taken in daylight. It was unclear whether the A-7Es would be able to find them at night.

Lastly, there was the element of surprise. If Westbrook's forces could approach unseen by Libyan long range radar systems, they could attack their targets from very close to the ground where medium and short range radars would have difficulty targeting them. It was possible that the Libyans would not realize an attack was taking place until American jets were within visual range. However, the flight plan to Libya took Westbrook's jets very close to Morocco and Tunisia. It was possible that Gaddafi could be forewarned of an attack.

There was little doubt that Operation Eldorado Canyon was complicated. A huge amount of tanker support was needed to support the mission. Over twenty K-10 and KC-135 refueling tanker aircraft would be involved. With air combat patrols, SAM suppression, attacking jets and tankers, the air space over the theater of operations would be congested.

Chapter Forty-Two

EARLY MONDAY AFTERNOON, April 14th, 1986, tanker and fighter crews arrived at their respective bases for mission preparations. Support staff mounting live ordinance on the fighters were given no information about the mission. Their work was completed late in the afternoon and at 5:30 p.m., the tanker aircraft took off in radio silence from the Mildenhall and Fairford airfields in the U.K., fully loaded with fuel, destined for rendezvous points in the Atlantic where they would meet their assigned F-111s. Just before 6:00 p.m., the F-111Fs, loaded with live ordinance, began to take off from Lakenheath in similar fashion as did the F-111As from Upper Heyford. Under the guise of NATO exercise Salty Nation, which started a few hours before, not even air traffic controllers knew of the mission or its flight plan.

At approximately the same time, the Navy's aircraft carriers, America and Coral Sea, began to move toward their assigned positions, hoping to avoid Soviet intelligence vessels by maintaining radio silence and using the cover of night to disguise their movements.

Once airborne over the Atlantic, Westbrook's fighters found their assigned tankers in radio silence, three to each tanker. They flew to the first refueling point where fighters refueled amid darkness. Once completed, pilots ran through a system check, after which six were sent home and the rest proceeded in formation on a very long and arduous journey around the continent, through the Strait of Gibraltar and into the Mediterranean.

Flying in formation was no easy task for aircraft grouped so close together. Planes tend to drift while on autopilot and constant correction was needed to maintain spacing and keep the groups together. Military planners thought that by flying in close formation, radar operators on the continent would interpret the images as benign tankers on their way to an unknown destination. The pilots took food along with them in the cockpit and wore plastic bags to urinate.

Flying through the Strait, the attackers were seen by radar scopes on both sides of the Strait. The British, at the Naval Base in Gibraltar, who had been advised of the traffic in advance, did nothing. Authorities in Morocco, accustomed to watching traffic in the Strait, thought a large inbound force was unusual for that time of evening, but decided to stand down and avoid interfering.

As the fighters and tankers rounded the tip of Tunisia, they executed their final refueling for the bombing run. Simultaneously, the carriers America and Coral Sea began launch operations of their own. Both were seen, the F-111s by spotters on the Tunisian coast and the carrier launching from the coast of Malta.

The call came into Gaddafi's headquarters at 1:38 a.m. Gaddafi had fallen asleep in his quarters. An aide woke him. "Beg your pardon, Colonel, but you have an important call waiting on the private line in your office." Gaddafi, somewhat perturbed at the intrusion, asked, "How dare you interrupt me at night? Who has the authority to wake the Leader of the Libyan people after his day's labor?"

"The caller did not identify himself, Sir, only to say it's of a national security nature and it's urgent," the aide replied as something of an excuse.

"I'll take the call in a moment."

Gaddafi slapped the behind of one of the women beside him. "Move," Gaddafi shouted in anger. The woman groaned and rolled over. Gaddafi pulled a robe around his shoulders, grabbed the briefcase from the nightstand and walked down the hall to his office. He sat behind his desk, lifted the receiver and said, "Yes, what's the problem?"

"Colonel, you may have trouble headed your way. The American carriers off Malta are putting their entire force in the air as we speak."

"How long do we have?"

"I'm guessing that you have no more than fifteen minutes," the caller said, "perhaps less."

"Thank you," Gaddafi replied and hung up.

Gaddafi looked at the clock; it read 1:41 a.m. He drummed his fingers nervously on the desk, wondering whether he should call a full alert on the basis of a phone call. The caller was known to be reliable, but Gaddafi thought it best to get an independent confirmation. He decided to order the S-200 SAM systems turned on to find out what was going on. He pulled the launch codes from his briefcase, found the phone numbers to each pod and dialed the direct line to each control trailer. He read the launch codes to the commanders, ordering them to turn on the radars and arm the missiles. Only four commanders answered the call; the phones in the other two pods rang without answering. Gaddafi made a note to deal with those two negligent commanders tomorrow morning.

If the report was true, Gaddafi reasoned, the Americans would hit installations around Benghazi. Those were the closest facilities to the carriers, which usually positioned themselves in the Gulf of Sidra. He picked up the phone again and called his commander at the Jamahiriyah Barracks in Benghazi. The duty officer picked up, "Jamahiriyah Barracks, Corporal Boutros speaking, may I help you?"

"Corporal, this is the Leader of the Libyan People, Colonel Muammar Gaddafi. There have been reports of American aircraft activity in your area. Inform your commanding officer he is to put all military installations around Benghazi at full alert. Inform the commander at Bennina that he is to have all his fighters in the air within the next fifteen minutes. Do you understand?"

"Yes, Sir. I'll do so at once. Thank you, Sir."

"Salam, Corporal. May Allah be with you," Gaddafi offered.

"And with you, Sir."

Gaddafi hung up the phone and glanced at the clock; it was now 1:57 a.m. *Surely, the Americans will not attack Tripoli. It isn't civilized to attack the sitting leader of a country at his residence,* Gaddafi thought. *What about my family? I don't have time to move them. It doesn't matter. Tripoli won't be attacked, anyway.*

Gaddafi was wrong. After the last re-fueling, the F-111Fs made one last course correction to align themselves to pass over Tripoli Harbor where their terrain following radar would pick up a needed landmark. The F-111As turned on their radar jammers to prevent radar lock from SAM installations in and around the city. At fifty miles out, the jets turned off their navigation lights. The jets would be heard and their exhaust plumes seen, but the jets, themselves, would be difficult to see at night with the naked eye.

One jet, which had trouble refueling, was late so it cut a corner to catch up, putting it slightly off course over the harbor. It never found its landmark and dropped out of the attack. One other plane dropped out due to a malfunction. Seven others came screaming over Tripoli Harbor at 600 mph, skimming the wave tops at 200 feet. They were joined by the Navy A-7Es, the Corsairs, as they approached the harbor. What they saw astounded them. They found a city completely unaware of what was about to happen. Downtown buildings were lit, street lights were on and traffic on the streets seemed normal for a late evening. None of the Soviet S-200 long range radars had been turned on and the Libyans were caught completely by surprise.

However, once the jets traveled over Tripoli Harbor, Libyan short and medium range radars found the jets. SAM missile sites and anti-aircraft placements became active. Libyan radars were attacked by the Corsairs to plow the road ahead for the attacking F-111Fs. Libya's SA-2s, the SA-3s, SA-6s, and SA-8 SAM sites all began firing. Libyan Crotales and ZSU-23/4AAA anti-aircraft batteries began to light up the sky. Many fired blindly. They filled the sky with deadly force, too late to counter the first few F-111s, but each succeeding jet encountered more enemy fire.

The first planes through the gauntlet had clean shots at the Bab al-Azizia military compound. Using their 2,000 lb. Paveway II laser guided bombs and their Snakeye high-drag munitions, they pummeled the Azizia complex. Gaddafi's military headquarters building was heavily damaged by a direct hit. Bomb after bomb tore through the Azizia complex. However, each following jet found more dust and debris in the air, making it difficult for jets to find their targets. The fifth jet had a malfunction of its computer aim point and dropped four 2,000 lb. bombs in a nearby residential neighborhood, leveling many homes and damaging several foreign embassies. The sixth jet over Azizia was hit by either SAM or anti-aircraft fire. It turned out to sea, where it crashed, killing the two pilots. The last jet aborted the run due to a combat system malfunction.

At the Murat Sidi Bilal terrorist training camp, the attack caught terrorists sleeping in their beds. The pilots missed hitting their targets directly, but the sheer power of the ordinance damaged buildings around the camp and tore through their training facility.

Approaching the Tripoli Military Airfield, pilots were surprised to find the terminal lights on. Their attack would be a complete surprise. One jet aborted due to a malfunction of its terrain following radar and four others suffered minor malfunctions, but were able to complete their run. Only one jet scored a direct hit, destroying two transport aircraft and damaging three others, but ordinance dropped by the others damaged helicopters and an operations building. A number of subsequent fires and explosions erupted at the airfield.

In Benghazi, American pilots were surprised to find the Bennina Airfield runway lights on and Libyan MIG fighter jets sitting on the tarmac. The attack squadrons pummeled the airfield, cratering runways, destroying three MIG 23s, two helicopters, one transport and one other small aircraft. Several other planes were heavily damaged, including a Boeing 727 transport and two other transports. Hangers, buildings and equipment were either destroyed or heavily damaged in the attack. The Jamahiriyah Barracks sustained a direct hit. Multiple SAM sites received direct hits and were destroyed.

The attack ended as abruptly as it had begun. Within fifteen minutes, all American planes had exited Libyan airspace. Although a few Libyan fighters managed to take off, none engaged the force. All Navy planes returned to the carriers safely. Among the F-111s, one plane was lost, along with both pilots after being hit by Libyan fire and one other diverted to an airbase on the way home due to a malfunction. Hours later, the rest safely returned to their U.K. bases.

Chapter Forty-Three

RASHID NAZARI DROVE around the American Hospital in Paris several times in the early morning hours on Tuesday before deciding to park a block away from the hospital emergency entrance. It was close enough to observe the entrance, yet far enough away to avoid attention. He looked at his watch; it was after midnight and the shadows between the occasional streetlights hid his presence. Nazari was to meet a contact, a bearded man named Ghalib Assaf, who would give him information on two targets that evening, an American woman in one of the hospital's rooms and a French DST agent at another location.

Nazari was Western educated, having lived much of his life in London. Born into an upper class family in Alexandria, Egypt, Nazari's father was a prominent doctor who married an English woman during his medical studies in England. His family owned homes in Alexandria and London. Nazari traveled extensively during his youth, often vacationing with family in Italy, southern France, and Greece. He was a bright young man, spoke several languages and was seemingly destined to follow in his father's footsteps. Yet Rashid yearned for more excitement than a medical profession provided, so he joined the Egyptian military at age eighteen. Being an athletic young man, Nazari enjoyed combat training and was known to be an excellent marksman. With his natural gift for languages and experience abroad as a youth, his commanders recommended him to Egypt's intelligence service, the GID, where he learned the street tactics of kidnapping, coercion, and torture. His superiors noticed that Nazari had no particular political philosophy or religious belief, just a disdain for people of lower economic classes, an attitude prevalent among Egyptian military officers.

He rose within the ranks of the intelligence community quickly, catching the eye of Yasser Arafat, who offered Nazari a job as a member of Arafat's traveling security team. It was during one of Arafat's trips to Tripoli when Muammar Gaddafi noticed him. Gaddafi became impressed with Nazari's professionalism and language skills.

Nazari left Arafat and entered into the employ of Muammar Gaddafi where he found what he enjoyed most: murder for profit. As his reputation grew within the tight, secretive community of professional killers, he began accepting jobs from several governments; a free agent doing the dirty acts of diplomacy that governments sometimes required, but could not do themselves. Nazari was well paid, respected by his peers and over the next few years, developed an international reputation as an assassin. Nazari was on Interpol's top ten wanted list, right alongside Carlos the Jackal. He was one of the world's best assassins.

As Nazari watched the bearded man approach the car, he discreetly folded the newspaper he had been reading over his weapon and trained it on the man. When the man knocked on driver's side window, Nazari was ready to fire if anything seemed amiss. He had never met Assaf and was highly suspicious of new contacts. After Assaf identified himself, Nazari motioned Assaf to the other side of the car and unlocked the passenger door, keeping his weapon pointed at the man. Assaf opened the door, climbed in the passenger seat and put a small black bag on his lap. He kept his hands on top of the bag in full view.

"Are you armed?" Nazari asked.

"No, Sir," Assaf replied.

"Keep your hands where I can see them." Nazari studied Assaf for a few seconds. He decided this man was no killer. "What business do you have with me this evening?"

"Mr. Nazari, I have been tracking your targets. If you would allow me to open the bag, I have the material you requested." Assaf figured Nazari had a weapon underneath the newspaper and he intended no quick or unusual movement.

"Go ahead, but do it slowly."

Assaf opened the bag, put one hand inside and Nazari immediately reacted by putting the barrel of his pistol next to Assaf's ear. "I said slowly," he reminded Assaf.

Assaf pulled a file from the bag and tried to hand it to Nazari. "Put it on the dashboard," Nazari said. "Tell me what's in the file."

"Information on two targets, a woman and a man, both currently in Paris. I don't have a picture of the woman, but her name's Laura Messier. She's an American, early thirties with long blond hair, currently in room 346 at the hospital. She's well guarded," Assaf advised.

"I know about the DST personnel at the entrances. She has others guarding her?" Nazari asked.

"Yes, Sir. A military guard sits outside her room."

"Fine. Tell me about the second target," Nazari asked.

"The second target is a French national named Jean Broussard. He works for French Intelligence and operates a nightclub in the Marais district. He lives within a few blocks of his club. The address of the club and his home are in the file, as well as a recent picture of him. He is well guarded also," Assaf advised.

"How so?" Nazari asked.

"Broussard never travels without an escort of some kind," Assaf replied.

"You have the other materials I requested?" Nazari asked.

"Yes, Sir. A white lab coat is in the bag along with the name tag of one of the woman's doctors."

"And the payment?"

"Yes, Sir. Unmarked U.S. currency inside an envelope at the bottom of the bag."

"Tell your employer the job will be completed by morning. I will send confirmation by the usual method. Please close the bag and lay it at your feet. Keep your hands in view the entire time," Nazari ordered. Assaf closed the bag and slowly laid it on the floorboard of the automobile. "Thank you," Nazari said politely. "Exit the car and walk away. Do not turn around or look in any particular direction. If you do, I'll kill you immediately. Leave the area. Go now, slowly," Nazari said with an emphasis on the word slowly.

Assaf exited the vehicle and sauntered away as though he were taking a late evening walk. Once Assaf was out of view, Nazari pulled his vehicle away from the curb, circled the hospital a few times, and then parked again in a different spot near the emergency entrance. Nazari planned to wait for the arrival of an ambulance and enter the hospital along with emergency personnel. He glanced at his watch; it was just after 1:00 a.m.

Nazari read the file on his targets. He wasn't worried about the woman; she would be easy. No one would take notice of a doctor inside the hospital; the target would be asleep and the guard at her door would not be expecting an attack. Exiting the hospital would be straightforward.

The other target could be difficult. Broussard was an intelligence agent, a professional like himself. He would be alert to danger and sense Nazari's presence. After reviewing the file, he decided to use the roof of the building across the street from Broussard's club as a firing position. As Broussard entered his club tomorrow morning, he would be a stationary target as he opened the front door. Nazari would use the long range sniper rifle he obtained earlier in the day from a discreet contact. Nazari would finish the hospital business, proceed to the club, scout his shooting position and then wait for morning. He would drive out of the country tomorrow.

Nazari pulled the envelope from the bag and counted the payment, then placed the money in the glove compartment. He took a fore-in-hand tie from the compartment and tied a professional looking knot over his white dress shirt. Pulling the white lab coat from the bag, he shook the out the wrinkles and attached the name tag. He put on the coat and buttoned it to make sure his weapon would be invisible tucked into the front waistband of his pants. Satisfied that he was ready, Nazari picked up the newspaper and continued to read while waiting for an ambulance to pull into the Emergency entrance.

Laura woke in the middle of the night. With the lights out and the door shut, she listened carefully before getting up. She was moving a bit better despite being attached to the IV. She opened the door to the room and stepped outside, rolling the IV stand alongside her.

The Marine guard stood and said, "Ms. Messier, can I help you?"

"Hi. I couldn't sleep. I was wondering if you knew the time?" she asked.

"Sure, it's Zero One Hundred, Ma'am." He looked alert and focused.

"We haven't met. I'm Laura Messier."

"Nice to meet you, Ma'am. I'm Corporal Mitch Jameson, United States Marine Corp."

"Are you one of the guards at the embassy?"

"Yes, Ma'am."

Jameson was an attractive young man, tall with blond hair and blue eyes. He had a kind look about him and smiled when he saw her.

"I'm surprised we've never met," she said. "I'm in and out of the embassy frequently."

"I usually pull night duty, Ma'am."

"So you're used to this late night stuff," she said with a smile.

"Yes, Ma'am. It isn't so bad. The shift change is at Zero Four Hundred, so it's a piece of cake really." He smiled at her.

"Do you mind if I ask you a question, Corporal?" Laura wanted to broach the subject gently.

"Not at all, Ma'am."

"I just wondered if you knew all the doctors and nurses on this shift."

"I think I've seen everyone who is supposed to be here tonight."

"What happens if you see someone you've not seen before?" she asked.

"I have the authority to use force, if necessary, to protect you, Ma'am," he said.

"Mitch, I need you to stay alert this evening. Would you do that for me?"

"Yes, Ma'am."

"Thank you so much, Mitch. I'm going to rest for a while. Please have the doctors and nurses knock before they enter the room, okay?"

"I will, Ma'am. Have a nice evening."

Laura climbed into bed, turned out all the lights and focused her vision until she could make out the black hands against the white background of the clock face. It was 1:15 a.m.

Tuning her hearing to concentrate on every sound, she heard occasional footsteps down the hall, the far away voices at the nurse's station and the hum of electronic devices. She tried to identify each sound and its location. Watching the light that spilled into the room from underneath the door, she could see the shadow of nurses walking past. She held the weapon in her lap.

At 2:00 a.m., Laura imagined U.S. warplanes roaring into Libyan airspace just atop the waves. *They'll be firing missile after missile at SAM installations in Benghazi and Tripoli,* she thought, *lighting up the nighttime sky, rendering the Libyans helpless against the awesome power of the American military.* She imagined chaos at the airfields where she pictured bombs destroying aircraft as they sat on the ground, barracks burning, men running for their lives. She pictured the F-111s screaming over Tripoli, using laser guided munitions to pound the Azizia compound, the Tripoli military airfield and the terrorist training camp. She pictured Gaddafi huddled underground, the ground shaking above him. *Instead of killing defenseless civilians, he had to face a real military.*

At 2:15 a.m., she pictured it being over with American pilots returning to the carriers or flying home to England. It was the righteous power of America defeating the evil Gaddafi regime. She laid her head back on the pillow and thought of everything that had happened over the weekend: Jean, Yani, Gaddafi, Markus, Henri, the escape.

Chapter Forty-Four

THE PERCEPTION OF time can become distorted in the silence of night. Absent the sun moving across the sky and the rhythmic patterns of daily activity, people are left to mark the passing of time by random sounds. Laura glanced at the clock; it was 2:40 a.m., but it seemed like an hour had passed since it read 2:35, and it might as well have been 3:40 or 4:40. When she heard a thump in the hallway, the sound of something unidentifiable, she thought she might have imagined it. Except it was followed by metallic sounds as though chair legs had scraped the floor so she knew it was real. Then it was gone and she heard nothing. However, her consciousness was raised. Her breathing became shallow and she began to sweat. *Relax,* she told herself. *Slow your breathing.* Laying her hand on the weapon, she felt fear. Field agents have an instinct for danger and although she had no reason to believe it, she sensed her killer was close by. Fear comes from the waiting, not from the doing.

Laura felt the fear drain away as she saw two small shadows come first, feet blocking the light underneath the door. The shadows lingered; someone stood in front of the door. Then, the slow, soft sound of the door latch being opened, after which light began to slowly flood the opposite side of the room as the door opened wider. Time stood still in that moment as Laura watched the shadow on the floor grow into the elongated shape of a man. She raised her gun and wondered whether it could possibly be a nurse. *No, a nurse wouldn't enter this way; neither would Mitch.* When Laura saw the full silhouette standing in front of her, she fired.

Nazari wasn't ready. The bullet struck his left shoulder. She heard him groan. The impact threw him back, but he was right-handed and he raised his weapon to line up his shot. She realized he could see her against the white background of the sheet and pillow.

She rolled off the bed to her left as he fired. She heard a thud as the bullet passed through the pillow behind her. "Fuck," she said when the IV stand came crashing down on top of her. Laura was entangled by tubes hanging off the IV stand. She was face down, weapon underneath her. The force of the fall caused her broken ribs to sear with pain.

Move, she thought. *Keep moving or die.* She kept rolling as he fired again. He lined up that shot perfectly, except she moved as he fired. The shot struck her in the side and she felt the burn of it, like she had touched the burner on a stove top. The wound in his shoulder had slowed him just enough to allow Laura to roll onto her back and free the weapon from underneath her.

She grabbed the handle with both hands, pointed the weapon in his direction and fired just to get metal flying in his direction. They were about eight feet apart now and neither would miss. Laura's shot found its mark, this time in his right shoulder. He yelled; she hurt him worse that time. His weapon dipped slightly after the round hit his shoulder. He had to recover his firing line which gave her a split second.

Laura improved her aim, right at the center of his chest. The slight pause gave Nazari time to aim and both of them fired simultaneously. Her shot was a kill shot. By luck, skill or an act of God, it hit him dead center in the chest. The impact threw him back against the wall and he exploded in blood.

His shot hit her as well, but due to the wound in his right shoulder, he didn't quite raise the barrel enough. She felt the burn as the round tore through the flesh of her leg.

Laura watched him struggle against the wall from the chest wound while he slowly slid down the wall into a sitting position. He wasn't dead, but he was too weak to stand. He raised his weapon and fired again, but could no longer aim properly. The bullet went wide, bouncing off the bed frame and into the wall. The floor was becoming covered with blood, but Laura could not tell whether it was hers or his.

She crawled toward him to make sure her last shot wouldn't miss. She was dizzy, weak, and didn't believe she could stay conscious long enough to kill him, but the blood on the floor allowed her to slide as much as pull herself to him. Nazari fired again, this time his round bounced off the floor and embedded itself in the closet door behind her. Laura reached out to slap his gun away as he lifted it to fire again. He held on and fired, but her hand had already moved the gun aside. She could see his face, blood oozing from his mouth. Nazari raised a hand to fight her, but he was too weak. Laura propped herself up, pushed his hand away and leaned over him. He looked at her and as Laura rested the barrel of the Sig on his forehead, he knew it was over. "I know you can still hear me," Laura said. "Lady Liberty says hello." She pulled the trigger; blood and bone and hair flew in all directions as the explosion tore into his head. That's all she remembered.

Epilogue

WHEN LAURA AWOKE, she knew time had passed, but it seemed like days rather than hours. It was impossible to take an inventory of her injuries; she was heavily bandaged and couldn't feel much due to pain killers. Steve appeared to be standing at the foot of the bed, however, she had difficulty speaking.

"What happened?" Laura whispered more than spoke. She pulled a tube from her nose. Steve walked to her side and smiled.

"Honey, let me help you put the tube back on. It helps you breath."

"I can breathe without it. What about the kid guarding my room? Is he okay?"

Rick walked over from the other side of the room. "Laura, we can talk later. You need to rest."

"Tell me, Rick. Mitch is his name, isn't it?"

"I'm sorry, Laura. He never saw it coming. The shot was taken from the nurse's station at the end of the hall."

"Nurses?" she asked.

"Two down in their chairs behind the counter."

"Anyone else?"

"One DST agent was found dead in the stairwell," Rick said.

As Laura realized how many lives had been lost, she began to sob uncontrollably. The Marine guard, the nurses; they were all known to her. "They were taking care of me," she said softly.

"This is not your fault, honey. None of it," Steve said.

"That's right, Laura. This is the work of Gaddafi," Rick added.

Laura was too exhausted to stay awake any longer.

The next time she woke up, it seemed to be a different day. Steve had changed his clothing. Rick, Henri and Steve were standing at the foot of Laura's bed talking among themselves.

"What day is it?" Laura asked.

"It's Thursday morning, sweetie," Steve said. He glanced at the clock, "10:15." He walked over and held Laura's hand.

"Am I going to be okay?" she asked.

"Yes, dear. The bullet that passed through your side fractured a rib, but that may have saved your life. It changed the trajectory of the round and none of your vital organs were hit. The round you took in the thigh clipped your bone, but the surgeon thinks he removed all the fragments. You lost a lot of blood before you were found. It will take a while, but you'll make a full recovery."

Henri and Rick came close to the bed. Laura looked at Rick. "Who was he?"

"His name was Rashid Nazari," Rick said, "one of the most notorious assassins in the world. He was on everyone's top ten list. Gaddafi sent the very best, Laura."

"He just stood there and kept firing. He was a machine."

"Do you feel strong enough to tell us what happened," Henri asked. "We brought a forensics team in, but we're unsure about the firing sequence."

"I don't remember it all, Henri," she said. "He came at me just as you said he would. I fired first, then I rolled off the bed. We kept firing at each other and I can't remember much else."

"We counted the shots," Rick said. "He shot six times, you took two rounds. You shot four times and hit him four times. No Ranger or Navy Seal could have done better, Laura."

"I remember now," she said. "Rick, he made me shoot the last shot."

"You mean the head shot?" he asked.

"Yes. He wouldn't stop firing."

"Laura, that wasn't cruel. He would have gone on killing innocent people until someone stopped him. I'm sorry that responsibility fell to you. It shouldn't have. But, God chose you, Laura. Remember that."

The nurses kept running visitors out of the room each time they found them, all except Steve. He was Laura's constant companion. He gave her a reason to live.

By the time John Brownley visited, Laura knew it was Friday evening. He spoke briefly to Steve and she opened her eyes when she heard his voice.

"Hi, John."

"Hi, Laura, how are you feeling?"

"I'd feel a lot better knowing what happened in the attack," she said.

"It was a success. The Air Force hit their targets around Tripoli and the Navy hit theirs around Benghazi."

"What were our losses?"

"Only one plane, an F-111 out of Britain. EUCOM is reporting it went down from mechanical failure, but the latest I heard, it was hit by a SAM."

"Probably the last one to do its run. The Libyans likely had everything firing by then. The pilots?"

"We think they were killed."

"What have the Soviets done in response?" she asked.

"Nothing, other than condemn the raid."

"I was worried about that. The Soviets had been flying in and out of Benghazi."

"The President notified them as the attack occurred. I'm not sure whether they had anyone there that night or not," Brownley said.

"Collateral damage? Some of the sites in Tripoli are in congested areas," she said.

"There was some, but it's impossible to know whether we did it or the Libyans did it themselves. The French Embassy was damaged."

"What about Gaddafi?" Laura asked.

"He lived."

"Probably stayed in his underground office. What about his wife and kids?"

"We're not sure. The Libyans claim one of his kids was killed, but we have no verification of that," Brownley said. "How are you feeling?"

"Me? I'm okay, John. It looks like I'm going to be off work for a while."

"We're going to send you back to the States when you're able to travel. You're due for a long vacation. You've earned it."

"I think I'd like to do nothing, except bake cookies for a while," she said.

Brownley laughed. "I'd like to make an apology to you, Laura, before I leave."

"For what?"

"Completely underestimating you. You're one hell of an operative. The best I've ever seen. I'll get out of here and let you rest. Take care." He kissed her cheek.

Marie Colvin stopped by a few days later. She smiled as she entered the room. "Hey there," she said. "I had a hell of a time getting in to see you."

"Sorry, Marie, my fault. I should have put you on the list. How are you?" Laura asked.

"Me? I'm fine. How are you doing?"

"I'm going to be okay; it's just going to take a while."

"There's a rumor going around town about a shoot-out here at the hospital the other night. There was nothing in the papers about it, but from the looks of you, I'd say the rumor was true."

"You know I can't talk about that, Marie," Laura said.

"You know I had to ask."

"When did you get back?" Laura asked.

"Yesterday."

"What happened?"

"Well, they tore the shit out of Azizia," Marie said. "The Libyans set up a press tour so we could see the damage. A lot of their missile sites were hit, too. It happened in the middle of the night, the next night after I saw you."

"Collateral damage?"

"We toured the neighborhood around Azizia." Marie said. "Some of the embassies were hit, homes, that sort of thing. It might not have been the Americans, though. Libyan missiles were falling all over the place."

"What about Gaddafi?" Laura asked.

"I managed to talk to him by phone afterward. He's okay, but he said one of his kids was killed."

315

"He probably left them above ground during the bombing," Laura said.

"You didn't look well at the party, Laura. Did he rape you?" she asked gently.

Laura looked out the window and tried to block it from her mind. When Marie saw Laura look away, she simply said, "I'm sorry."

"It wasn't supposed to happen that way. The mission fell apart. I was lucky to get out alive."

"I'd like to write the story when it's declassified," Marie said.

"You'll be the first one I call if they do."

"Thanks."

"Marie, you do a great thing when you report the horrors of conflict," Laura said. "The world needs to know about that. I want you to know we're trying to prevent terrorism in the first place. We don't always get it right, but I believe in what we're doing."

"I know you do," Marie said as she held Laura's hand. "You're a good person, Laura. I'm sorry I can't stay longer, I've got to get back to work. I wanted to stop by and see how you were doing."

"Thanks, Marie. I really appreciate it."

Marie started to walk out, but stopped, turned around and said as an afterthought, "Gaddafi's pissed off at you. He knows you're CIA."

"Yeah, well, Muammar and I have some unfinished business."

Marie smiled. "You take care, Laura."

"You, too, Marie."

Laura stayed ten days at American Hospital before being released. Steve slept in her room, talked with her doctors and managed her care. He stopped by her apartment every few days, too. Laura asked him to watch for blue chalk marks on the wall, but he found none. Gaddafi must have had enough on his mind. Laura thought they'd be safe and they were.

Henri stopped by once more before he returned to Tripoli. The French Embassy had been severely damaged in the bombing, but since the attack occurred at night, there were few injuries. Rick Williams stopped by often and she enjoyed his visits immensely. The Minister of Foreign Affairs, Laura's boss at her cover job, dropped by. Her job would be waiting when she felt strong enough to return.

Laura had only one other visitor of note, Jean Broussard. He poked his head in the door one day and said, "Mademoiselle?" She knew instantly it was Jean.

"Jean, I'm so glad to see you. Thank you for coming." She stretched out her arms and he gave her a big kiss on each cheek. "You're looking wonderful today. I've never seen you look so beautiful," he said.

"You need to get an eye exam."

"Mademoiselle, I look with my heart and you're the most beautiful woman in the world."

"Stop it, Jean! You're going to make me smile," she said, already beaming. "You must tell me how you've been."

"I am fine and the Mademoiselle is so kind to ask about me when such misfortune has befallen her."

"I want to introduce you to the love of my life, Jean. This is Steve Tilton."

Steve stood and stuck out his hand. "Laura speaks highly of you, Mr. Broussard," Steve said.

"It is such a pleasure to meet you, Mr. Tilton. The two of you look like you belong together."

"Why don't I leave to allow you two some privacy," Steve offered. "I would imagine you've got a lot to talk about."

"No, no, I do not want to tire the Mademoiselle today," Jean replied. "She and I will get together soon and have our little chat over coffee, won't we?"

"Yes, Jean," Laura said with a smile. "At the coffee shop where we went before."

"Exactly. Mademoiselle, I wish you a full recovery and please call me when you're feeling better. We have much to discuss."

"I will, Jean."

"Oh, I nearly forgot," Jean said, digging into his shoulder bag. "Pierre Doucet asked me to give you this."

Jean smiled as he handed her a large padded envelope. Both of them knew its contents. Laura opened it and held the jewel up so the light could reflect off of it.

"I estimate its value to be nearly two million of your U.S. dollars, Mademoiselle," Jean said. "The Ambassador says it belongs to you."

"What about the other item. The ring?" Laura asked.

Jean laughed. "That item had no value, Mademoiselle. I threw it in the Seine this morning," he said.

With that, it was Laura's turn to laugh. "That's a great place for it."

"Monsieur Tilton and Mademoiselle, I will take your leave. We will talk again."

"Thank you, Jean, for everything. You're the reason I'm here today," she said.

"We saved each other, Mademoiselle." He kissed her again on both cheeks before leaving.

Laura held up the jewel to look at its beauty. The sun was shining through the window and when the light caught the stone just right, it reflected its color onto the walls. She looked at Steve. "They say it's one of the largest cut emeralds in the world."

"You going to keep it?" Steve asked.

"No, I just wanted to look at it one more time before I return it."

"Jean mentioned a ring. I'm sure there's a story there," he said with a smile.

Laura shrugged, "Maybe, maybe not."

"By the way, I like what you've done with your hair," Steve said.

"Really?"

"I think blond is your color,"

"You know, I'm beginning to like it, too," she said.

The next morning, Laura pulled the tray table across her lap, took a piece of stationery and wrote a note to the Colonel.

Dear Muammar,
I am returning the jewel. I expect you to leave me
alone. If you send anyone else, no power
on earth will stop me from killing you. If you respect
my right to live in peace, I will respect
yours. I would like your children to grow up knowing
their father.
Sincerely,

Laura Messier

Steve wrapped the package and dropped it off with Brownley, who promised to have the package delivered. Laura never heard from the Colonel again. It was a long time before she felt safe, but it looked as though Gaddafi ended the matter with the return of the stone.

***

When the hospital released her ten days later, Steve and Laura returned to the apartment where they packed her things to travel back to the States. Laura noticed the new locks.

"Hey, Steve, did you put new locks on the doors?"

"No, Rick Williams had the embassy do it. I got the keys from him."

"Very thoughtful," she said. "What time's the flight this afternoon?"

"Oh … whenever we show up," Steve said coyly.

"What are you talking about?"

"You'll see." He would say nothing more about it.

An embassy car showed up, they left for de Gaulle, but instead of dropping Steve and Laura off at the terminal, it pulled onto the tarmac beside a Boeing 747.

"Where did this come from?" she asked as Steve helped her up the stairs. She was still using a wheelchair.

"Bill Casey sent it. We're not putting you at risk again."

"How's he planning to get this past the bean counters in accounting?" she asked.

Steve shrugged, "To tell you the truth, it's probably slush fund money," he said with a laugh.

Three Days in Tripoli

Once back in Washington, Laura relaxed for the first time in weeks. Steve left for work each morning, came home at a decent hour and Laura imagined this to be what married life might be like. She did physical therapy every other day, cleaned house, cooked meals and baked those cookies she'd been thinking about. Laura visited a mental health counselor each week, learning how to manage the emotional scars that lingered. Clair George delayed the debriefing interview which helped her recovery. She would be haunted by the experience, but in time she'd return to normal.

***

In early June, Laura felt strong enough for Steve to take her to their usual vacation spot in Ouray, Colorado, for a couple of weeks. The beauty of the mountains, the leisurely pace they adopted there and the coolness of the weather lifted her spirits after a tough year. On the Thursday morning before they returned to D.C., a call came into the cabin early in the morning. As usual, Laura was still sleeping, but Steve, who always got up at the crack of dawn, was at the kitchen table planning the day's activities.

"Hello," Steve said.

"Hi, Steve; its Clair calling from Langley. Sorry to be calling so early, but I need to speak with Laura."

"Okay, hold on a minute," Steve said.

"Laura?" Steve said loudly, sticking his head into the bedroom. "Phone call, dear. It's Clair George."

"The last time I took a call from Clair at the cabin, I ended up getting shot, Steve. I'm not taking the call."

"Come on, be a good sport about it."

"Steve, I'm serious. Clair George can go fuck himself," she said.

"My hand is over the receiver, Laura, but I think he heard that."

"Oh, all right." Laura lifted the extension. "Hello?"

"Hi, Laura. Sorry to disturb you so early in the morning, but I wanted to remind you that we're having our wrap-up meeting on Eldorado Canyon next Monday at 10:00 a.m. I'm sure Steve told you."

"Clair, Steve never tells me a damn thing. I had no idea. You're saying I need to be there?"

"Yes, I'm sorry; the meeting's mandatory."

"So if I don't show up, I'm fired, right?"

"You and I both, Laura," Clair said. "I don't want to be fired, so show up, please?"

"All right, I give up; I'll be there. Can I go back to sleep now?" she asked.

Clair laughed. "Enjoy the rest of your vacation and I'll see you on Monday."

Laura hung up and turned to Steve. "That man annoys the hell out of me!"

"Come, I have something to show you," Steve said.

Laura put on her bathrobe and made her way to the kitchen with great difficulty because her right leg was still healing. Steve poured coffee.

"I want you to see this," he said. Steve had legal documents spread across the table.

"Surely, you can't be working on vacation, dear?" she asked.

"These are the closing documents for a piece of property I'm buying. I'm closing next Tuesday," Steve said.

"What are you buying?"

"Here, take a look," he said.

Laura looked at the address on the closing sheet. "Are you kidding me?"

"I know how much you love the place," Steve said. "I fell in love with the view of the Eiffel Tower from the kitchen window, so I found the owner and made an offer. After Tuesday, we own it."

"You're amazing," she said.

Returning to Georgetown late Sunday night, Laura was exhausted and when Steve forced her up on Monday morning for the trip out to Langley, she refused to be rushed.

"Laura, dear, please, we can't be late this morning."

"If we're late, they'll start without me."

"Today, I don't think they will, so hurry up."

The working group for Eldorado Canyon had already gathered when Steve and Laura walked into Clair's office. The group immediately walked together downstairs to the small lecture hall on the main floor, another of the rooms at CIA where Laura had never been.

When they exited the elevator on the ground floor, Laura realized security had become tight during the short time she'd been upstairs. When she entered the building twenty minutes ago, everything seemed normal. Now, all access points were monitored; hallways, doors, elevators, and the entrances to the auditorium were guarded by men checking ID badges. Floating security teams wandered about watching employees walk through the lobby. They didn't appear to be CIA and as Laura walked through the lobby, she asked Steve, "Are those guys Secret Service?"

"Don't know," he said, a little too casually. Steve knew what was going on, but he wasn't going to tell her. Frankly, that bugged the hell out of her.

The auditorium was more akin to a small college lecture hall. The light wood colored flooring, quasi-theatrical lighting and carpeted walls made the hall seem out of place amid the sterile decor of the building. The meeting was lightly attended because Eldorado Canyon had been a classified operation with only a minimum of people involved. Only the first two rows were filled. Steve grabbed a couple of seats up front which Laura appreciated as she still had difficulty negotiating stairs. Laura settled in for a boring recap of the mission and at 10:00 a.m. sharp, Director William J. Casey walked to the podium to speak.

"Good morning ladies and gentlemen. Thank you for coming today. The greatest honor I have in my role as Director of the Central Intelligence Agency is to acknowledge the achievements of the great people who work here. We have gathered here today to honor one of those people. The Intelligence Star is the highest award given at the CIA. It has been awarded only a few times in the history of the agency and only to those who have shown acts of great courage performed under conditions of the gravest risk. The outstanding achievements of the person we honor today set the standard by which all of us at the CIA aspire to. We have a special guest today to present the award. Ladies and gentlemen, please rise and welcome the President of the United States."

President Ronald Reagan entered through one of the side doors. Laura had never seen him before in person. He was taller than she had imagined him to be, big with broad shoulders and he looked larger than life itself. He wore a huge smile and waved as he walked to the podium accompanied by the enthusiastic applause of those present. Standing behind the podium, he looked very much like Laura had seen him on television, hugely confident and comfortable in front of people. He waved the applause down.

"Thank you everyone, thank you," he said as he waited for the applause to finish. "It's great to be with you this morning for this special occasion. It isn't often that I have the privilege to meet a true American heroine. But I have that privilege today. It is my deepest honor to present this award today to someone whose acts of courage and self-sacrifice in the face of grave danger saved the lives of American pilots. Miss Laura Messier, would you please step forward to allow me to present you with the Intelligence Star?"

Laura was shocked. *How could this be happening?* she thought. Steve nudged her and whispered in her ear, "Here, honey, let me help you up." Steve helped her rise, but the President shooed him away. "Here, let me help you, Laura," the President said as he walked her to the podium. Still limping and weak kneed from the revelation, she could hardly walk. Tears came to her eyes as everyone kept applauding and whistling. The group rose to their feet as she stood next to President Reagan. The President pulled the Intelligence Star from its holder, unfolded the blue ribbon from which the Star hung and lifted it over her head.

"Congratulations, Laura," he said warmly, taking her hand. He smiled, turned to the audience and said, "Ladies and gentlemen, I present Laura Messier, one of the bravest people I've ever met." The applause started anew.

Bill Casey stepped to the podium and said, "Thank you, Mr. President and congratulations, Miss Messier. We ask that everyone join us in the Executive Dining Room where brunch will be served." With that, Ronald Reagan took Laura's arm and escorted her to brunch. "Mr. President," she said, "you'll have to excuse me, but I'm not able to walk very fast."

Reagan laughed. "Well, I can't either, Laura, so we'll just walk slowly and you know what? I think they'll wait for us." Laura leaned on him quite heavily as they walked down the hall, but the President didn't seem to mind. "Laura, I was updated frequently while you were in Libya and I want you to know that Nancy and I prayed for your safe return."

"That's very kind of you, Mr. President. I believe God had a lot to do with me getting out of there."

"You know, we lost those two pilots," Reagan said, "and I feel a terrible responsibility for their loss. I'm glad we didn't lose you, too."

"I had a lot of help, Mr. President and a lot of luck," Laura said.

"You've done a great, great service for your country, Ms. Messier. I want to convey my personal thanks for your contribution," the President said.

There was an impromptu receiving line in the dining room where everyone wanted to meet the President and offer their regards to Laura. As Steve came through the line, Laura introduced him. "Mr. President, this is the special man in my life, Steve Tilton, the Assistant Director of Intelligence here at the agency.

"Very nice to meet you, Mr. Tilton. I'm hoping that you will keep this young lady out of trouble from now on," the President said with a smile.

"I intend to do just that, Mr. President."

The President didn't stay long, but one of his aides informed Laura that the President wished to speak with her before he left. "Laura, I wondered if you would be kind enough to do me a favor?" the President asked.

"Absolutely, Sir," she said.

"We are having a formal State dinner this fall at the White House for the President of France. I was hoping you'd agree to sit at the table with us and serve as interpreter. He doesn't speak English and I don't know a word of French."

"Of course, Sir, I'd be happy to do that."

"Please bring that gentleman of yours with you, too. He seems like a nice fellow. The White House social secretary will be in touch with you in a couple of months about the dinner. Once again, congratulations on your award."

As the lunch crowd began to thin, Clair came over to offer his congratulations. "Laura, I want to express how proud we are. It's a well-deserved honor that, unfortunately, I must take away from you and store in the agency vault until you retire," he said.

"You're kidding, right?" she asked.

"The award is classified, Laura, just like the mission. I'm sorry, but neither you nor the agency can reveal that you've been awarded the Star." Laura took the Star off and gave it to Clair.

"We'll keep it safe for you," he assured her.

"That's fine, Clair," she said. "Thanks for your support. You were the only one who believed in me."

"Everyone's a believer now, Laura. Go home, rest, let Steve take care of you and let us know when you're ready to go back to work."

"Thank you, again, Clair, for everything."

Steve walked over. "Are you ready to go? Let's get out of here and go buy some property in Paris tomorrow."

"Nothing would please me more, Mr. Tilton."

***

The next day, Steve and Laura would buy the building at 51 Rue Cler, 75007, in Paris, where the lights from the Eiffel Tower would twinkle at them out the kitchen window for many years to come. Laura and Steve planned to get married later that summer so Laura could be back in Paris by next September, doing the usual things, in her usual way, at the usual places. She'd stop for a croissant every morning on her way to work, look for chalk marks on the wall down the street and slip out the through the butcher shop once in a while. She'd continue working for the Ministry of Foreign Affairs and for CIA, too, where John Brownley would continue to complain about her lack of tradecraft.

Steve planned to work out of his Washington office, but he'd spend plenty of time in Paris. Laura would finally get the chance to sit with a true friend, Jean Broussard and they'd sip coffee out of cheap paper cups and talk about whatever came to mind. She might finally cook Rick

Williams a mess of biscuits and gravy because he was another true friend.

And Laura Messier planned to continue her involvement in events that would shape the destiny of nations because as someone once said, with a hundred like her, they could rule the world.

Thank you for reading my book. If you enjoyed it, won't you please take a moment to leave me a review at your favorite retailer?

Thanks!

Lawrence Scofield

Follow me on Twitter:
http://twitter.com/LScofieldAuthor
Friend me on Facebook:
https://facebook.com/LawrenceScofieldAuthor
Favorite me at Smashwords:
https://www.smashwords.com/profile/view/LawrenceE
Scofield

Author's Notes

The American government had been planning an attack on Libya for months as a last resort to stop Muammar Gaddafi's support for terrorist activities. After Libya's involvement in the December, 1985, attacks on the Rome and Vienna airports was proven, President Ronald Reagan warned Gaddafi that military force may be necessary if Libya continued its support for terrorism. The American military action against Libya in the early morning hours of April 15, 1986, was in direct retaliation for the bombing of a West Berlin discotheque, April 5, 1986, planned and executed by the Libyan Embassy in East Berlin. The attack killed three and injured 230. Two American servicemen were killed and another 79 servicemen were injured.

In the aftermath of the American attack, it was reported that Muammar Gaddafi lived on a bus for months, never spending more than a day at any location fearing another attack. The bombing did not damage Libyan installations as extensively as press reports in Tripoli claimed, but moderate damage was later seen in Pentagon aerial photographs. Homes and embassies nearby in Tripoli were accidentally damaged by errant bombs, although it is likely that some of the destruction was caused by Libyan missiles that missed their American targets.

Several American pilots on the mission believed it was the Pentagon's intent to kill Gaddafi, who was present inside Libya's Military Headquarters in Tripoli at the time. Pilots complained that the Pentagon's insistence on a precise manner of attack increased the likelihood their planes would be hit by enemy fire. One American F-111 was shot down, although there are varying claims about where and how the jet was actually hit. The plane crashed in the Mediterranean Sea and its two American pilots, Paul F. Lorence and Fernando L. Ribas-Dominicci, lost their lives.

Libyan long range surface to air missile systems were shut off during the attack for an unknown reason. The lack of Libyan long range radar contributed greatly to the success of the attack. American warplanes were not seen on Libyan radar screens until intermediate and short range radars picked them up over Tripoli harbor. It has been suggested that Gaddafi frequently kept them off to prevent his own military from instituting a coup by shooting down his own aircraft as it traveled in and out of Tripoli. The absence of Libyan long range radar that evening gave me the opportunity to create a fictional CIA mission to intentionally turn them off.

It is likely that Gaddafi had advance warning of the attack, however the source of the warning is disputed. The Italian Prime Minister was implicated, but there are other possibilities as well. An American military research paper accuses an unnamed American journalist, presumably Marie Colvin, of warning Gaddafi, although I do not see how that was possible. Prior knowledge of the attack was limited to just a few people inside the American government. A third possibility is military coast watchers, either on Malta or in Tunisia, saw the American planes as they approached the Libyan coast. This is the source I used in the novel.

The United Nations General Assembly condemned the bombing afterward. The action was strongly supported by American allies and some privately suggested the attack should have been more severe. Gaddafi's support for terrorist groups continued afterward, although not publicly admitted. It was the 1988 bombing of Pan Am flight 103 over Lockerbie, Scotland that ultimately brought a cessation of Libyan support for terrorism, although the incident took years to resolve. Two Libyans were charged with the crime and in 2002, Libya finally accepted responsibility for the bombing, which killed all 259 people aboard the flight and 11 people living in the town of Lockerbie. As a result of negotiations with the Libyan government, in 2008, the United States entered into a comprehensive settlement agreement with Libya to compensate the victim's families for the 1986 United States bombing of Libya, the 1988 Lockerbie airplane bombing, the 1986 Berlin bombing and American casualties resulting from an additional airline bombing. Muammar Gaddafi died in 2011 at the hands of militants after a coup.

Marie Colvin, the legendary American journalist for whom the Marie Colvin Center of International Reporting at the Stony Brook School of Journalism is named, was in Tripoli at the time of the bombing and contacted Gaddafi by telephone immediately after the attack, as stated by Colvin herself. Some of the material used in the novel about Gaddafi came from Colvin's written statements and interviews. Additional information was derived from recorded interviews with former members of Gaddafi's personal staff, and other published sources. Colvin was later killed in Syria in 2012, reporting on Syrian government atrocities against its own people. It has been suggested that the Syrian government intentionally targeted Colvin and her cameraman.

William J. Casey, Director of the CIA and Clair George, the Deputy Director of Operations at the time of the attack, became embroiled in the 1987 Congressional Iran-Contra investigation. Casey was hospitalized with a brain tumor before he could testify as to his knowledge of Iran-Contra. He died shortly after. George did testify before Congress and was convicted of giving false statements to congressional committees. He was later pardoned by President George H. W. Bush, himself a former Director of the CIA. George died in 2011.

Among the various materials I used in researching the novel are two excellent volumes, "Qaddafi, Terrorism, and the Origins of the U.S. Attack on Libya," by Brian Lee Davis and "Eldorado Canyon: Reagan's Undeclared War with Qaddafi," by Joseph T. Stanik. For those interested in further reading about the bombing, one can hardly do better than to read those wonderful accounts.

###

About the Author

Lawrence Scofield holds degrees from the University of Missouri at Kansas City and Northwestern University in Evanston, Illinois. Early in his career, he enjoyed performing with major symphony orchestras and opera companies. He has appeared on Grammy Award winning recordings and has international touring experience. Following a career in the performing arts, Mr. Scofield served in the administrations at colleges and universities. After retirement, he turned his attention to the written word and now writes novels, articles and columns.

Sneak Peek

Next in "The Laura Messier Files" Series

One Day in Lebanon

A Spy Thriller

By Lawrence Scofield

Prologue

September 22, 1988

When William Sharp left his rented townhouse Thursday morning in the diplomatic section of Damascus, Syria, he had no reason to suspect this day would be different than any other. After negotiating the congested downtown Damascus traffic, Bill, as his friends called him, pulled up to the back gate at the American Embassy a few minutes before nine. "How are you this morning, Harry?" he asked the American Marine stationed at the gate.

"Very good, Mr. Sharp," the young Marine replied as he pressed the button that slid the electronic iron gate open.

"Thanks, buddy," Bill said before driving through the gate and parking behind the building.

Bill entered the double doors at the back of the Embassy and took the stairs two at a time up to his office on the second floor. He threw his briefcase on the desk, hung his jacket on the back of the door and then walked down the hallway toward the front of the building to check in with the duty officer and retrieve messages. "What's up this morning, Richard," Sharp said to the clerk.

"Morning, Bill. Brooks left this for you," Richard said, handing Sharp an interoffice envelope. Franklin Brooks was the Ambassador and Bill, in his mid-thirties and a former Army Delta Force officer, served as his assistant.

"Thanks," Bill said, grabbing the envelope. "See you later," he said before heading back to his office.

He sat down behind his desk, propped up his feet and opened the envelope. It was a one page itinerary with a handwritten note by Brooks scribbled across the top. "Cover this for me. I've got a conflict," the note said, signed "FB."

Sharp scanned the page. Nicholas Buck, the Under Secretary of State for Political Affairs was flying in from Brussels this morning to meet with President Hafez al-Assad. Brooks wanted Sharp to meet the Secretary at Mezze Air Force Base, accompany him to the Presidential Palace for the meeting and return him to the airport afterward. Sharp immediately picked up the phone. "Richard, I thought Brooks was supposed to babysit the Secretary today," Sharp said.

"Apparently, something came up, Bill. Brooks is already gone."

Sharp looked at his watch. "All right. Tell Henry to bring the car around to the back and I'll be out in a couple of minutes."

"Henry went with Brooks."

"Who's my driver then?" Sharp asked, surprised that the Embassy's best driver was unavailable.

The clerk looked at a list. "It says here it's Ahmed."

"Who the hell's Ahmed?"

"A new hire. He's a local guy."

"Come on, Richard," Sharp said, slightly frustrated at the violation of policy. "You know we never put foreign drivers with visitors. Can't one of you guys drive us?"

"Everyone's busy this morning, Bill. Ahmed will be okay. He knows the city."

"Does he even speak English?"

"Of course he does. You won't have a problem. What time you think you'll have the car back?"

"I have no clue." Sharp glanced at the itinerary. "It says here the meeting's at ten. You know how these things go. They can last fifteen minutes, they can last two hours. You need me to check in?"

"I'd appreciate it. We need the car later in the day."

"All right. See you later." Sharp hung up the phone and stared at the itinerary. Why do they always keep us short staffed around here? Bill asked himself.

Sharp took his jacket from the back of the office door, walked downstairs to grab a cup of coffee from the cafeteria, then walked out into the parking lot where he found his driver, a diminutive young Syrian man, leaning against a black embassy limo with diplomatic plates.

"Are you Ahmed?" Sharp asked, approaching the car.

"Yes, Sir."

"You got a last name, Ahmed, or are you one of those rock stars with only one name?"

"It's Kalami, Sir. Ahmed Kalami."

"Are you related to Safa?" Bill asked. Safa worked on the housekeeping staff at the Embassy.

"Yes, Sir. I'm her brother."

"That's the best way to get a job, my friend. Connections."

"Yes, Sir," Ahmed said.

"You have a full tank of gas?"

"Just filled it now, Sir."

"Okay. I'm gonna ride in front with you. You know where you're going?"

"No, Sir."

"Mezze Airport."

3

"The Air Force base?" Ahmed asked.

"Yep. Let's go."

The men climbed into the limo and Ahmed pulled out of the Embassy gate. *With Henry, this trip would be routine,* Bill thought. *With this guy, who the hell knows?* He watched Ahmed negotiate his way through traffic, eventually turning onto the thoroughfare that led to the airport.

"How long have you been working at the Embassy, Ahmed?" Sharp asked, seeking to break the ice and get to know Ahmed.

"A week," Ahmed said.

"You certainly know your way around the city," Sharp said, watching Ahmed make his way through downtown Damascus.

"I've lived here my entire life."

"Really? What part?"

Ahmed pointed off to the south. "Over there."

I thought the Kalami's lived northwest of the city. "Are you living with your parents?"

Ahmed nodded, "Just until I get my own place."

Maybe I'm wrong, Bill thought. *Perhaps they do live south of the city.* "You certainly speak good English," Bill said.

Ahmed chuckled. "I studied in America for a while. A foreign exchange student."

"Where did you go to school?"

"Harvard University."

Sharp whistled. "No shit? Damn, you must be smart." Why would a Harvard educated kid work a driving job?

"Just an average student, Sir," Ahmed said, glancing over at Sharp.

4

One Day in Lebanon

The Kalami father runs a business in town. Why wouldn't he hire his Harvard educated son? Let's get through the day and I'll find out more about this kid when we get back. Ahmed was taking the proper route to the airport so Sharp decided to let the matter drop.

As they swung around the cloverleaf in front of the airport, Sharp pointed toward the north end of the terminal. "You need to go to that end, Ahmed. You're looking for a gate with a guard shack."

"I know where it is."

"You've been out here before?"

"Many times."

Who is this kid? Bill wondered.

Ahmed found the gate and spoke to the guard in Arabic. He turned to Sharp. "He wants to see your embassy identification." Sharp held it up and the guard bent over and took a cursory look. The guard gave Ahmed his approval and pointed to the Jeeps waiting inside the gate. Ahmed turned to Sharp. "The guard says we must follow the escort."

"Go ahead and pull in behind them," Sharp said. "They know where we need to be."

The automatic gate slid open and as they drove through the gate, one Jeep pulled in front, the other behind. Sharp and his driver were led around the terminal and onto the tarmac where the Jeep in front abruptly stopped. Sharp could see a row of MIG fighter jets parked at the opposite end of the tarmac. *It's an Air Force base, but Assad's personal airport, too. It must be nice to have your own airport.*

One of the soldiers climbed out, walked back to the limo and knocked on Sharp's window. Sharp opened the

5

window and smelled the strong odor of jet fuel wafting through the air. "Wait here. Plane pull up," the soldier said in broken English.

Sharp nodded. "Okay."

Ahmed kept the engine running and the air conditioning on high during the wait. The day promised to be sunny and hot, typical early fall weather for Damascus. It was after nine and the temperature was already in the upper 80s. Sharp watched the plane land fifteen minutes later, a white Boeing 747 with the words "United States of America" printed in white on a blue background above the windows. "Stay in the car," Sharp said as the plane taxied toward them. "When they get off the plane, walk around and open the back door for them," Sharp said.

"Yes, Sir."

Airport maintenance wedged blocks under the tires and rolled portable stairs up to the plane's door. Sharp could hear the whine of the engines decrease as the pilots shut the craft down. The door opened and two men and a woman walked down the stairs. Sharp got out of the limo and immediately felt the heat radiating off the pavement. As he walked toward the plane, he saw two MIG fighters land on the runway in the distance.

Sharp met his party halfway across the tarmac. He extended his hand to the older man. "Bill Sharp, American Embassy here in Damascus."

The older gentleman, in his late 50s with wire rim glasses, smiled weakly. "Nicholas Buck, Under Secretary for Political Affairs, State Department."

"Nice to meet you, Sir."

"This is my assistant, Melissa Clarke," Buck said, gesturing toward the woman, "and Harry Acker, my interpreter."

Sharp shook the hands of both. "Nice to meet you. Would you step this way?" Sharp held his hand out toward the limo. Ahmed opened the back door and all three squeezed into the back seat.

"When we pull out," Sharp advised Ahmed as they climbed back into the limo, "keep some distance between you and the vehicle in front. No accidents today."

The Jeep made a U-turn on the tarmac and proceeded around the terminal to the gate while the Jeep that trailed the entourage followed closely behind. The guards had left the gate open and all three vehicles sped through and onto the expressway ramp that led to the private two lane road between Mezze Airport and the Presidential Palace.

Nicholas Buck glanced at his watch. "How long is the drive, Mr. Sharp?"

"Should be just a few minutes, Sir. This road takes us directly to the Palace." The air base and the palace sat beside each other on a plateau northwest of the city. Sharp looked to the south over the downtown area that sat below a large cliff that separated the Palace from the rest of the city. *It's a pretty view from up here*, he thought.

To the north, the plateau stretched for miles; nothing but scrub brush and small trees dotted the arid landscape. The government prevented commercial development around the base and the palace for security reasons. This was one of the safest parts of the city.

Fifteen minutes later, the Syrian escort led the entourage onto the Palace grounds, which included three large modern buildings set around an elongated roundabout

7

driveway. The largest building, set in the middle at the end of the drive, was the palace. "When we pull in front of the palace, you stay with the car," Bill said to Ahmed. "Keep the engine running and the air on. I have no idea how long we're going to be. It could be fifteen minutes; it could be an hour."

"Yes, Sir."

The entourage pulled up to the steps in front of a tall façade made of gray marble and glass. Ahmed exited the limo, walked around and opened the back door for the occupants. Sharp led his contingent up the stairs to the massive bronze double doors by which they entered the foyer of the palace, a huge marbled room with a red carpet running the length of it. A man walked down the carpet toward them smiling broadly. "I'm Masoud Fakhoury, Foreign Minister. Welcome to the Presidential Palace, Secretary Buck," the man said in fluent English.

"Mr. Foreign Minister, it's so nice to meet you," Buck replied. "This is my assistant Melissa Clarke," Buck said gesturing toward her, "and my interpreter, Harry Acker." Fakhoury nodded and turned to Sharp. Much to the surprise of Buck, the two embraced warmly.

"Good morning, Masoud. How are the tennis lessons going?" Sharp said, pounding Fakhoury on the back.

"Dreadful, Bill, just dreadful. I'm wasting my money."

"Can't be going that badly. You beat me every time we play."

The Minister smiled. "I suspect you lose intentionally."

"Just doing my part for diplomacy." The two men erupted in laughter.

The Minister wagged his finger at Sharp. "I'm going to have to keep my eye on you, Bill," he said with a smile.

Fakhoury returned his attention to Buck, who looked uncomfortable at Sharp's close relationship with the Minister. "Step this way, Mr. Secretary," Fakhoury said, "and I'll accompany you to the President's office." He led the party up the interior stairs and turned left down a hallway where a guard blocked their path. Buck and the Minister walked past, but the guard stepped in front of the others. "Wait here," he said.

Buck turned. "I need my interpreter," he told the Minister.

"Of course." Fakhoury spoke to the guard and Acker was allowed to pass. "Bill," the Minister said, "I hope you don't mind waiting in the next room."

"Not a problem, Sir," Sharp replied. Melissa Clarke and Sharp were ushered into a side room where the guard motioned them toward seats along the walls.

"Sit please," he said in barely understandable English.

Clarke and Sharp sat on opposite sides of a large room adorned with same gray marble and a wood parquet floor. It looked to be some kind of reception area. Sharp settled in for what he thought might be a long wait. He looked around at the high ceilings and wood inlaid floor. *It looks like an American corporate lobby.*

The room was quiet, no light or noise coming into the room. Bill heard a faint buzzing sound that he presumed came from the overhead fluorescent lights. After a lengthy time, he looked at his watch. *It's been an hour already.* Bill shifted his attention to Melissa Clarke on the other side of the room. *Maybe early 30s? Long blonde hair. I should talk to her.* He was about to speak, when she looked up and gave him a blank stare. *Maybe not.*

Bill glanced at his watch when the door opened. It had been an hour and fifteen minute meeting. *Return the Secretary to his plane and I'll be back at the Embassy by noon,* Bill thought. A Syrian guard stepped into the room and motioned them into the hallway. Outside the waiting room, Bill saw Buck and Assad standing in the hallway shaking hands. *They're not smiling. It must have been a tough meeting, probably about the Palestinians, those poor bastards.*

As Buck and his interpreter walked in Bill's direction, President Assad eyed Sharp and waved. Sharp and Assad walked toward each other. Buck turned around to watch.

"Hello, Bill. Good to see you again," Assad said, shaking Bill's hand firmly.

"You, too, Sir. How's your lovely wife?" Bill asked.

"Very good. When are we having you for dinner again?"

"You know me. Anytime you're serving food, I'm there, Sir."

Assad laughed. "I'll make a note on my calendar. Perhaps sometime next week?"

"Thank you, Sir. It'd be a pleasure," Bill replied.

"My secretary will call you."

President Assad strode away in the opposite direction and the guard motioned Sharp and his associates back down the hallway toward the front entrance. Two guards posted inside the outer doors swung them open and the group paused outside for a second at the top of the stairs, adjusting their vision to the bright sunlight. *Damn,* Bill thought, digging for his sunglasses. *It's getting hot.*

Ahmed stood by the car holding the rear passenger door open. The escort soldiers piled into their vehicle and Bill heard the engine crank on their version of a military Jeep. Bill stopped and looked around. The second Jeep, the one behind them, had vanished. Buck, Clarke and Acker climbed into the back seat of the limo. After Bill and Ahmed got into the front seat, Ahmed turned and looked back at Buck. "Back to the airport, Sir?"

"Yes," Buck said impatiently as though the question was unnecessary. "Where else would we be going?"

"Sorry, Sir. Just asking."

The Syrian Jeep started down the long driveway toward the exit and Ahmed accelerated to catch them. Bill looked out the window as they exited the palace grounds, wondering how, in a country with so little water, the Syrians managed to make the huge Palace lawn look as green as the grass on a major league baseball field. He glanced between the buildings at the sprawling city below the cliff. A mid-day wind kicked dust into the air, clouding his view of the city.

Bill heard Buck speak to his aide. "Melissa, hand me that briefing book, would you? I want to make a couple of notes. When we get on the plane, start transcribing these. SecState will want a report as soon as we get back to Brussels."   "Yes, Sir," she said.

Bill looked back at Buck. "Tough meeting, Sir?"

Buck, annoyed that Sharp seemed to have better relations with the Syrians than he enjoyed, frowned as though it was none of Bill's business. "Just an exchange of views, Mr. Sharp. Nothing more."

They should have let me talk to Assad, Bill thought.

Buck took the binder, opened it, pulled a pen from his shirt pocket and began writing. Bill concentrated his view out the window as the car gained speed exiting the Palace grounds. *Really shitty place for a palace if you ask me. They should have put it downtown in the old part of the city. It's pretty down there.*

Ahmed suddenly began to slow down as the Jeep in front of them slowed.

"What's wrong?" Bill asked, looking over at the driver.

"There's a wreck in the middle of the road." Ahmed pointed at a disturbance a few hundred yards ahead. "Look!"

Bill saw smoke far ahead of them. "I see it now. Hang back a little. We might have to go around it."

The Jeep stopped close to the accident, where a truck lying on its side blocked the two lane roadway. The soldiers climbed out to assist the truck driver who staggered around, dazed and bleeding. Ahmed stopped the limo a hundred yards back from the scene.

"It must have just happened," Ahmed said, leaning forward to get a better look at the accident. "He probably swerved to avoid something and cut his wheels too fast."

Bill saw the box truck lying on its side, the kind of vehicle commonly used for food deliveries. Smoke was coming up from underneath the hood, although it didn't appear to be on fire. Two soldiers assisted the driver while another walked around the truck doing an inspection. The fourth soldier ran back to the Jeep and began talking on the radio.

Buck looked up from his briefing book. "What's the problem? Why are we stopping?"

Bill looked back. "There's an overturned truck in the roadway. Let's drive around it on the shoulder."

Buck looked at his watch. "Go ahead. Let's get on the way."

12

One Day in Lebanon

Bill became nervous whenever he experienced something out of the ordinary. Although he'd never known an American to come to any harm around Damascus, Buck wasn't an ordinary American. Bill turned his head side to side, studying the landscape for approaching danger. "Ahmed, do we have room to pull around on the shoulder?"

Bill rolled down his passenger window and stuck his head out to get a better look. In the distance, some yards away from the roadway amid the brush and trees, Bill watched two men stand up from behind a bush. Bill watched as one of the men rested a long cylindrical object on his shoulder. Bill turned toward the back seat. "We've got trouble. Everyone duck down in the seat." Bill quickly rolled up the window. "Get the hell out of here, Ahmed. Now!" Bill screamed. Ahmed made no attempt to drive away. The car sat motionless. "Ahmed!" Bill shouted.

The man holding the object kneeled and pointed to what looked to be a weapon at the Syrian jeep. Bill recognized it and shouted, "Everyone down! Down! RPG! RPG!" as the men fired and the projectile screamed toward the Jeep leaving an exhaust trail behind it. A huge fireball of yellow and red enveloped both the truck and Jeep ahead of them, followed by a thunderous sound. Metal shrapnel flew into the air in all directions. A wave of sound, fire and air hit the limo, lifting it off the ground and slamming it back down askance in the roadway. Large chunks of smoldering metal crashed against the vehicle, one large chunk glancing off the bulletproof glass windshield, putting a large crack across it. The occupants were thrown against the roof and then landed on the floorboard as the limo dropped to the ground

"Fuck," Bill shouted, lifting his head to watch the aftermath. A second explosion, not as strong as the first, erupted and sent clouds of thick, black smoke into the air.

Bill ducked down again, then raised himself up and looked in the back seat. "Anyone hurt?" He waited. The occupants seemed to be in a state of shock, stunned and shaken. No one answered. "Is anyone hurt?" Bill asked more forcefully. Bill put his hand on Ahmed's shoulder and shook him. "Ahmed!" He waited a second, then repeated himself. Ahmed! Is the car still running?" Ahmed didn't answer. "Ahmed!" Bill shouted. "Is the car still running?"

Ahmed looked at the dashboard. "Yes."

"Get us the fuck out of here. Now!"

Ahmed pressed the accelerator and the car lurched forward, bare metal grinding on the pavement. Ahmed let up on the pedal.

"I think the tires are blown," Ahmed said.

"I don't give a shit. If it'll move, get us the fuck out of here," Bill shouted.

Ahmed pressed the accelerator and the car began to lurch forward. Ahmed aimed for the shoulder attempting to drive around the burning pile of wreckage.

"I can't see where we're going."

"Drive, Ahmed!" Sharp pointed at the shoulder. "Get far enough off the road to get around the wreckage. If we hit anything, keep going. Move!" Bill put one hand on Ahmed's shoulder and the other on the dashboard to brace himself as Ahmed drove completely off the roadway, churning up dust and debris. The car tipped at a precarious angle as it passed the wreckage.

The limo pushed large chunks of metal aside as it made its way around the burning mass of twisted metal. Large pieces of debris became lodged underneath the car and the grating sound caused Bill to wonder if they were even capable of getting to the airport. Bill glanced at the men who had fired the RPG. They were running toward them with the weapon aimed at the car. "Get your ass going, Ahmed!"

Ahmed pulled back onto the roadway but could go no farther. He stopped, seeing a white pickup truck sideways in the roadway blocking their path. A 50 caliber machine gun mounted in the bed of the truck was pointed straight at them. Four men in green military uniforms and black masks walked toward them with AK-47s pointed at the car. A fifth man was in the bed of the pickup behind the machine gun. One of the men shouted something. The man shouted again and pointed at them.

"They want us to get out of the car," Ahmed said.

"Your Harvard education help you figure that out?" Sharp asked, looking suspiciously at Ahmed. "Are you working with these guys?" Sharp pushed him in the shoulder. "How the fuck did they know we'd be here?" Sharp asked, raising his voice. Ahmed looked straight ahead and wouldn't answer.

Three of the masked men opened fire, pouring bursts of ammunition into the grill of the limo. Smoke began coming out from under the hood and the engine died. The fourth man, who appeared to be their leader, walked to the passenger side, looked at Sharp and pounded on the window with the butt of his rifle. He shouted again, gesticulating with his hand. Bill looked into the back seat.

Buck, his assistant and interpreter were piled together on the floorboard. Melissa whimpered softly.

"They want us to get out of the car, Mr. Secretary," Bill said to Buck. He received no answer.

The leader looked around and pointed to the truck mounted machine gun. Bill dove for the floor. The men stepped away from the limo before the 50 caliber erupted, putting several rounds through the front windshield. Glass shards and blood spread everywhere. Bill looked over and saw Ahmed's head was a mass of bone and blood, slumped over the steering wheel. *Bye, bye, you little bastard.* Bill peeked over the dashboard and saw the leader take the sidearm from his belt and walk back to the passenger side of the limo. He kept shouting words Bill couldn't understand. Bill kicked at the door, finally opening it enough that he could exit the car. The leader of the group walked up to him and pulled down the mask which covered his nose and mouth. He motioned with his rifle at Bill and pointed toward the ground. Bill saw the toothless grin of his attacker. "Go see a dentist, you towel-headed motherfucker," Bill said before someone hit him from behind with a rifle butt. Bill's knees buckled and he collapsed to the ground where the leader kicked him in the stomach.

Buck, his aide and interpreter were forced from the limo, punched and kicked until they stopped struggling. All four were forced to the pavement, all in a row on their knees facing the leader. The other masked men walked back and forth behind the group.

The leader nodded to his men and Bill heard the first pistol shot, so close that the sonic blast stung his ears. His head immediately ached, but that was the least of his problems. Even with his head bowed, he saw the splatter of blood on the ground in front of him. *You fucking bastards.* Acker, the interpreter, fell forward onto the ground and Bill stared at his limp body. The next shot was even closer and the force of the sound drilled through Bill's skull, but it was Melissa's limp body falling forward that caused Bill's anger.

Bill saw the shadow of the man who stepped behind him. He turned his head and looked into the man's eyes. "You better make sure I'm dead or I'll kill every last one of you motherfuckers," Bill hissed. He felt the blow to his head, then saw nothing. He struggled to remain conscious, but a second blow ended that hope.

Buck was hit over the head as well and knocked unconscious. Black bags with drawstrings were put over their heads, tightened in the fashion of a noose and their hands were tied behind them. Sharp and Buck were lifted up and thrown into the bed of the pickup. The masked men climbed in around them while the leader rode in the cab with the driver. Sharp regained consciousness briefly, bouncing around the truck bed as the vehicle drove straight across the desert. *I'm not dead. Buck must be alive, too.* Sharp rose up slightly before being struck again in the head with a rifle butt. Everything went black as he slumped back onto the truck bed.

William Sharp, an American diplomat working out of the United States Embassy in Damascus, Syria, and Nicholas Buck, the Under Secretary for Political Affairs at the United States Department of State, in Washington, D. C., had been taken captive. The date was Thursday, September 22nd, 1988.

Made in the USA
Columbia, SC
25 March 2021